To Have and to Hold

Leo McNeir

Enigma Publishing

Copyright

First published by Endeavour Media Ltd in 2019
This edition published 2021 by Enigma Publishing
© Leo McNeir 2019

Leo McNeir has asserted his rights to be identified as the author of this work.

All rights reserved. No part of this publication may be reproduced, stored in any retrieval system, or transmitted, in any form or by any means, electronic, mechanical, photocopying, recording or otherwise without the prior written permission of the publishers.

This book is a work of fiction. Names, characters, businesses, organisations, places and events other than those clearly in the public domain are either the product of the author's imagination or are used fictitiously. Any resemblance to actual persons, living or dead, events or locales is entirely coincidental.

Dedication

For Geoff and Carol with love

About this book

A young woman flees in desperation when her family decide her future ...

Interior designer Marnie Walker runs her own business from a renovated farm close by the Grand Union Canal. She also owns some beautiful cottages she rents out.

But the bucolic bliss of rural Northamptonshire is shattered by the arrival of secretive tenant Samira Khan. The mysterious Asian beauty stumps up six months' rent and then locks herself into her canalside retreat.

Marnie tries to win Samira's trust – but gets more than she bargained for as a harrowing story unfolds.

What lies behind a series of racially-motivated attacks in nearby Northampton? Can she find Samira's family and allay fears about so-called 'honour killings'? How does Marnie find herself accused first of attempted murder, then murder itself? And who exactly is the victim?

Index

To Have and to Hold

Chapter 1

Summons

The sun was shining down on Little Venice. The confluence of waterways in the heart of London looked beautiful that warm Thursday afternoon in late May.

Soon spring would be easing its way gently towards the first days of summer. Dappled shade from the plane trees splashed down on the narrowboats that lined both banks of the Regent's Canal. Birdsong masked the hum of traffic in the background. The water sparkled. Those fortunate enough to have a mooring there regarded this as the most attractive section of the entire canal network.

One such boater was Roger Broadbent, solicitor. As senior partner in the firm and in his late fifties, he enjoyed the luxury of taking the occasional day off from work. That was one such day, and he had spent the previous two hours applying a final top coat of paint to the roof of his narrowboat, *Rumpole*. Now he was looking forward to cleaning up and relaxing on board with a gin and tonic. He stepped back on the towpath, wiping both hands on a rag and surveyed his work, satisfied with a job well done.

He was advancing towards the stern deck of the boat, when he heard a cry. A man was hurrying in his direction a short way along the towpath, one arm raised, brandishing a piece of paper. Roger frowned. He recognised the man as Albert, a retired merchant seaman who lived aboard the 'security boat' with his two cats, also retired. The frown was because Albert rarely moved with any appearance of urgency. Something must be serious if it caused the old man to attempt a marathon run of almost forty yards.

Just then, Roger's mobile began vibrating. He fished it out of his pocket and pressed the green button. As he listened intently to the voice on the line, his frown increased.

Meanwhile, Albert shuffled to a halt, waving the paper in front of him. He was bent double and panting. "Have you ... seen ... this ... Roger?"

Roger half turned, pressed the mobile hard against his head and put a finger in his free ear.

"Say that again?" He furrowed his brows as he listened. "Dear God ... yes, yes ... surely ... I'll be on my way, soon as. Right. Leave it with me. Say nothing until I get there, not a word."

Roger disconnected and gave his attention to Albert for the first time. He nodded at the paper.

"What's that, Albert?"

"Haven't you ... seen it?" The old man was still breathing heavily. "Here, have a ... read."

Roger shook his head. "Sorry. Can't stop now, old chum. Gotta go."

"But they're going to double our mooring fees ... just like that! Not so much as a ... well, I don't know what."

"Sorry, old love . Something very important has cropped up. I really must go."

"But ... but ... why so sudden?"

"Remember Marnie Walker? Used to have the mooring by the tunnel ... *Sally Ann?*"

"Course I do. We all know Marnie ... lovely girl."

"She's the reason."

"What can possibly be ... more important than ... having our mooring fees doubled?" Albert protested, wheezing.

"Marnie's been arrested."

"*Arrested?* What ever for?"

"Attempted murder," Roger said bluntly. "That important enough for you?"

Albert gaped. "Bloody hell! You'd better get going, boy."

****

2

Roger's wife, Marjorie, laid out his casual day-off clothes on the bed in the sleeping cabin, while he made a quick phone call. Marnie had asked him to ring home and let her partner, Ralph, know what had happened. The police allowed one call only, and she knew Roger would sort things out. Marjorie relieved him of his overalls while he held the phone, explaining the situation to Ralph. That was simple; Roger only knew the nature of the charge and the police station where Marnie was being held.

Marjorie held up Roger's slacks and he climbed in. She tucked his shirt into the trousers and zipped him up.

Ralph sounded incredulous. "Who's she supposed to have attempted to murder, for God's sake?"

"That I can't tell you, my friend. The line was crackly, and I just got the bare minimum. All I know is, she's at the cop shop in Milton Keynes. I'm on my way."

"I'll meet you there," Ralph said.

"Don't bother. They won't let you see her. I'll come on to Glebe Farm and fill you in after we've had a talk. Er, Ralph ... don't take this the wrong way, but –"

"Of course I don't know. The idea's *absurd*. Marnie wouldn't harm a *fly*."

"So you've no idea what this is –"

"Oh, yes. I can guess what it's all about in general terms. But who the actual victim is, is frankly anyone's guess."

On that enigmatic note, they hung up. Marjorie eased Roger into his jacket, handed him his briefcase – it never left him, even when away from the office – and held up the car keys. She kissed him on the cheek and wished him a safe journey.

"You've got cash for a taxi home, darling?" he asked.

"No need to worry about me, Roger. I'll be fine."

"You'll lock everything up all right?"

"No need to fuss now."

"Sorry to have to dash off."

"That's okay, dear. I'll just have to sit and have my gin and tonic all by myself." She sighed. "It's a hard life."

3

Roger groaned and clambered out of the boat. He waved at Marjorie through the window and hurried along the towpath towards the entrance gate.

****

Fifteen minutes later Roger reached the motorway and set cruise control to a steady seventy. Traffic was light by the standards of the M1, and he was able to relax a little. Only then did he think back to Albert and his letter. Doubling our mooring fees, had he said? Outrageous! That would mean another meeting of the Regent's Canal Boat Owners' Association in the Little Venice pub; more heated discussions, more righteous indignation, more protests. Hey ho ... *plus ça change*, and all that.

Nonetheless, Roger knew where his first priority lay. What the hell was Marnie up to this time? Attempted murder? Ridiculous! On the other hand, she had run into more than her share of trouble over the past few years. In fact he had sometimes thought of her as a walking disaster zone. It had all started after she left her job in London and set up her own interior design business in the country. He recalled her saying at the time that she was hoping for a 'more laid-back lifestyle' in rural Northamptonshire. Some hopes! But an attempted murder charge ...

Roger smiled to himself. What had Albert called him? *Boy.* That was a new one. Roger had settled into comfortable middle-age, complete with expanding waistline and incipient balding patch. He was hardly anyone's idea of a *boy.* But to Albert, doyen of Little Venice and well into his seventies, every boater along the cut was his junior. He even had the most senior cats.

Roger's thoughts strayed back to Marnie. He hoped she would have the good sense to follow his advice and say nothing. More than anything, he wished he had some inkling of what had happened so that he could arrive better prepared. He told himself there was no way Marnie could have committed such a crime, or indeed any kind of crime worth the name. And yet, his years as a London solicitor had taught him that in life

4

nothing was impossible, and things were often not what they seemed.

****

Meanwhile, fifty miles to the north of London in the canalside village of Knightly St John, there was frenzied activity in Marnie's home, Glebe Farm. Despite Roger's advice, Ralph was making preparations. To Marnie, he was her partner, lover, fiancé, significant other. To the outside world he was Professor Ralph Lombard, visiting professor of economics and Fellow of All Saints' College in the University of Oxford.

He was not alone. Helping him was Anne Price. To Marnie, she was her work assistant and closest friend. Anne was a student at art school, just completing her foundation year. She looked up to Marnie as her role model and inspiration and regarded herself as her apprentice. She also loved her like a sister, and the feeling was mutual.

At that moment the two of them were on the phone. Ralph was speaking with Marnie's sister, Beth; Anne was talking to her mother. Their message was the same: you may hear on the news that Marnie has been arrested. It's all nonsense and we're doing everything we can to sort things out. Don't worry, whatever you hear. They both had their fingers crossed for luck, but after Roger's call they had to take action, rather than sit at home and wait passively for news. Anne knew that Marnie adhered to what she had called the Royal Marines School of Management; *Seize the High Ground*, was her motto. Assuming that Marnie might be held overnight by the police, they optimistically put her sponge bag and a box of cereal bars in a carrier bag to keep her going.

Ralph brought the car round from the garage barn, while Anne quickly put out a saucer of food for their cat, Dolly, and locked up. She raced out and met Ralph's Jaguar as he turned the corner to line up for the ascent of the field track. Anne leapt aboard, and they took off. The track climbed up to the village from the cluster of buildings that constituted Glebe

Farm. At the top, Ralph slowed to pass through the field gateway and accelerated out onto the road.

They drove past the primary school, the church, the pub, the village shop and the collection of stone houses and cottages that lined the high street. Anne took a series of deep breaths when they left the village and followed the narrow, winding country road that led to the dual carriageway. Only then was Ralph able to speed up as they headed for police HQ in the town that called itself the 'New City of Milton Keynes'.

****

Finding the police station was easier than they expected. Anne had spotted a town plan for Milton Keynes in the map pocket behind her seat. She gave Ralph concise directions, and they located the building, fronted by a spacious car park.

"Loads of room here, Ralph," she said. "You can park practically outside the door. No probs."

Ralph made a non-committal kind of sound and, to Anne's surprise, drove past the main entrance and slotted the car into a space round the corner a short walk away. This puzzled her, but she made no comment. Ralph switched off the engine and turned in his seat to face her.

"I've got an idea," he said.

"You have a master plan?"

"Presumably no-one will be allowed to visit Marnie, apart from her solicitors."

"Is there a clue to your master plan in the use of *solicitors*, plural?" Anne asked.

"You've got it. If we wait till Roger gets here, we could go in together and perhaps he might be able to take me in as his assistant. What d'you think?"

Anne nodded. "Must be worth a try. Let's go for it."

****

They lurked in the car park for quite some time before Roger's Volvo swung into view. Before he was out of the car, Ralph was beside him, with Anne in pursuit.

6

"Ralph." Roger climbed out and closed the door. "Now there's a surprise ... I don't think."

"You didn't really expect us sit at home twiddling our thumbs, did you?"

"I suppose not." Roger opened the rear door and retrieved his briefcase from the back seat. "But you do realise —"

"Ralph has a master plan," Anne said.

Roger looked suspicious. "Which is?"

"You introduce me as your assistant, clerk, co-counsel, paralegal or whatever, and we go in to see Marnie together."

Roger considered this. "Rather irregular," he said at length. "But we can give it a whirl. The main thing is, what can you tell me in advance that I ought to know? I'm totally ill-prepared for this."

Ralph shrugged. "You're the one who phoned us. We didn't have a clue about any attempted murder charge."

"Except that it's utter nonsense," Anne added.

"I'm sure you're right," Roger said. "But there must be some sort of background."

"Oh, there's plenty of background, all right," said Ralph. "But why don't we go in and let Marnie explain?"

Roger looked Ralph up and down. In contrast to Roger, who was wearing an open-neck shirt, slacks and a casual jacket, Ralph had changed into a navy pinstripe bespoke tailored suit, with a white shirt and dark red silk tie. His black semi-brogue shoes were polished to a brilliant sheen. Ralph looked every inch the distinguished academic authority that he was. He could certainly pass for a city solicitor.

Roger sighed. "Come on, then. We can but give it a try." He had an afterthought. "They don't know you here, do they?"

"Not at all."

"Good," Roger said. "It really would be Sod's Law if you were recognised. Let's go. You can carry my briefcase."

Ralph took it and smiled. "Certainly, sir."

They hurried across the car park and up the steps to the main door. As befitted his station, Ralph opened it and stood aside to let his 'boss' through. Anne followed them in.

7

It was one of those days when Sod's Law prevailed. The first person they encountered in the entrance area was DC Cathy Lamb heading for the door. Ralph and Anne had known Lamb for virtually all the time they had lived in Northamptonshire, and their paths had crossed on several occasions. She had a moment of hesitation before recognition dawned.

"Ralph, Anne, hello. What are you doing here?"

Ralph tried not to sag visibly. "Hi, Cathy. It's ... well, a trifle awkward actually."

Lamb grinned. "I heard there was someone in being charged with attempted murder. Nothing to do with you, is it?"

There was no quick-and-easy answer to that question, even for an articulate university professor.

"Well, in fact ..." Ralph's voice tailed off.

Seeing his expression, Lamb became serious. She looked from Roger to Anne and back to Ralph. Her gaze took in the whole of the entrance area. Her expression darkened.

"Marnie not with you?" she asked suspiciously.

****

Ralph and Anne walked back to the Jaguar and climbed in.

"So much for the Master Plan," Ralph said. "My disguise was blown before it even got started."

"You weren't to know Cathy would be there for a meeting," Anne said.

"Par for the course just lately. Everything seems to be going awry these days."

Anne agreed. "Certainly is. Roger's in there being briefed by Marnie who's on an absolutely *ridiculous* charge, and we don't even have a clue as to who the victim is."

Ralph stared at Anne for a long moment. He said quietly, "It's not even easy to hazard a guess, is it?"

Anne reached over and took Ralph by the hand. "It's weird."

Ralph nodded. "Our lives have been turned upside down ever since Samira arrived."

They fell silent, both thinking back to the day not many weeks earlier when Samira Khan had come into their lives.

8

Interrogation 1

In the police station Roger Broadbent was escorted along a corridor and shown into an interview room on the ground floor by a detective sergeant. It was the room routinely used by solicitors in conference with their clients. A constable in shirtsleeves was standing inside the door, assigned there to keep watch over the person – the *suspect* – who was seated at the table, occupying one of the four straight-backed chairs. The suspect was Roger's friend and client, Marnie Walker. She stood up when he entered and they embraced briefly. The constable made a disapproving sound in his throat. The detective sergeant shook his head.

Roger set his briefcase down on the table top and turned to the police officers.

"I should like some time alone with my client."

"Certainly." It was the detective who replied.

"And our discussion is private, so I want your assurance that our meeting will neither be overheard, recorded nor in any way observed. If you can't give me that assurance I shall insist on moving to another room."

"I can give you that assurance."

"Very well." Roger smiled an encouraging smile. "And how about a cup of tea?"

The detective nodded, and both officers withdrew. Roger turned back to Marnie, pulling out a chair for her. They sat.

"Well, Marnie, you're a big worry and no mistake. What's this all about?"

"They haven't explained anything?"

"No, but they wouldn't. All I know is you've been arrested and cautioned, and the charge is attempted murder. I'm starting from the premise of course that it's complete nonsense."

Marnie took a deep breath, staring down at the table. Roger heard her breathe out and saw that she had her eyes closed. He continued.

"This is meant to be where you look me straight in the eye and deny everything, okay?"

"I'm just trying to work out where to begin," Marnie said, looking up.

"I suggest you —"

"I know, I know … start at the beginning. How far back should I go? That's the question."

"The police will want you to go back to the time when it all started, and you have to decide when that was. Don't be in any doubt, Marnie, that the officer who interrogates you —" At the word *interrogates* Marnie sat up straight. Roger went on, "Oh yes. That's what it will be, though everything will be done to make it seem like a conversation. I don't know why I'm telling you this. It's not as if you haven't been through it before."

"I've not actually been charged with attempted murder before, Roger."

"True, but you know they probably won't believe a word you say."

"Then why interrogate me if they aren't going to believe me?"

"The purpose of interrogation is only partly to establish facts, Marnie. The other aim is to trip you up, to probe for any inconsistencies in your statements, even to trap you. That's the point I was trying to make, so just answer the questions succinctly. Don't embellish. That's important, okay? Ultimately, they'll want to wear you down, bombard you with any evidence they've been able to gather, so that you confess to whatever it is they believe you've done. Why don't we start there? Tell me who they've accused you of trying to murder, then we'll work out where the story begins."

Marnie frowned. "That's what's so odd, Roger. No-one's told me a name. They just drove me here and told me I could make a phone call, which is when I rang you. Then they sat me in here to wait for you."

"Did they caution you, Marnie?"

"I seem to remember one of the officers cautioned me in the car on the way here."

10

"You seem terribly vague about everything, Marnie."

"It all happened so quickly. One minute I was walking into the kitchen, the next thing –"

"Okay. Suppose you just tell me everything you can about what happened. Start with arriving at the house and take it from there."

Marnie spent the next half hour going over the events that had led up to her arrest. The only interruption came when the constable arrived with two cups of tea. There were no biscuits.

****

The interrogation began as soon as Roger indicated that his client was ready. The interrogating officer was not the sergeant who had brought Marnie in but a woman of about forty, accompanied by a man perhaps ten years older. She switched on the recording machine and introduced herself as DC Shirley Driscoll. Her colleague as DC Harry Rabjohn. The opening was relaxed.

"Would you give your names, please."

"Marnie Walker."

"Roger Broadbent, Mrs Walker's solicitor."

Driscoll leaned forward as if to share a confidence. "Is it all right if I call you Marnie?"

"Yes."

"Thank you, Marnie."

Marnie added, "Though I'll find it irritating if you tag that onto the end of every sentence or question."

Driscoll smiled. "I'll try not to. I'm going to ask you to go right back to the beginning, to when the events leading up to today first started. It's up to you to decide when that was, but I may have to prod your memory. All right?"

Marnie nodded. Driscoll said, "For the recording, please."

"Yes. That's all right."

"Thank you. So where do we begin?"

Marnie sat back in her chair and stared at the opposite wall for a long moment before speaking.

"I suppose it all began on the day that Samira came to the village."

"Samira?"

"Samira Khan. This is all about her, really. The rest of us just got drawn in. We didn't want to, but that's how it was."

"Okay, Marnie. So tell me how Samira Khan came into your life."

Chapter 2

Enter Samira Khan

It was one Tuesday in early May. Molly Appleton, proprietor of the shop in the village of Knightly St John, noticed the taxi driving slowly past. She broke off her conversation with Richard, her husband, the village post-master, and diverted her attention from behind the counter to the shop window. It was an infrequent occurrence for taxis to appear in the village. Moments later the cab drove by again, this time accelerating in the opposite direction. Presumably it had either dropped off or picked up a fare. Molly was not one for gossip, but she had what she regarded as a healthy curiosity about anything that happened in the village.

Her *healthy curiosity* was soon satisfied. With a loud ring of its bell, the door opened to admit a young woman, a stranger. Molly guessed she was probably in her early twenties, tall, attractive and with long black hair. Most noticeable about her was her complexion, a warm light coffee colour, and her large dark brown almond-shaped eyes. It was rare for any Asian woman to appear in Knightly St John.

Molly treated the visitor to her warmest smile, but even as she did so, she sensed an unease about this newcomer.

"Good morning," Molly said brightly. "Can I help you?"

"Er … I'm looking for a house called …" She consulted a piece of paper. "… er, Glebe Farm. I've driven through the village but I haven't been able to see it. I'm guessing it's somewhere out in the country."

She was well-spoken, Molly thought, pronouncing her words clearly in unaccented English, like a news reader on television.

"You want Marnie."

Again the woman looked down at the paper. "The name I have is … Mrs M Walker."

"That's right, Marnie Walker. You haven't long missed her. She was in here not ten minutes ago. Is she expecting you?"

The woman checked her watch. "Yes, but not until eleven. I'm rather early."

"Well," Molly began, "Marnie can't be far away. You see that car parked outside the door, the dark blue one, the Freelander? That's hers."

"But I didn't see anyone in the street. Could you describe her for me?"

"Marnie? She's … about five-seven and slim like you, with dark hair down to her shoulders but a bit wavier than yours. Oh, I should mention she has someone with her."

The woman suddenly looked wary. "Someone Asian like me?"

"Oh no, quite the opposite in fact."

"What does that mean?"

"Just that the girl with her has a pale complexion and light blonde hair, cut very short. Quite different, you see? She's called Anne, and I say *girl* but she must be about twenty now."

"She's Mrs Walker's daughter?"

"No. She works for her and also lives at Glebe Farm."

The young woman turned and walked back to the door, looking out through the glass to left and right.

"I can't see anyone apart from an older lady coming this way."

Molly smiled again and nodded. "That will be Mrs Faulkner coming to collect her pension. She always comes later than the others."

The young woman stepped back towards the counter.

"Would you have any idea where I might find Mrs Walker … or perhaps I should go straight to Glebe Farm?"

Molly turned to her husband. He was seated a short distance away in a glazed cubicle.

"Richard, did Marnie say anything to you about where she was going?"

"I think I heard her say something to Anne about seeing Margaret."

Molly looked at her visitor. "That would be Mrs Giles. She's the head teacher at the village school. That's probably why Marnie left the car; double yellow lines outside the school entrance. It's just along the street after the church. You can't miss it."

"You think I should go there?"

"You could ask in the office if she's there or if she has been."

The young woman frowned. Before she could reply, the bell over the door rang again, and an elderly woman came in.

"Morning, Molly," she said cheerfully. Noticing the young woman, she added, "Morning, my dear." She turned towards Molly. "I say, did you know someone has left a bag outside on the pavement?"

Molly shook her head. "What sort of –"

"Oh, it's mine. I'd better be on my way." Turning to leave, the young woman had a sudden afterthought. "Is there a public telephone in the village?"

Molly pointed towards the front window. "Just round the side of the building, past the post-box, an old-fashioned red kiosk."

"Thank you for your help. I'll try the school."

Molly said, "If you miss her and I see her first, what name shall I tell Marnie?"

A hesitation and the wary look again. "Samira ... Samira Khan."

"What a pretty name," said Molly.

If Samira heard the compliment she made no reaction. She was already leaving, retrieving her bag and heading for the corner past the post-box. Molly and Mrs Faulkner looked at each other.

"A nice bag," said Mrs Faulkner.

Molly said, "Odd thing to do, leave your handbag outside on the pavement."

"Oh, it wasn't that sort of bag, Molly. It was the sort you might use for a weekend. It looked good quality, too ... brown leather ... shiny, like new."

"For a weekend?" Molly repeated. "That's interesting."

It occurred to them both that it was Tuesday.

****

15

Samira Khan opened her shoulder-bag and pulled a receipt out from under her mobile. She checked a number, went into the kiosk and dialled. After a brief conversation she hung up and set off along the pavement, carrying her weekend bag. It was heavy with as many clothes and extras as she could pack in. She hoped fervently that Glebe Farm was not far away, or that she would track down Marnie Walker and be offered a lift. The road ran on for about a hundred yards before curving away to the right. She was now approaching the perimeter wall of the village church. It occupied a slightly elevated site and was neatly kept with the grass well-trimmed between the many gravestones and occasional larger tombs. She stopped to read the name board by the gate and noticed a war memorial just inside the yard. To Samira's surprise, the rector was a woman: *The Reverend Angela Hemingway BA, BD.*

Samira shifted the bag from one hand to the other and walked on. The churchyard wall gave way to a chain-link fence bordering a playground beyond which stood the school. It was a single-storey Victorian building with a modern extension to one side. Samira read the name board which confirmed that here too the person in charge was a woman: *Mrs Margaret Giles, BEd.* Samira lowered the bag to the ground and looked around her. There was no-one in sight. Even so she felt uncomfortable standing in the open.

She turned back to look at the school. The entrance doors were in the modern extension, and a row of windows to their left suggested office spaces rather than classrooms. Was it allowed to walk into a school, just like that? As Samira dithered by the school gate, she heard a car approaching slowly from the other end of the high street. It was a dark colour, grey or blue and low-slung. Suddenly, she felt exposed and threatened, standing there alone on the pavement. Samira hesitated no longer, but grabbed her bag and set off briskly across the playground. She reached the entrance and yanked open the door just as the car cruised by. The driver was a man, though she couldn't make out his features or any details about him. Of one thing she was certain: as he drove by, he turned

16

his head and looked in her direction. She pressed herself against the wall in the lobby and prayed he had not seen her.

From the corner of her eye, Samira caught sight of movement. She suppressed a gasp and mentally shook herself. *Get a grip!* Beyond the entrance, through double half-glazed doors, she could see a hall across which a woman was walking. She was carrying some folders under one arm and wearing a simple floral dress with a white cardigan draped over her shoulders. The head teacher?

On impulse, Samira lurched forward, dropping her bag and pushed open one of the inner doors. She called out.

"Mrs Giles!"

No reaction. The woman carried on walking, reached a classroom door, knocked and went in. Samira turned back into the entrance lobby. She was puzzling over what to do next when she heard footsteps. For the second time that morning she was greeted in a bright, friendly voice.

"Good morning. Can I help you?"

Samira looked up from her bag to find herself faced with not one but three women who had emerged from a short corridor.

"I was looking for the head teacher."

A warm smile. "Then you've found her. I'm Margaret Giles. Let me just take leave of my visitors and we can go to my office."

Samira shook her head. "Sorry. I'm not explaining myself properly. I'm actually looking for Mrs Marnie Walker. The lady in the shop said she might be here."

"Molly was quite right," said Margaret. She half turned towards her companions. "This is Marnie Walker and her assistant, Anne Price."

Marnie advanced and held out a hand. They shook. "Miss Khan, I presume?"

"I'm sorry to arrive so early."

"No problem. Let's get out of Margaret's way and head for Glebe Farm."

After leave taking, Margaret watched the entourage crossing the playground. She was about to return to her office when a woman appeared at her side. It was the person Samira had seen crossing the hall.

"What did she want?" she asked.

"Valerie, her name is Samira Khan."

Valerie Paxton was the school secretary. She scowled, watching the three women go through the school gate and out into the street.

"I saw her through the window," Valerie said. "Not a prospective parent, I hope."

"No, but a perfectly charming person."

"If she doesn't want a place in the school for a child, what was she doing here?"

Margaret sighed. "Since you're so curious, Valerie, she was looking for Marnie Walker."

"Why am I not surprised? And since when are we acting as Marnie Walker's receptionists?"

"Valerie ..." Margaret decided not to press the point. "Molly Appleton suggested she might be here, which she was. Now I think we should both return to our desks. The school won't run itself."

Valerie Paxton didn't move. "I suppose we should be grateful for small mercies."

"What do you mean?"

"Well, the Asian woman –"

"Samira," Margaret interjected. "That's her name. It's a lovely name."

"Whatever. She might've been wanting us to enrol a kid, or more likely *hordes* of them."

"In which case we would have been pleased to accommodate her children."

With that, Margaret Giles turned and walked back towards her office. With one last glance across the playground, Valerie Paxton pursed her lips, frowned and followed on.

****

"Can I help you with your bag? It looks heavy. I'm Anne, by the way. That's Anne with an 'e'."

18

Samira looked confused. "Anne Withaney? I thought Mrs Giles said you were –"

Anne laughed. "No, I'm Anne *Price*."

Samira cottoned on. "Oh, I see. Anne spelt with an 'e'. Is that it?"

For the first time, Samira smiled. It was a brilliant smile, revealing white even teeth, which contrasted with her light brown complexion. Beside her, Anne was pale and blonde, as Molly had described. Her hair was ultra-short, almost sculpted to her head. With her thin boyish figure she looked somehow vulnerable, though her walk was fluid and confident. As they made their way along the pavement, Anne reached down and took hold of one of the carrying handles. Samira's first reaction was to withdraw, but Anne gave an encouraging nod, and Samira relented.

"I'll go ahead and you can follow us down," Marnie said. "It's not far."

Samira stopped suddenly. Anne almost lost her grip on the handle.

Marnie said, "Something wrong?"

"I was hoping to ride with you." Samira added, "if you have room."

Marnie looked up and down the street. "How did you get here?"

"By taxi."

"But your luggage?" Marnie said.

Samira half raised the handle of the weekend bag. Marnie knew that Samira had signed a tenancy agreement for a minimum of six months. She was on the brink of mentioning this, but standing in the middle of the high street was not the best place for a discussion.

"Okay. That's my car, the dark blue Freelander up by the shop."

They resumed their walk. Samira was scanning the street for signs of any activity. Anne was thinking that if this was the sum total of Samira's luggage, it was not so heavy after all.

19

Marnie was mulling over her first impressions of Samira: she was elegant; she was attractive; she was an enigma. What bothered Marnie most of all was a growing suspicion that Samira Khan could be trouble.

DC Shirley Driscoll had listened carefully to Marnie's account of the day when Samira arrived in Knightly St John. Marnie found it slightly unnerving that Driscoll made no reaction to her statement, no nodding of the head, nothing. She just sat immobile and expressionless looking into Marnie's face while she spoke.

Eventually Marnie said, "I hope that answers your question about how things started."

"Yes, thank you, Marnie. That's all very helpful. I'd just like to clear up one or two points. You said that Samira arrived without any luggage. Didn't that strike you as unusual?"

"Highly unusual, yes. That's why I mentioned it."

Marnie was on the brink of expanding her answer when she recalled some advice given to her by Roger. *Keep your replies simple and to the point.* No purpose was served by elaborating; it only gave the interrogator more scope for probing. That way lay confusion, even when you were being completely accurate and truthful. Driscoll waited for a few moments – no doubt to give Marnie time to say more – before she continued.

"How would you describe Samira Khan, Marnie? What impression did she make on you?"

Before Marnie could reply, Roger interjected.

"I don't really see how that's relevant, officer. You're asking my client to give subjective opinions. I think it would be more appropriate to confine your questions to factual matters."

"Very well. You've mentioned, Marnie, that Samira was Asian. Can you add a few more facts?"

"She was smartly dressed. I would say she was quite elegant, even beautiful really."

"In what way did you find her *elegant?*"

"Her bearing. She walked with her head held high and moved rather gracefully, though she also seemed to be wary, as if on her guard."

Marnie heard Roger clear his throat. It was a warning.

21

"What made you think she was 'on her guard'?" said Driscoll, adding, "Please just stick to the facts."

"She kept looking round, up and down the street, as if looking for someone."

"Or expecting someone?" said Driscoll.

Roger said, "Now I think you're putting words in my client's mouth."

"As a witness, Marnie is well placed to give us an insight into Samira's state of mind when she first came on the scene."

"Nevertheless I think it would be more appropriate to keep to factual matters."

Driscoll turned back to Marnie. "Let me just get this clear. You said you were surprised how little luggage Samira had with her and that bothered you."

Roger sighed loudly. "We've been over this. My client said it was unusual." He looked across at DC Rabjohn who had been taking notes throughout. "You won't find any reference in your notes or in the recording to her being 'bothered', will you?"

Driscoll persisted. "It would be a perfectly natural reaction to sense that something was seriously wrong when a person who has arranged to rent a cottage for six months turns up with a weekend bag." She glanced across at Marnie with a shrug. "Isn't that right?"

"I suppose."

Marnie froze. She felt as if she had been tricked and could have bitten her tongue, though at that moment she couldn't think why. Before she could collect her thoughts, DC Driscoll moved on.

"Once you'd met Samira in the village, what happened next?"

"We went to Glebe Farm and I showed her round the cottage."

"That would be the cottage she had undertaken to rent for half a year without previously having seen it?"

"Yes."

"I'd like you to tell me, Marnie, how that went."

Chapter 3

Cottage Number Three

G lebe Farm was a cluster of buildings largely screened by trees, nestling at the foot of a steeply sloping field track. The main farmhouse fronted onto a cobbled courtyard, with three terraced cottages aligned at right-angles on one side, facing a small detached stone barn on the other. This latter building was the *office barn*, the base for Marnie's company, Walker and Co, interior design consultants. Its frontage comprised a tinted plate glass window, like a shop front, with a single semi-glazed door beside it. When the office was not in use, large timber sliding and folding doors could be pulled across to close it off. The office barn had one further facility: its loft area had been adapted to create a spacious bed-sitting room for Anne. This attic was accessible by means of a wall-ladder climbing up to an open trap door.

When Marnie and Anne brought Samira down to Glebe Farm, they escorted her to cottage number three. It was the nearest to the farmhouse, in which Marnie lived with Ralph Lombard. Samira stopped in the courtyard and stared at the little cottage. Like all the buildings in the Glebe Farm complex it was built of cream-coloured limestone under a roof of Welsh blue slate. Like the other two cottages, its window-frames were white and its front door was painted a glossy deep blue. Under the door knocker was the number 3. Both were made of heavy polished brass.

"Is this it?" Samira asked.

"This is it," Marnie confirmed. "I realise it's quite modest, but –"

"Can I see inside?"

Anne stepped forward and turned the key in the lock. Standing aside, she gestured to Samira to enter. The front door led into a small hallway. To its right a door opened into a sitting room, furnished comfortably but simply with two armchairs, a low table and a television. In the wall looking towards the front window stood a small Victorian fireplace.

Either side of the chimney breast were fitted bookshelves above built-in cupboards. Beyond the sitting room was a kitchen equipped with modern shaker-style units, including a separate hob and eye-level electric oven, a fridge, a washing machine and a useful amount of built-in storage. A small table and two bentwood chairs completed the furnishing.

From the hall a staircase rose to the first floor. Without speaking, Samira climbed the stairs. She found two bedrooms, each fitted with a double bed and free-standing pine wardrobes, plus a tiled bathroom with a shower unit over the bath. On both floors the colour scheme was designed to unify the whole cottage. The walls were emulsioned in apricot white, the doors were of stripped and varnished pine and the floors were covered in a biscuit-coloured woven carpet.

When Samira came down, she walked past Marnie and Anne and went to look through the semi-glazed door leading from the kitchen out into the small walled patio garden. It was furnished with an outdoor table and chairs and a furled parasol. The end wall was almost totally covered by a climbing rose, which was heavy with buds.

Samira turned to face Marnie and Anne who had followed her into the kitchen.

Marnie said, "Miss Khan, if it's not what you —"

Before Marnie could complete her sentence, Samira's eyes filled with tears. She took two steps quickly forward and hugged Marnie tightly. Slowly Marnie raised her arms to hold Samira, gently patting her back. She cast a surprised glance at Anne who looked on, bemused.

"Not as bad as that, is it?" Marnie said, attempting levity to lighten the atmosphere.

Samira snorted, released Marnie from her embrace and stood back, wiping her eyes, smiling through her tears.

"I'm sorry, both of you. You must think me ..."

The sentence went unfinished. Samira sniffed and made to rummage in a pocket of her slacks. Anne held out a paper tissue. Samira took it and dabbed her face, smiling again in embarrassment.

"I really am sorry ... tears of joy. I think your cottage is beautiful, Mrs Walker. It's so lovely and I'm really grateful."

"I'm glad you like it ... and it's Marnie."

"Thank you ... Marnie. Do please call me Samira."

Marnie handed her a front door key and added, "There are some things in the fridge to get you started: milk, bread, butter, eggs, cheese ... that sort of thing. I would've offered you a bottle of wine, but I thought perhaps that might not be appropriate."

"Very thoughtful of you, Marnie." Samira reached for her shoulder-bag. "Let me pay you for them."

Marnie held up a hand. "No. That's not necessary. They're just a few basics to make you feel welcome."

Samira took a deep breath, blinking rapidly. "Oh dear ... any more kindnesses and I'll be back to tears of joy." She laughed self-consciously.

Anne said, "Much more of this and I'll be joining you. Lucky I've got some more tissues."

They laughed together.

Marnie said, "I hope you'll be very happy here, Samira. Let me know if there's anything you need or if you have any questions."

Samira finished wiping her eyes and stuffed the tissue into her pocket.

"The other cottages are occupied?"

"Two young couples, very pleasant. They're out at work all day. I'll introduce you some time."

Samira nodded thoughtfully. Anne had been wondering what more she could do to help and suddenly realised there was something obvious. She left the kitchen and, seconds later, could be heard slowly climbing the stairs.

Marnie said, "There's something else I should explain. There are Chubb bolts on front and back doors."

"What are they?" Samira asked.

"The key's hanging on a hook in the kitchen. There's a spare for you in the cutlery drawer and we also keep all our keys on a board at the rear of the office. You just push the Chubb key

25

into the round holes at the top and bottom of the doors and turn it to fasten."

"Okay. Thanks."

Anne returned, slightly breathless and smiled at Samira.

"I've taken your bag upstairs. It's on the landing. I wasn't sure which bedroom you'd want to use."

"Oh really, you shouldn't have. That's very kind of you ... Anne."

"No probs. I've opened the windows a little in both bedrooms, front and back, to let in some fresh air."

Samira shook her head slowly. "You are both so kind."

"Don't mention it," Marnie said. "Now we're going to leave you in peace to unpack and settle in. Is there anything you need before we go ... information, a hug, more tissues ...?"

They were all smiling as Samira showed them out and closed the front door behind them. Outside, Marnie told Anne she needed to type something into the diary on her computer before she forgot. They were turning to cross to the office barn when they heard the bolts being fastened on the front door of the cottage. It was the first time they had ever known a tenant use them.

In the office barn, Marnie occupied herself at the keyboard while Anne took a fresh yellow folder from the store cupboard and labelled it:

Sally Ann
School visit, 11 July

Into the file she slotted the notes she had made in their meeting that morning with Margaret Giles. Anne always enjoyed the visit by school children in the summer term. It had become a village tradition since Marnie arrived with her boat, *Sally Ann*. Anne was already thinking up new ideas to make their educational trip a fun day out for the children.

By now it was time to close the office for lunch. Marnie was locking the office door behind them when they heard a strange sound in the air. It seemed to be coming from the other side of the courtyard. They advanced a few steps and stopped, their heads cocked to one side. The sound they heard was sobbing. Looking up, they realised that it was emanating from the front bedroom of cottage number three, Samira's cottage.

Of one thing they were certain. Those were not tears of joy.

"I'm not sure I understand the question." Marnie looked puzzled. She glanced to her side at Roger, who raised an eyebrow in the direction of DC Driscoll. Marnie continued. "What do you mean by 'how it went'? I showed Samira the cottage, and she moved in. That was it."

"Not quite," said Driscoll. "I was interested in her reaction. Did she enthuse about the cottage? Did she bombard you with a thousand questions on practical matters? On the other hand, did she seem disappointed? Might it have been too small? She must have made some reaction."

Marnie shrugged. "She said she liked it and wanted to move in straight away."

"She'd arrived by taxi with one piece of luggage, so what else was she going to do but move in there and then?"

"That's true."

"And what about food? If she only had a weekend bag, how was she going to organise provisions? Or hadn't she thought of that?"

"I'd put some food plus milk and mineral water in the fridge for the incoming tenant."

"Even though you had no idea that Samira Khan was going to be arriving that day?"

"I aim to make all my tenants feel welcome. When you first move in, things can get overlooked. It's nice to know you have some basics waiting for you; one less hassle to think about."

Driscoll sat back in her chair and stared over Marnie's shoulder at the wall behind her. Marnie waited in silence.

"Did you already know Samira Khan, Marnie?"

The question came as a surprise.

"Of course not."

"But you had things prepared in advance for her arrival."

"For *anybody's* arrival, at short notice."

"Weren't you worried that, for example, the milk might go off if left too long?"

Marnie collected her thoughts. "Look, first, my cottages are let as soon as they become available. It's not unusual for someone to move in straight away. That's how it is with good property for rent around here. There's a lot of demand for such accommodation, and the agent knows my cottages are top quality. Second, if the food wasn't going to be needed for a few days, I'd simply take anything that might be perishable and use it myself."

"You're sure you didn't know her before, Marnie?"

"Positive. Until that day I'd never set eyes on her."

"Shall we move on?" Roger said. "I think that point has now been firmly established."

"Then let's go back to how Samira settled in to her new temporary home. Can you take us on from there, Marnie?"

Before speaking, Marnie took a sip of her tea. It was now cold, but it gave her the space to clear her thoughts, to recall the events of Samira's arrival at Glebe Farm and work out what details she should describe and what was best omitted.

Chapter 4

Invitation

Ralph Lombard was fairly certain that he was the only academic in Britain who carried out his research and writing in a study on a canal boat. A few years earlier, he had sought a change of direction in his career. He had bought a boat and converted it into what he termed his own 'floating Oxford college'. He had retained his status of professor at the university – now as a *visiting professor* – at All Saints' College, one of the oldest, smallest and most prestigious institutions in Oxford. All its Fellows were eminent in their fields, and all its students were post-graduates and research associates. Such was Ralph's international reputation that, in addition to his university stipend, he was able to earn a more than comfortable living from writing books and articles and undertaking lucrative lecture tours around the world. His advice on matters of economics was sought in high places; he was frequently engaged as a consultant by a number of governments.

Ralph had conceived the idea of living and working on a narrowboat as a result of his first contact with Marnie, some years earlier. They had met in unusual circumstances when she pulled him out of the river in Oxford one summer night. It was to be a summer and an encounter that changed both their lives. Eventually it led to them living together in the recently renovated house at Glebe Farm. Ralph also owned a cottage in the village of Murton near Oxford, which he let to visiting academics.

His boat, *Thyrsis*, was moored on the canal close to Glebe Farm, a few yards away from the docking area in which Marnie kept *Sally Ann*. The canal was separated from the farm complex, a distance of about fifty yards, by a spinney, the two areas linked by a footpath through the trees. Ralph made his way along this path each morning at around ten-thirty to join Marnie and Anne for coffee in the office barn.

On the Thursday morning, two days after Samira arrived, Ralph came into the office for his short break and asked a question.

"She does exist in reality, does she, your Samira lady? She's not just a figment of your imagination, Marnie?"

"What a curious idea," Marnie said. "Why d'you say that?"

At the rear of the office Anne was making coffee in the kitchen area.

"I know what Ralph means," she said. "I was almost beginning to wonder about that myself, and I've actually met her."

Marnie said, "Ralph, you did say you thought you saw a young Asian woman going into the school the other day."

"True. So perhaps I'm hallucinating, too."

Marnie looked thoughtful. "Mm ... come to think of it, we haven't seen her since that day when she arrived. That would be ... Tuesday? I hope she's all right."

"Perhaps we could invite her over for coffee," Ralph suggested.

Marnie got up from her desk. "Good idea. I'll pop across and ask her."

Anne was already taking a fourth mug from the cupboard as Marnie reached the door and went out. The weather was cool for early May with a hint of rain in the air. Marnie knocked on the door and took a step back. She waited for a while and was wondering if Samira might have gone out when she heard a sound in the hallway. A tentative voice called through the door.

"Who is it?"

The tone was anxious. Marnie wondered again if Samira was paranoid.

"It's me, Marnie."

"Who?"

This was ridiculous. Who did she think it was?

"It's Marnie, Marnie Walker."

There was a rattling sound, the Chubb bolts being unfastened. The door opened a crack and Samira peeped out.

Seeing Marnie, she opened the door and peered to left and right, her dark eyes even wider than usual.

"Is everything all right?" Marnie asked.

"Yesterday I heard men's voices outside," Samira said in a suspicious tone.

"Those were the builders. They've been laying the terrace behind the house."

"You know them?"

"They're called Bob and Lenny and they've been working here on and off for the past few years. They were part of the team that renovated your cottage ... and my house, and all the other buildings here. So, yes, I know them quite well."

"They're not here today."

"No. That's because they've finished what they were doing."

What on earth is the matter with this woman? Marnie thought. She didn't mention that there would be more men coming from Monday onwards to work on the garden. That news might send her running to a fall-out shelter.

"Is everything all right, Samira? We haven't seen you since you arrived and we did wonder ..."

"I'm fine, thanks, Marnie. Everything is fine. It's all just lovely."

"What about food? You surely can't have enough, unless you brought something with you."

"You left things for me in the fridge."

"Yes, but they were just standbys. Actually, I came to ask if you'd like to come across for coffee. We take a short break at this time of day."

If Marnie expected a fulsome reply, she was disappointed.

"Erm ..."

"No pressure," Marnie said. "Some other time, perhaps?"

"That would be nice."

"Samira, it's entirely your choice how you live, but while you're here I feel bound to do what I can to make your life agreeable ... without in any way interfering. I know how much food I left for you and I'd like to make a suggestion. Either I can take you with me to the supermarket so that you can stock up when we do or, as a start, perhaps you'd like to join us this evening for supper."

Samira frowned. "Supper?"

"Dinner, evening meal ... that kind of thing. What d'you think? After all, you do have to eat."

With a quick glance round the empty courtyard, Samira surprised Marnie by relaxing into a smile.

"That would be great, Marnie. What time shall I come?"

DC Shirley Driscoll sat looking thoughtful for a few moments before turning to confer with her colleague, DC Harry Rabjohn. She whispered into his ear, and he in turn pointed to the notes he had been writing. Driscoll slowly read a page or so, muttered something inaudible to DC Rabjohn, then swivelled back in her seat to face Marnie.

Marnie and Roger had looked fleetingly at each other before watching the detectives.

"You haven't really told us very much about your first meeting, Marnie."

"I've told you what there is to tell. What do you want me to say? That she turned cartwheels round the courtyard, fell on the floor frothing at the mouth in ecstasy, or perhaps sniffed and said it would do?"

Roger said, "I think that subject has been pretty well covered, don't you? Surely it's time to move on."

Driscoll smiled. "That will be for me to decide, won't it?"

Marnie said, "I'd tell you more if I could but it was just a routine meeting: new prospective tenant views rental, likes it, moves in without delay. That's what usually happens. Fair rent, good accommodation, lovely surroundings – what do you expect? Places like that don't stay empty. They get snapped up at once."

Roger pointedly looked at his watch. Driscoll ignored him.

"How did you get on with Samira, Marnie?"

This new change of direction took Marnie by surprise. "All right."

"Not more than that?"

"She was a tenant. I did what I could to make her feel at home and welcome."

"How did you do that?"

"I've told you already. I put some basics in the fridge and –"

"I meant once Samira had moved in."

"After a day or two we invited her to join us for a meal."

"After a day or two, you say. In between times you got on –
to use your term – all right?"

Marnie was wary. It had not quite been like that.

"Look, I have a business to run and a lot of work. I'm not in
and out of the cottages checking up on my tenants. I let them
settle in and get on with their lives."

"But Samira was a new tenant. Did you enquire how she
was settling in?"

"After a short while, yes."

"How soon?"

"I think it was about two days after she arrived."

"But you didn't speak to her in the meantime?"

"I didn't see her in the meantime."

"Not at all?"

"No."

"Even though she lived just a few feet from your home and
just opposite your place of work?"

"No."

"Didn't that strike you as odd?"

"I told you. I'm very busy at work."

"I've seen your office, Marnie. You have a window like a
shop front. Surely you couldn't miss seeing someone in your
yard. And wouldn't it be normal for a new tenant to come to see
you with minor queries?"

"Some do, some don't. And I don't spend time looking out of
the window. In fact, my desk is positioned so that I face
inwards. It's ergonomics: daylight comes in over my left
shoulder."

Am I rambling? Marnie wondered. Remember Roger's
advice, she thought. *Don't elaborate. Keep it brief and to the
point.*

"How did it go?" Driscoll asked suddenly.

Marnie looked blank. "How did what go? Sorry, I'm not with
you."

"Your meal with Samira. How did it go?"

"Fine."

Driscoll stared at her. "Nothing out of the ordinary?"

35

Marnie opened her mouth to speak and closed it.

"Well?" said Driscoll. "It was a simple enough question."

"Apart from a small incident, everything was as I said ... fine."

Chapter 5

Small incident

The doorbell to the farmhouse rang promptly at seven. When Anne opened the door she was astonished at what she saw. Samira looked utterly stunning. She was wearing a calf-length full-sleeved dress in purple with a broad musk-rose hem and gold detailing over tight purple leggings and gold sandals. Her hair was worn over one shoulder in a thick plait, and the whole effect was complimented by discreet make-up that emphasised her colouring and especially her dark almond-shaped eyes.

Is everything all right?" Samira asked, her tone uncertain.

At first, Anne could not find words. She gawped. Eventually, still gawping, she said, "Blimey ..."

Er ..."

"Sorry." Anne opened the door wide and stepped back. "Didn't mean to keep you standing on the doorstep. Please come in. You look ..."

Anne gave up on finishing the sentence and led the way to the sitting room where Ralph was setting out glasses and nibbles on the coffee table. He looked up as Anne and Samira entered. He smiled and straightened his shoulders. The connecting doors to the dining room were open, and at that moment Marnie came in carrying two bottles.

"Samira, welcome. You already know Anne, of course. Let me introduce Ralph. They have a number of things in common including, as you've no doubt noticed, a very broad smile."

Samira looked uncertain. "Am I perhaps not ... appropriate? I only have one set of –"

"You look wonderful," Marnie reassured her.

Ralph stepped forward, still smiling, and they shook hands.

"Ralph is my partner," Marnie explained.

"You're also a designer?" Samira said.

Not that sort of partner," said Ralph. "I'm an economist."

Marnie offered Samira a place on the sofa. "Ralph's my ... fiancé."

Ah, yes." Samira turned to Ralph. "And do you live near here?"

"I live here, actually."

Samira lowered herself in one graceful movement onto the sofa. "Of course, yes. I understand."

Ralph asked, "Would you like something that describes itself as sparkling ginger with lemongrass as an alternative to white wine?"

"The sparkling, er … whatever, sounds lovely."

Samira accepted the 'sparkling whatever' from Ralph, who then poured wine in the other glasses. She was touched when Marnie raised hers and offered a toast to their new guest and neighbour. Marnie sat beside her on one sofa, while Ralph sat on the other and Anne took the armchair. Samira sipped her drink.

"This is delicious," she said.

"Good. We also have still and sparkling mineral waters and something based on elderflowers. Am I guessing correctly that you don't drink alcohol?"

"That's right. Thank you for being so considerate."

Anne grinned across the room. "We haven't got pork either. And I'm a veggie."

Is that on religious grounds?" Samira asked.

"Not really." Anne laughed. "I just find meat disgusting."

Hastily changing the subject, Marnie said, "So, Samira, tell us about yourself. What brings you to this neck of the woods?"

"Well, er … I just felt like a change of scene for a while."

"You're not here on account of a job?" Marnie said.

"No." Samira sipped her drink again. "But I did pay the agents for six months in advance, as well as the damage deposit, and I gave them my references."

Marnie looked puzzled. "Did you? I wasn't thinking along those lines, Samira. I was just naturally curious … just wanted to get to know you a little."

"You're probably not used to having the third degree," Ralph said.

Samira took another sip of her drink. Marnie was just thinking that she was using the drink as a kind of shield, when Samira jumped so violently that half the contents of her glass splashed over her dress. Anne was on her feet racing to the kitchen before Marnie realised what had caused the upset. Dolly the cat had jumped up to sit on Samira's lap. This had startled her. Samira was by now standing, staring down at the damp stain that covered the front of her dress.

"I'm so sorry," Marnie began. "I didn't know Dolly was even in the house."

"No, it's my fault," Samira protested. "I'm not used to having animals around. The cat surprised me and I over-reacted."

Anne hurried back clutching a towel in one hand and a roll of kitchen tissue in the other. She offered them both to Samira, who took the towel and wiped her hands as Anne took the glass from her.

While Samira was using tissues to wipe her dress, Marnie said, "We'd better treat that straight away. The colours are fast, aren't they?"

"Yes. I'd better change. I'm afraid I only have slacks and tops with me."

"Don't worry about that," Marnie said. "Go and change and bring the dress back with you. I'll deal with it here. I think it needs rinsing in slightly soapy water, then clean water. After that I'll put it in the dryer."

Anne went with Samira to the hall and opened the front door for her. When she returned, Marnie was already running water into the sink in the utility room. Anne checked the carpet for marks and went off to fetch a damp J-cloth. She had just finished rubbing the spot-marks away when the doorbell rang. This time Samira's arrival was less jaw-dropping. She was wearing a pale yellow smock top over black trousers, holding her dress over one arm. Marnie quickly took it and disappeared into the kitchen. On entering the sitting room, Samira noticed that the cat was curled up on an armchair. Dolly looked up appraisingly at Samira and, unconcerned, lowered her head onto her front paws.

"Come through to the dining room," Ralph said. "Marnie will be with us in just a moment."

Marnie reappeared, smiling. "I think your dress will be fine, Samira. It's in the dryer and will be good as new before the end of the evening."

Samira shook her head. "I'm sorry to make so much fuss. It's just that —"

Marnie raised a hand. "It's not a problem. No harm done. Let's eat."

****

"Lovely meal, darling." It was later that night. Ralph was towelling his hair dry after the shower, sitting on the bed in his dressing gown. "Though for a time I was beginning to wonder if the incident with Dolly and Samira's dress was going to be the high point of the evening. She wasn't very forthcoming."

Marnie emerged from the shower room in her bathrobe and padded across to sit at the dressing table. She began brushing her hair.

"I think she comes from a rather traditional background. Was that your impression, Ralph?"

"Definitely. She seemed taken aback to learn that we were living together and not married, though she just about managed to take it in her stride."

"She's certainly a beautiful girl and, whatever her background, she's not hard up. That dress of hers ... really top quality."

"And did she say she'd paid six months in advance for the cottage plus the damage deposit?" Ralph asked. "You don't usually ask for that, do you?"

"No. The agents must have insisted for some reason. I'll speak to them tomorrow. Ralph, how old do you think she is?"

Ralph considered the question. "Early twenties?"

"That's what I thought. Yet she's paid the agents around four thousand pounds, but doesn't seem to have a job."

Ralph said, "Did you notice she made no mention of her family, either?"

40

"You think that's odd?"

"I think the whole situation's odd. She's obviously a well brought-up young woman from a conservative religious background and she's moved into a small fairly remote village. Hardly her natural habitat."

Marnie agreed. "Since you put it like that ..." She continued brushing her hair. In the dressing table mirrors she could see Ralph lost in thought. After a while she said, "We really didn't learn much at all about her this evening, did we?"

"Hardly anything," said Ralph.

"Have you come to any other conclusions?" Marnie asked.

Ralph shrugged. "All sorts of questions are going round in my head, but not many answers, at least nothing definite. One thing's for certain. She's as nervous as a kitten."

Marnie stopped brushing and looked across at Ralph in the mirror.

"Even as a kitten, I can't imagine Dolly ever being quite that nervous," she said.

DC Shirley Driscoll conferred once again with her colleague. He thumbed back through his notes and finally tapped one page with a finger. Driscoll studied the text, murmured something indistinct to DC Rabjohn and turned back to face Marnie across the table.

"I have to say, Marnie, you're not really giving us much to go on. If you don't fill us in on the details, it makes it harder for us to help you."

Roger Broadbent interjected. "May I remind you, officer, that you have arrested my client and charged her with attempted murder. She is fully aware that your aim is to gather as much evidence against her as possible. May I also remind you that she is not obliged to tell you anything. I have advised her to cooperate with you as much as she can in order to help your enquiries and in the knowledge that she is entirely innocent of the charge."

While Roger was speaking, Driscoll did not cease staring at Marnie.

"So who was the man in black?"

"What?" Not for the first time during the interview, Marnie was thrown off balance.

"I think you know who I mean, Marnie. I know there was an incident concerning a 'man in black'. What can you tell me about him?"

Frowning, Marnie leaned over and whispered to Roger. "I don't get it."

"In what sense?" Roger's voice was barely audible.

"I can't see how this fits in with anything."

"You have no idea what she means? If that's the case you can make no comment, but remember, that could come back to bite you."

Marnie turned back, still frowning.

"Take your time," said Driscoll. "And while you're thinking about it, you might consider why you discriminated against Samira Khan."

Roger spoke quickly. "I fail to see the relevance of these questions. In fact, I think this interview is little more than a fishing expedition. We're trying to cooperate with your investigation, but you're obviously hunting in the dark. I'd like a break so that I can confer with my client."

"May I remind you, Mr Broadbent, that your client was arrested with the murder weapon in her hand. That is rather more than just circumstantial evidence, don't you agree?"

While this exchange was taking place, Marnie was thinking back to the events of the previous weeks. *The man in black?* Okay. But *discriminating against Samira*? How did they work that out? The whole situation was becoming more and more bizarre. Marnie was only vaguely aware that someone was talking to her ...

Chapter 6

A Man in Black

These were busy times for Walker and Co, interior design consultants. The next day, Friday morning, Marnie was gathering together papers and drawings for a meeting with clients; a barn conversion in a village near Daventry. Anne was sorting the post. The junk mail was already in the bin, and she was opening the letters. The first caused her to stop, sit back and look puzzled. Marnie noticed her reaction from across the office.

"Something up?" she asked.

"Not sure." Anne held up a cheque. "This is from the estate agents in Towcester."

"Cheques usually make you turn cartwheels. What's the problem?"

"First month's rent for cottage number three, in advance, plus damage deposit, less agency handling charge."

"Okay," said Marnie.

Anne shook her head. "Not okay."

"Why not?"

"Last night Samira said she'd paid *six* months' in advance. Wasn't that odd? Or had you asked for that?"

"Course not." Marnie set her briefcase down on the desk. "Usual terms: payment in advance, one calendar month at a time; refundable damage deposit with first month's rent. You know the score."

"Then why has Samira had to pay for six months from the start?" Anne asked.

"*Very* odd," Marnie agreed. She checked her watch and grabbed the briefcase. "Gotta go."

Anne said, "Shall I phone the agents and ask why?"

"Mm ... could do. Second thoughts, no, leave it to me."

"I'll remind you when you get back."

****

Marnie needed no reminding. On the road to her meeting she puzzled over the mysterious payment demand on Samira by the agents. Later, the thought troubled her on the way back to base. As soon as she arrived in the office, she dropped the briefcase beside the desk and reached for her address book. It was then that she spotted the yellow Post-it note stuck on the phone. She winked at Anne and began pressing buttons.

"Blackey and Johnson, Carla speaking, how may I help?"

"Carla, it's Marnie Walker, hi. Is Tony Dyson available?"

"I'll put you through, Marnie."

Dyson came on the line. "Marnie, lovely to hear from you. All well in Knightly St John?"

"You tell me. There seems to have been a policy change recently."

"A policy ... oh yes. You mean the Asian lady."

"Miss Samira Khan," Marnie said. "For some reason she has to pay up for the whole tenancy in advance. Why is that? I thought we'd agreed on the lettings policy. Or am I missing something?"

"Oh, Marnie." Dyson sighed. "Please don't be annoyed."

"Who says I'm annoyed? But I do admit I'm curious."

"You see, Marnie, it was like this. We noticed her outside, looking in the lettings window. Then she came in carrying an overnight bag and asked if your cottage was in a secluded location. I assured her it was, and she said she'd take it if she could move in straight away. I don't mean to be rude, but there was something really odd about her behaviour. She seemed somehow ... shifty."

"When was this?" Marnie asked.

"Tuesday morning, as soon as we opened."

"Okay. Go on."

"I thought she might be a time-waster. That's why I suggested paying for six months in advance."

"You thought you were calling her bluff."

"In a way, but she accepted without arguing. I told her we needed to check references. She gave me two names and phone numbers on the spot and said we could check them while she

45

sorted out the money. Well, you could've knocked me down with
a –"

"And did she? I mean, sort out the money?"

"I was astonished. She went out and came back half an hour
later with *cash*."

"*Cash?*" Marnie repeated. "That would be about four
thousand pounds. The references were kosher?"

Dyson chuckled. "Well ..."

"Yeah, yeah," Marnie said. "You know what I mean."

"Everything in order. All very satisfactory. She filled in the
tenancy agreement forms, and that was that."

"Then what did you do?"

"I left a message on your answerphone to say she'd be with
you around eleven."

"Actually, Tony, I meant what did you do with her money?"

"Ah, well." Dyson cleared his throat. "We er ..."

"Presumably," Marnie said, "you paid it into your holding
account."

"Yes."

"Which earns your company interest."

"Well, yes."

"At what rate?"

A pause. Then in a quiet voice, "Six per cent."

"And yet you sent me one month's rent plus deposit."

"As per our contract." His tone had become increasingly
sheepish.

"But our contract doesn't require full payment in advance,
does it?"

"Marnie, like I said, it was all on the spur of the –"

"Tony, let me tell you how it's going to be."

****

Over a sandwich lunch in the farmhouse kitchen, Marnie
outlined to Ralph the story of Samira and the cash payment,
plus a blow-by-blow account of how she dealt with the
situation. He was impressed.

46

"So," he said, "Dyson's sending you a cheque for the remaining five months' rent."

"He is ... today ... by first class post."

"And you're giving the money back to Samira."

"That's the idea. She can pay one month at a time, like any other tenant. I was appalled that Dyson should treat her like that."

"You don't think he was being –"

"No, nothing like that. I'm sure he's not prejudiced. He just thought her manner was suspicious."

Anne laughed. "He's not alone there." She choked on her sandwich and reached for the glass of mineral water, patting her chest. "Poetic justice," she muttered between croaks.

"I'm sure getting all that money back will cheer her up," Ralph said.

"I'm hoping it might bring her out of her shell," said Marnie.

"Oh, she's already out. In fact she's been out twice today."

Marnie stared at Ralph, incredulous. "Are you sure?"

"I saw her on the towpath this morning on my walk. Then a moment ago as I closed the front door."

Just then the phone began ringing. It was Marnie's sister. Beth was two years older, a book illustrator, married to a lecturer in physics at University College, London.

"Tell me your news, Marnie, then I'll tell you mine."

"You go first. You're obviously aching to tell me."

"Well, it's Paul's news really. He's going to take part in a research exchange project with ... wait for it ... the University of ... da-dah! ... Crete, no less."

"That's nice," Marnie said. "They have a university in Crete?"

"Huh! Tell me you're not jealous."

"Beth, I'm not –"

"I didn't mean that *literally*. Don't you think it's *great?*"

"I'm sure it's very interesting for Paul, but where do you come in?"

"I don't, actually. In fact, I go out."

"Now you're losing me."

"I'm going with him! For me it'll be like a holiday, three weeks or so, on the sun-soaked island of Crete. I can't wait."

"And you can be away from work for that time?"

"Sure. I've got a lull till the next book arrives. No problemo!"

"Isn't that Spanish?"

"So funny! Anyway, what news from the rural backwater? Oops! I mean idyll."

"I have a new tenant next door."

"Tell me more."

"She's early twenties, beautiful, quite well off and Asian."

"That's different. Where's she from?"

"Luton."

"Is this a wind-up, Marnie? I meant which part of Asia?"

"She really is from Luton, but obviously her origins are in Pakistan."

"What's she like?"

"Actually, she's of a rather nervous disposition."

Marnie outlined the incident with Dolly and the spilt drink.

"You've got to be careful there, Marnie."

"Just because she's a Muslim doesn't mean –"

"I didn't mean that. I'm just wary of anyone who doesn't like cats."

"Beth, I really have to go. I'm pleased about your news but I have a crust to earn."

After disconnecting, Marnie turned back to Ralph. "Sorry about that interruption. Where were we? Oh yes. I was impressed. You said you'd seen Samira twice in one day. That must be a good –"

She was interrupted by an urgent banging on the front door. It had turned to frantic by the time Marnie reached the hall, with Ralph and Anne close behind. Samira almost fell on top of her. Her expression was pure terror. Marnie took her in her arms to calm her down.

"Hey, hey, hey, Samira. What is it?"

Samira broke free, turned and slammed the door shut, leaning her back against it, panting heavily. Her voice, between gasps, was barely a whisper.

48

"Oh my God ... oh my God ... even here ..."

"Even here what?" Marnie asked.

Samira gulped. "Even here I'm not safe ... even here ..."

She closed her eyes, her chest heaving, both palms flat against the door behind her. Ralph stepped forward.

"Of course you're safe here, Samira," he said. "Why wouldn't you be?"

Samira shook her head, but did not reply.

Marnie said, "Ralph's right. You're perfectly safe here with us. Come on." She reached out and took Samira by the hand. "Come and have some water. Sit with us in the kitchen. Tell us what's scared you."

Samira reluctantly allowed herself to be coaxed away from the door. Marnie sat her down near the comforting warmth of the Aga while Anne poured a glass of sparkling water. She added two ice cubes and a slice of lemon and set it down in front of Samira who stared at it without moving. Her breath was now returning to normal, but she still seemed anxious. Marnie sat beside her, held her hand and offered her the glass. Samira took it and sipped. She breathed out heavily.

"By the canal on the path just now," she blurted. "I saw a man dressed all in black. He was coming this way."

Marnie, Ralph and Anne exchanged glances. Anne said, "Did he have blonde hair almost as fair as mine?"

Samira shook her head. "No. His head was covered ... a balaclava, I think."

"Are you sure about that?" said Marnie.

"I don't know. I ... I came away in a rush."

At that moment the doorbell rang. Its two-tone ringing sounded totally mundane, but Samira reacted as if it came from the depths of hell. She leapt to her feet, knocking over the chair, wildly scanning around her.

"I'll go," Ralph said calmly.

He went out to the entrance hall. Voices were heard.

Samira strained to listen, completely on edge. "It's a man."

Marnie said, "Samira –"

"No. Listen."

To Samira's dismay Anne's expression brightened. She quickly walked to the door and went out.

"What's she doing?" Samira asked in a whisper.

Marnie stepped forward and put a hand on Samira's shoulder.

"She's going to say hello to her boyfriend. He's your man in black."

****

For Samira there had been enough excitement for one day. Marnie suggested a restful afternoon in the cottage, and she agreed. That left Marnie and Ralph free to continue with their work, while Anne and her boyfriend retreated to Anne's loft to read companionably for their college and university courses.

It had become a regular pattern in their lives that Donovan would join them for weekends, unless Anne was visiting her parents and brother in Leighton Buzzard. Most often Donovan drove up from London in his venerable 1970s VW Beetle or, on rare occasions, in his classic 1950s Porsche sports car, both black, both inherited from his late parents. Though for that weekend he had travelled up over several days in his narrowboat. The name painted on its bows was *XO2*. It was pronounced *Exodos*.

As it was the last day of the normal working week, Marnie suggested that they get together at five o'clock for a kind of afternoon tea. When Samira asked what Marnie meant by 'kind of', Marnie said she would have to wait and see. She hastily added that it involved no unpleasant surprises.

****

At about four o'clock Anne heard Marnie downstairs getting afternoon refreshments ready for the men clearing out the farmhouse garden. Minutes later she heard Marnie go out. While Marnie was outside the phone began ringing in the office. Anne was on her feet in a second.

"I'd better get that."

50

Donovan glanced up from his own reading and saw her scramble down the wall-ladder. She managed to reach the phone just before the answerphone cut in, and was writing a message for Marnie when Donovan came down the wall-ladder.

"I've got things to fetch from the boat," he said.

Anne waved a slip of paper. "Can you give this to Marnie? She's left a note on the desk to say she's gone round to the garage barn."

It was a short detour for Donovan on his way to the boat. He expected that Marnie might be doing some work on her 1930s MG sports car, but he found her sitting in the Freelander with the driver's door open. She was immersed in an instruction manual of some kind, holding in one hand a small object about the size of a camera. She looked up when she heard his footsteps.

"Hi, Marnie. Phone message from Anne. What's that you've got there? New toy?"

"Sort of. One of these new satnav things. Present from Ralph. I thought I'd install it and try it out over the weekend."

"Satellite navigation," Donovan said. "Is it complicated?"

"Don't think so. Just plug it into the cigarette lighter and press a few buttons. Seems quite intuitive."

"Useful for going to meetings, I'd imagine."

"That's the idea." She glanced at the phone message. "Thanks for this."

"No trouble. I'm on my way to the boat for some goodies."

Marnie said, "For *Kaffee und Kuchen*?"

"Your accent's definitely improving."

"Can you find your way to the canal?" Marnie asked. "Wanna borrow the satnav?"

"I'll manage."

****

Samira rang the bell promptly at five, and Donovan offered to answer the door. Anne protested.

"No, I'll go. The sight of you might scare her off."

51

"So now I look like Quasimodo?" Donovan hunched forward, one arm dangling loosely, the other held up crooked and withered, muttering, "The bells, the bells ..."

Marnie said, "If someone doesn't go soon, the poor girl will have taken off in alarm." She looked at Donovan. "Isn't that your Richard the Third impression?"

Anne skipped past Quasimodo, alias Richard III, and out into the hall. Samira's entrance this time was not as spectacular as on her first invitation, but she wore an embroidered pashmina in gold and burgundy over a loose top of gold satin and black trousers. More than a hint of star quality. She was holding a small posy of yellow roses.

"I know this will seem like an awful cheek – offering you your own flowers – but these lovely roses are just coming into bloom in the cottage garden. I thought it would be nice to share them with you."

"A kind thought, Samira," Marnie said. She was occupied with kettle and teapot while Anne and Ralph were laying the table. Over her shoulder she said, "Donovan, be an angel. Can you deal with the flowers? There's a small vase on the window sill."

"Sure." He took them from Samira. "These are *Maigold*," he said, pronouncing the name as *my golt*. "They're always the first to come out in our garden at home."

Samira watched him discreetly as he set about filling the vase and arranging the roses. He was slightly taller than she was, she guessed around five-ten, with a slim build and blonde hair. In colouring he was similar to Anne, though not nearly as pale.

Samira remarked on this. "If I didn't know you were Anne's friend, I could have taken you for brother and sister."

Anne said, "I do have a brother. He's not like Donovan, though he does have the same nice nature."

Donovan added, "And unlike me he doesn't look like Quasimodo."

Anne stuck out her tongue at him.

Samira was surprised that she had ever found Donovan threatening. After placing the vase on the table, he bent down and picked up his black rucksack.

"What have you got there?" Anne asked.

Donovan smiled. "You know what I've got: my secret weapon."

Samira's brows furrowed. Marnie quickly explained.

"Donovan has just came back from visiting relatives in Germany. That usually means only one thing."

"So first I was compared to Quasimodo, then Richard III, now I'm boringly predictable. Can't think why I bother coming here."

"I can," Anne said coquettishly, trying not totally successfully to look vampish.

Samira quickly asked, "What's your secret weapon?"

Donovan said, "In this case *Linzertorte* – a sort of raspberry tart – and *Marmorkuchen*, which is like a marbled sponge cake. I can't bring some of the more exotic varieties because they contain cream. It would go off."

"Believe me, Samira," Marnie said, "they're all delicious and utterly dangerous."

Samira smiled. "That's the kind of danger I can handle."

Amid laughter they took their places at the table. Donovan set out the cakes while Marnie poured tea for Samira and herself. Ralph and Anne joined Donovan in coffee, which had also been brought from Germany. Samira admired the table decoration which comprised her roses and an ornately carved candle that Donovan lit, even though it was broad daylight.

"There's one thing we need to clear up," Marnie said. "Donovan was *not* wearing a balaclava."

Hearing this, Donovan reached down into his rucksack and produced a black knitted woolly hat. Quoting Sir John Falstaff, he said, "*Ecce signum.*"

"You needed a hat in this weather?" Samira said.

"I set off this morning at sunrise when it was pretty cool. I suppose I just left it on without thinking about it."

53

Marnie reached across the table and squeezed Samira's hand. "You see, you can relax. Not a balaclava at all."

"Mind you," Anne said, "It's a good job you didn't see him on his boat. That's even *more* spooky! It's painted dark grey – *battleship* grey – with a matt black hull. We even call it the U-boat."

"Why is it painted like that?" Samira asked. "I thought barges were supposed to be colourful." She noticed a slight reaction from the others. "Er ... have I said the wrong thing?"

Marnie smiled at her. "A cardinal sin. We don't have *barges*. We have *narrowboats*."

"Oh dear. Is that serious?"

Ralph was suddenly transformed into Long John Silver, intoning in a hoarse voice, "Oh aarh ... to the loikes of Oi, 'tis a sin against Creation, me 'earties."

Samira put a hand to her mouth and laughed in a manner that was heartfelt yet elegant. "Narrowboat, *not* barge," she spluttered. "I won't forget."

"Yee've got it, moi flower," said Long John Silver.

****

Afterwards Marnie insisted on escorting Samira back to the cottage, a distance of less than fifty feet. Samira asked if Marnie would like to come in, and was surprised when Marnie accepted. They walked through to the kitchen and perched against the units.

"Samira, is there anything you want to talk about?"

"Why do you ask, Marnie?"

"Well, you're obviously very anxious about something. You seldom leave the cottage, you were spooked by Donovan and you seem to have left wherever you came from in a hurry."

"In a hurry?" Samira repeated.

Marnie nodded. "You only brought a weekend bag. Or perhaps your luggage is being sent on separately?"

Samira unhitched the pashmina from over one shoulder and let it hang down like a cloak. She answered quietly, "I just need some time and space to work things out. You see, Marnie, it's rather complicated."

Marnie said. "I'm not wanting to pry into your life, Samira."

"But you did ask me."

"I asked if there was anything you *wanted* to talk about. I wasn't trying to meddle in private matters. Just remember we're here for you if ever you need help or want to talk. That's all."

"Thanks, Marnie."

"There is one thing, though."

"What's that?"

"I'm worried that you can't have any food left in the fridge. I'm going to the supermarket tomorrow. Would you like to come with me to stock up?"

A warm and dazzling smile lit up Samira's attractive face.

"You're always so practical and helpful, Marnie. You're like ... I don't know ..."

"Don't say I'm like your mum!"

Samira's smile began to fade. "No, I wouldn't say that. I was thinking more along the lines of ... a guardian angel."

"I can live with that," Marnie said. "I wasn't meaning to intrude into your own family."

"But it's like being with a family here, isn't it?" Samira said. "You and Ralph, Anne and Donovan."

"I suppose we are, really."

"I felt a fool, mistaking Donovan for a ..."

"For a what?" Marnie asked.

"For a ... sinister person. In fact, he seems very nice."

"We're all very fond of him, especially Anne, of course. Obviously."

Samira's demeanour suddenly changed. Her expression became wistful, even coy.

"Marnie, can I ask you something?"

"Go ahead."

"When Donovan comes, does he ... well, does he stay on his boat?"

"Not usually. Sometimes he does, but most often he stays with Anne in her attic room."

Samira lowered her gaze. "And you approve of that?" Before Marnie could reply she added, "What do Anne's parents think? She said she has a brother. What would he say?"

"Don't take this the wrong way, Samira, but I wouldn't think that was anyone's business but Anne's ... and Donovan's of course. And I'm sure no-one would expect her brother even to have a view, least of all him."

Samira nodded slowly. "Interesting..."

"Does that surprise you ... or shock you, perhaps?" Marnie asked.

Samira hesitated. "In my world things are very different."

"You've led a rather sheltered life, you mean?"

This time Samira's smile was rueful. "I wouldn't quite put it like that."

DC Shirley Driscoll was getting on Marnie's nerves. She had begun in a relaxed conversational style, as Roger Broadbent had predicted, but her questions were surrounded by tripwires. Marnie had been questioned by the police on other occasions and knew her track record in handling them was poor. She had a knack of saying the wrong thing, of appearing deliberately to be trying to mislead, of giving a false impression. As the interview wore on, she could feel herself slipping into old habits. Mentally she gritted her teeth. *Keep it simple, Marnie*, she told herself. Short succinct accurate replies were all that was needed. But it wasn't easy.

"So, Marnie, you maintain you at no time discriminated against Samira Khan."

"Why would I want –" Marnie hit the brakes and stopped abruptly. "No."

"No?"

Marnie shook her head.

"For the tape, please, Marnie."

She's trying to get me to expand. "I think it heard me first time."

Beside her, Roger cleared his throat again. Marnie knew he was warning her not to get rattled. *Just take it calmly*, he was saying. She gave him a quick smile to show she understood.

"No discrimination, then," Driscoll went on. Another change of tack. "Would you say you took an interest in Samira's financial affairs, a *personal* interest?"

"Not in the way you seem to be implying."

"Then how would you describe the way you became involved?"

"I don't know what you mean. I didn't *get involved*, as you put it." Marnie turned to Roger. "Do I have to answer this? What possible bearing does it have on my arrest?"

"Good point, Marnie. I was beginning to wonder about that myself. Well, officer?"

"As you can surely see, I'm trying to establish the way in which your client began insinuating herself into the personal affairs of Miss Khan. That is entirely relevant to what subsequently happened."

"But I did no such thing," Marnie insisted.

Another side-step from Driscoll. "How would you describe Samira's state of mind at that time?"

Marnie saw red lights flashing. She thought back to the day she had advised Samira about money and was pleased she had evaded that question, even though her involvement was completely benign and innocent. But Samira's state of mind, that was tricky. Marnie saw the trap the detective had laid for her and had no intention of falling into it. DC Driscoll was looking at her expectantly.

Chapter 7

Pure Gold

Anne had dealt with the Saturday morning post and was filing the previous day's correspondence when she looked across the office to Marnie.

"What time did you say you were taking Samira shopping?" she asked.

"I said I thought we might go about nine."

Anne checked her watch and smiled to herself. The hour hand was bang on nine; the minute hand was just coming up to nudge twelve. At that moment there came a faint knock at the door and Samira looked in.

"Morning, Marnie. Hope I'm not late. Hello, Anne."

"Hi," Marnie and Anne chorused with one voice.

Marnie glanced up at the wall clock. "You're spot-on, Samira. What's it like out?"

"Pleasant."

"Then I'll come as I am." She switched the computer to *Sleep* mode, grabbed her shoulder-bag from the floor and stood up. "But first, there's something I have to give you."

"Give me?"

Marnie gestured her over. "Yes." From the desk she took a cheque and held it towards Samira. "This is for you."

Frowning, Samira took the cheque and studied it. "Three thousand ..." Her voice fell away as she lifted her eyes to stare at Marnie. "I don't understand. This must be several months' rent."

"Five months to be precise. You'll notice that the cheque is from the estate agents."

"But I paid for everything in advance. That's what Mr Dyson asked for." Samira looked baffled. "Are you giving me notice, Marnie?"

"No, of course not! It's a refund. He had no right to ask for so much all at once. You've paid for the first month and from now on you'll pay one month's rent at the start of each calendar month, the same as the other tenants."

"Are you sure that's all right?"

"Absolutely. We can call in at the bank on our way out shopping, so you can pay it in. They open on Saturday mornings."

Samira took a wallet from her bag and opened it to slot in the cheque. Marnie was amazed; the wallet was bulging with fifty pound notes. She stepped forward and placed a hand on Samira's arm.

"Why on earth do you carry so much money around with you?"

Samira quickly pushed the wallet back into her bag. "I ... I didn't know when ... I thought it would cover all possibilities."

"Even so ..." Marnie turned towards Anne. "What's our most secure storage?"

"How much are you talking about?" Anne asked.

"Rough guess, a few thousand."

"In *cash?*" Anne shook her head. "We've only got lockable drawers in our desks or the filing cabinet." She added, "You said you were going to the bank."

Marnie turned back to Samira. "Anne's right. I think you should pay in most of that, as well as the cheque."

Samira hesitated. "I don't know ..."

"Presumably you have a debit card?"

"Yes."

"Good, that's settled."

They were in the Freelander halfway up the field track when Marnie said, "No wonder you always bolt the door, with all that cash in the house. It's hardly surprising."

Samira began, "That isn't why I ..." She stopped in mid-sentence and turned her head away to look out of the window.

She did not speak again on that journey, and Marnie let it pass without comment. She could almost feel the inner conflict and anxiety emanating from the passenger seat. As they drove in silence along the dual carriageway, Marnie kept seeing flashbacks to that wallet bursting with money. Where did it all come from? What was it for? She could think of even more questions about Samira herself, but put them aside to concentrate on driving ... for the time being.

****

Meanwhile, back in the office, Anne phoned Donovan's mobile. He had gone out after breakfast to move his boat to the Glebe Farm moorings. On Friday he had moored further up the canal so as not to impede *Sally Ann* or *Thyrsis*. When Donovan answered the call, there was no engine rumble in the background.

"All done?" Anne asked.

"Safely stowed away. I'll be with you in five."

Five minutes came and went. Ten minutes. After a quarter of an hour Anne became curious. Nothing odd about it really. There were always things to do on a boat, but it wasn't like Donovan to be imprecise. Anne picked up her mobile and wondered about ringing him. She decided to be patient.

One minute later she stood up and headed for the door. Outside there was no sign of Donovan. Anne turned the corner and set off along the footpath through the spinney. She had gone no more than a few paces when she heard a strange swooshing sound. She stopped and listened. Then she saw movement in the trees about twenty yards off the path to one side. Donovan was kneeling in the undergrowth. He signalled to her to get down.

Anne leapt off the path and squatted among the trees, scanning the spinney, wondering what had caused Donovan to conceal himself. Then she saw it: two men standing close together towards the outer edge of the trees, talking quietly. Both were dressed in woodland camouflage gear with drab green woolly hats. Each had a pair of binoculars slung round his neck.

Anne stifled a gasp as Donovan materialised suddenly and silently beside her.

"Who are they?" she whispered.

"No idea. I spotted them as I was getting off the boat. I don't know how long they've been here."

61

"Could they be birdwatchers?" Anne asked.

"Dunno. We've never had any round here before, at least not in my time. And I don't remember seeing any unusual birds in these parts."

"Perhaps they don't realise this is private land."

"There are no public footpaths here. I'd expect serious twitchers to have maps of the area."

"Twitchers?"

"Fans of our feathered friends."

"Look!" Anne pointed. "They're going."

The men skirted the spinney, walking rapidly past the moored boats in the direction of the accommodation bridge. Donovan and Anne slowly stood up.

"Did you get a good look at them?" Donovan asked.

"Not really. They were mostly covered up and standing too close together for me to see what they looked like. You?"

Donovan shook his head. "The same. There's only one thing for it."

Anne stared back, deadpan. "Put the kettle on?"

****

Marnie's timing was right. By the time they reached the high street, the banks were open. By coincidence Samira used the same bank as Marnie, which turned out to be an advantage. They found an available cashier without waiting, and Samira quickly filled out a paying-in slip while Marnie chatted to the young woman behind the counter.

"Anne not with you today, Marnie?"

"No, Anita. Her boyfriend's come for the weekend, so she has other fish to fry."

"Is she still with that rather nice-looking young guy ... black clothes, blonde hair, attitude?"

Marnie smiled. "That's the one."

Samira slid the paying-in slip with the cheque and bundle of cash into the tray. Anita reached through and gathered up the items. She read the slip, studied the notes and looked up at Samira with a quizzical expression.

62

"Quite a large sum," she observed.

Marnie said, "I thought you could handle cash up to ten thousand. Isn't that right?"

"Normally, yes."

"But?"

The cashier looked embarrassed. "We've had a memo round about ... don't laugh ... about money-laundering."

A sudden intake of breath from Samira. "You don't think I'm ..." She turned to look at Marnie. "Surely ..."

Anita said, "Marnie, you obviously know this lady ..." She looked down at the paying-in slip. "... Miss Khan."

"Yes. She's renting one of my cottages for a while. That money's a refund. There was a misunderstanding with the estate agents."

Anita nodded. "Ah, I see." She smiled. "That's fine."

Samira and Marnie waited in silence while the cashier counted the notes, dividing them into bundles of a thousand pounds each. She stamped and initialled the slip and its stub and passed the latter back to Samira with a friendly smile.

"Anything else I can do for you, Miss Khan?"

Samira shook her head without a word and turned to go. Anita looked at Marnie.

"Nothing for you today, Marnie?"

"Could you just check the balance in my current account?"

"Sure." She consulted her screen and wrote the balance on a slip of paper. She folded it and passed it back through the tray. "Have a good weekend. Say hi to Anne ... and her *beau*."

Outside on the pavement, Samira was looking thoughtful.

"Fancy a coffee?" Marnie asked. "There's a very good coffee shop round the corner."

Samira did not seem to hear the invitation. "If you hadn't been there, Marnie ..."

Marnie shrugged. "It's obvious what happened. The bank had an instruction from head office, and they didn't know you personally at this branch. You were paying in thousands in cash. Very unusual, but that's all it was."

"You think?" Samira looked troubled.

"Absolutely. Why else?"

"You don't think it's because … I'm Asian?"

Marnie laughed. "No, definitely not!"

"What makes you so certain, Marnie?"

Marnie looked Samira straight in the eye. "The manager of this branch is Mr Pranab Patel. He's been in charge for some years, and he was a great help to me when I first set up the business."

"Oh dear, I think I over-reacted. Perhaps I should go back and apologise to … what was her name? Anita?"

"Don't worry about it. Come on. Let's get coffee before we hit the supermarket."

"Okay, but it's my treat. After all, I'm the moneybags round here." Samira grinned. "That's official. Ask the bank if you don't believe me."

They linked arms and set off down the street, laughing.

****

Donovan turned the two visitors' chairs round to face each other by Anne's desk while she brought mugs of coffee from the kitchen area. By the time they returned to the office barn they had given up speculating about the strangers in the spinney, though they would both be wary about possible intruders in the future.

Anne changed the subject and told Donovan about Samira's money.

He was amazed. "*How* much?"

Anne nodded. "Yep. Several thousand, according to what Marnie saw."

Donovan looked impressed. "The milky bars are definitely on Samira."

"Too right."

"Any idea how she came to have so much?"

"None at all. In fact, she's frankly a bit of an enigma all round. We don't know where she's from, what she does, why she's here or anything about her."

"Except that she's loaded," Donovan murmured.

"Why would someone carry so much around in *cash*?" Anne asked.

Donovan pondered. "Perhaps she's sold a car. That can involve large amounts of cash. Or maybe for some reason she's taken out her life savings. Did you see the notes, Anne? Were they all pristine as if they'd just come from a bank?"

"You're not seriously thinking she might have robbed a –"

"Course not. But suppose she'd been saving money from, maybe, holiday jobs. The notes would probably all look used, as opposed to drawing out a lot of cash from a bank, in which case they could come in new batches."

Anne sipped her coffee. "There's no way of knowing, is there?"

"Probably not and, in any case, it's not really any of our business."

"That's true." Anne smiled wistfully. "But it is very intriguing."

****

Samira insisted on getting the coffees while Marnie found a vacant table. The coffee shop was always busy on a Saturday morning, and Marnie was lucky to find a small table for two just vacated in the furthest corner from the entrance. She waved at Samira as she left the counter carrying a tray. For a moment it felt to Marnie as if they had been friends for a long time. She noticed that Samira's expression had become serious as she set the coffee cups down on the table. When they were settled, Marnie had the impression that Samira had something to say. She waited.

"Marnie?"

"Yes?"

"Look, there's something I ought to tell you."

"You don't owe me any explanations."

Marnie stirred her cappuccino without looking up. Samira glanced round at the other patrons before speaking in a hushed voice.

"It's about the money. You were wondering why I was carrying so much cash."

"Only natural curiosity," Marnie said. "It was more than I've ever carried around ... much more."

"I had savings in a building society. I began putting money away from holiday jobs, then carried on when I started work. Later, I inherited from grandparents and other relatives. We're quite a large family. Some of it was special gifts."

"How special?"

Samira stared down at the table. When she eventually spoke, her voice was barely a whisper.

"There were gifts from family members towards ... my dowry."

"I see."

"Perhaps you don't, Marnie. In my community it's quite a big deal, the dowry. And there's more to it than just money."

"Okay."

Samira briefly looked again around the coffee shop. She leaned forward slightly in her chair and gently pulled aside the collar of her top. Marnie saw that she was wearing a chunky necklace, a thick chain of gold.

"You see this, Marnie?" she said softly. "It's pure gold. I mean literally. There aren't many places in the world where you can get actual twenty-four carat gold. It's not common in this country, for example, but it's highly prized in the Middle East and the South Asia."

"It looks beautiful," Marnie said.

"I have a collection of gold jewellery; gifts. I've brought them with me. They're in the cottage."

Marnie frowned. "Blimey. I don't think my insurance policy for the cottages covers that kind of value."

"I don't suppose anyone would expect to find such things in a small country cottage, Marnie. I shouldn't worry if I were you."

"Ah ..." Marnie began. The light dawned. "Now I understand why you always keep the doors locked and bolted. It explains a lot."

"No, Marnie, you don't understand, not really. But that's another story."

Marnie waited, but Samira offered no further explanation.

****

The Freelander with its cargo of provisions descended the field track shortly before one o'clock. Samira and Marnie loaded themselves up with carrier bags and trudged round from the garage barn.

"Samira, join us for lunch."

"Oh, I really couldn't impose."

"It's no great feast on a Saturday," Marnie protested. "My guess is probably soup and maybe some cheese, a salad."

"But you're not sure?"

"Anne and Donovan will be preparing something, or maybe Ralph will."

They turned the corner into the courtyard between the office barn and the farmhouse.

"Yours is a very democratic household," Samira observed.

"I suppose it is. I've never really thought about it like that. We just get on and do what's needed."

Samira said, "I can't imagine my brother making a meal for the rest of us." She laughed. "What a thought!"

"I didn't know you had a brother," said Marnie.

"He's the baby of the family. Tariq. He's fifteen with two sisters and a doting mother – well, usually – so he's hopelessly spoilt."

"You have a sister, too."

Samira nodded. "Rashida. She's lovely, still at school studying for A Levels."

"So you're the eldest."

"Big sister, that's me."

Samira smiled. Marnie was pleased at how she was becoming more relaxed. They arrived at the front door. Marnie put down one of her bags and pulled out the key. They entered the hallway and heard the chugging of a food processor. The door of the kitchen was ajar, and a faint odour of garlic wafted through.

"What did I tell you?" Marnie said. "They're making soup. Do stay."

"I'd love to, if there's enough to go round."

"There will be, don't worry."

They were lowering their shopping to the floor when the machine in the kitchen stopped and they heard voices, Anne at first.

"I think you've been very calm about it, but I must say I'm a tad concerned about those men appearing out of the blue like that. You don't really believe they were bird-watchers, do you?"

Donovan said, "I don't know what they were, but I think it would do no harm to be on our guard without making a song and dance of it. I shouldn't mention it to you-know-who."

"Shouldn't that be you-know-*whom*?"

Donovan's reply was a loud raspberry. Marnie pushed the door further open and walked in.

"Hi, folks. We're back."

"Didn't hear you arrive," Anne said.

Marnie announced. "And we have a guest for lunch."

She turned to one side and smiled as Samira appeared in the doorway. In contrast, Samira was not smiling. She was staring.

"What men?" she said without preamble.

"Oh, just two guys in the spinney," Donovan said casually. "They looked harmless enough ... bird-watchers, I reckon."

Marnie said, "Samira, come and sit down. You like quite ... pale."

Marnie hoped that statement didn't seem too strange, given Samira's colouring. She guided her to a chair. As she sat, Samira stared up at Marnie.

"I can't ... nowhere is ... oh, Marnie."

"Sorry, Samira, I don't follow."

Anne came over and stood beside them. "Look, there's really nothing to worry about."

68

Samira looked unconvinced. "No? Then who were the men you saw?" She seemed close to tears. "Why were they snooping around?"

Donovan joined in. "They stood by the trees for a bit, then moved on. That's what people do in the country, Samira. It's not uncommon."

Samira stood up. "Forgive me if I don't stay for lunch after all. It was kind of you to invite me."

The others looked on as Samira hurried out of the room to pick up her shopping. They heard the front door shut, and the house fell silent.

****

They were clearing away the dishes after the soup-and-sandwich lunch when the doorbell rang. Marnie had a foreboding that all was not well as she made for the entrance hall. She was right. Opening the front door, she found Samira on the doorstep. On the floor beside her were her weekend bag and the shopping from that morning.

"I'm really sorry about this, Marnie." She held out a slip of paper. Marnie saw it was a cheque. "I don't have much actual cash now, but this covers the rest of my six months in line with the agreement I signed."

Marnie shook her head. "What are you doing, Samira?"

"I'm giving notice that —"

"Yes, I can see that, but why? I don't understand."

"Those men ... the ones who were here this morning. I'm sure they —"

"You don't know anything about them. Donovan was right. Out here in the country people are always tramping around. They go for walks, look at birds, wildlife, flowers. They're just out to enjoy nature and the open air."

"Why did they come into your spinney, Marnie?"

"Who knows? It's how *I* came here in the first place a few years ago. I was on the canal and I saw rooftops through the trees. I was curious, so I came to explore. There are no *Keep*

Out or *Private Property* signs here. I don't go in for that kind of thing."

Samira looked doubtful.

"Come on," Marnie said. "Be practical, Samira. Where are you going to go?"

Samira's expression changed from uncertain to desperate.

"I need to go somewhere where I'll feel safe. Those men in the trees have unsettled me. To be honest, Marnie, I can't really think of anywhere safe right now. I only know I –"

"I can."

It was Donovan who spoke. He stepped out from behind Marnie. Samira stared at him, took in his confident no-nonsense bearing, his steady gaze, his you-can-have-faith-in-me attitude. For all that, everyone knew she would take some persuading.

****

They stood on the bank between *Sally Ann* and *Thyrsis*: Marnie and Samira, Ralph and Anne. The afternoon sun was flitting between high clouds bringing just enough warmth into the air to make the day pleasant and comfortable. Samira's weekend bag lay on the grass beside her.

Donovan had asked the others to give him fifteen minutes' start before following him down to the canal. Marnie had noticed that on leaving he had grabbed Samira's bags of provisions from the hall. While they waited, Marnie had coaxed Samira into eating a bowl of soup and a crusty roll. This had had the effect of calming her down, but only by half a notch. Now, grouped together beside the moorings, Samira was gradually working herself back into a state of nervousness.

"I don't get it," she said, looking round in all directions. "Isn't this where you saw those men, Anne?"

Anne's reply was totally nonchalant. "That was then. There's certainly nobody here now. Look around you. The place is deserted."

"Even so, I ... what's that?" Samira cocked her head to one side.

They all heard it at the same time, a low rumbling, trembling in the air, followed by the short blast of a horn. Samira was startled when without warning Anne sped off round *Sally Ann*'s docking area and jogged towards the bridge a short distance away. Everyone looked on as Anne came to a halt, raised both arms in the air and began waving in a semaphore criss-cross motion above her head. Almost at once the prow of a narrowboat appeared through the bridge hole. *XO2* emerged slowly, her engine note picking up. Donovan brought his boat expertly to a halt alongside *Thyrsis*, where Ralph was standing on the gunwale, ready to make her fast.

Samira had been frowning until then, but now began to understand what was happening. The thought did not seem to bring her much comfort. Donovan and Ralph clambered over *Thyrsis* and hopped down onto the bank. As the five of them regrouped beside the boats, Samira was the first to speak.

"I don't think so."

"You don't think what?" said Marnie.

"Donovan's got a plan to take me somewhere on his boat. It wouldn't be a good idea. In fact, it could make matters a whole lot worse, believe me."

"That isn't what I have in mind," Donovan said. "I wouldn't be so stupid."

"Then what do you have in mind?"

Donovan outlined his plan. It evoked a mixed response. Marnie thought it sounded a little reckless and therefore typical Donovan. Ralph wondered if Samira could possibly go along with it; on the whole he thought probably not. Anne was the least surprised, but tried to look on the bright side. It was better than Samira just leaving on her own without any notion of where she was going or what she was going to do. Once again Samira spoke first.

"Are you serious, Donovan? Or are you teasing me?"

Anne interjected. "Donovan wouldn't do that."

"Anne's right," said Ralph. "Whatever you think of the idea, his reasoning is actually quite sound."

71

Marnie often thought Ralph sounded like a text book, but she was sure he was right. She said, "I think it's worth a try, Samira. After all, what have you got to lose? And do you have a better plan?"

Samira shook her head. "No, I don't. It's just that Donovan's idea is practically the last thing I'd ever think of doing."

Donovan permitted himself the faintest smile. "Exactly. That's the beauty of it. So what do you say? It's entirely your decision."

It fell to Marnie to speak for them all. "Let's go for it."

****

Donovan manoeuvred *XO2* round to face northwards, and within minutes the small convoy slipped under the accommodation bridge and headed up the Grand Union Canal in line astern. Donovan led the way on his boat with Anne and Samira, followed by Marnie and Ralph on *Thyrsis*. As they set off, Samira announced that she had never been on that kind of boat before, or in fact any other sort. She stared around her at the slowly passing countryside, her expression an intrigued smile.

They cruised steadily on, watched only by the occasional fawn-coloured cow drinking at the water's edge and random sheep grazing in a meadow on the opposite side. No other gaze fell upon them, not even the unblinking stare of a lugubrious heron. Away to the far horizon the country was only pierced by a distant church steeple, and once or twice they caught a glimpse of a rooftop in among trees beyond the fields and woods. The towpath was undisturbed by jogger, stroller, hiker or angler. They were in the middle of England barely fifty miles from London, yet they saw no-one and, more importantly for Samira, no-one saw them.

About fifteen minutes passed, and the sky was clouding over when Donovan turned round in the leading boat and signalled to Marnie that he was slowing down. He held up both hands with palms facing *Sally Ann*. Marnie responded by pushing the heavy gear lever into reverse and pressing down firmly on the

72

accelerator, bringing the boat smoothly to a halt in mid-channel. She and Ralph looked on as Donovan steered *XO2* to the left, over to the non-towpath side of the canal. There, a cluster of spreading willow trees reached out to trail their fronds in the water.

Slowly and carefully Donovan slid the boat in under the projecting greenery until the entire vessel was virtually concealed from view. The grey and black paintwork looked no more than a shadow in amongst the new and abundant foliage of the trees and the thick bramble bushes that partly skirted the field beyond.

On board, Donovan let Anne escort Samira through the boat on a conducted tour of its facilities. In the gathering half-light under the lowering sky and with the curtains drawn to cover the port-holes, it was necessary to turn on the lights as they progressed from one space to the next.

"Okay?" Donovan said. "Have you got all that? I'll put clean linen on the bed so that you can make it up fresh. I'll pull the current sheets and pillow-cases off and take them back to Glebe Farm to wash. You've got the shower room and loo through there. The rest is obvious: galley, dinette and study all together ... open plan."

Samira looked embarrassed.

"What is it?" Donovan asked. "I'm sorry to be standing so close to you in this confined space. I realise that's not your preference, but I've made sure Anne was here as –"

"No, no, it's not that," Samira protested. "It's ... I couldn't help noticing ..."

She glanced at a matt black metal bookcase mounted on the wall near the galley. On the side of it were three photographs of silver racing cars from long ago. One of them was clearly marked with a black swastika inside a red circle.

"Donovan's not a Nazi," Anne said quickly.

Donovan smiled. "No, quite the opposite. Those photos were taken by a great-uncle I never knew. He was a photo-journalist, worked on German magazines before the war. We believe the

Nazis killed him in 1939. I keep them as mementoes of his work, a reminder of what he was up against."

Samira looked even more embarrassed. "I'm so sorry. I didn't realise."

"How could you?" Donovan reassured her. "Now, what do you think of this location? No-one's going to think of looking for you here."

In the few seconds of silence that followed, they became vaguely aware of the rumble of an engine outside. The boat rocked gently at its mooring.

"You think that's what's worrying me?" Samira said.

"Of course it is. It's obvious. I thought this would be a good place for you to take time out in total seclusion. All your food and stuff is already on board, and you're welcome to anything of mine in the cupboards and fridge. I keep the boat well stocked all the time. There's a mini-hi-fi, including a radio plus a load of CDs so you shouldn't get bored." He pointed to the shelves at the far end of the study area. "Quite a few of the books are in English, too. Any questions?"

Samira looked close to stunned. "Er … no … nothing I can think of."

"Good. Then we'll leave you to settle in. If you need anything, just give us a call."

Donovan shook Samira's hand, and Anne stepped forward to give her a hug. As they made their way out, Donovan showed Samira how to lock and bolt the stern doors. She noticed with interest that Donovan was as security-conscious as herself. The three of them stepped up onto the stern deck to find that Marnie had turned *Sally Ann* round and brought her close by so that they could easily step across from one boat to the other.

As they were leaving, Donovan turned to Samira. "For as long as you need to be on my boat, what's that blessing you have … may peace be upon you?"

Samira's eyes moistened. She raised a hand to her chest and briefly bowed her head. "And upon you also," she murmured.

74

With that, she turned and stepped down into the cabin. Donovan heard the lock turn and the bolts slide home, top and bottom.

The police officers left the interview room for a short break. As they went out, Marnie thought Roger was chancing his luck when he asked for a second time if they might have some refreshment, but to her surprise two plastic cups duly arrived. This time it was coffee. Marnie sipped hers and found – second surprise – that it was drinkable. While they were alone together she wanted to compare notes with Roger but knew they would be under surveillance. There were two small dark blue inverted glass domes in the ceiling at opposite sides of the room. Marnie knew they housed CCTV cameras. She guessed that the room was wired for sound.

Roger leaned forward and whispered in her ear. "You do realise someone is watching us, don't you, Marnie?"

"Yes, but it doesn't seem fair."

"They don't want the interviewee to be coached by their solicitor."

Marnie nodded. "How's it going, d'you think?"

"They seem confident, but I suspect they don't yet have results of forensic tests. They've probably gone to check on progress with that. They're probably also conferring with their Senior Investigating Officer."

"Is it significant that I'm being interviewed by a constable and not someone more senior?"

Roger shook his head. "Driscoll's trained in this kind of work. It's quite normal, I believe. But remember, Marnie, I'm not a criminal law specialist."

Marnie was about to reply when the door opened and Driscoll and Rabjohn re-appeared. They resumed their seats.

"Thank you for the coffee," Marnie said.

"That's okay. Before we start recording again, does either of you need a break for the loo?"

Marnie could not refrain from smiling. It seemed a very British kind of interrogation. She had seen films where suspects in other countries were routinely beaten up, wired with electrodes or at least shouted at, yet here it felt almost like a minor social occasion. Both she and Roger declined the offer. DC Rabjohn switched on the recording machine; Driscoll announced their names and the time, and the interrogation started again.

"Would you say it was normal to let someone who was virtually a stranger stay on your boat?"

"I don't think I've ever let anyone, stranger or otherwise, stay on my boat," said Marnie.

"I'm thinking of Samira Khan staying on the boat of your friend, Mr Donovan Smith."

"It didn't strike me as odd in the circumstances."

"How would you describe the circumstances, Marnie?"

Marnie shrugged. "Samira wanted some peace and quiet, and Donovan offered his boat."

Driscoll looked sceptical. "Peace and quiet in comparison with the noise and bustle around her cottage at Glebe Farm?"

"Samira wanted solitude to think over her ... situation. At Glebe Farm I have contractors coming and going, working on the renovation project, so there is some disturbance there."

"She just asked out of the blue if she could use his boat?"

"It came up in conversation that she'd like some time to herself, and Donovan made the offer."

"So that's how it came about?"

"As I recall." Marnie turned to Roger. "I really don't –"

"My client has a point, officer. I can't help thinking you're just playing for time."

Driscoll said, "We have formally charged your client, Mr Broadbent. We aren't under any time constraint at this stage."

"But nevertheless, your line of questioning seems – I know I've said this before – more like a fishing exercise than a focused interrogation."

"This is a complicated matter, Mr Broadbent. We need to establish the background, the events leading up to the attempted murder and the relationships between all the people involved. One minute Samira Khan is staying in a cottage in a small country village; the next, she's up the canal staying on a

77

boat belonging to someone she hardly knows. Surely you can see that is an unusual occurrence. I'm trying to find out how it happened."

"And I think I've told you," Marnie said in an even tone.

Even as she spoke, Marnie knew she was lapsing into her old ways. Once again she wasn't telling the whole story and she wasn't sure why. Would it help her position if she told the police everything she knew, or would it plunge her deeper into the mire? It was all desperately confusing and there seemed to be no clear way forward.

At that moment she didn't even know if Samira was alive or dead.

Chapter 8

Special Delivery

That weekend Marnie thought that Shakespeare got it right. Rough winds certainly could shake the darling buds of May. Marnie and Ralph lay in bed on Sunday morning listening to rain beating against the window panes. Across the yard in the attic over the office barn Anne and Donovan awoke in each other's arms, unaware of the weather that morning until they descended the wall-ladder to the floor below. The only window in the attic was a narrow vertical slit in the stone end wall into which double glazing had been fitted. It was recessed with the result that no rain reached it even in stormy times, and the roof was heavily insulated. In hooded cagoules they had raced across the shiny wet cobbles to the farmhouse where the warmth of the Aga beckoned, and breakfast awaited them.

For the rest of the day they had all settled down to reading in the sitting room where Ralph lit the wood-burner. Occasionally their thoughts had turned to Samira on board *XO2*, but no-one was over-concerned about her. They reasoned that she would feel cosy and secure on her secluded mooring, far from the haunts of other people, especially on such a day as that one.

****

By Monday morning the weather had improved, but only slightly. Donovan, like Anne, was well advanced with his final course-work of the year and decided to stay on rather than return to London. He would deal with the writing-up stage using his laptop on the kitchen table while Marnie and Anne worked in the office, and Ralph continued with research in his study on *Thyrsis*.

The phone rang mid-morning. Marnie took the call and listened for a few moments, her expression puzzled. She pushed the button for speakerphone so that Anne could hear. The caller was Molly Appleton up at the village shop.

"I'm sorry, Molly, but I'm not sure I follow. You say you've had a delivery to the post office but you think it might be for me. Is that what you're saying?"

"Not you exactly, Marnie, but for Glebe Farm."

"So it's addressed to Glebe Farm?"

"No, it's addressed here, but I think the name on the label might be your tenant. Isn't she Sam ... something or other?"

"You mean Samira? Samira Khan?"

"Yes, that's the one."

"Okay, so you have something delivered for Samira, care of the post office. Is that right?"

"Well, yes."

"You don't seem very certain. Isn't it just *poste restante?*"

"No, you see, it's not a service we provide these days, and nobody's said anything to me about receiving a delivery."

"Well, you've got it now, so you just need to decide what's to be done with it."

"That's why I'm phoning you, Marnie."

Marnie hesitated. "Does it need a signature?"

There was a silence on the line. Marnie guessed that Molly was checking with the delivery driver. She came back on.

"Yes, it does."

"Does Samira have to sign in person?"

Another silent interval before Molly returned.

"No, it seems anyone can sign for it."

"Okay, Molly, Samira's not available, so I'll come and get it. What is it, by the way?"

"Well, it's sort of ... luggage. The label says something about an airport in Karachi."

Marnie shook her head in bewilderment. "I'm on my way."

They disconnected as Donovan came into the office. Anne quickly explained the situation.

"Need any help?" Donovan asked. "Shall I come with you?"

"No, I'll be all right, thanks. Back in a trice."

As Marnie exited the office, Anne called out, "I'll have coffee ready by the time you get back."

Marnie's parting shot was, "Good thinking, Batman!"

In the kitchen area Anne set out mugs for the workmen and poured their tea. Donovan volunteered to take the mugs out while Anne got on with making coffee. He was picking up the tray when Anne said, "A delivery of luggage sent to the village post office here, somehow connected with an airport in Karachi. Not exactly an everyday occurrence in Knightly St John. It's all very curious."

Donovan turned to go, but hesitated. "Not really," he said. "It's all starting to make sense."

"How d'you work that —"

"Here's Ralph," Donovan said, heading for the door. "You'd better get that coffee made."

****

Marnie pulled up in line with the Parcel Force van outside the shop and hurried in. Drizzle had started to fall. Inside, she found a cheerful West Indian in uniform leaning against the counter. Beside him on the floor stood the luggage: two large black suitcases, each bound with a purple strap. The Parcel Force driver handed Marnie a device like a chunky version of a mobile phone and gave her a pen with a plastic tip. He asked her to sign on the glass screen. Marnie looked at her signature. It was completely unrecognisable. She passed the device back.

"Is that really acceptable?" she asked incredulously.

The driver shrugged and grinned. "Frankly, darling, you could sign Mickey Mouse and nobody would take any notice."

Marnie replied deadpan. "I did."

The driver laughed out loud, blew Marnie a kiss and went out, whistling a happy if tuneless song. On the other side of the counter Molly was looking bemused.

"I don't understand what Karachi airport has to do with it, Marnie. Do you think the cases have come from there?"

Marnie examined the label and shook her head. "No. I think they were supposed to be *going* there."

81

"Then how did they end up here?" Mollie asked.

"That," Marnie said, "is a very good question."

She bent down, turned the first case onto its side and pulled out its extension handle. She wheeled it to the door, pulled up the hood on her parka and hurried out to the Freelander. She wished she had accepted Donovan's offer. The case was heavy, seriously heavy. It took all her strength to hoist it up into the luggage space. Only pride prevented her from phoning Donovan and asking him to join her to tackle the second one. It was as heavy as the first. Puffed, damp and panting, Marnie climbed into the driving seat and fastened her safety belt. On the short run to Glebe Farm she resolved not to reject any offer of help in future from anyone. Ever.

****

Marnie arrived back at the office to find Anne poised with the cafetière. After Ralph and Donovan humped the suitcases from the Freelander, the four of them sat round the luggage and contemplated the next step. The drizzle was now backing off.

Ralph said, "I suppose the first question is what we should do with the luggage, and that depends on what Samira plans to do next."

Marnie looked doubtful. "Isn't the first question to ask where Karachi airport fits in?"

"You don't think that's rather obvious?" Donovan said.

"Obvious or not, I suppose the best way to find out is to ask her."

"You've got her mobile number," Donovan said.

Marnie shook her head. "Better face to face, I think."

Just then Marnie's mobile warbled. It was Samira, sounding concerned but not panic-stricken.

"I've got a problem, Marnie ... well, not so much a problem – at least I don't think so – more an issue, a query."

"Go ahead."

"It's just that every now and then, there's a strange sound, a sort of humming ... quite loud but in the background, if you see what I mean."

"When did it start?" Marnie asked.

"Early on this morning, I think."

"You're not sure?"

"Not exactly. It might have been what woke me up at around half past six, or then again perhaps I just didn't notice it and it started earlier."

Marnie said, "I'm going to hand you over to Donovan, as it's his boat. I'm pretty sure I know what it is, but he might have another idea."

Marnie explained the issue-cum-query and passed the mobile to Donovan.

"Hi Samira. Sounds like the water pump to me."

"Is that serious?"

"Well, you're not likely to get flooded and sink, if that's what's worrying you. On the other hand, it does need looking at."

"Can you do that?"

"Sure. Don't worry about it. Sorry if it's annoying, but I should be able to fix it quite easily. I'll be with you as soon as I can get there."

Silence on the line.

Donovan said, "Samira?"

"Er ..."

"I'll be bringing Anne, of course."

"Oh yes. Thank you."

Donovan hung up and turned to Marnie. She spoke first.

"I agree about the water pump and do I guess right that you need a chaperone?"

"You guess right," Donovan said. "We all play by Samira's rules these days. There's something else. I need to get across the canal."

"Sure. Take *Sally Ann*."

"Thanks, Marnie."

Anne took the boat's keys from the hook in the kitchen and followed Donovan out.

****

83

The rain had eased off completely as *Sally Ann* chugged northwards. Even at her maximum cruising speed of four miles per hour she made very little wash. Anne was at the tiller, with Donovan perched facing her on the wooden lid of the gas bottle container. He had one foot on the stern deck, the other resting on the gunwale, and he was staring back with a far away expression that Anne recognised very well.

"What are you chewing over?" she asked, adding, "as if I can't guess."

"You tell me, then."

"It's obvious. It has to be the luggage."

"And what are my conclusions?"

"Not sure, but my guess is, you're wondering where it came from and how it found its way to Glebe Farm."

Donovan made a face. "Partly right. I've worked out where it came from."

"What about the rest?"

"That's the unknown part. And, by the way, it didn't come to Glebe Farm. It came to the post office, remember. That's significant."

"So it did. D'you want some coffee? Only, I didn't bring any milk."

"Let's have it when we reach *Exodos*. There are plenty of provisions on board."

"Even milk?"

Donovan gave her a look. Anne changed the subject.

"Are you going to ask Samira about the luggage?"

"No."

"You sound very definite about that."

Donovan stared thoughtfully at the passing countryside. "I think that's something for Marnie to decide. After all, she's the one who took delivery of it. In any case, I think if we told Samira about it, it might spook her out."

"You're not going to mention it at all?"

"No. Are you?"

Anne thought for a moment and shook her head.

They cruised on for several minutes without speaking, while *Sally Ann's* engine thumped beneath their feet and they passed through fields and meadows with distant views of woods under a sky of leaden clouds. After a while Donovan pulled out his mobile and pressed buttons.

"Who are you phoning?" Anne asked.

"Samira. I don't want her freaking out when we bang on the door." He listened and almost immediately hung up.

"Changed your mind?" Anne said.

Donovan shook his head. "Straight to voicemail, as I expected."

He kept the phone in his hand, one finger poised over the green button, and smiled at Anne when it began ringing a few seconds later.

"Hi Samira. Just wanted to let you know we'll be with you in a few minutes. Anne's with me ... good idea. See you soon." He pressed the red button.

"What was the good idea?" Anne asked.

"She said she'd put the kettle on. Amazing."

"What is?"

"She sounded a different person ... calm, relaxed, confident ... normal."

"That's quite something," said Anne. She craned her neck forward. "I think we'll see *Exodos* after this next bend."

Anne was right. It was a long left-hander, and as soon as they cleared it they caught a glimpse of the boat concealed almost completely under the willows. Anne eased back on the accelerator and steered *Sally Ann* to a halt with the stern of both boats close together, separated only by trailing willow fronds. At once the rear doors of *XO2* swung open to reveal Samira smiling out at them. Donovan had not been exaggerating. She really did seem a different person. Gone was the haunted look, the nervousness, the furrowed brow. In their place was a cheerfulness they had scarcely seen before.

While Anne kept *Sally Ann* steady, Donovan stepped across onto his own boat and fastened the two craft together with mooring ropes from cleat to cleat, fore and aft. Anne pulled on the engine stop lever and held it firmly while the Lister slowed, sighed and expired with a final clank. She joined Donovan on *XO2* to be welcomed by Samira with a hug.

In the cabin there was a further sign of Samira's return to normality. She had laid the table in the dinette, and a packet of Bahlsen *Leibniz* chocolate-coated biscuits lay unopened in the centre. On the stove the kettle was hissing softly. As they entered, it began whistling, and Samira laughed.

"Good timing or what?" she said in a cheery voice.

"As usual with you," said Anne. "Spot on!"

For a brief moment, Samira looked anxious. She turned to Donovan.

"I hope you don't think I'm being cheeky, but I found the biscuits in the cupboard and I thought ..." She shrugged.

Donovan smiled. "Good choice. That's what they're there for."

"I'll open them, then. Oh ... I don't have – I mean *you* don't have – any milk on board. Shall we have black tea or coffee instead? Is that all right?"

Donovan stepped round her and opened the fridge. He produced a small tin of evaporated milk.

"In Germany we use this in coffee. In fact, it's usually known as *Kaffeesahne*, coffee cream. It may be an acquired taste, but I think it goes well with my coffee, which is also German."

"I like it," Anne said. "But that's maybe because I find black coffee too bitter."

Samira grinned. "Then I'm game, too."

Donovan said to Anne, "D'you want to sort out the coffee while I check the water pump?"

And so, a division of labour was agreed. Donovan knelt down with his toolbox to investigate pipework in the under-bench units; Anne measured coffee into the filter; Samira sat elegantly on the black-and-grey tweed banquette at the table. Anne and Donovan could hardly believe that Samira was humming quietly to herself as she neatly arranged the biscuits on a plate.

Donovan said, "Anne, can you get the torch in my rucksack."

86

"Sure." Anne delved inside and pulled out the torch, a Maglite in black steel, surprisingly heavy. The design had become an American classic. Anne smiled to herself as Donovan ducked back into the unit, knowing how much he liked classics of all kinds, cars, cameras, watches, everything.

"Got it!" A triumphant cry from Donovan with his head in the cupboard.

"Is it what you suspected?" Anne said.

"Yep. Can you pass me a J-cloth, please?"

Anne did as requested and hovered behind Donovan until he held up the sodden cloth. She wrung it out in the sink and passed it back to him. The sound of a wrench gripping a joint could be heard, accompanied by soft grunts from Donovan. Two more wipes with the J-cloth, one final grunt, and the job was done. He reversed out from under the workbench, switched off the Maglite and packed the toolkit away.

"Did I cause the problem?" Samira asked hesitantly.

"No. Such things happen all the time on boats: expansion, contraction, heat, cold ... just one of those things."

"Talking of heat and cold," Anne said, "are you ready for coffee?"

Settled together at the table, Anne asked Samira how she liked being on a boat. When Samira replied, her expression was almost sublime.

"The peace, the tranquillity, the ... I don't know how to describe it ..."

"Serenity?" Anne suggested.

"Yes, absolutely ... wonderful. I completely understand why people like to live on barges ... oops, I mean, *narrowboats*. Did I get it right?"

Anne smiled and nodded; Donovan winked.

"I'm glad you like it," he said.

"I love it. Last evening I sat on the roof and looked out between the branches of this beautiful weeping willow. I just listened to the sounds as the night came down. Far away I heard a sheep bleating. Then suddenly, quite nearby, I saw a fish jump right out of the water and splash back down. I've never been so close to nature in my life."

Donovan said quietly, "Feel free to stay as long as you wish, Samira."

"Ah, but that's just it," she said. "I feel more than just refreshed. I feel renewed. Being on the boat for the weekend has made me feel free in a way I've never felt before."

Anne said, "Marnie always says that the waterways have a liberating effect on her, almost like a kind of magic."

"And I know just what she means." Samira sighed. "Yes. I've loved this short stay on the boat but I'm ready to come back now, back to the world, well to the cottage at any rate, to Glebe Farm."

"Are you sure that's what you want to do?" Anne said.

"Yes, quite sure." Samira's tone was firm, determined, resolute.

****

It was Donovan's decision. Anne had expected the two boats to return in convoy, but he insisted on leaving *XO2* concealed in the willows. He reasoned that it was too much bother sliding the boat out of its mooring, and their time would be better spent cruising home together on *Sally Ann*. Anne suspected that his motives were otherwise. Her chance to quiz him came when Samira uncharacteristically accepted a turn at the tiller and proved to be capable of steering the boat without constant supervision.

Anne stood close beside Donovan a few feet from Samira. They were both facing forwards and, with the sound of their voices drowned by the rumble of the engine, Anne murmured softly, "Was that your real reason for leaving *Exodos* back there?"

"What do you mean?"

"I think you had an ulterior motive."

"Such as?"

"You tell me."

He smiled at her. "Are you forgetting what's waiting for her back home? When she sees the luggage, who knows how she'll react? She might feel like beating it back to her bolt-hole."

Their talk was interrupted by Samira. "What should I do now?" She pointed ahead. Another craft was approaching.

"Keep a steady course," said Donovan. "When you get within a boat's length veer slightly to the right so that you pass, keeping them on your left. They'll do the same."

He watched closely and, at the appropriate time, said, "Okay, tiller towards you now ... not too much ... just leave a few feet between you. Steady now ... steer straight ahead."

The boats passed each other smoothly, and the other captain gave Samira a friendly wave. She waved back, the very picture of expertise and confidence. Anne and Donovan were impressed by her boatcraft and still bemused by her change of character.

"Bring her back into mid-channel now," Anne said.

Samira followed instructions and took up station mid-stream. She smiled broadly at her companions. There was an aura of brilliance surrounding her. An atmosphere of joyful camaraderie hung over the boat as *Sally Ann* cut effortlessly through the water, bearing them back to Glebe Farm. For Samira it felt as if she was turning a corner in her life and not just negotiating the gentle bends of the Grand Union Canal. She raised her head and shook out her silky dark hair, relishing the sense of freedom conferred on her by the waterway.

Briefly, Anne's eyes met Donovan's, as they shared a single thought: the luggage and its link with Karachi airport, and what it might mean to Samira.

****

The sun was parting the clouds by the time they neared the bridge on the approach to Glebe Farm. Samira handed the tiller to Anne for the final manoeuvre into *Sally Ann*'s dock. It was a narrow side arm of the canal a little more than seventy feet long and about eight feet across, wide enough to accommodate the boat with a few inches to spare on each side.

Anne slotted her in with practised ease. As soon as she stopped the boat, Donovan leapt onto the bank and set about tying the mooring ropes to the bollards fore and aft.

Samira stepped nimbly down from the stern deck and turned to face Anne who was pulling the engine Stop lever. "Anne, that was brilliant. You made it look so *easy*."

Anne shrugged. "I've done it many times before. Mind you, on my first attempt I think I bumped into every bank in sight! You should watch Marnie do it, if you really want to be impressed … silky smooth."

Donovan came to join them. "On our next trip, Samira, we'll teach you how to do it."

Samira raised both hands in alarm. "I don't think so."

Anne grinned. "We'll make a boatman of you in no time. Next thing you know, you'll be wearing a greasy cap and a red-and-white spotted necker."

"And smoking cheroots," Donovan said.

Anne added, "Or even a pipe!"

Samira joined in the laughter. "You two have a very easy-going relationship. You're so relaxed together. Are you planning to get –" She stopped abruptly. "Sorry, I didn't … I mean …"

Anne reached down and touched Samira's arm. "We're young, we're both students and we're together when we can be. That's how it is right now."

Donovan said, "That's how it's been for a couple of years or so. We'll let the future take care of itself when it comes along."

Samira looked from one to the other. "Well, you're certainly thriving on it, however strange it may seem."

"Why strange?" said Anne.

Samira reflected. "Yes, why indeed? It's just so different from everything I've ever known. It's all so …"

"Free?" Anne suggested.

Samira nodded. "Yes, free … and a little bit scary." After a moment's pause she said, "Are we going in now?"

Anne said, "I can't yet. There are things to do on the boat before I can leave her. It won't take long, but you won't want to

hang around while I mess about in the engine compartment."
Anne pointed down at the stern deck below which the
machinery was situated. "Why don't you go along with
Donovan and I'll come as soon as I'm ready?"

Samira looked hesitant. "Are you sure?"

"Yeah. I'll be maybe ten minutes, max."

Donovan turned towards the spinney and said, "Coming?"

Samira nodded and followed. Watching her go, Anne
wondered if she had ever before walked alone with a man of
roughly her age who was not a relative. Samira may have
experienced a new sense of freedom, but they never forgot she
was from a different world.

****

The spinney smelled of fresh wet vegetation. They walked
through in silence, skirting puddles on the footpath. When they
rounded the office barn and came into the courtyard Samira
veered off towards her cottage.

"Thanks, Donovan. I enjoyed staying on your boat. And
thanks for the ride home."

"No problem. See you later on."

Samira looked blank. "Later on?"

"You'll be joining us for supper, won't you?" He paused.
"Sorry. I should've mentioned it earlier. Marnie would like you
to eat with us."

"Oh, er ... that's very nice." She smiled. "Everyone seems to
want to feed me these days."

"About seven?"

"About seven," Samira repeated. "Thank you. See you later."

Samira was fiddling with her keys when she heard Donovan
close the door to the farmhouse. She inserted the key into the
lock at the moment the thought struck her. When could Marnie
have said she wanted to invite her to supper? It was only when
Anne and Donovan came to see her that she told them she
wanted to return to Glebe Farm. Until then, the idea had never
been mentioned. Samira's familiar frown was back in place

when she went into the cottage, closed the door and bolted it behind her.

****

The breeze must have shifted direction for as Samira crossed the courtyard that evening she heard the church clock ring out for the first time since she arrived at Glebe Farm. The tolling floated on the air, faint like distant wind chimes. The clock was striking seven. She was carrying a small plate covered with a square of kitchen roll. On it was a mound of cheese straws, made especially as a thank-you gift for her hosts. She was wearing the primrose yellow smock-top and loose black trousers that she had worn on a previous visit. Both were now freshly washed and ironed, The clock was still sounding when she pressed the doorbell.

Moments later the door was opened wide by Anne, who was smiling in welcome.

"Bang on time, as always. Come on in."

"It's not rude to arrive on time, is it?" Samira said, momentarily unsure of herself.

"Course not. We're all glad to see you any time."

"Thank you, Anne. And I'm always –"

Samira stopped so abruptly that Anne had to lunge forward to grab the plate before the cheese straws tumbled to the ground. As Anne gently took hold of the plate, she saw that Samira was staring open-mouthed beyond her. Anne glanced back and saw what had so startled Samira into silence.

"What ... how? I don't understand ... it's not ..." Samira was stammering.

Anne took her by the elbow and guided her through the hall. Samira didn't resist, but tottered forward, her gaze all the time fixed on the two black suitcases with their purple straps, standing innocently by the wall.

"Are you all right, Samira? You look as if you've seen a ... well, never mind. Let's go through to the kitchen."

Samira allowed herself to be ushered out of the hall. When the door to the kitchen swung open Marnie, Ralph and

Donovan looked up smiling to see their friend. Their smiles faded when they saw her face. Marnie quickly wiped her hands on a towel and rushed forward.

"Come and sit down."

Samira did as she was told and settled unsteadily on the nearest chair. Marnie knelt beside her. By now, Anne was already taking a bottle of mineral water from the fridge. Within seconds she was thrusting a glass into Samira's hand. Samira held it up and gazed at the rising bubbles, the ice cubes and the slice of lime.

Samira began stammering again. "It's ... I don't ... it's ..."

"The luggage," Marnie said. "You weren't expecting it, were you?"

Samira shook her head slowly.

Marnie continued. "You didn't ask for it to be sent here for you?"

"No," Samira croaked. "How did it ... find me?"

Anne glanced in Donovan's direction. His expression was inscrutable.

"You don't know how it followed you here?" Marnie said.

"No."

"Can you tell us the connection with Karachi airport?"

Samira focused on Marnie. "What connection? What does that mean?"

"The labels on the luggage refer to Karachi airport as their ... that must mean *your* ... destination."

"But it doesn't explain how they came here," Samira said.

Then Donovan spoke up. "I think it does, and I think it's pretty clear. What isn't so clear is what triggered the process."

"I agree with Donovan," said Ralph. "Look, why don't we all have a drink and talk things over calmly? I'm sure we can get to the bottom of this."

"Good idea," said Marnie. "We can have supper after that, by which time you should be feeling better, Samira. Does that sound like a plan?"

"I suppose so."

****

93

The five of them sat round the kitchen table, each staring into their drink. Marnie, Ralph, Anne and Donovan were contemplating glasses of white wine from which a few sips had been taken. Samira was gazing morosely at her glass from which she had taken not a drop and in which the ice cubes were melting. Marnie had begun by asking Samira to outline the course of action which had brought her to Knightly St John. Samira had stumbled through an incomplete and partly incoherent narrative which the others struggled to grasp. Ralph broke the silence.

"We want to understand what's happened, Samira, each of us for different reasons. You want to know how your luggage came back to you. We want to try to get the full picture, for no other reason than that we want to help you."

"No-one can help me," Samira said in a hoarse voice, without raising her eyes.

"Samira," Marnie began, "we seriously don't want to pry. That's not what this is about. Some things are fairly clear, but there are more matters that don't add up. We can't tell what they are. Only you can join up the dots."

Samira shook her head miserably. "I just don't understand."

The others sat back in their chairs. Marnie sighed.

Donovan said, "Yes, you do. Of course you do."

The bluntness of his tone caused Samira to look up, startled. She opened her mouth to speak, but no sound came out. Marnie was about to intervene when Donovan raised a hand.

"Marnie says there are some things that are fairly clear. Shall I spell them out?" He did not wait for a reply. "You were supposed to be travelling to Karachi. That's why your luggage is labelled like that. For some reason you changed your plans."

"That's what I meant, Samira," Marnie said. "Those are the things that are clear."

"There's more than that," Donovan said. "I think we can make a fair guess at why you changed your mind about travelling. What we can't do is work out about the luggage, unless you arranged for it to be delivered to the post office.

94

Your shock at seeing it makes it clear that you didn't make any such arrangements."

Ralph said, "Is Donovan right about that? And if so, can you try to join up the dots, as Marnie puts it?"

"No. You've got to believe me. I have no idea how anyone knew to send the luggage here ... unless someone is tracking me."

"Let's assume that isn't the case," said Marnie. "Think hard about what could have happened."

"Did you tell the estate agents anything about your luggage?" Anne asked. "Surely they're the only people who knew where you'd be going."

"Good point," said Ralph. He turned to Samira. "What d'you think?"

"No. I didn't tell them anything about anything, apart from wanting to rent your cottage. I saw it advertised in their lettings window and asked about it. I signed the papers, made the payments and that was that. Then I caught a cab and came here direct."

"You didn't chat with the cab driver?" Anne asked.

"Not a word all the way here."

"Was he Asian?" Marnie asked.

Samira's eyes widened. "Yes. How did you know that?"

"A lot of the drivers round Milton Keynes are from the subcontinent. I know several of them by name from when they've taken me or my visitors to the station or the airport."

"You think he might have recognised me?"

"It did cross my mind. Did you recognise him?"

"I'd never seen him before ... but it's a thought."

Donovan slumped forward in his chair with his head in his hands.

"We're missing something here," said Marnie.

Ralph agreed. "There must be a link that's eluding us."

Donovan sat up suddenly. "Did you come straight down here when you arrived?"

Marnie said, "Samira came looking for us in the school. We were talking to Margaret Giles about the children's summer outing on *Sally Ann*."

Donovan looked at Samira. "What gave you the idea of going to the school?"

"The lady who runs the shop said I might find Marnie there. She told me —" Samira stopped sharply and put a hand up to her mouth.

"What is it?" said Marnie.

"There's the missing link," Donovan said quickly. "We know the airline sent your luggage. So how did they know you were here? How did you cancel your flight?"

"I ..." Samira's voice tailed off.

"Samira?" Marnie prompted.

"I phoned them to say I wouldn't be travelling. I didn't want to hold everything up while they located my luggage and took it out of the hold. That's what happens if you're a no-show."

"They wouldn't have the means of tracing your mobile," Ralph said.

"I didn't use the mobile. The lady in the shop told me where the public phone box was. I rang the airline contact number from there. The woman at the other end started asking me questions, so I hung up."

"How did you book your tickets?" Ralph asked. "You'd have to give an address together with all your other details."

Samira said, "My father made the booking at a travel agent's in Luton. I said on the phone that I wasn't now living at that address."

They all looked thoughtful.

"And that's when you disconnected?" Ralph said.

"Yes."

"Did you tell the airline you'd be staying here?" Marnie asked.

"No."

"Then how could they —"

"Caller ID," Donovan murmured. "It's a new feature on phones. The person you call can see your number. They must have thought you'd been cut off, so they sent your luggage to *poste restante*, care of the post office. They knew that's where the phone was located. So they assumed that was your temporary contact address. That way, you'd be certain to get it via the local post-master."

"You really think that's all it was?" Samira sounded as if she wanted to believe it.

"Sounds logical to me," Marnie said.

"Me too," Ralph agreed.

"Right," said Marnie. "It looks as if we've solved that little conundrum. No-one is tracking you, Samira. The airline did what it thought best to reunite you with your luggage after you changed your plans."

Samira breathed out audibly, a long sigh. "Yes. That's what must've happened."

Marnie continued. "Okay. That's sorted out at last. Let's eat."

She was heading for the fridge when Donovan spoke again. "You were going to Pakistan to get married?"

The words fell like a bomb into their midst. Samira stared at Donovan. The others all stared at her.

"That's what this is all about, isn't it?" Donovan said.

Samira looked about her, as if she felt trapped. "It's not as straightforward as that."

Marnie said, "We don't wish to pry into your –"

"But you're the only people I can talk to. You're probably the only people I know who'd understand."

"Presumably you don't think you can get your family to help with the problem?" said Marnie.

"Marnie, my family *is* the problem."

Ralph said, "May I suggest we start our meal and have a little time for calm and reflection?"

"Thank you, Ralph," said Samira. "That would be lovely. To be honest, I don't have much of an appetite right now, but perhaps if we made a start ..."

That evening's supper was a *salade niçoise*. The meal began in contemplative silence. At one point Samira glanced up to find Donovan eyeing her with a speculative expression. He averted his gaze, but she had the impression that he could read her mind. She put down her knife and fork and stared across the table at him. He noticed her attention and stopped eating.

"What is it?" he asked.

"You know, don't you? You've got everything worked out, haven't you, Donovan?"

"It's only an inkling, Samira." Donovan glanced quickly at Marnie. "I think Marnie's right. We shouldn't be probing into matters that don't concern us."

"But what if they *do* concern you, or perhaps could end up concerning you?" Samira said. "Sorry, I don't mean to talk in riddles."

Marnie said, "Samira, it sounds like you're calling out for help. You know we'd do anything we could for you, but there's a fine line between help and interference."

"I know, and getting involved could put you in danger."

"Danger?" Marnie said. "You mean actual, *physical* danger?"

Samira nodded. "Yes. That's exactly what I mean."

"Coming back to my earlier question," Donovan said. "Were you going to Pakistan to get married?"

Samira bit her lip. "No ... or perhaps I should say, yes. Sort of."

"But you changed your mind," said Marnie.

Samira shook her head. "I told you it wasn't really like that."

Donovan raised the glass to his lips but, instead of drinking, said, "Either you spell it out or we just have to drop the subject. No-one here wants to interrogate you."

The others were taken aback by Donovan's bluntness, but knew he had a point. They were skirting round a subject, going in circles, getting nowhere.

Marnie said, "Samira, why don't you tell us what you think we ought to know? By doing that, we won't be treading on your toes or prying into things you don't want to talk about. Does that make sense?"

"Yes, it does, though I'm not sure where to begin."

"Tell us about Pakistan," said Donovan. "That's where it all begins, surely."

Samira gazed for some moments into space, delving back in time to the events that led her eventually to Glebe Farm. She said, "Okay. I haven't been to Pakistan since I was eight years old. I was born in Britain, not many miles from here, actually. So was my mother. My father was born near Lahore and moved here when he was about ten years old."

"You have dual nationality?" Ralph asked.

"No. I'm British only, so are my brother and sister, but we have family in Pakistan. That was the idea, or so I thought. I was going back to visit them and stay with an uncle and aunt for a month."

Ralph said, "Do you mind me asking what you do? I mean, are you a student or do you have a job?"

"I graduated in Business Studies at university."

"Where was that?" Ralph asked.

"Leicester. Since then I've been working for a big accountancy firm in Luton on the management consultancy side. I've just got a promotion that involved transferring to a new branch in Birmingham. The position would be available in a month or two. My parents thought this seemed a good time to visit the family abroad, and the firm agreed to a leave of absence."

"A generous firm," Ralph said.

Samira nodded. "Absolutely. I've been earning a good salary for almost three years while living at home, and even after contributing to the housekeeping, I've managed to save quite a bit."

"And you've had some generous gifts," Marnie said.

Samira fingered her gold necklace. "Yes, and I should have realised what they implied. Anyway, the holiday was all arranged, and I was looking forward to seeing my relatives again. But something my sister said made me wonder. She's seventeen. She said she didn't want to get *married off* until she was thirty. She wanted a proper career like me, and what the other girls in her class at school wanted. Her ambition was to

99

run her own business, designing and selling clothes in her own boutique."

"Sounds wonderful," said Anne.

"It's the way she said it ... getting *married off*. It got me thinking. Also it upset my mum. She said there was nothing wrong with bringing up a family. It was natural for a girl to want to have children."

"That doesn't stop you having a career as well, does it?" Anne said.

Samira looked thoughtful. "Not in your world perhaps."

"How did your mum react to what your sister said?" Marnie asked.

Samira sighed. "They had a row. Rashida said they'd never pack her off to marry some cousin she hadn't seen since she was a child. They were both in tears and soon made up, but as the time came for me to pack for the journey, I noticed Rashida looking at me in a funny way. It was as if she wanted to say something but couldn't find the right words. The day I left the house to go to the airport she hugged me really tight and was quite emotional. I waved at her as my father drove me away and saw that she was clinging to my mum. It looked like she was crying."

"You must be very close."

"Marnie, I was only going away for a few weeks' holiday."

"But you had some suspicions," Marnie said.

"Yes. My father stayed with me at Heathrow till I went through to the departure lounge, then he left to get back to work."

"And that's when you made your decision."

"Yes, Marnie, and I've been fretting about it ever since."

Donovan said, "Why did you say getting involved could put us in danger?"

"Perhaps that was over the top, but ..."

Marnie reached over and touched Samira's arm. "You think you might be regarded as bringing dishonour on your family if they'd come to an arrangement with someone to marry you, someone you couldn't accept?"

100

"Yes," Samira said softly.

"Are you sure that's what they really had in mind?"

"Not a hundred per cent, but it all seems to add up."

"Leaving you in a tricky position vis-à-vis your family," said Ralph.

"Yes ... in all sorts of ways."

D C Shirley Driscoll looked at her watch and smiled before framing her next question. Marnie didn't smile back. In fact, she was becoming increasingly wary and wondered if Driscoll's colleague was going to join in as the other half of a good-cop-bad-cop routine. Did they do that in Britain? she wondered. Or was it dreamt up by the directors of American movies?

"Did you see much of Samira while she was staying in your cottage, Marnie?"

Marnie dragged herself out of her reverie. "Not really."

"Why was that?"

"I think I've already explained that I was busy with my work and I didn't spend time gazing out of the window."

"But you could have gone across to see if everything was all right, couldn't you? After all, you did all you could to be a caring landlady."

"A caring landlady who didn't interfere in the lives of her tenants," Marnie added.

"How often did your paths cross in an average week?"

Marnie shook her head. "A few times, I suppose."

"And you invited her for meals?"

"Occasionally."

"Would it be fair to say you went out of your way to make her welcome?"

"No more than for any other new tenant living alone."

"What about shopping? You took her with you sometimes, didn't you? She didn't have transport, so I suppose you felt obliged to drive her."

"No."

"You didn't take her shopping? I thought we'd already established that you did."

"I meant no, I didn't feel obliged to drive her, not every time she needed things from the shops."

"So how did she manage?"

"She could take a taxi."

"Did she often do that?"

Careful, Marnie. You're digging yourself into a hole.

"I don't think so, but it would be a possibility, and there's a bus service in the village."

"Do you remember the time she went shopping in Milton Keynes, that rather *unusual* time?"

"I wasn't there at the time."

"But you went afterwards and became involved, didn't you?"

Marnie looked at Roger. "This has surely nothing whatever to do with what happened later and why I'm here, falsely accused of something I didn't do."

Roger said, "Officer, I really fail to see where you're going with this line of questioning."

"Do you really, Mr Broadbent? I can't believe you don't see that I'm trying to piece together all the incidents that took place during the time that Samira Khan stayed at Marnie's cottage. That period of time led to a set of circumstances that resulted in an attempted murder. Anything we can learn from those incidents might help us to see the full picture. No crime happens in a vacuum. You know that. Every murderer brings something to the scene of the crime and takes something away. Any events that led up to that crime may be relevant."

"But I'm not your would-be murderer," Marnie said firmly. "Whatever events took place while Samira was staying in my cottage, they can't have any bearing on your investigation."

Driscoll looked Marnie in the eye. "That's for us to determine, Marnie, and if you are innocent, as you maintain, you must see it's in your interests to cooperate with us to get at the truth."

"That's why I'm doing my best to answer your questions," Marnie said wearily.

"Then let me ask you to think back to that particular Friday when Samira went into town. It was certainly no ordinary shopping trip, was it?"

"I wasn't there," Marnie said emphatically.

"Indulge me, Marnie. Just cast your mind back and try to remember what happened. I'm sure you can."

Chapter 9

Thin Air

Had things really changed? After the meal they had shared together on Monday, Samira seemed more at ease. When she returned to her cottage at the end of the evening she hugged everyone in turn and thanked them for making her feel better. Just being able to talk about her worries had lifted a great weight from her shoulders.

The rest of the week passed as normal from then on. Donovan went home by train on Tuesday. It was not until Wednesday afternoon that Anne remarked that she had not seen Samira since Monday evening. Marnie detached her concentration momentarily from design work.

"Mm ... I think you're right. What is it today ... Wednesday? D'you think we should check if she's okay?"

Anne shrugged. "I did wonder. Ralph might have noticed if she'd gone out for a walk along the canal."

"I wouldn't count on it," Marnie said. "Once he's got his nose buried in statistics, we could be invaded by Martians and he'd be none the wiser."

"Very true! Should I pop across or do you want to go?"

"A friendly enquiry from someone close to her own age might be best, perhaps?"

"Sure," Anne said. "Maybe I should have a reason for going. Do we need any shopping? I could ask if she wanted to come."

"Give it a whirl."

Anne skipped across the courtyard and pressed the doorbell at cottage number three. While she waited, she turned her face to the sky. A hazy sun was making its presence felt. Anne was thinking that summer might soon be on the way, when she was brought back down to earth by the sound of bolts being released and the lock being turned.

"Hello, Anne."

"Hi. Thought I'd come and see if you needed any shopping. We could go together."

"Ah ... I'm actually quite well stocked up for now."

This was not the script Anne thought they'd be following.

"I see. So ... how are things? I notice you're making use of the new wardrobe."

Samira looked down at her clothes, a blue sweater and jeans.

"You're right, though I could use a few more things. I don't seem to have packed enough ..." She lowered her voice, "...tights or underwear."

Anne was on the point of offering to lend Samira some of her own when she had a brainwave.

"We could go into town and you could get some things there."

Samira frowned. "Into town? What town?"

"Milton Keynes? There are loads of shops in Centre MK. They've got a Marks and Sparks, a John Lewis, a Debenhams, a House of –"

Samira raised her hands in surrender, smiling. "I get the picture."

"So you'll come?" Anne said in an encouraging tone.

Samira's smile faded. "Not sure. Er ..."

Anne knew better than to press the point. "Okay. Just let me know when you're ready. We can go in my car."

"You have your own car?"

"Yep. Or we might go with Marnie in hers. No pressure, no hassle. See you, then."

Anne was turning to go when Samira said quickly. "No, wait. It's a great idea. I do need those things, only ..."

"What is it?"

"Could we go ... er ... on Friday ... sort of late in the afternoon?"

"If you want. What sort of time would you have in mind?"

"Say, after five o'clock? Or would that be the rush hour?"

"No. It'd be all right. The traffic usually flows in MK."

"That's fine, then."

Anne said goodbye for a second time and was just turning to go when she had an afterthought.

"I took it as a good sign when you didn't call through the door to ask who it was."

Samira smiled sheepishly. "To be honest, I peeped through the front room window."

Anne laughed. She was shaking her head as she walked back to the office.

****

On Friday morning Anne popped a note through Samira's letter-box:

See you this afternoon around 5.00 -shopaholics are us!

    Anne X

Marnie had been rather surprised when Samira accepted Anne's invitation to go into town and she thought it was a strange time to choose. Ralph on the other hand saw the logic. It was the time reserved in Samira's world for Friday prayers, so few if any Muslims would be about. Marnie and Ralph had other commitments, but Anne was looking forward to a girls' outing to the shops.

"I hope it'll be fun," Marnie said shortly before five o'clock.

"We're just going on a shopping spree," Anne said breezily. "What can possibly go wrong?"

Marnie made no reply, but glanced up at the wall clock.

Anne noticed this and said, "I'm all ready for off. You know how punctual Samira always is. I think she believes it's polite to arrive dead on time."

The clock was a replica of the ones used by Swiss Railways, and Anne watched the red second hand climbing towards the top of the dial. With three seconds to go she switched her gaze to the window through which she could see Samira's front door. The hand swept up to the twelve, and the minute hand clicked to the vertical position. There was no movement across the courtyard. The second hand continued on its journey, heading south. Five o'clock had come and gone, but only by a few seconds.

106

"No big deal." Anne stood up. "It's still technically five, not even one minute past." She looked at her watch. "I suppose the clock is accurate."

"Sure," Marnie said. "It goes like clockwork."

Anne groaned and pulled a face. She wandered over to the door and peered out through the glass panel. "You don't think she's forgotten, do you?"

"She'd need to be suffering from terminal amnesia to have forgotten the note you dropped in this morning."

Two minutes past five. Anne walked back to her desk and sat down. When the clock showed five past the hour she stood up again.

"I think I'll go and bring the car round. It'll give me something to do."

"Alternatively, you could put the kettle on," Marnie suggested.

"Fine." Anne got up and went to the kitchen area. She poured enough water into the kettle for Marnie and scooped ground coffee into the filter. The kettle boiled and switched itself off. Anne waited, watching the second hand sweep round for a full minute before pouring the water onto the coffee. It was a dictum she had learnt from Donovan to allow the water to come off the boil for a minute so as not to release free radicals in the coffee. She had never known sixty seconds take so long.

It was now ten past five, and Anne was pouring coffee into Marnie's mug when the door opened and Samira came in.

"Hi. Hope I'm not late."

"No probs," Anne said. "I'll be ready in a jiffy."

"Oh, you're making coffee. I can come back a bit later." Samira turned to go.

"No, you're all right." Anne crossed the office and put the mug down on Marnie's desk. "Shall we go?"

Samira hesitated. "Er ..."

"Problem?" Anne asked.

"No, I er ..."

Marnie looked across at her. Anne waited.

"Forgotten something?" Anne prompted.

"I ... I think perhaps I'll just pop back to the cottage and use the bathroom before we, er ..."

Marnie pointed to the rear of the office. "We have a bathroom through there. Why not use that?"

"Oh ... yes. Thank you. Good idea."

"That reminds me," Anne said suddenly.

"What is it?" Samira looked momentarily anxious.

Anne smiled at her. "Car keys. I'll fetch them from the board in the kitchen."

Samira said, "You keep your car keys in the kitchen?"

"Sure. All our keys, on a board. Why not?"

"Nothing. I just thought you'd want to keep them with you."

Anne shrugged. "Donovan suggested I keep a spare set near the car, too. Less risk of misplacing them."

"Near the car?"

"Yeah." Anne grinned. "Top security. They're under an old oil can at the back of the garage."

"You don't think someone could take them, Anne?"

"Someone who just happens to be passing by and wanting to steal a car?" Anne said.

Samira nodded. "Good point. It's not as if anyone does come by, I suppose."

"Shouldn't you two get going?" Marnie said.

Anne smiled, turned and skipped to the kitchen area. Behind her, Samira put down her shoulder bag, walked slowly across the office and disappeared into the shower-room. When Anne reappeared with her keys Marnie glanced over at her and raised an eyebrow. Anne shrugged. She spoke in a low voice.

"Am I missing something?"

"Beats me," Marnie said softly. "Something's bugging her, that's for sure."

A few minutes passed before Samira emerged again. She smiled brightly.

"Sorry to keep you."

Marnie wished them a happy trip and watched them as they passed the plate glass window; two young women off to the shops. What could be more normal, she thought. What had Anne said? *What can possibly go wrong?*

As Anne reached the car and opened the door, one thought was going through her mind. Samira had been in the shower-room for longer than she had expected, but at no time had she heard the loo flushing.

****

The office phone rang twenty minutes later. With a sense of foreboding, Marnie reached for the receiver, but it was Ralph using his favourite new toy, the car phone. He was ringing to let her know that his meetings in Oxford had finished earlier than expected and he'd be calling in at the village shop on his way home.

"Did the girls get off all right?" he asked.

"Yes."

"You don't sound very sure."

"Oh, they got off all right, but there was something ..."

"Something Samira said?"

"No, nothing like that. I can't quite put my finger ... ah, yes. You know how punctual Samira always is?"

"She's a consultant to Big Ben, I believe."

"Correct. Well, today she didn't arrive until almost a quarter past five. Doesn't that strike you as odd?"

"A certain lack of enthusiasm, I'd say."

"Me too."

"Did she seem all right otherwise?"

"I think so, though she did decide to go to the loo."

"My God!" said Ralph. "How very sinister."

Marnie laughed. "You're thinking I may be making too much of this?"

"Surely not. But it is just a shopping trip. No harm can come to them in MK."

After the call ended Marnie sat back in her chair and looked up at the clock. She watched the red hand sweeping round for a few seconds. They should be arriving in Centre MK about now, she thought. Ralph was surely right. What harm could possibly come to them there?

****

Anne easily found a parking slot. The two of them crossed the road and entered Centre MK, one of the biggest covered shopping centres in the country. It comprised two long avenues of shops with exotic trees planted in the middle of each broad walkway. In addition there were side streets linking the two main thoroughfares, plus two large squares, one covered, the other open to the elements.

Anne suggested they walk to the far end to start their expedition in what she always called *Marks and Sparks*. She noticed that Samira was staring all around her in wonder. Or was it apprehension?

"Haven't you ever been here before?" Anne asked. "I thought everyone for miles around knew this place."

"I think my parents brought me here when I was little. Can't say I remember it very well. I seem to recall it was busier than this."

"The advantage of coming at this end of the afternoon," Anne said. "I thought that's why you suggested this time."

Samira looked confused. "What? Oh, yes. I see what you mean. Probably. What time do the shops close?"

"They stay open quite late. We've got plenty of time. No need to rush."

"I don't want to make you late for supper, Anne."

Anne stopped to look at a display in the window of Past Times, one of her favourite shops.

"Don't worry about it. We'll find you some tights and undies and be back well before –"

Anne turned to face Samira, only to find that she was talking to herself. Samira was nowhere to be seen.

****

Marnie was pleased with the progress she had made on a scheme design that day, a complete makeover of a small manor

110

house. She was checking the floor plans when the phone rang. For a moment she was tempted to leave the call to voicemail, but she recognised the caller's number as Anne's mobile and grabbed the handset.

"Walker and Co, advisers on underwear to ladies of discerning taste."

"Marnie, it's me."

"I know that, otherwise I wouldn't –"

"I've lost Samira."

Marnie was jolted back to reality by the urgency in Anne's tone.

"*Lost*? What d'you mean?"

"One moment she was beside me, the next, she was gone."

"Where are you?"

"Centre MK, the square, the covered-in one."

"And she disappeared … you mean like thin air?"

"That's about it, Marnie."

"You're not thinking someone could have abducted her, are you?" *I'm getting paranoid*, Marnie thought.

A pause on the line. "Can't see how. Surely I would've noticed."

"Is it crowded?"

"Not really. We were just looking in a shop window and then … bingo!"

"She must've gone into another shop, Anne. What else could it be? Have you checked?"

"I've looked everywhere, the shoe shop, the clothes shop, even Mothercare. Surely she would've said something, not just leave me standing there."

"Okay, listen. Here's what we'll do. You go on searching and keep me posted on my mobile. I'll bring Ralph – he's just getting home – and we'll come into town. We'll be with you in twenty minutes or so. I'm sure she'll turn up. Don't worry."

After disconnecting, Anne walked into the middle of the square and did a full three hundred and sixty degree scan of the area. No result. *Where the hell could Samira be?* Anne tried to think logically and clearly. She could hear Donovan's voice: *the answer is probably staring you in the face.* Anne tried to reason it out. If anyone had snatched Samira away, that would have resulted in a scuffle, a disturbance, noise. So Samira must have done something of her own accord. Okay so far.

If she had bolted, where would she go? *Staring me in the face* ... Anne found herself looking in the direction of the large department store. It was vast and filled with nooks and crannies, an Aladdin's cave of merchandise, a cave ... a *refuge.* Anne set off at speed across the square. As soon as she entered the store she could see it offered Samira protection and concealment, but that also made it difficult to track her down.

And then it happened.

Anne was wandering hopelessly through the women's clothing section when she spotted bustling activity up ahead. A group of people was hustling across the shop floor: a man and a woman, both dressed like members of staff. Between them walked another woman. She was fairly tall, with long dark hair and an upright bearing. She was clearly Asian. She was clearly Samira Khan.

"Can I help you, miss?"

The voice startled Anne. She half turned to find an assistant hovering beside her, an encouraging smile on her face.

"Sorry if I made you jump. You seemed to be hesitating over one of our new lines, the summer collection."

Anne was surprised to find that she was holding the sleeve of a silk top between her fingers.

"Oh, yes ... well, it's lovely, though really for someone a little older than me?"

"Yes, perhaps you're –"

"Can I ask you something?"

"Of course."

Anne looked over her shoulder to where the trio was now disappearing across the store. She noticed that the woman accompanying Samira had a number of garments over her arm.

"What's going on over there?"

The saleslady leaned towards Anne and spoke quietly.

112

"That young woman, she's been arrested for shoplifting."

Anne was incredulous. "*Arrested?*"

"Well, not technically, not yet, but that's what will happen."

Muttering to herself, Anne began to walk away, stunned. Nothing made sense. She had barely gone two paces when the saleslady spoke again.

"'Strange, really."

Anne stopped and turned around. "How strange? In what way?"

"I saw it all. She just walked in. Well, I say *walked*. She sort of *rushed* in, stopped by that rail over there, grabbed half a dozen items and made for the side exit. Unbelievable!"

"So you reported her?"

"Oh no. She did it right in front of the floor manager when she was talking to one of our store detectives."

"Was that the lady carrying the clothes?"

"That's her."

Anne said, "What will happen now? Will someone take her to the police station?"

"I shouldn't be talking about this, really."

Anne shrugged. "I'm just curious. Nothing I can do about it."

"No, I suppose not." The saleslady lowered her voice again. "They'll take her to what's called a *holding room* until the police get here."

"Is it like a cell?" Anne's imagination was in overdrive.

"No. It's just a room, not unpleasant, up on the second floor with the offices. She'll be treated properly. The company has a duty of care towards people, even shoplifters."

Anne nodded. She guessed the saleslady was quoting from a staff training course. "Well, after all that drama, I'd better be going." She smiled. "I'll keep my hands in my pockets in case anyone suspects me, too."

The saleslady shook her head. "No danger of that."

"Glad to hear it," Anne said. "Goodbye."

Anne was about to leave when the saleslady's expression clouded over.

"Everything all right?" Anne asked.

113

"It's odd. I was just thinking ... what you said about the clothes in this section being too old for you. Then it struck me."

"What did?"

"The clothes she took, that young woman, the shoplifter."

"What about them?"

"They were in the outsize section."

"She wasn't outsize," said Anne. "Very slim, I'd say."

"So would I. Peculiar, isn't it?"

****

Anne sat in the outside seating area of the Costa coffee shop while she waited for Marnie and Ralph. She stirred a cappuccino, her mind in turmoil. Something was bothering her, and it was not just the odd choice of clothes – *outsize* fitting – that Samira had taken.

When Marnie and Ralph burst into view, Anne stood and waved them over. She gave a rapid account of the events that had taken place in the store.

Marnie looked at her watch. "It happened when? Twenty minutes ago?"

"Something like that."

"Come on, then. We'd better get moving."

They walked quickly across to the store, and Anne led the way to the lifts.

Ralph pressed a button and the 'Up' symbol lit up in green. "Don't you think the police will already have come for her?"

Marnie shrugged. "What else can we do?" She glanced at Anne who was frowning in deep concentration. "Don't worry, Anne. They'll treat her properly, I'm sure."

Anne stared back. "That's it!"

"Go on."

"There was something strange about the whole scene."

"You mean taking clothes that were obviously not her size?" Ralph said.

"No. Well, yes, that was pretty weird, but that's not what was bothering me. It was her ... what would you call it? ... her

114

whole *demeanour.* You know how nervous she gets. I was worrying that she'd be *terrified* at being arrested."

"And she wasn't?"

"No, Ralph, not a bit. She seemed totally relaxed about the whole thing, just walked calmly along with the people who'd arrested her. It was almost as if ..."

"She wanted to be arrested?" Ralph completed the sentence for her.

"Exactly."

The lift took them to the second floor, and two minutes later they were waiting outside the office of the store manager. It felt like being summoned to see the head teacher at school.

****

After handshakes and introductions they sat facing the manager across his desk. He looked younger than they expected, somewhere in his thirties like Marnie, clean-cut and business-like. Beside him sat a middle-aged woman in a dark suit.

"You asked to see me on what you described as *an important matter,*" he said. "So what can I do for you?"

Marnie glanced sideways in Ralph's direction and said, "Perhaps Professor Lombard can speak for all of us." She hoped the tiny pause after Ralph's title would serve to emphasise his rank and, by association, his respectability.

The manager's eyes narrowed for a split second as he turned his attention to Ralph. Marnie knew her point had been registered. It amused Anne that before speaking Ralph steepled his fingers. Very much the academic.

"We believe you have apprehended an apparent shop-lifter within the last half hour or so. May I ask if she's still in your custody?"

The manager frowned. "You have a particular reason for asking?"

"I do, but before making any further comment, I wonder if you'd mind answering my question."

115

"We are holding a person with a view to pressing charges. I should perhaps make it clear that it's company policy to seek prosecution as a matter of course. That is the norm in the retail industry."

"I fully understand that," Ralph said, lowering his hands to his lap and leaning slightly forward. "Would you, however, be willing to take into account mitigating circumstances of a highly exceptional nature?"

The manager sat back, clearly intrigued. "You're a professor," he began. "May I ask where?"

"I'm professor of economics at All Souls College, Oxford."

The manager looked impressed. It was the result Marnie had hoped for.

Ralph nodded towards the nameplate on the front of the manager's desk. After the name D W Christie were the letters BSc (Econ). "I see you too are an economist."

"Actually I did Business Studies and Finance at Oxford Brookes University."

"Ah yes," said Ralph. "Under Professor Templeman. I know him well."

Marnie was starting to feel impatient. At any moment the police might arrive to cart Samira away in handcuffs, and here was Ralph making academic small talk with the manager. She decided to intervene.

"Would you be willing to hear us out, Mr Christie?" she asked.

Christie turned his gaze on Marnie, and he liked what he saw. He smiled.

"Please, go ahead."

"We have reason to believe that my tenant, Miss Samira Khan, came into your store to seek refuge ... what you might almost call *sanctuary*."

"Refuge from ...?"

"It's a long story but, in brief, we believe she's run away from home to avoid an arranged marriage and she fears her life may now be in danger as a consequence."

"Your *tenant*, did you say?"

Marnie nodded. "I run my own business at Glebe Farm in Knightly St John. Samira rents one of my cottages. That's how I know her."

Christie was frowning again. "Sorry, I can't see the connection between her family circumstances and this store."

Anne got in first. "Samira was out shopping with me. I think someone spooked her and she ran in here to hide."

"By shoplifting?"

"Yes. I think she must've realised that she'd be taken to a place where no-one could reach her, where the police would be coming and she'd be safe."

"This is all very odd," Christie said.

Anne persisted. "The things she took, those dresses, they'd be *miles* too big for *her*, wouldn't they?"

Christie looked for the first time at his colleague.

"Actually, they would," she said. "They were all size sixteen and above. The young woman would be about size ten or twelve, in my judgment."

"There's something else," said Marnie. "When Samira was ... what's the word? ... arrested, apprehended? ... how did she react?"

Christie's colleague replied. "Now that's another strange thing. I've been head of security here for twelve years and I've never known *anyone* react like that before."

"What did she do?" Christie asked.

"Nothing. She sort of sighed and handed me the dresses."

"You don't think she sighed because she'd been found out?"

The security manager shook her head. "No. She seemed quite relaxed about it all, even somehow relieved, I'd say."

"Obviously she made no attempt to run away or struggle?" Christie said.

"Not a bit. I called Mr Fleming over to escort her with me, and she just stood there waiting patiently till he came. Then we walked through the store together, and she came quietly with us. No fuss, no bother."

"Not the kind of reaction you'd expect, I think you'll agree," said Ralph.

"Not at all. Some shoplifters try to make a run for it, others start yelling and screaming, some burst into tears. A few years ago I had one who fainted."

"Mr Christie," Marnie said, "Samira has a very nervous disposition. Acting so calmly like that was completely out of character. She wanted to be taken into custody because it –"

Before Marnie could finish the sentence there came a knock at the door and a young woman entered. She walked briskly up to Mr Christie and handed him a note. While he read it she stood in silence beside him. He glanced up at her, muttered thanks and she left. Marnie felt a knot in her stomach as Christie sat back in his chair and stared into the distance. After a few moments he reached forward, pressed a button on the intercom and spoke.

"Pauline, would you phone them back and say the situation has been resolved. No further action needed. Thanks" He looked at his visitors. "That message was from the police. They're overstretched. There's been a pile-up, an accident on the A5, so they can't send anyone at the moment."

"You're willing to accept our explanation?" said Ralph.

Christie glanced again at his colleague. She gave an almost imperceptible nod.

"Very well," said Christie. "In the circumstances I'm able to exercise my own discretion." He stood up. "I'll arrange for Miss Khan to be escorted to the nearest exit. It's by the customer collection area on the ground floor. You know where that is?"

"Of course," said Marnie. "Thanks for your understanding."

While they were shaking hands, the security manager left the room.

****

"It's over there." Back on the ground floor, Marnie pointed across the store. They threaded their way to the customer collection area.

Situated next to a side entrance, it comprised a service counter where pre-paid goods were handed over to customers, plus a row of seats where they could wait for their items to be

118

fetched from storage. There was no sign of Samira, so the three of them sat and waited for her to appear, while customers came and went.

"What's this place for?" Ralph asked.

Marnie said, "If you buy something and you don't want to traipse around carrying it, you can arrange to have it brought down here. It's handy, especially if you want to buy a number of things in different departments."

"Like when we bought the TV for my room and a printer for the office," Anne added. "I waited here while Marnie brought the car round, so we didn't have far to carry things."

Marnie looked at her watch. "I thought she'd be here by now."

Anne grinned. "Perhaps they have to fetch her from the stock-room. Shall I go and ask at the counter? There are no customers there for the mo."

Anne walked across and spoke to the young men on duty. She was frowning when she returned.

"She's not here, I mean not here *any more*."

Marnie leapt up from her seat and strode over to the counter.

"We're waiting for a friend," she said to the group of men. "She's Asian, about my height, slim with dark hair over her shoulders. Have you seen her?"

One of the men, himself Asian, said, "Yeah. She was here just now. She came with Mr Fleming."

"And?"

He shrugged. "She walked out."

"Quite quickly," another man said. "It was like she had a bus to catch."

"Definitely in a hurry," the third man added.

****

In the car on the way home Marnie and Ralph were racking their brains to think what might have become of Samira. On the back seat Anne was almost sick with worry after losing her for a second time. They had split up and spent half an hour searching the shopping centre from one end to the other. They had drawn a blank and called off the hunt after checking every shop and café, every department store and even the banks that stayed open later than normal business hours.

A pale tremulous voice emanated from the rear. "It's all my fault."

"Of course it isn't, Anne," said Marnie.

"How can it *possibly* be your fault?" Ralph said.

"If I hadn't suggested this silly shopping trip, she'd be safely tucked away in cottage number three instead of ... I don't know."

They travelled on in silence.

"**D**o you think you did everything you could to find Samira, Marnie?"

Marnie was shocked. "We all did." Then she remembered things that Donovan had suggested to Anne and felt deflated. "I mean I did what I thought had to be done at the time. Perhaps we could've tried harder."

"You just searched from shop to shop."

Marnie nodded.

"For the tape please, Marnie."

"I took it as a statement rather than a question. Yes, we searched high and low."

"And afterwards?"

Marnie shrugged. "We went home."

Driscoll said, "You didn't think to report Samira as missing."

"No! Why would we? Samira was a grown woman, not a child who'd wandered off. We weren't in charge of her."

"But you were concerned, worried for her safety."

"Not in the way you're implying. There was obviously something wrong, something troubling her. We realised it was something serious, but we didn't know the details, not then anyway."

"She eventually returned," said Driscoll.

"I wouldn't quite put it like that."

"How would you put it? In your own words, Marnie. Take your time."

Chapter 10

Questions to be answered

Samira didn't return to Glebe Farm that Friday evening. Saturday morning was cool and overcast, threatening rain, and Marnie nipped out before breakfast to knock on the door of cottage number three. No reply. Over coffee, toast and orange juice in the farmhouse they held a council of war.

"We can't just stand by and do nothing," Anne said. She had slept only fitfully and had dark smudges under her eyes. "What can have happened to her?"

Marnie said, "At times like this Donovan's always full of ideas." She turned to Anne. "Is he coming for the weekend, d'you know?"

"Not sure. I'll ring him after breakfast."

"I suppose we could report Samira to the police as a missing person," Ralph said.

Marnie looked less than enthusiastic. She had seen enough of the police to last a lifetime, though the idea made sense.

Anne looked shocked. It was the first time anyone had called Samira a *missing person*. For Anne it brought up visions of a captive in some dark and dingy cellar, bound to a chair, beaten and battered with no hope of escape. Or worse. She hastily chewed and swallowed a last piece of toast, gulped down a last mouthful of coffee and headed for the door.

****

Anne didn't normally go up to her attic room to phone Donovan in private, but on that day she had forebodings about Samira and wanted a quiet chat, just the two of them together. He picked up the phone after two rings.

"Hi! Deadlines department."

"Hi Donovan. How are ... what did you say?"

"Deadlines are the name of the game. My tutor has slipped in an extra project and I'm writing an application for a placement. I'm chained to the desk here."

"Oh ..."

"That sounded a bit flat. What's up, Anne?"

"Have you got a minute while I fill you in about Samira?"

"Fire away."

Anne gave a blow-by-blow account of the aborted shopping trip to Milton Keynes and the subsequent disappearance of Samira. "So that's it, and we haven't seen her since." She waited in silence, wondering what Donovan's reaction might be. When he spoke, it surprised her.

"You really just went looking in the shops? That's all you did?"

"Not just shops but cafés, restaurants –"

"You didn't think of checking with security?"

A pause. "Er, well, no. How would we do that?"

"Anyone managing a shop in Centre MK would be able to tell you how to find the security office."

"But what could they do?"

"Okay. First, they could tell their own security personnel to look out for her. That way you'd have several more pairs of eyes working for you."

"Would they do that?"

"Why not? Worth asking. But there's more. They could put out an announcement, asking her to go to a meeting point."

"But what if she'd run away or been abducted by someone? In either case she'd hardly present herself, just like that."

"Maybe not, but if she was in hiding she'd know you were trying to trace her, and it might give her something to think about. If she was being held it would tell her captors that pursuit was at hand, or at least that she had some sort of back-up."

Anne was frowning again. "I don't see how that would work."

"That's the point, Anne. You have to throw various options at a situation. You never know what might happen.

Everything's worth trying. You need to exploit every opportunity you can get. And there's more."

"Oh gawd. What else did we fail to do?"

"They have CCTV in the centre. Their staff could watch for her on their monitors. They might even allow one of you into the control room to see if you could spot her."

The airwaves between London and Knightly St John fell silent. Anne was the first to speak, her tone downcast.

"We messed up big time, didn't we?"

"Look, Anne. It's easy for me to sit here and pronounce words of wisdom. Quite different when you're in the thick of it."

"Marnie said it would have been better if we'd had you with us."

"Not necessarily."

"And, being realistic with your deadlines, you'll not be coming up this weekend, will you?"

More silence as Donovan surveyed the papers that were littering his desk and the draft text that covered his computer screen.

"You can't, can you?" Anne continued. She heard Donovan breathe out in a sigh.

"Being realistic ..." he began. There was no need to finish the sentence.

****

Back in the kitchen the phone rang, and Marnie picked it up. It was her sister, and immediately obvious from Beth's tone that not even the gloomy weather could dampen her spirits.

"So, how are things going, Marnie? I expect your new tenant has settled in by now."

"Not quite. She's er ... gone missing."

"You mean a moonlight flit? Had she paid her rent?"

"Not like that, Beth."

"Then like what?"

"It's a complicated story."

"Tell all. What am I here for?"

"Do you really want me to answer that?"

124

"Just get on with it."

"Okay. Condensed version. She went shopping with Anne in MK then just vanished. Anne spotted her being arrested for shoplifting, and we had to persuade the manager that she was doing it to avoid being found. So they let her go."

"But she was found, surely. You said she'd been arrested."

"I meant to avoid being found by anyone who might be pursuing her."

A pause. "You've lost me."

"I told you it was complicated."

"What had she stolen?"

"Half a dozen dresses."

"Why did they let her go when she was caught red-handed?"

"She wasn't."

Beth said, "She was wearing gloves?"

"I'm going to ignore that."

"But seriously, Marnie."

"The dresses were size sixteen and above."

"There's an amnesty for overweight shoplifters?"

"No, you ninny! And Samira's probably a size ten."

Beth groaned. "I'm really sorry I asked about this."

"So am I," said Marnie.

Beth made one last valiant effort. "You said they let her go."

"Correct."

"Then what did she do?"

"She went." Marnie heard something on the line that might have been a scream or a groan or both. She tried to put things right, adding, "I meant she disappeared, went off, legged it, whatever."

Some seconds elapsed before Beth spoke again. "Have you found her?"

"No. Not yet."

"Well, I would say I'm looking forward to the next instalment, but thankfully we're flying to Crete tomorrow."

"I hope Paul's research project goes well. Wish him good luck from me."

"I will. You know, Marnie, there is one thing."

125

"What's that?"

"I'm now wishing I asked for the full-length version of the shoplifting saga."

"Yes," Marnie agreed. "It would probably have been a lot quicker. Have a nice trip."

****

Glebe Farm's own private black cloud floated over them all weekend. There was no word from Samira, nothing further from Donovan.

On Monday Anne struggled to concentrate on the firm's VAT returns, her thoughts returning to the conversation with Donovan. She felt guilty at not taking enough action to find Samira. Then it struck her. He had said something about a placement application. The second year placement was an important part of his university course, and she had not even asked him about it. Another reason to feel guilty.

Soon after ten Anne was glad to do something practical to take her mind off things. She got up and put the kettle on; coffee time for the men working in what was laughingly called the farmhouse garden or, as she preferred, 'the jungle'. Pasting a friendly smile on her face, she set off with the tray to encourage the contractors.

Marnie waited until Anne was out of the office before getting up from her desk. She knew her friend would spend a couple of minutes chatting to the men while they took a breather from their exertions. Such small considerations helped keep up morale and, in any case, Anne liked the men. She liked to hear about their progress in clearing away years of neglect.

Marnie grabbed the spare keys for cottage number three from the board in the kitchen area and skipped across the courtyard. Normally she would never enter a cottage after letting it unless invited or requested by the occupants, but these were exceptional circumstances.

She opened the front door and stepped into the hallway, standing in silence for a few moments, listening to the house breathing. Marnie had an overwhelming sense that the cottage

126

was empty. She took a few deep breaths before going from room to room on the ground floor. In the kitchen she looked through the semi-glazed door into the patio garden. On the end wall a mass of yellow *Maygold* roses covered the trellis.

She returned to the entrance hall and called up the stairs. "Samira! Samira, are you there? It's only me, Marnie."

There was no reply, and she expected none. Alone in the cottage, Marnie was overcome with anxiety.

Where are you, Samira? The question haunted her. *What has become of you?* She shuddered when a third question came into her mind. *What have they done to you?*

****

Later that afternoon Anne was glad of another distraction. She bundled up that day's correspondence and headed off to the post-box and village shop. There she bought a few basics and presented them at the counter where Molly Appleton bagged them up. Handing the change to Anne, she looked at her appraisingly.

"You all right, my dear? You're looking a bit peaky. There's a flu bug going around at the moment. Hope you're not going down with it."

Anne sagged. She had hoped that putting on her smiley face might have camouflaged her true feelings. Now she felt almost relieved that her cover had been blown.

"No, Molly. It's not a bug. I've got an attack of the Samiras."

"Ooh, that sounds nasty. Is it, like ..." She lowered her voice and mouthed, "diarrhoea?"

Anne could not help but laugh. "No, it's nothing like that. I just meant I've been worrying about *Samira*. You know, Samira, our new tenant?"

"Oh yes. The pretty lady with the pretty name. Of course I know her. Why are you worrying? Isn't she well?"

And so it all came out. Anne told Molly about the shopping trip, the apparent shoplifting episode and Samira's disappearance. Not normally one for gossip or indiscretion,

Anne just could not help herself, and Molly had always been a sympathetic listener.

"Please don't tell anybody about this, Molly. There are more things in the background that I can't talk about, and frankly the whole thing is wearing me down."

"You can trust me, Anne. You know that. Village shops are supposed to be centres of gossip, but I know when to hold my tongue."

****

Donovan phoned that night and asked about Samira. It took Anne less than a minute to sum up their progress. Non-progress. Before he could enquire further, Anne changed the subject.

"You mentioned a placement application earlier. Tell me all about it."

"I'm supposed to spend a term with a film or television company as an intern."

"How exciting! And how's your application coming along?"

"Well, it's ..."

"It's what?"

"Rather tiresome, really."

"Why?"

"I have to fill in this long form then write a *two thousand* word proposal, outlining what outcomes I want to achieve, what skills I have to offer, what experience I've had, what areas I want to develop, what ... You get the picture. Waffle, waffle, waffle."

"It won't be waffle when you write it, Donovan. You're always so precise. It'll be brilliant."

"No pressure, then. But thank you for that comforting thought."

"And it'll be a marvellous opportunity to develop your skills with all that extra experience."

Donovan laughed. "Yep. I can't wait to brush up my technical skills."

"Did I say something funny?" Anne asked.

128

"I have a sneaking suspicion that the skills involved will be sweeping floors and making tea."

Marnie was beginning to wonder if DC Driscoll was performing both parts: good cop and bad cop, rolled into one. Driscoll put her questions in a quiet voice as if they were enjoying a friendly chat. At the same time she stared into Marnie's eyes as if provoking her into making a mistake, trying to trip her up, goading her to commit some inconsistency that she could seize upon.

"You must have been very worried about Samira, Marnie. You said she made no contact for several days?"

"I've already told you I was concerned about her. We all were."

"And you really had no idea where she was during that time?"

"No." *Keep it brief, Marnie. Don't embellish.*

Driscoll looked down at her notepad. "You must have had some idea about what provoked her into disappearing like that."

Marnie sighed. "I thought I'd made it clear that I wasn't there, so I couldn't have an opinion on that."

"Though you formed an opinion after thinking about it and talking about it with your friends. No?"

Marnie frowned. "Look, any opinion I had or might have had is surely immaterial. The fact is, Samira was missing. That was all that concerned me at the time. I don't know what more I can say about that."

Before Driscoll could continue there came a knock on the door and a face appeared. Marnie thought she recognised one of the other detectives she had seen earlier.

"Can I have a word?" he said to Driscoll.

She announced for the recording that the interview was being suspended and left the room. Marnie looked sideways at Roger Broadbent. DC Harry Rabjohn glanced at her across the table as Roger stared down at the desk in front of him with the slightest shake of his head. Marnie took the hint and said nothing. Five minutes passed before Driscoll re-entered the room. She did not look happy as she sat and passed a slip of paper to Rabjohn. He read it but made no reaction. Driscoll switched the recording machine back on, announced the time and stared at Marnie.

"I have to inform you, Marnie, that there has been a development," she said. "The charge you are now facing is murder."

Marnie sat back in her chair, stunned. Once again she turned to Roger.

"In the circumstances," he began, "I would like to talk to my client in private."

Chapter 11

The key to the problem

The rest of the week passed with no news of Samira and a succession of restless nights for Marnie, Ralph and Anne. Saturday dawned cloudy and grey but by mid-morning the sun was poking through, and Marnie began making plans. She liked weekends. They were a good time to press on with projects; no business phone calls, no meetings. But fine weather made Marnie realise she was desperate for some R and R, and a chance to get away from worrying about Samira. She rang Ralph on *Thyrsis* and suggested an outing

****

They decided to eat lunch on the boat. Anne volunteered to throw together a picnic. She hopped across to the farmhouse while Marnie tidied her desk and Ralph finished off his statistics. Slotting some papers into a drawer, Marnie came across the keys of cottage number three. She had forgotten to hang them up on the board in the kitchen area. She grabbed them and headed over to unhook the keys for *Sally Ann*. As she did so, a thought pinged distantly in her head. She was focusing on it when Anne burst into the office clutching a shopping bag.

"Am I holding us up? There isn't much for lunch, just a few sandwiches – cheese and pickle – some yogurts and fruit, nothing exciting, apples and pears. We've got coffee and some of Donovan's tinned milk on the boat. Oh and some wine, of course. Not sure what it is. Red, I think."

"You are allowed to pause and take a breath, Anne."

"What? Oh yes, good idea." Anne breathed in deeply. "Right. Have you got *Sally*'s keys?"

"Yep, and I'm sure your picnic will be fine. Come on. Let's go before the weather changes its mind."

****

The weather didn't change its mind. It kept its promise for the whole afternoon. A few puffy white clouds drifted lazily across the sky, scarcely troubling the sun. And the picnic lunch was enlivened by the wine, a big red Aussie shiraz, that hit the spot perfectly. Marnie pointed the boat's prow southward, down to the lock at Cosgrove by the Buckingham Arm, on to and over the Iron Trunk aqueduct and beyond to the varied landscapes around Milton Keynes. Cruising on *Sally Ann* soothed away their anxieties. It always did, but they all knew they would have to face up to the problem of Samira once that peaceful interlude was over.

Pleasantly relaxed by their few hours in open air and sunlight, they brought *Sally Ann* home and settled the boat into her dock. While Ralph dealt with the engine compartment, Marnie and Anne headed off through the spinney.

At the end of the path Anne walked over to the farmhouse to investigate the larder and devise a menu for supper; Marnie opened the office barn to check the answerphone. Before locking up, she crossed to the kitchen area and hung the boat keys on their hook. It was only then that she recalled what had struck her earlier in the afternoon.

Marnie and Ralph arrived together at the farmhouse door. In the kitchen Anne met them with a suggestion.

"How about fresh tuna marinated in orange, lemon and olive oil then baked in the oven, plus new potatoes and a mixed salad, followed by banana fool?"

Ralph said, "I'm drooling."

Marnie agreed. "Sounds good to me."

Anne smiled. "Great. I'll make a start on the marinade. Anything on the answerphone from Samira?"

Marnie shook her head. "Nothing."

Ralph said, "I suppose the old adage about no news being good news springs to mind."

"I want to change the subject," said Marnie. She turned to Anne. "Did Donovan take his boat keys with him when he went back to London?"

"He sometimes does. He'll probably ring tonight. I can ask him."

****

Anne was reading in her attic room, eyelids drooping, when her mobile began warbling soon after ten.

"Hello you. How's it going? Application all sewn up? Project completed?"

"You sound weary, Anne."

"Blame it on my new boyfriend."

"Too lively for you?"

"Not quite. He died in 1852."

"My commiserations. Must have been a terrible shock."

Anne laughed. "Idiot!"

"You started it. Anyway, who is – or was – this guy?"

"Feeling jealous?"

"Thinking of sending a belated sympathy card, actually. And, yes, I have completed the application, and the project is progressing. How's your day been? Any news of Samira?"

"A pleasant tootle on *Sally* and no, in that order. Before I forget, I have a question from Marnie. Did you take your boat keys with you when you left?"

A pause on the line. "Not sure. Have you checked the board in the office kitchen?"

"Not there. That's why we're asking."

"Leave it with me. I'll check and ring you back. How urgent?"

Anne yawned. "I don't –"

"It's okay. I've got the message. You can get back to grieving for Pugin."

"How did you know it was –"

"Google. Sleep well. See you soon."

****

Marnie and Ralph also decided on an early night. At the time when Anne and Donovan were talking, Marnie and Ralph were in the shower together. They enjoyed that.

134

They were drying themselves with capacious white towels when Ralph made an announcement.

"I'd like to make a proposition."

"I rather thought you might."

Ralph said, "I suppose there's a semantic difference between a proposal and a proposition?"

Marnie reflected. "Well, in my life I've had two of the first sort and quite a few of the other. Which is it to be?"

"How about a *suggestion*?"

"Keep digging."

Ralph cleared his throat, so Marnie knew it was going to be serious.

She said, "You do remember you've already proposed to me, don't you?"

"How could I forget?"

"So what do you have in mind?"

"Let me come straight to the point," Ralph said.

"Praise the lord!"

"How about –"

"That's how propositions begin, in my experience."

Ralph persisted. "How about getting married very simply, no fuss?"

"That's it, is it, your proposal-proposition-suggestion? Very romantic."

Ralph added, "Then going to Venice on the Orient Express?"

Marnie was speechless.

Ralph continued. "Unless you'd like a big wedding ... posh frock, swanky venue, marquee, champagne reception, sit-down meal, dancing till the early hours?"

Marnie found her voice, eventually.

"Er ... you've taken me by surprise."

Ralph had a twinkle in his eye. "I was hoping that might come later."

"I mean it. I hadn't really been thinking about our wedding. It's crossed my mind from time to time but we've all just been so busy it's never come to the fore. What would we do to

135

celebrate with friends and family? Presumably we'd do something?"

"Perhaps we could have a big party when we get back. How about a summer garden party?"

"Wow," said Marnie. "I certainly like the idea of Venice and the Orient Express. Yes, and the garden party sounds great."

"If you like, I could get down on one knee and make my proposal-proposition-suggestion. What d'you think?"

Marnie cast off her towel and playfully threw it at him. In reply, Ralph cast off his towel and did the same. They collapsed into bed in each other's arms, laughing. For that night neither of them spared a further thought to a missing person or her pursuers.

M arnie and Roger were escorted to a small meeting room down the corridor. They were given fifteen minutes together before the formal interview resumed.

Once left alone, they hugged each other and sat at the table side by side. Marnie was breathing steadily and deeply, in a state of shock.

"Nothing can really prepare you for something like this," she said. "I've seen people charged with murder on television and in films, but the reality is something else. It just hits you like a runaway train."

Roger reached over and placed a hand on hers, squeezing it gently. "We're going to have to find you a solicitor experienced in criminal law, Marnie, and a good barrister."

"I've got *you*, Roger. You're a rock, always supportive, always dependable."

He withdrew his hand. "Marnie, you've got to face facts. I'm fine at general law. Someone needs a divorce or wants to buy a house, draw up a will, any of the run-of-the-mill stuff on which key parts of our lives depend, then I'm your man. But this ..."

Marnie put her head in her hands and sighed deeply.

"Interesting," said Roger.

Marnie looked up. "What is?"

"Driscoll informed you of the changed situation, but she didn't formally charge you."

"Is that significant?" Marnie asked.

"I'm not sure. I would've expected something more. But perhaps that isn't necessary at this stage."

"What's going to happen next, Roger?"

"No doubt DC Driscoll will want to carry on establishing the facts in the case by interviewing you. Others in the same team will be assembling all the evidence needed to go to the Crown Prosecution Service. Once they're satisfied they tick all the right boxes against you, that's when it moves on."

"How does it work?"

"I expect you'll appear before a magistrate tomorrow. That's a formality. Nothing happens there. The case will simply be referred to the Crown Court and a date will be set for the trial."

Marnie leaned forward, both elbows on the table and murmured, "Bloody hell!"

"Marnie, I want you to know I'll do everything in my power to help you. That includes finding a good defence team."

Marnie looked up sharply. "And I want you to know, Roger, that I absolutely did not commit this crime."

"You don't need to tell me that, my love. I've never doubted it for a second."

"But you do look worried."

"This is a big deal, Marnie. It's bigger than anything that has ever come my way. I don't want to let you down."

"I know that." She made a passable attempt at a smile, leaned over and kissed him on the cheek.

As she withdrew, the door opened and a uniformed policeman stepped into the room.

"Time's up," he said and opened the door wider.

Chapter 12

Bolt-hole

Anne had showered in the office barn on Sunday morning and was rubbing her hair dry when her mobile chirped. She wrapped the towel round herself and padded through to the kitchen area. The phone was on the workbench.

"Hi, Donovan."

"Hi. Not too early?"

"I've just come out of the shower, but I'm decent."

"Pity. Listen, I've checked high and low. I *definitely* didn't bring the boat keys back with me. You're really sure they're not hanging up on the board?"

"Positive. I can see it now."

"So what's the problem? You think you might've lost them?"

"Possibly. I'm really sorry."

"Don't be. I have my spare set, and I expect the others will –" Donovan stopped abruptly.

Anne found herself listening to silence. "Donovan? Hello?"

"Has anyone else had access to the kitchen area?" Donovan asked.

"No. No-one ever comes ..."

Silence on the line again.

"Anne?"

"Just thinking. The other day, when we were going shopping ..."

"Samira?"

"Yeah. She said she wanted to use the loo. She was back here for a few minutes. But why would she take the keys? She seems so much more relaxed these days."

Donovan said, "Insurance policy? Fall-back position? Just in case? You know how paranoid she is."

"But the boat's moored on the opposite side to the towpath, out of reach. That's the whole idea."

"And behind it?" Donovan said.

"It backs onto private land. There's no access on that side, and a sign, 'no admittance'."

"So what?"

****

Over breakfast in the farmhouse Anne relayed her conversation with Donovan. As soon as they opened the office Marnie checked the diary for the following day. She had no meetings scheduled for Monday. Ralph needed to spend time preparing for a seminar at Warwick University, so Marnie and Anne decided they would take *Sally Ann* to investigate *XO2*.

Under an overcast sky threatening rain, Marnie took the helm and steered northwards. Despite having been there before, they were both surprised by how well concealed Donovan's boat was. It was barely visible under the trailing branches of the spreading willow trees.

Marnie held *Sally Ann* steady against *XO2*, stern alongside stern, and Anne stepped across. She tapped gently on the door, softly calling Samira's name. There was no immediate response. It seemed they had had a wasted journey. Anne looked across at Marnie and shook her head. The curtains in the portholes were all drawn shut. The boat seemed abandoned and deserted.

Marnie was not one to give up at the first sign of adversity. She fastened a mooring rope to a cleat on *XO2* and joined Anne on the stern deck.

"What now?" Anne asked.

"We could walk along the gunwales and check all the portholes in case there's some way of looking in."

"I suppose so."

Anne sounded less than enthusiastic. Marnie felt much the same. Progress would be slow and awkward, elbowing their way through the willow branches. As they stood there looking at the boat for inspiration, Marnie's gaze fell on the door handle and lock and she had the germ of an idea. She knelt down and leaned forward.

140

"Looking through the keyhole?" Anne said. "I'd have thought it would be too dark inside to see anything."

Marnie turned her head and smiled up at Anne. "On the contrary, my dear Watson. It is *very* revealing."

"What can you see, Sherlock?"

"It's right under my nose."

Anne looked baffled. "You can see inside?"

"No, I mean literally under my nose." Marnie pointed at the lock. "Have a peek and tell me what you see."

Anne knelt beside Marnie and leaned towards the door handle. She shook her head. "It's no use. I can't see a thing. The keyhole is ... Ah."

"Exactly," said Marnie. "*Ah.* The keyhole is blocked by the key ... on the inside."

"Which means ..."

"Quite. You know something, Anne? I'm getting rather impatient with our tenant."

With that, Marnie thumped firmly on the door three times with the side of her fist and called out in a loud voice.

"Samira, we know you're in there. It's Marnie and Anne. Let us in, please, for goodness' sake."

Still no response. Marnie thumped three times again. Harder.

"Now!"

After a few seconds they heard the bolts being drawn and the key turning in the lock.

****

They sat in Donovan's saloon drinking his coffee. Anne had put some of his German biscuits out on a plate. No-one touched them. Samira looked at Marnie as if fearful of what she might say, but Marnie was in no mood for an argument.

"I'm sorry, Marnie, to cause you so much trouble. You must think me a real pain."

"True."

Samira looked downcast. Marnie continued.

141

"I know you're scared, Samira, but you must see you can't keep running away. How long do you think you can go on like this?"

Samira sipped her coffee. "I don't know. What do you think I should do, stay in the cottage and wait to be found?"

Marnie sighed and took a biscuit from the plate. "This kind of situation is unlike anything I've encountered before. Perhaps if you stay in the cottage for long enough your family will get things in perspective and you'll be able to resume your normal life. Is that what you're hoping?"

"I don't think it works like that, Marnie. The longer I'm away, it can only make things worse. I'd be seen as bringing even more disgrace to my family."

"Samira, it's almost the twenty-first century. What you're saying sounds like something from the Middle Ages or ancient history. You have the right to live your own life, take your own decisions."

"Not if I'm dead."

Marnie looked aghast. "You really believe it could come to that?"

Samira stared at Marnie without speaking.

Anne cleared her throat. "Can I make a suggestion?" she asked. "Why don't we all put our heads together, sit round the table, the five of us, with Ralph and Donovan? That way we might work out what's to do for the best."

Marnie looked at Samira. "Could you handle that? Could you come back with us and we'll get everyone together to talk things over?"

Samira looked haunted. "Do I have a choice?"

"You have several choices," Marnie said. "But you must realise that sooner or later you'll have to return to the real world."

Samira drank more coffee, staring ahead into a bleak future.

When the interview restarted, Marnie had a surprise. DC Shirley Driscoll and DC Harry Rabjohn had changed places. She now found herself sitting opposite the male detective and wondered if this was how a good-cop-bad-cop routine worked in practice. Marnie braced herself for an onslaught. Instead, she had another surprise. Rabjohn spoke quietly, and his tone was courteous.

"We need to establish, Marnie … Oh, is it okay if I call you by your first name?" Marnie nodded. "Thank you. As I was saying, we need to establish if we can what the reason was for Samira's alarm in the MK shopping centre. Can you help me with that?"

Marnie wanted to scream, *I've already told you I wasn't there, so how could I bloody well know? How many times do I have to tell you?* Instead, she said simply, "I really couldn't say, not being there at the time."

"I understand, but you must have talked about it afterwards with Professor Lombard and Miss Price and possibly with Mr Donovan Smith as well. You must've come to some conclusions."

"Nothing of any use. I don't think Samira recognised anybody in the shopping centre, if that's what you mean." *Careful, Marnie. This man could lead you into too much elaboration.*

Rabjohn sat in silence for a few moments, then eventually said, "You'd been to the Shahs' house in Luton before?"

Marnie sat up. "The Shahs?" She looked confused.

Rabjohn said, "Shall I repeat the question?"

Marnie hesitated. "No. Er, no, I'd never been there before."

"You're sure of that?"

"Positive."

"For how long were you at the house today?"

"I'd just arrived … a few moments before the police turned up."

"But you knew the house well enough to go round to the back door."

Marnie shook her head. "No. Well, yes, I did go round the back, but it was only ..."

"Yes?"

"It was a sort of impulse."

Rabjohn and Driscoll exchanged looks.

"Okay," Rabjohn said. "Tell me something. How did Samira get on with Mr Donovan Smith?"

This second sudden change of tack caught Marnie unawares. "Well ... I think ... er, at least ... Yeah. I think they got on fine." *Hold it there, Marnie! You've said – or blurted – enough.*

"Are you sure about that, Marnie."

"I am. Yes, really."

"Mr Donovan Smith will confirm that, will he?"

"Can I say something?"

DC Rabjohn smiled. "Please do. That's what we're here for."

"It's just that his surname is Smith. It's not double-barrelled or anything."

"So Donovan is his first name?"

"It's one of his forenames, the one he always uses in Britain."

"What else does he use? Do you mean he has an *alias?*"

Marnie's turn to smile. "No! He's half-German, and over there they call him Nikki or Nikolaus. His father was half-Irish, and Donovan is an old family name."

"So how did *Donovan* get on with Samira?"

"Like I said, fine. He let her use his boat, remember."

"Let's explore that a little."

Roger was about to ask what was the relevance of Marnie's account of Samira's use of Donovan's boat when the door opened again. The uniformed policeman entered and passed a note to DC Rabjohn. This time there was a decided reaction. He jerked his head sideways and thrust the note at DC Driscoll. She read it quickly, and the two detectives stared at each other for a long moment. Driscoll then announced that the interview was being suspended and switched off the recording machine.

The detectives excused themselves hastily and abruptly left the room.

Marnie turned to Roger and spoke quietly. "What d'you make of that?"

Roger shook his head. "Beats me. Something's certainly got *them* excited."

Marnie lowered her voice to a whisper. "Do you think we're being observed, Roger?"

"Most likely, but I doubt if there's much we can say that will make a difference to anything."

"What do we do?"

"There's not much we can do but sit and wait."

They didn't have long to wait. The detectives reappeared a minute or two later. As soon as they entered the room they looked far from happy. Roger's antennae began twitching. If the detectives were displeased for some reason it could well be good news for Marnie. She on the other hand had no such intuition. The sight of their scowling faces brought a lump to her throat and a heavy weight in the pit of her stomach.

Chapter 13

Guests at the table

"You did *what?*"

Marnie was struggling to suppress laughter. It was Wednesday morning at the breakfast table in the farmhouse.

Anne was grinning. "I gave her some knickers."

Ralph and Marnie laughed in unison.

"When was this?" Marnie asked.

"When we brought Samira back on Sunday. I found an unopened pack of four pairs in a drawer." Another grin. "I think of it as my … drawers drawer."

More laughter.

"I think it emanates from a kind of repressed prudishness," Ralph began. "Probably dates back to the Puritan era, or perhaps Victorian times."

He often sounded like a textbook.

"What does?" Anne asked.

"Laughing at the word *knickers*," Marnie said. "So you took them over to Samira?"

"Yep. She said she was running out of tights and … undies, so I gave her my spares, new ones. That was the whole point of the dreaded shopping trip to Milton Keynes, remember? She said she didn't want to run the washing machine for just a few pairs of pants, and washing them by hand in the sink didn't seem very satisfactory."

"Very helpful of you, Anne." Marnie changed the subject. "Did Donovan say what time he'd be coming today?"

"Not exactly. He just said he had to drop his project off at uni and then he'd head this way."

"Let's assume he'll be here for supper at least," Marnie said. "D'you want to pop over to Fort Knox and invite Samira to tunnel her way out and join us for the evening?"

Anne nodded. "Okay, but I think I'll call her on the mobile. It's starting to drizzle and I don't want to get soaked standing on the doorstep while she undoes seventeen bolts and chains up the guard dogs."

****

"Good evening, Samira. Do come in." Marnie held the door open for her to enter. "As usual you look *absolutely* stunning."

In a tunic that seemed to be tailored in pure gold, with a pale gold silk-chiffon scarf draped over her shoulders, no-one could argue with Marnie's compliment. Samira made a self-deprecating gesture as she stepped into the hall and handed Marnie a small package. It too was wrapped in gold paper and tied with a deep red ribbon.

"A small gift of thanks for you, Marnie. You're always so good to me."

"That's very kind of you." Marnie kissed Samira on the cheek.

She ushered her guest through to the drawing room where Ralph was placing a tray of drinks on the coffee table. As Samira sat down, Anne appeared from the adjacent dining room carrying a tray of nibbles: olives, cashews, pistachios and pretzels.

"Don't get up, Samira," Anne said. "Lovely to see you."

"Lovely to be here, Anne. No Donovan this evening?"

Anne's smile faltered. She camouflaged it by removing the bowls from the tray and transferring them to the low table in the centre of the Oriental carpet.

"He's, er ... coming on shortly."

Ralph intervened. "Samira, what can I offer you to drink? We've got that cordial you liked, based on ginger and lemongrass."

"Wonderful, thanks."

"Ice and a chunk of lemon?"

"Perfect."

While Ralph mixed the cordial with sparkling mineral water, Marnie poured three glasses of chilled white *gewürztraminer* from Alsace. They clinked glasses.

"How are you feeling, Samira?" Marnie asked.

Anne began handing round the nibbles. Samira selected a single cashew and bit it in half.

"I'm fine, thanks." She looked at Ralph. "Your cordial's delicious."

"You look marvellous," Marnie said. "But with your colouring you'll always look better than us with our pale skin."

Anne made a mock-indignant *huh!* sound and pretended to pout. Samira laughed.

"Actually," she began, "I do feel well. After what happened in town the other day you must think me *completely* stupid."

Marnie shook her head. "Think no more of it. Obviously something spooked you. You wouldn't have just taken off like that without good reason."

Samira smiled self-consciously. "You know how jumpy I am."

No-one could disagree with her.

"I was totally baffled," said Anne. "When I looked round I saw a few boys in football shirts, and suddenly you weren't there any more."

"I expect I was just being silly."

They waited, expecting Samira to elaborate. She seemed to be on the brink of saying something, but instead took another sip of her drink. At that moment the doorbell rang.

Anne leapt up. "I'll go. It'll be Donovan."

Samira placed the remaining half of the cashew in her mouth.

Anne let Donovan come into the hall and drop his weekend bag on the floor before hugging him.

"You're later than we expected. Did you get your project in on time?"

"Project? Oh, yeah. That seems a long time ago now."

They kissed.

"Come on through. Samira's here, and Ralph's found this really nice wine with an unpronounceable name. I don't think I've had it before." As she turned to lead the way, she looked at his face. "Is that a smudge on your cheek?"

Donovan shrugged. "Probably just a shadow. Let's try this unpronounceable wine."

Donovan gave the wine his full approval and, as everyone expected, he was able to pronounce its name without difficulty. The meal also didn't disappoint. The starter was tomato *bruschetta*, an old favourite, but the main course was something they hadn't eaten for some time. Swordfish was one of Donovan's favourites and went well with *dauphinoise* potatoes and glazed carrots. Even so, Anne was not the only one to notice that he seemed somewhat tense. Apart from praising the food, he said even less than usual.

For dessert Marnie had made a lemon sorbet and, as she handed round the glass bowls, she looked at Donovan.

"Is that a bruise on your cheek?" she asked.

He shrugged it off. "It's nothing."

"Looks like a bruise to me," Ralph said. He smiled. "What have you been up to?"

"I think I caught it while I was shutting the car door. Tough beasts these Beetles."

"Beetles?" Samira looked surprised.

"It's Donovan's car," Anne explained. "It's an old VW Beetle."

"Not *old*," Donovan corrected her. "*Classic.*"

Anne poked her tongue out. "If you say so." She turned to Samira. "Donovan likes classics. Can you by *any* chance guess what colour it is?"

Samira considered this while looking at Donovan. He was wearing a black shirt, dark grey jeans and black trainers.

She smiled. "I think I probably can, especially as I've spent some time on *Exodos*."

Marnie said, "That was Donovan's choice of decor, of course. Actually, Samira, I must say I was surprised when you agreed to use *Exodos* as a hide-away."

"Me too, if I'm honest," said Anne.

Donovan looked across the table at Samira. "I wasn't. You needed a refuge. Where else were you going to run to?"

"As a matter of interest," Ralph said, "I was wondering how you got to the boat and how you came to have the keys in the first place."

Samira looked uncomfortable.

"After I was ... released in the store I used a payphone to call for a minicab. That got me to the pub by the canal near Yardley Gobion."

Ralph nodded. "And you'd borrowed the keys in case of need, presumably."

Samira lowered her eyes and said softly, "Yes." She quickly added, "Then I climbed over a low wall at the rear of the car park and skirted the fields until I came to the boat."

"That was quite a walk," Marnie said.

"Yes. It took well over half an hour, but I knew I'd reach Donovan's boat as long as I kept going. Eventually I saw water on my right through the bushes, then the willow trees and I knew I'd made it."

"And that's where you felt safe."

This time a wistful smile. "Yes. That's where I felt safe."

While Samira spoke, Donovan concentrated on the sorbet. Sitting beside him, Anne cast a glance in his direction just at the moment when he raised a hand and gently touched his cheek. The bruise was plain to see.

****

The evening went well, though Samira could not be drawn on her intentions, and Donovan was equally reticent about the bruise on his face. As the next day, Thursday, was a working day they split up soon after ten.

In the farmhouse Marnie emerged from the bathroom to find Ralph sitting up in bed reading. He looked up at her.

"You're looking very thoughtful. Let me hazard a guess about what's on your mind. Would it be Samira, by any chance?"

"Wrong."

"That's gotta be a first these days. So what have you been thinking about?"

"Doing something exciting we've never done before."

Ralph laid aside the book he had been reading. He smiled broadly. "Tell me more."

150

"I've been thinking about your idea, the trip to Venice on the Orient Express."

Ralph tried his best – and almost succeeded – not to look too crestfallen.

"Ah that, yes. Go on."

"I think it's terrific. Let's do it."

"And the rest of the package?" said Ralph.

"I agree with that, too. Just a simple ceremony with two witnesses."

"Anne and Donovan?"

"I think so. But we'd perhaps better not check with them tonight. They're probably ... otherwise engaged."

****

But Marnie was wrong. Over in the office barn Anne could sense that Donovan was feeling drained and, while she showered, she wondered what could have happened that day to sap his energy. When she climbed the wall-ladder to her attic room she found him in bed fast asleep. Unusually for him, he was wearing a T-shirt.

Anne was frowning as she climbed into bed and turned out the light.

The two detectives returned, but stayed only long enough to take their seats before being called away again. They had not even had the time to switch on the recording machine before a uniformed constable put his head round the door and asked them to step outside. Marnie and Roger sat alone in the interview room for the next twenty minutes. Roger looked at his watch and sniffed.

"Can they just keep us here like this?" Marnie asked.

"Yes. You've been formally charged and you're in custody. The procedures being followed are all in accordance with PACE rules."

"With what?"

"The rules originally laid down by the Police and Criminal Evidence Act, 1984."

"Okay. Any idea why we're being left like this?"

Roger leaned closer and spoke softly. "When they came back just now did you notice how worried they looked?"

"Sure. I thought I was in for a hard time."

"Not necessarily, Marnie. If they'd been looking less tense that would have been different."

"So what, then?"

"Hard to tell, but something's rattled their cage."

Chapter 14

Doubts

On Thursday morning Samira went into the front sitting room to open the curtains. To her surprise she saw several people standing together in the courtyard. Her first instinct was to draw back out of sight, but her curiosity was piqued. She peeped out and saw Marnie and Ralph, Anne and Donovan, plus a young couple she had not met before. It was obvious that the young couple were heading off to work; they were both in office clothes and carrying brief-cases. With a cheery wave to the others they went on their way.

Next to leave was Ralph, smartly dressed in a charcoal grey suit and also carrying a briefcase. He kissed Marnie, said something inaudible and walked off briskly towards the garage barn. Marnie then spoke urgently to Anne, who nodded as she listened. In the background Samira thought she could just make out the sound of car engines. The residents of Glebe Farm were on the move.

When Marnie went on her way, this left only Anne and Donovan. He was speaking in a low voice which put Anne in nodding mode again. The two then walked off together to complete the Glebe Farm exodus.

It was a day for travelling. Samira herself had been invited by phone to a meeting with her bank manager, Mr Patel. He wanted to discuss her 'not insignificant current account balance'. Had she realised that all her newfound friends were heading off, she might have asked for a lift into Northampton. Instead, she took out her pay-as-you-go mobile and ordered a taxi.

****

Samira sat well back in her seat as the cab drove into town. She couldn't help thinking that her last journey by taxi had been in flight from an invisible enemy, escaping to a strange boat on a remote canal mooring. The thought made her shudder. Now here she was all dressed up in a dark blue jacket and slacks on her way to discuss financial matters with a bank manager. Life seemed slightly surreal.

The traffic in town was moderate, but there were junctions aplenty and progress was sporadic. The cab braked to a halt at yet another red light. Gazing idly out of the window, Samira saw something that made her sit up with a start. A group of young Asian men was strolling along. Most of them were wearing western clothes, but one was in a pale grey *shalwar kameez* with a white *kufi* skull cap. Walking towards them was the distinctive figure of Donovan in his habitual dark clothing.

Samira gasped as the young men accelerated towards him. The man in the *shalwar kameez* burst from the group and practically ran forward. To her surprise, on reaching Donovan he embraced him warmly, while the others caught up and gathered round them. Jubilation was in the air. Straining forward, Samira was convinced she heard at least one of them call Donovan 'brother'. At that moment the lights changed to green and the taxi pulled away. Samira swivelled in her seat and peered through the rear window, staring at the group. As the cab turned a corner she slumped back. *What on earth was that about?*

"All right, love?" The driver had turned to face her as he stopped at the kerb.

"Why wouldn't I be?" Samira replied.

The driver smiled. "No. I meant is this all right for where you want to be? That's the bank you asked for on the corner."

"What? Oh, yes, this will do fine."

She thrust the driver a note and scrambled out.

****

It had been a productive day for all of them. Marnie's meeting had brought final approval to her design for converting an old industrial block in town into stylish apartments. Ralph's meeting had resulted in broad agreement on an exam marking scheme. Anne had enjoyed lectures in college on post-war German industrial design, and Donovan had taken one of his *classic* Leica cameras to a specialist shop for servicing.

154

At supper time Ralph was as usual entrusted with the task of choosing the wine. He put two bottles of Chilean *sauvignon* on the table and made an announcement.

"I found out something interesting today. Well, more than just interesting, rather chilling in fact."

Marnie, Anne and Donovan gave him their full attention. He continued.

"At lunchtime I was sitting next to Sarinda Hamid."

"Don't think I know her," said Marnie. "Not a colleague from Oxford."

"No. Dr Sarinda Hamid is reader in Modern History at Warwick, and it's *he*, by the way. He came here as an undergraduate from Islamabad and he's made a good career for himself. He still has family in Pakistan and goes back about every two years to see them."

"You told him about Samira?" said Marnie.

"No details initially, just that she was from the sub-continent."

"Initially?"

Ralph nodded and set about opening a bottle. "He told me he'd married a local girl, meaning English, and that his family had eventually come to accept her. He added that it would be different – much more of a problem – the other way round. I mentioned that Samira was having that sort of problem."

"And his reaction was interesting or – what was the word you used? – *chilling?*"

"I mentioned that she'd run away from her family to avoid what she believed was an arranged marriage. He said that was quite a serious matter; shame on the family, and so on. I said she was obviously nervous about the whole situation and added that she'd recently been spooked when there was no-one near her but some teenage boys. That's when he said it."

The three were hanging on Ralph's every word. He placed the wine bottle in the middle of the table.

"Go on," Marnie said.

"It's almost incredible." Ralph hesitated. "He asked if any of the boys were Asian. I said I thought it wasn't impossible. He

155

then told me it's not unknown for children to be used in certain countries to carry out ... honour killings."

Marnie gasped. "Seriously? Children?"

"Apparently."

"What?" said Anne. "Teenage boys in football shirts in the middle of Centre MK? But that's incredible."

Donovan said softly, "In some countries minors can't be prosecuted."

"That's right," said Ralph, "but that's not the case in Britain. Here they can be taken into custody, put on trial and detained in secure units. Sarinda made the point that in some Muslim countries they can be subject to detention but are released once they reach sixteen and they don't even have a criminal record."

"Which Samira almost certainly knows," Marnie added. "Just the thought would be enough to spook her out."

They sat down to eat in silence, each lost in their own thoughts. Eventually Marnie spoke again.

"This so-called *honour killing*, what kind of crazy idea is that?"

Donovan said, "It's the kind of crazy idea that can scare a young woman half to death and put her in fear of her life. It's obviously what this is all about."

****

At roughly the same time, Samira was sitting in the kitchen in cottage number three, slumped at the table, head in hands. Her mind was a jumble of confusion. Once upon a time her life had been orderly, governed by routines and schedules. Her future had seemed full of promise. She had known where she was going and had a measure of control over her affairs. Why had everything gone wrong? What had she done to bring so many problems down on her head? She knew the answers, of course. For her the main question was, most importantly, whom could she trust?

Marnie for one seemed solid and reliable, Ralph straightforward and dependable. Anne was just lovely, always anxious to please, always helpful. But Donovan, he was a strange one. Samira never quite knew where she stood with him. He could be remote, as if something was going on in his head the whole time. The others were obviously very fond of him, especially Anne. But could their judgment be misplaced? Samira wanted to accept him, to like him, if only because they did.

Into her mind floated the image of Donovan in the street that afternoon, surrounded by young Muslim men treating him as a close friend. More than that, to them he was special, a 'brother' they had called him. *Brother!* She was sure they had said that. But why?

And there were those books on his boat. Some of them were frankly a weird choice. One was actually 'Mein Kampf' by Adolf Hitler. Samira remembered the photos of the silver racing cars from the Nazi era, one of them bearing a swastika symbol on its headrest. Anne had said that Donovan wasn't a Nazi. Yet when Samira had opened some of the German books out of curiosity, she found that several of them were stamped inside with a catalogue number and the emblem of an eagle clutching a swastika in its talons. What could that signify? No Nazi sympathiser could be regarded by Muslims as a *brother*.

Samira didn't know if she was coming or going. Then she recalled that it was Donovan who had given her shelter, a refuge on a boat where no-one would be likely to look for her. He had seemed like a normal friendly young man wanting to help her through a difficult time, and she had even felt relaxed in his company. That in itself was quite something. It was also quite confusing.

For Samira there seemed to be no way back to a settled regulated life. Her head was spinning. She had never felt so isolated, so miserable, so abandoned.

Slowly she rose from the table, stepped into the hallway and climbed the stairs. Reaching her bedroom, Samira knelt down, pulled a suitcase from under the bed and rummaged in it until she found a mobile phone. She had not seen it since the day she left home. For some minutes she sat gazing at it. Slowly she reached back into the suitcase and pulled out the mobile's

157

charger. Biting her lip, she plugged the charger into a wall socket, sat on the bed and connected it with the phone. She had imagined she would never use it again, but now hypnotically watched the charging symbol in the tiny screen. Was this really the right thing to do? As with so much in her life these days, she had no idea.

****

Donovan was midway through pulling off his shirt when he stopped and looked across the attic room at Anne. She was sitting on the bed, watching him. It was night, and the room was lit only with a few table lamps over which were draped light cloths in rich colours, sapphire, emerald and gold. They created an exotic intimate atmosphere.

"What are you doing?" Donovan asked.

"Looking at you," Anne said quietly.

"As in, looking at me while I get undressed?"

"Yes."

"Don't tell me you've turned into some kind of pervert."

"Perhaps I've always *been* one."

Donovan laughed. "That's very reassuring! My girlfriend the deviant. Seriously, though. Why are you staring at me?"

"To quote you: I'd have thought that was rather obvious."

"Well, it's not because I'm what you'd call Man Mountain Super-thingy, is it?"

"Donovan, you know why I'm looking at you. I saw bruises on your ribs, like the bruise on your face. I think it's time you explained how you got them, and I won't be satisfied with you telling me you bumped yourself on the car door."

Donovan finished pulling off his shirt and went to sit beside Anne on the bed. Studying his torso, she lightly ran a finger down his ribs.

"Is that sore?" she asked.

"Not too bad."

"So are you going to tell me about it?"

Donovan paused for a moment before speaking. Sitting with her arm round his waist, Anne listened attentively without interrupting until he finished his narrative.

The door to the interview room opened, and DC Driscoll came in alone. Instead of taking her seat and switching on the recording machine she remained standing. Marnie stared up at her expectantly. Roger got to his feet. Marnie feared he was bracing himself for bad news.

"There's been a development," Driscoll said. She looked down at Marnie. "We're releasing you on police bail."

Marnie looked bewildered. "What does that mean?"

"It means you're free to go for the time being. Release is conditional on you continuing to reside at Glebe Farm. At the moment we're not requiring you to report to your local police station or hand over your passport. But you must not contact the Shah or Khan families at any time. Do you understand?"

Marnie had no idea what was happening. She gazed up at Roger whose only response was to raise an eyebrow. "I suppose so," she said.

"There's a form for you to sign when you retrieve your belongings at the desk."

Marnie felt Roger's hand under her elbow. He nodded towards the door. She stood and they went out followed by the detective. A hundred questions were going through her mind, but they were for another time and another place.

****

Outside in the car park Marnie sat in Roger's Volvo while he put her shoulder-bag in the boot. He climbed in beside her.

"I don't get it, Roger. Why have they released me? Have you had to pay bail? Am I still charged with murder? What's going on?"

"Whoa, Marnie! I'm still trying to come to terms with things myself. Obviously something has happened that alters the situation."

"But Driscoll said that —"

"I know, but they haven't actually charged you with murder." Roger looked pensive. "It's interesting."

"What is?"

"My understanding of police bail is that it isn't normally an option if you're charged with a serious crime. It doesn't get much more serious than attempted murder."

"So ...?"

"I'm just wondering if they might be going to drop the charge altogether, Marnie."

"What about the bail?" Marnie asked.

"For police bail there isn't a bond to be paid. Had you appeared before a judge, it would be a different matter."

"Roger, now I'm totally confused."

Roger took a few breaths. "I'm surmising that somewhere some new evidence has turned up. Maybe forensics have produced something, or a witness has come forward or some other development has taken place."

Marnie shook her head. "There can't be a witness to something I didn't do, that's for sure."

"Obviously not," Roger agreed.

Marnie continued. "I thought they were hoping that forensic evidence would nail me."

Roger made a non-committal gesture. "From my limited experience, Marnie, I'd say that forensics are usually used to eliminate suspects rather than zero in on a suspect."

"So you think they might've found something that exonerates me?"

Roger shrugged. "It's possible."

"And the police won't enlighten us on that?"

"No. If they find something that goes against you, they will in time confront you with that."

"So it looks like they've found something that gets me off the hook?"

"I can't think of any other reason why they'd release you like this. But what that something might be is anybody's guess at this stage."

"So we're groping in the dark," Marnie said.

"I'm still very much in the dark," said Roger. "There's a lot more to this case than I've gathered so far. We need a proper

161

discussion about everything that's happened since that incident in Milton Keynes that led to Samira's hiding out on Donovan's boat."

"There's quite a lot to tell."

"Yes, and I'd prefer to hear it with a clear mind when I've had time to digest what I know so far. I'm going to take you home then head back to London where Marjorie is waiting for me –"

"Of course, Roger."

"– with a gin and tonic."

Marnie smiled. "You've certainly earned it. Thanks for coming so promptly and for all you've done."

"Marnie, my love, we aren't out of the woods yet, not by a long chalk." He started the engine. "Let's get you back to Glebe Farm. Then I'll make a fresh start on things tomorrow morning, including getting advice from a barrister friend. We have to be prepared for any eventuality."

Roger's words gave Marnie little comfort. She stared gloomily ahead as Roger drove out of the car park and steered towards the western by-pass round the new city of Milton Keynes.

Marnie turned to look at Roger. "There is of course still one great unknown."

"Yes, I know," said Roger.

"So far the police haven't even told us the name of the victim."

Roger glanced quickly sideways at Marnie. "Quite," he said.

Chapter 15

Donovan's story

Donovan told his story that night, sitting beside Anne on her bed. It began with a message left on voicemail at his home in London.

"This is for Mr Donovan from Grayson's of Northampton. Can you call us on this number, please. We have something that we think will be of interest to you. Thank you."

Grayson's? The camera shop had processed film for Donovan in the past, one of those specialists rarely to be found in an age of franchises and chains. It was a small family-run business where the staff were experts and took a pride in their service. Without hesitation Donovan returned the call.

"Thanks for getting back to us, sir."

"I was intrigued. What have you got?"

"To cut a long story short, we had a lady in the shop this morning. Her father died recently and she was clearing out his house when she came across a box of camera items."

Donovan's pulse quickened. "Leica?"

"Not entirely. All sorts of stuff. But included in the find is a Leitz Hektor lens for the Leica Mark Three camera. We think it's from around 1937."

"Condition?"

"You'd swear it was brand new; leather case and all. Would you be interested, sir?"

"At the right price, I might. I'd like to see it."

Donovan was due to travel up to Glebe Farm the following day, so he made an appointment. Grayson's agreed to put the lens to one side until he came in.

****

The next day, Wednesday, Donovan drove from London direct to Northampton and found a slot for the Beetle in a multi-storey a short walk from the camera shop. Shouldering his rucksack, he locked the car and set off. Outside on the pavement, waiting to cross the road, he noticed a group of women on the opposite side of the street. They were dressed in *niqabs*, covered in black from head to foot, with only narrow slits for their eyes. Coming towards them were four young men in hoodies, jeans and heavy boots. Donovan watched with a sense of unease. To his surprise they walked past the Muslim women without a second glance.

Donovan turned his attention back to watching for a gap in the traffic to cross the road. A sudden scream sounded above the noise of passing cars. Donovan's head snapped round. In that moment he saw one hoodie tugging at the head-dress of one of the women while another lifted the back of a *niqab* high up, exposing bare legs and underwear. The women were spinning round to escape their assailants, clearly distressed. Donovan stepped quickly onto the roadway, ready to launch himself forward, already pulling open the rucksack.

Before he could advance, an angry shout rang out from nearby, a man's voice filled with outrage. Donovan glanced sideways to see someone of about his own age running into the road heedless of the traffic. He was tall with a short dark beard and wearing a *shalwar kameez*. Vehicles were braking sharply to avoid him as he raced towards the commotion.

Arriving on the scene, he seemed to have no regard for his own safety. He grabbed one of the attackers by the shoulder and roughly pulled him away. Releasing his grip, he seized another by the arms and jerked him backwards. The element of surprise was in his favour, but not for long. An almighty blow from behind caught him on the side of the neck and he staggered forward only to collect a heavy kick to the stomach which doubled him over. By now the four attackers had lost interest in the women and were turning all their aggression on this newcomer.

The spectacle of the fracas on the pavement had caused the traffic to slow almost to a crawl, giving Donovan the openings he needed to pick his way across the road. As he ran he reached into the rucksack and pulled out his torch. It was a four-cell Maglite about a foot long, solidly engineered, of hard black steel, an excellent weapon for hand-to-hand combat.

164

Donovan swung the torch in a sweeping curve. It hit the first hoodie on the ear with a sickening thud. He was seeing stars as he crashed to the ground. Donovan flicked the torch round to bring it heavily down on the crown of the next man. It took him completely unawares as he was occupied with lining up a kick to the head of his victim. He never knew what had hit him as he too fell in a heap.

Donovan stepped over the man and was raising his arm to deliver the next blow when he was punched hard in the face. Simultaneously a boot crashed into his chest. Had he not been reeling backwards from the first blow, the kick could have broken his ribs. Even so, it caused tremendous pain. Defensively, Donovan thrust the torch forward in a desperate lunge. It connected with the face of the third man, punching out his front teeth. As his head went back he was spitting blood through split lips. That left number four, the one who had delivered the kick, but he turned and fled before Donovan could tackle him.

Donovan was breathing heavily as he bent down to examine the man in the *shalwar kameez* who was groaning softly. The women gathered round, in shock after being engulfed in so much violence. As Donovan touched his shoulder the young man flinched.

"It's okay, it's okay. They've gone. You're safe. Are you all right?"

The man was holding his stomach with both hands. "I don't … I don't know." His voice was little more than a croak.

"Can you stand up at all?" Donovan asked.

He supported the man in a supreme effort to get up.

One of the women held up her mobile. "Shall I call for an ambulance?"

Donovan couldn't see her face, but her voice was young and it quivered as she spoke.

Donovan pointed. "My car's over there. Quicker if I take him to A and E." The thugs lying on the ground were moaning. To the women Donovan said, "You'd better get away from here as quick as you can."

The young woman said, "And you'd better be very careful from now on. What you did, both of you, was very brave, but asking for trouble."

****

In the Accident and Emergency department Donovan led the young man by the arm to reception. While they waited for the nurse on duty to finish a phone call, the man bent forward and rested his forehead on the counter, holding his chest. Donovan put an arm round his shoulder. The nurse put the phone down and looked up.

"Can I help you?"

"He's been attacked. I'm worried he might have internal injuries."

"Can you give me his name?"

Donovan shook his head. "I don't know him. I've just brought him in."

"Your name?"

"Donovan."

Before the conversation could go any further a brisk young doctor came by and looked at them. She turned her gaze on Donovan.

"What's happened to him?"

Donovan explained briefly about the fight and his concern about internal injuries. The doctor took the man's arm. She nodded to the nurse on duty.

"Okay," she said. "We'll take a look at him." She bent forward and said quietly. "Come with me. We'll get you sorted out."

As they turned away, the young man caught hold of Donovan's arm.

"Thank you ... Donovan," he said hoarsely, looking up. He squeezed Donovan's arm feebly. "Thank you, my friend."

****

"I don't know how you do it," Anne said. "You seem to attract trouble like a magnet."

166

"I was walking along, minding my own business," Donovan said reasonably, "thinking of nothing more than the price of that special camera lens."

"And you just happened to see some Muslim women being attacked by a gang of yoboes."

Donovan looked dubious. "That's how it was."

Anne sighed. "I despair, I really do."

"I had to help them. What else could I do?"

Anne leaned forward and kissed him. "Nothing. You did exactly the right thing. You might really be Man Mountain Super-thingy, after all."

Chapter 16

Rashida

That evening, while Donovan was telling Anne his story, Samira was bracing herself for the unthinkable. Staring down at the mobile, her face bore the expression of Lady Macbeth contemplating the dagger. Was it such a big step? After all, she was only thinking of calling her sister. What could be the harm in that? Yet it was a step into the unknown. Who could tell what that simple call might unleash?

Samira tried and failed twice before she could bring herself to complete the number of her sister's mobile, only succeeding at the third attempt. When finally she did press the green button, she was on the brink of cancelling the call yet again when the ringing tone stopped and a tremulous voice was heard at the end of the line.

"Samira?" The voice was little more than a whisper. "Is that really you?"

"Oh, Rashida. It's me, yes."

For several seconds neither of them could speak. It was as much as they could do to hold back their tears. Eventually Rashida sniffed and cleared her throat.

"Where are you?" she said, her voice still hushed.

"I'm somewhere safe, at least for the time being."

"But where?" No reply. "No, of course. You can't tell me. You don't know who you can trust."

"Don't say that! It's not like that at all."

"What then? D'you think I might let it slip out?"

"Honestly, Rashida, I don't know what I think. It's just … I don't know. I miss you so much, all of you. I'm lonely. I want to come home, but I can't do that until everything has died down. All I know is I had to hear your voice again."

"What are you going to do, Samira? What are your plans?"

My plans? Samira thought. Good question.

"I think I have to lie low for a while, at least until the main problem has blown over."

"Main problem? By that you mean what?"

168

"The plan to get me married off in Pakistan."

"You guessed about that, then."

"I suspected it when I saw how emotional you were when I left for the airport. You knew what was planned, didn't you, Rashida?"

"I overheard mum and dad talking in the kitchen. They didn't know I was in the hall. I wanted to tell you, but I didn't dare."

"I wondered how you knew. Do you know who they had in mind?"

A moment's hesitation. "It's our cousin, Javid."

"*Javid?* The last time I saw him I was just a little girl. He was in his teens. You're sure it's him, Rashida?"

"They said his name. I heard them clearly. So what are you going to do now?"

"I'm going to keep out of the way for a while. I hope things might get better. Tell me how is everybody."

"Worried about you, obviously. Mum and dad are desperate to know where you are, what you're doing."

"And Tariq?"

There was a pause. "He's ..."

"What is he, Rashida?"

"I think in some ways he's even more of a worry than you are."

"What d'you mean?"

"Didn't you notice before you went away?"

"Notice what?"

"He's become more ... not sure how to put it. He said he wants to grow a beard. He's becoming sort of, more orthodox."

"A *beard?* Rashida, he's fifteen years old. He's hardly even ... What d'you mean, *more orthodox?*"

"He's started going to these meetings at the mosque. They have lectures, visiting speakers, study groups. He's always got his nose buried in the Koran, and taken to reciting whole passages in Arabic."

169

"So he's become quite devout. Kids go through phases like that. I seem to remember you got quite religious when you were about twelve."

"Not like Tariq, Samira. He's become more ... not sure how to put it ... *intense ... extreme.*"

"Enough to get you worried?"

"He's been arguing with dad, saying he's not observant enough. He thinks we've become too westernised."

"What? We live in Luton. It's in England. What does he expect?"

"I know," Rashida said. "But that's what he says."

"It sounds ominous. On the other hand, it could just be an adolescent phase he's going through. Has he said anything about me going away like that?"

"Not that I've heard."

"So you don't think he's likely to run off and join the Taliban?"

"Don't even joke about it, Samira! Last week a boy from the mosque did just that."

"My goodness! And here's me thinking that after the dust has settled maybe things will get better and I can come home."

"Oh, Samira ..."

"What?"

"I've got to tell you this and then I've got to go. Things aren't going to get better. In fact, they've just got a whole lot worse."

"How can that be?" But Samira was already guessing the answer.

Rashida said, "Javid is coming from Pakistan to find you. In fact, he's arriving any time now. He's determined to marry you. He said you were *promised* to him."

Samira felt the room sway before her eyes. "I don't know how much more of this I can take."

"You've got to be strong, Samira. It's the only –" An abrupt silence. A sharp intake of breath. "Ooh. Gotta go. Be strong, big sister."

And that was it. Rashida's last words echoed in Samira's brain as she sat listening to silence.

170

Chapter 17

Dark stranger

Marnie laughed at breakfast on Friday morning.
"Donovan, you really don't have to ask. Of course you're welcome to stay for the weekend. You're family. Well, in a manner of speaking. In fact that's how Samira described us ... like a family."

"And I'm sure that's how we feel," Ralph added. "Although in actual fact, we're none of us technically even related."

"Though ..." Marnie looked at Ralph. He nodded. "That may change shortly."

Anne's smile lit up the room. "You're getting married?"

"We've been thinking about it, so Ralph said it was about time we got on and did something about it."

"Shall I start writing lists?" Anne asked.

"We're not thinking of an elaborate event," Ralph said. "Just a simple ceremony."

"Is that all?"

Ralph smiled at Anne. "Then a short honeymoon."

"So everything really low-key." Anne tried to hide her disappointment. "Fine."

Marnie said, "Ralph's suggestion for the honeymoon is to go to Venice."

"That's nice."

Marnie added, "On the Orient Express."

Anne's eyes widened. "Wow!"

"What about a celebration?" Donovan asked. "Assuming you don't get stuck in snowdrifts in the Balkans and end up murdered."

Anne grinned. "He's been reading Agatha Christie: *Murder on the Orient Express!*"

"Thanks," said Marnie, "but I've had enough murders to last me a lifetime."

Donovan repeated his question.

"We've been thinking of a garden party in the summer," said Ralph.

171

"Give me a few weeks' notice, then, if you can," Donovan said.

"Is your social calendar likely to be congested?" Marnie asked.

Donovan shook his head. "No, but Herr Geretzky will appreciate having time to prepare."

Marnie and Ralph looked quizzically at Donovan.

Marnie was puzzled. "Herr ...? Who is he and where does he figure in all this?"

"There's a custom in Germany that after the wedding ceremony everyone has *Kaffee und Kuchen*, coffee and cakes, whatever else is planned for later. In your case we'd better do it at the garden party."

"Coffee and cakes, right. You're on. And this Herr Ger-wotsit?"

"Herr Geretzky has a bakery near me in London. He's a master cake-maker, and as a contribution to the party, I'd like to order a *Prinzregententorte* from him."

Anne laughed. "It's easy for you to say that!"

Donovan made a face at her.

"So he's German?" Marnie said.

"Austrian. I think his grandfather was some sort of aristocrat in the old days."

"And he needs a period of notice because ...?"

"*Prinzregententorte* has seven layers of chocolate cream and seven sponge layers, and he'll want to make it fresh just before it's needed."

Anne grinned. "We wouldn't want a stale Prinz-thingy from Herr Ger-wotsit, would we?"

"So this cake is Austrian?" said Marnie.

"German. From Bavaria, I think. It's a classic. Quite a rarity, even in Germany."

"It's a lovely thought, Donovan," said Ralph. "Thank you."

Ralph glanced in Marnie's direction, expecting her to add her thanks. Instead, she was lost in thought.

"Marnie?" Ralph said. "Are you all right?"

172

Marnie looked up. "I was just thinking. Here we are, planning a wedding, all smiles and banter and looking forward to doing special things ..."

Ralph completed the thought. "And Samira's dreading being forced into a marriage against her will, desperately worried about what her life has become, all because she's offending her family by not accepting the partner they've chosen."

"Not just *her* family," said Marnie. "She's offending the family of the man who's been chosen for her – whom she doesn't want – and probably upsetting their whole community. She must be terrified of repercussions."

"With good reason, I'm sure," Ralph said.

****

Friday was a busy day. The weather continued dull and overcast with moisture in the air, a good day for working. Ralph left straight after breakfast for postgrad student tutorials in Oxford, leaving Marnie and Anne to work on designs. Donovan waited for the rush hour traffic to subside then drove to Northampton to visit the camera shop.

At ten-thirty Anne made tea for the men working in the farmhouse garden and called in on Samira in the cottage. She thought Samira looked more drawn than usual, and so was surprised when she invited her in for coffee. They sat together at the kitchen table.

"You said you were going to the bank yesterday," Anne began. "He's a nice man, Mr Patel, very helpful. How did you get on?"

Samira nodded. "Yes, he was helpful." She smiled. "He said I was a *young woman of some means* and said I should give some thought to *putting my resources to work*."

"Cool. And how will you do that?"

Samira pointed to a pile of papers on the workbench. "To start with, he's opened a savings account for me so that I can get some interest on what he called my *surplus*."

"Good start."

173

"That's what he said. Then he gave me leaflets on personal equity plans, unit trusts and something called a TESSA. I can't remember what the initials stand for." Samira sighed. "I find it quite confusing, having all this money."

"Still, it's better than being hard up with no *resources* or *surplus*," Anne said. "Can't you ask Mr Patel to advise you on a plan for saving? Surely he'll know what's best."

"That's the story of my life, Anne ... men taking decisions for me."

"In this case it makes sense. He can help you with your savings." Anne grinned. "I can help on the other side."

"What other side?"

"I can help you *spend* some. I'm going to the supermarket. Wanna come?"

Samira made as if to speak, then hesitated and drank some coffee. To Anne's surprise she said, "What time are you going?"

Anne said, "I know it's Friday, but I can't wait till later this afternoon. How about half-eleven?"

Be strong, big sister. Rashida's words echoed in Samira's mind. It was only a trip to the supermarket, so hardly a big deal, but she thought it would at least be a step in the right direction.

"Half past eleven," she said decisively. "I'll be there."

****

Donovan returned soon after eleven with a spring in his step, pleased with his new lens.

"Well, not *new* exactly," he said. "In fact it's about sixty years old, but I doubt if it's been used very much at all."

He produced it from a Grayson's carrier bag and removed it from its box, which also looked as good as new.

"Is that box sixty years old as well?" Marnie asked. "Amazing."

"How can it be so old and in such good nick?" Anne asked.

Donovan shrugged. "Camera enthusiasts buy stuff because it takes their fancy. This was bought some time in the thirties. Who knows what became of its owner?"

174

"Sobering thought," Marnie said.

Donovan put the lens back in its box. "Look, I don't want to disturb your work by fiddling with this in the office. All right if I mess about with it up in your room, Anne?"

"Sure. Make yourself at home."

Donovan was placing one foot on the wall-ladder when he paused and turned. "Strange thing. When I was in town I had the odd feeling that someone was watching me."

"Who?" said Marnie.

Donovan shook his head. "Dunno. It was, like I said, more a feeling than anything else."

"Not the hoodies?" said Anne, concerned.

"Don't think so. I was probably just imagining things. Samira's making us all paranoid. See you later."

There was silence in the office after he left. Marnie was soon lost in concentration on her design project. Anne tried to work but found it difficult to focus. It wasn't like Donovan to imagine things. He was always wary, alert to everything going on around him. He had often faced danger, and his instincts had served him well. Anne's musings were interrupted by Marnie.

"Didn't you say you were going to the supermarket with Samira this morning, Anne?"

"Yes."

"Have you noticed the time?"

Anne looked up at the clock. Eleven-twenty-nine. "Blimey! I'd better get ready."

"Don't tell me you haven't written a list," Marnie teased her.

Anne waved a note in evidence. "Gotta pop to the loo!"

Anne was disappearing towards the bathroom when Samira knocked on the office door and entered.

"Sorry, Samira," Anne called out. "I'm just going to the —"

"Would you like me to come back in a few minutes?"

Anne looked at Marnie who was deeply engrossed in a design project. The last thing she needed was a further interruption.

"Er, no. I won't be a minute. Why don't you sit in the car? The keys are on my desk."

175

"Okay."

****

Samira was impressed that Anne had her own car. It was only a little Mini and a few years old, but it looked like new with bright red bodywork, a white roof and alloy wheels. She made her way past the farmhouse and was turning the corner heading for the garage barn when movement up the field track caught her eye. Her heart froze in her chest.

A man was walking down the track. Worse than that, a *man in shalwar kameez* was walking down the track, coming in her direction! Luckily, all his attention was focused on stepping over ruts and tussocks. Samira swiftly leapt back out of sight behind the house. Her heart had now evidently thawed because it was pounding as she turned and raced back towards the cottage. Reaching the front doorstep she lunged forward to push the key into the lock. Disaster! With trembling hands she realised she was trying to open the door with Anne's car key. She began fumbling in her shoulder bag, fearing that at any moment the man would arrive in the courtyard and she would be trapped.

It was no good. Samira's hands were incapable of doing what she wanted. In desperation she charged across the courtyard, pushed open the office door, spun sharp left and scrambled up the wall-ladder to Anne's loft. Just then Anne was walking across the office towards the door. She and Marnie stared at each other, bewildered.

Marnie began speaking. "What d'you think that was –"

"You haven't seen me!" Samira cut her off, a voice from on high, followed by what sounded like a gasp.

Marnie shrugged and looked at Anne. "What d'you reckon?"

Anne nodded towards the door. "I think we're about to find out."

Marnie turned her head in time to see an indistinct shape passing the plate glass window and reaching the office door. They heard two knocks, but the door did not open.

Marnie called out, "Come in."

It was not the first time that either Marnie or Anne had seen a man dressed in the traditional *shalwar kameez*, but it was their first close encounter face to face. He was tall with fine features and a short dark beard. Marnie felt she should say something like *salaam alaikum*, but contented herself instead with a simple *good morning*.

The man inclined his head and replied, "Good morning. Sorry to disturb you." He was softly spoken with an English accent and exuded politeness. "I'm looking for someone called ... Donovan." He hesitated over the name as if he was uncertain of it.

Marnie stood up. "Donovan?" she repeated a little more loudly than normal. "Would you mind me asking in what connection?"

The visitor took in the surroundings, the desks, filing cabinets, charts on corkboards, plus photographs and plans of buildings. It all looked very businesslike. He realised he had intruded into a place of work.

"I didn't know he worked here. I thought ... well, I'm not sure what I thought, really. I just wanted to ..."

Marnie came to his aid. "You see, it isn't our policy to give out personal information other than in exceptional circumstances. Have you come to talk about a particular project, perhaps?"

"No, it's not that. It's more a personal matter, and I'm thinking it might not be appropriate to raise it here in working hours, so to say."

Anne was watching this exchange with interest from across the office and admiring Marnie's way of stalling. She was also aware that Samira was not only hiding up in her attic room, but was in the company of a man who was not a relation. They were in fact alone together in a bedroom. She tried hard not to smile at this situation which reminded her of a television bedroom farce.

Marnie began ushering the visitor towards the door.

"Perhaps if you could explain what your enquiry is, I might be able to help. Would you like a cup of tea? We could join my husband over in the house and have a chat."

Anne tried not to frown. Husband? Ralph was neither a husband nor anywhere near Glebe Farm. Then Anne understood. It would certainly be improper for Marnie to invite the visitor into the house unchaperoned, but there was no obvious means of getting him out of the way. As Marnie and the man began stepping into the courtyard, Marnie turned to look back at Anne.

"You will remember to tidy things up, won't you."

With a subtle raising of her chin, glancing up towards the attic, Marnie hoped her meaning was clear. Anne's puzzlement morphed into comprehension.

"Of course," she said firmly and, she hoped, convincingly.

Anne waited until Marnie and the young man had entered the farmhouse and closed the door behind them before calling up the wall-ladder.

"Samira, all clear. You can come down now. You'd better be quick. We ought to get off before that man sees there's no husband around and excuses himself."

Samira descended the wall-ladder as quickly as she could.

"What should we do?" she asked Anne.

"Go shopping, as planned, straight away."

"What did Marnie mean about tidying up?" Samira asked.

"I think she wanted you out of the way, that's all. Come on, let's go."

"Coming down!" Donovan appeared at the top of the ladder and began a scrambled descent.

Anne and Samira moved aside to give him space. While Samira handed Anne her car keys, she turned to Donovan.

"Why was he looking for *you*? You know what this is about, don't you?"

"There isn't time now. Anne will explain."

"But I don't understand why you –"

Anne took Samira by the arm. "We've really got to get out of here if you don't want to meet that guy. Let's go!"

178

Anne all but dragged her out of the office. Samira was still staring back at Donovan as they passed the plate glass window. As soon as he was alone, Donovan assessed the situation. He turned on Marnie's answerphone and legged it across the courtyard.

****

In the farmhouse kitchen Marnie invited her visitor to take a seat at the table. While the kettle boiled she set out three mugs and a jug of milk.

"Do you take sugar?" she asked. "Sorry, I don't know your name. I'm Marnie."

"No sugar, thank you, and my name is Azim. May I ask, Marnie, is Donovan your husband?"

"No."

Azim continued. "Is that a first name or a last name?"

"Well —"

"It's rather more complicated than that."

The new voice surprised them both as Donovan came through the door. Azim leapt to his feet and rushed towards Donovan.

He embraced Donovan warmly. "It's good to see you, brother."

Marnie looked on in confusion. *Brother?* What was that all about? Azim's affection for Donovan was clear, and Donovan in turn seemed more than pleased to see the newcomer. The mystery was, how they had developed this close rapport.

"Tea, Donovan?" Marnie asked.

"I'd prefer coffee if that's on offer."

"Sure. And then I think it'll be time for some explanation. How about that?"

****

After Donovan finished his narrative the three of them sat in silence for a few moments.

"So you'd never met before the incident with the women wearing the *niqabs?*" Marnie said eventually.

179

Both men shook their heads.

Azim said, "It was a very fortunate meeting as far as I was concerned. If Donovan hadn't come to my aid I don't know what might have happened to me."

Donovan agreed. "It was a pretty stupid thing to try to take on those four without any back-up."

"Yes, but I just saw red. What they were doing was unpardonable, and who knows what else they might have done to those women? And, Donovan, you were surely just as foolhardy as me."

"But I was armed, don't forget."

Marnie was surprised. "Armed?"

Donovan looked across the table at her. "The Maglite. The big one I always carry in my rucksack."

"A kind of truncheon," Azim said. "I saw you use it from where I lay. A formidable weapon."

Donovan grinned. "It's not a weapon; it's just a torch, but it's very hard and solid and a good size. If you hold it down at the lamp end, the handle makes a useful club."

Marnie said, "Who were those people, Donovan? Were they skinheads?"

"I don't think so. They wore hoodies. Not our usual friends."

"Friends?" Azim looked amazed.

"I'm using the term ironically. We've had trouble in the past with neo-Nazi skinheads, fascists trying to cause trouble for ethnic minorities."

"We've had our share of trouble with them, too," said Azim. "We think they were probably the ones who tried to burn down our Islamic Centre last year."

"Your mosque?" Marnie said.

"Yes. We couldn't prove anything, so the police couldn't charge anybody, but some of our neighbours – not even members of our community – testified that they'd seen some skinheads hanging around a few days before. But without evidence or proper identification ..." He shrugged.

"Any trouble since then?" Marnie asked.

"Not so far. We've installed CCTV cameras. I'm sure that helps."

Donovan changed the subject abruptly. "Do you know anyone called Samira?"

Azim nodded. "Yes."

Marnie stiffened. She wasn't sure this was a wise direction to take.

Azim added, "I have a cousin called Samira. She's my aunt's daughter. They live in Islamabad."

"Is she married?"

Azim smiled. "I don't think so. She's six years old."

Another change of direction from Donovan. "You came all the way here to find me? How did you know where to look?"

"I spotted your car in town – it's not easy to miss it – and I set off to follow you. I almost lost you when I got held up by traffic lights, but then I saw that black shape in the distance. Anyway, I managed to get close enough to see you turn off into a field. I followed on foot because there was just a track."

"You were certainly persistent," Marnie said.

Azim was still smiling. "I had to thank Donovan for what he did for me in town that day, and for taking me to the hospital. I shudder to think what –"

"Don't," Donovan interrupted. "Don't think about it. Put it behind you."

"But ... No, you're right. You did what you did, Donovan, and I'm grateful." Azim put his hand to his chest. "Thank you, my friend. I think you probably saved my life. I will always be in your debt."

Donovan grinned. "Just do me a favour. Try not to get into that kind of mess again, okay?"

"I'll do my best. If ever I can do anything for you, you can reach me through the Islamic Centre in Grace Street."

"They know you there?" said Marnie.

Azim nodded. "Oh yes, they know me. My father is the imam."

****

181

"Is everything all right? You look rather tense."

Anne and Samira were getting out of the Mini in the supermarket car park. Oddly, the question was asked by Samira who was looking at Anne over the car's roof. Anne bit her lower lip.

"It's just ... I'm not sure how to put it, and I don't want to cause offence."

"Can I make a guess?" Samira asked. "Could it be you're worried in case I run off again?"

Anne shook her head and looked Samira in the eye. "I noticed you hadn't returned Donovan's boat keys to their place on the board."

Samira looked surprised. "Oh, haven't I?"

Still staring across the roof at Samira, Anne tilted her head to one side and raised her eyebrows. "I'm not going to ask you to give them back, Samira. It's up to you what you do. But it worries me. I'm only trying to be helpful and it saddens me that you don't trust me, or us. Sorry to be so blunt but someone has to be honest round here."

As soon as she finished, Anne regretted it. Samira swallowed and began delving into her shoulder-bag. She pulled out the boat keys and held them up, her expression somewhere between contrite and ashamed.

"You're right, Anne." Her tone was downcast. "Here. Let me give them to you."

"No. They belong to Donovan. You should hang them up or give them back to him. I'm sure you're welcome to stay on his boat any time, but I know he'd appreciate being told."

She shut the driver's door and locked the car. As they went to collect a shopping trolley, Samira squeezed Anne's arm and inclined her head towards her.

"Anne, can I promise you something?"

"You don't have –"

"No. Listen. I promise not to go into hiding when we're in the supermarket. You can relax. Truly."

"No skulking behind the baked beans display?" said Anne. "No quick getaway through the fast foods section?"

182

"'I mean it. I'm being serious."

The shriek of laughter from Anne that rang out across the car park caused several shoppers to turn and stare.

****

After Azim left, Marnie and Donovan crossed the courtyard to the office barn. Marnie looked up at the sky. The clouds seemed to be closing in, and there was a definite feeling of mizzle in the air.

Donovan held out a hand, palm upwards. "I think my new-found friend is going to get damp walking up to his car in that exotic dress thing he wears."

"*Shalwar kameez*," Marnie said. "That's what it's called. Exotic and rather elegant. I hope Anne and Samira don't get caught in a downpour, carrying their shopping to the car." She stopped on the threshold and turned to Donovan. "Talking of Samira, that must have been a surprise when she scrambled up the ladder to the loft and found you there."

Donovan grinned and turned the handle on the door. "I think *shock* would be more the word, at least as far as she was concerned."

They pushed the door open and went in. Marnie headed for her desk, while Donovan placed his foot on the bottom rung of the ladder.

Marnie said, "Yes, shock *is* probably the word. I'm just thinking, it could well have been the first time she'd ever been in a bedroom alone with a man."

"Probably enough to scare the pants off her," Donovan said with no trace of innuendo.

Marnie gave him an old-fashioned look. "Would you care to rephrase that?"

They were both laughing as they went their separate ways.

****

When they carried their bags to the Mini in the car park, Anne glanced up at the sky. It looked ominous. They quickly loaded the shopping into the tiny boot space and onto the rear seats.

183

On the journey home to Glebe Farm the atmosphere between them was much improved. Anne had bought some fruit gums to compensate for the dull weather, and they were both sucking on them contentedly.

"Anne, I've got to ask you something. I'd almost forgotten. What did Donovan mean when he said you'd explain about him and that Muslim man?"

"About what?"

"You know, about why he came looking for Donovan. I saw him with a group of them in town and they were calling him 'brother'."

"Oh, that ... The background is, I asked him how he came to have so many bruises on his body. He said he'd got them in a fight."

There was a gasp from Samira. "A *fight?*"

"Don't get the wrong impression. He's not a violent person, not normally."

"Then how did he –"

"To keep it short, that chap in the long robe thing who came into the office was trying to stop a bunch of hoodies in town from molesting some women in those long black head-to-foot robes, you know, with just slits for their eyes."

"*Niqabs.*"

"Right. Anyway, Donovan saw he was in trouble and waded in to help. He chased off the hoodies but got slightly roughed up as well."

"So Donovan rescued that man we saw?"

"I'm guessing it was him from Donovan's description. Did you recognise him, Samira, from the ones you saw in town?"

"Not really."

Anne glanced sideways and grinned. "No. You were too busy rushing up to the bedroom where my boyfriend was."

Samira's expression was mock horror. "Anne! What are you saying?"

They both laughed so much that Samira nearly choked on her fruit gum. When her coughing fit subsided she fell silent for a couple of miles before speaking again. Anne detected a coyness in her tone.

"You, er ... saw bruises, you said, on Donovan."

"I think he'd been punched or kicked in the chest. There were some quite nasty bruises on his ribs."

"You saw them when he was ... undressed."

"Undressing, yes," Anne said quietly, adding, "I'm sorry if that shocks you."

Another mile passed before Samira spoke again. "Perhaps you can see, Anne, why having an arranged marriage to a man I don't really know is quite a big thing to someone like me. I haven't been brought up with the kind of freedom that you've had."

To Samira's surprise, Anne braked sharply and pulled into a lay-by. She switched off the engine and sat in silence staring out of the windscreen.

"Anne, I hope I haven't offended you. I didn't mean to imply that your morals were –"

"No. It's okay. I'm fine with my morals and not offended. For Donovan and me it's not just a casual physical thing. It's not a formal arrangement either, though it is definitely a relationship. We can understand you don't want to be pushed into a marriage, and we realise that you're really scared of the consequences of your decision and your actions."

"It's more than just that, Anne."

"Yes, I see that now. What I can understand more clearly is the physical side to all this. With your upbringing you haven't had the same experience of life that Marnie and I have had. For you, having to sleep with a strange man must be like ... well, it could be a kind of ... rape, couldn't it?"

Samira made no reply. She reached sideways and took Anne's hand in hers. Anne wished that she hadn't spoken so bluntly. She looked at Samira who was sitting back against the head restraint with eyes closed, tears running down her cheeks.

Anxious to change the subject and lighten the mood, Anne gave Samira's hand a quick squeeze then removed it to reach for the ignition switch. As she pulled out of the lay-by she asked about traditional Muslim dress.

"You said those long black robes with eye slits were called ... *niqabs*? Is that the word?"

"Yes."

"What sort of girls or women would wear those?"

Samira's reply astonished her. "The ugly ones."

Anne shrieked with laughter and had to force herself to focus on the road.

"You're kidding! Is that really true, Samira?"

Samira exploded in laughter. "No!" She controlled herself. "I can't believe I said that, Anne."

"So it's not true?"

"Well, not altogether. In fact it's an old joke in my community, though you wouldn't say it in front of a man whose wife was wearing one."

Anne was grinning broadly. "Can't think why not. Then what's the real answer?"

"Often it's women, married or otherwise, from a conservative background. I don't mean politically."

"Is that part of Islamic law?" Anne asked.

"No, it's not in the Koran, or anything. It's more a tradition, a tradition imposed on us by men, probably."

"And the tunic worn by our visitor?"

"That's a *shalwar kameez*. It means he's probably from a quite orthodox family."

"Traditional and presumably not imposed on him?"

"Right in both cases."

"Smart gear."

"Very."

They came to the turn-off for Knightly St John, and Anne steered the little car towards the village.

"You must have been surprised when you climbed up to my room and found Donovan there. I heard you gasp and guessed you'd noticed him for the first time. Was it an awful shock?"

"It was certainly a surprise, not something I'm used to, but he behaved like a perfect gentleman."

186

"Naturally."

"He stood up and invited me to sit."

"On my bed?" said Anne, sounding shocked.

Samira replied quickly. "Yes, but it was all perfectly proper."

Anne laughed. "I'm teasing you."

"I know," Samira said. "But my family would be horrified."

They were both relaxed in each other's company as they reached the edge of the village.

****

It was mid-afternoon that Friday when Rashida took the call. She was at home alone revising for her A Level exams in business studies. It was a man's voice, one that she didn't recognise.

"This is Javid Shah. Who am I speaking to, please?"

"It's Rashida, Rashida Khan."

"You are the sister of Samira?"

"That's right."

"Is she at home?"

"No, she's away at the moment."

"Your parents?"

"My father's at work and my mother's out shopping."

After a pause Javid said, "I would like to speak with them. Can you suggest a good time to do that?"

"Perhaps you can give me your number and I'll pass on your message."

They exchanged details and disconnected. Rashida looked at the number she had written on the pad beside the phone in the hall. It was on the local exchange. She knew he had relatives in Luton. In her head she could still hear his voice. He spoke English with a slight accent, and his style was calm but gave the impression of a decisive person, someone who knew what he wanted. If what he wanted was Samira, he had certainly come a very long way to make that happen. This man would not be easily deterred. *Oh, Samira, how is this all going to end?*

Chapter 18

Javid

O n Saturday morning Donovan made an announcement as the Glebe Farm Four set off across the courtyard after breakfast.

"I thought I'd drive to the supermarket this morning. Anyone need anything?"

"Do you need to?" Marnie asked. "Anne did a big shop with Samira yesterday. We're fully stocked up for the weekend and beyond."

"The stores on *Exodos* are depleted after Samira's unscheduled visit. I thought I'd replenish. Perhaps as it's fine, if you're going for a tootle later –"

Donovan's mobile began warbling and he fished it out of his pocket.

"Hi."

"Donovan?"

"Yeah."

"It's Azim. Listen. My father wants to thank you personally for ... well, rescuing me like that."

"That's okay. No need."

"No. He really wants to meet you. Could you come into town?"

"Well, I suppose ..."

"It would mean a lot to him."

"Not today, obviously," said Donovan. It's a holy day for you, isn't it?"

"Friday is special for us, but for a Muslim every day is kind of holy. We pray five times a day."

"So when would suit you or him?"

"He has meetings on Monday. Would Tuesday be okay for you? Or will you be back in London?"

"I'll be here. I've handed in my last project, and that will be a so-called reading week."

"What's your course?"

"Media Studies at Brunel."

188

Azim said, "Isn't that supposed to be a soft option?"

Donovan laughed. "Not for those of us studying it. Every day is a kind of reading week."

****

For the rest of Saturday Glebe Farm was a busy day. Anne went to the shop with Donovan and on their return set about working on the accounts, the filing and cleaning the office. Marnie and Ralph buckled down to their own respective tasks.

Of Samira there was no sign all weekend. Marnie wondered about inviting her to join them for a tootle on *Sally Ann* on Sunday – which she unilaterally declared to be a *complete* day of rest, apart from delivering Donovan's stores to *XO2* – but then decided against it. Samira was after all entitled to her privacy and her space. Marnie was confident that if Samira needed anything she knew she only had to ask.

****

Samira's parents lived in a modest semi-detached house around thirty miles south of Glebe Farm. On Sunday morning the smells emanating from their kitchen were wonderful. Mrs Khan was preparing lunch while her husband was half-heartedly mowing the small lawn in the back garden. Not a keen gardener. When the phone began ringing, Mrs Khan was nearest to it but couldn't break away from stirring a pot on the stove. She hustled to the door and called up the stairs for her daughter Rashida to take the call. Rashida was only too happy to suspend her school work and skip down the stairs.

"Good morning. It's Javid. Presumably your father isn't at work today or your mother out shopping?"

Rashida gritted her teeth, but agreed to bring one of them to the phone. The first port of call was the kitchen. Her mother thrust a wooden spoon at her with instructions to keep stirring. She wiped her hands on her apron and picked up the phone. Hard as she tried, Rashida could not make out what her mother was saying in the hall. She wouldn't dare abandon the pot for fear of causing a culinary disaster. When Mrs Khan

189

ended the call and resumed her duties in the kitchen she was not in the mood to stop for a chat. She hurried Rashida out – *from under my feet!* – and ordered her back to her studies.

No mention was made in Rashida's hearing of the outcome of the telephone conversation, but the atmosphere over lunch was subdued.

****

At the end of the afternoon, when the good ship *Sally Ann* was safely tucked up in her docking area and Donovan's stores had been stowed on *XO2*, Ralph announced that he would be preparing supper. No-one demurred. While the others dealt with their ablutions and changed into comfortable clothes for the evening, Ralph mixed chopped tomatoes and garlic in olive oil with tomato paste while pasta was bubbling on the boiling plate of the Aga. He may not have had the culinary skills of Mrs Khan, but his efforts were always appreciated by fellow crew-members. While cooking, he switched on the radio to catch the BBC's evening news programme.

Marnie was the first to join Ralph in the kitchen. He looked up from stirring the tomato mixture as she began laying the table.

"Northampton was on the news just now."

"What was it?" Marnie asked.

"Local news?" Anne said, coming into the kitchen followed by Donovan.

"No, national," said Ralph. "I only caught the tail-end of the item, but I think it was a senior police officer making a statement ... an outrage leading to social tension, or something of the sort."

"It wouldn't be the first time," Marnie said. She put a hand over her mouth to stifle a yawn. "Sorry. I think it's all that fresh air. I feel quite dozy."

"Me too," said Anne.

Ralph turned from the stove. "Anyone got the energy to fetch some wine from the cellar?" He was referring to the wine rack at the rear of the pantry. "I think we've got some *Valpolicella* that should go with this."

Donovan manned up to the task and headed for the pantry door. "You didn't hear anything else of the report about Northampton, Ralph?"

"Are you wondering if it had anything to do with your Muslim ladies?" said Ralph.

Donovan shrugged. "There was a definite tension in the air in town last week. Not good."

He switched on the light in the pantry, went in and located the *Valpolicella*. In his mind he saw the group of women being molested by the hoodies. Judging by what he saw of their legs they were probably quite young women. *My Muslim ladies*, he thought. He was shaking his head as he turned out the pantry light.

Chapter 19

Tea

The Monday morning post brought not one but three cheques. From across the office Marnie heard Anne give a low whistle followed by a *wow!* She glanced over at her friend who was laying out the cheques in front of her on the desk. At that moment the door opened and Ralph looked in.

"Don't let me interrupt. I'm gonna be late. See you tonight."

He rushed in, kissed Marnie, waved to Anne and was gone.

Marnie smiled. "I wonder if that's what's meant by a whirlwind romance. So, Anne, what is the *wow* factor?"

Anne waved the cheques in front of her face like a fan. "Any more of this and we'll soon be as rich as Samira."

"Talking of which – or perhaps I should say *whom* – I suppose she's still in the land of the living. Perhaps she's training to be a hermit. She elevates keeping to oneself as a new art form."

Anne agreed. "Sure, but we know why, don't we?"

"I wonder if she can drive," Marnie mused. "She's certainly got enough money to buy a car. Then she'd be mobile, able to get out and about."

"I don't think she wants to get out. Surely her aim is to hide from the world."

"Mm," Marnie muttered. "All the same, she must get very lonely with nothing to occupy her. Talking of which – and I do mean *which* this time – I've got to press on. Busy week."

Anne checked the calendar. "Three meetings tomorrow. D'you want me to man the office or shall I come with you?"

"We'll go together. Three very different projects. Good experience for you."

"Great. No danger of us becoming hermits."

****

Some thirty miles south of Glebe Farm Rashida's mobile began ringing. She was in the kitchen making herself a cup of coffee; her mother was tidying the living room. Recognising the caller's number, she slipped into the hall to avoid being overheard.

"Samira?" she whispered.

"Yes. Can you talk?"

"Go ahead."

"Oh, Rashida. I'm missing you so much."

Rashida said, "Me too. Listen, can we meet somewhere, even if just for coffee?"

There was silence on the line.

"Samira? Are you still there?"

"I don't know about meeting. Not sure it's a good idea."

"*Please*," Rashida pleaded. "I'm really missing you."

"Well ..."

"You choose, Samira. Anywhere you like. I promise I won't tell anyone."

"Well, I suppose we could find a place somewhere. What about Northampton? You could get a coach direct from Luton. I could meet you at the bus station."

"No problem. When? Make it soon. How about tomorrow?"

Samira hesitated. "I'd have to fix transport."

"Can you do that?"

"Probably. Everyone's very helpful here."

"Where's here? You're staying with some people?"

"I'll tell you more when we meet."

"Okay. The bus station in Northampton. What time?"

"I don't know the times of buses, but say around eleven o'clock?"

Rashida stepped across to the table where the house phone was kept. Beside it was a notepad. She quickly scribbled the heading *Samira*, then added the details.

"Let me get this right. Tuesday, bus station, Northampton, eleven. Oh!"

"What is it?"

"A taxi has just pulled up outside the house. There's a man getting out. He's coming this way. Samira, I think it might be him! He's seen me through the window."

"Put the phone down, Rashida."

"Okay. See you tomorrow."

Before the newcomer touched the bell, Rashida had the door open.

"Hello." She was breathless.

The man stared at her. "Are you all right?" It was the voice she had heard on the phone, no doubt about it.

"Yes."

"It's just that you seem rather flustered."

"No, no. Not really. I was just a little surprised when you arrived. I wasn't expecting you."

"Your mother is expecting me, though."

"Please come in. I'll call her." Rashida closed the door behind him. "I won't be a moment." She walked to the living room door and looked in. "We have a visitor, mum. It's Javid."

There was a sound of bustle in the room, words spoken in a low voice. Standing in the hall, the visitor's gaze fell on the notepad. He had seen the girl through the window beside the front door as he walked up the path. She had been writing something, and his curiosity was piqued. He was reading her notes when Mrs Khan entered the hall.

"Rashida should not have kept you waiting like this. Come in, come in."

"It's not a problem, Mrs Khan. I'm very pleased to see you again after so many years."

"Yes, and it's lovely to see you again, too. Come into the living room. Rashida will make us some tea."

Chapter 20

Pursuit

Anne felt cool moist air on her face as she was crossing the courtyard. It was after breakfast on Tuesday and, when the others had left, she stayed behind to tidy the kitchen. She enjoyed those moments of calm, alone doing something useful. Now, closing the farmhouse door behind her, she paused on the doorstep and took in her surroundings, the cobbles coated with a film of dew, the cream stone of the buildings, the blue-mauve slates shining on the roofs. She closed her eyes and raised her face to the sky, breathing in deeply, relishing the cool smell of the damp air.

Her reverie was broken by the sound of a door opening. Samira was coming out of her cottage.

"Hello, stranger."

Samira smiled. "Did you think I'd done a runner ... again?"

"Not really. I know you like your privacy."

"Anne, can I ask a favour?"

"Sure."

"Any chance of going into Northampton with you?"

"When d'you have in mind?"

"This morning, perhaps?"

Anne's mouth turned down at the edges. "I'm out with Marnie for most of the day. Back-to-back meetings."

"Oh." Samira's disappointment was clear in just one syllable.

"If you want to go shopping, I could take you later this afternoon."

"I need to be in town by eleven. Not to worry, I'll call a taxi."

"Come into the office," Anne said. "Let's see what's what."

"I'm going there anyway." Samira made a sheepish expression. "Gotta put Donovan's boat keys back while I remember."

In the office Marnie was on the phone, her desk covered in drawings and colour swatches. Samira followed Anne to her desk where she booted the computer to check the diary. While

195

Anne waited for the machine to warm up, Samira headed for the kitchen area to hang the keys on the board. The sound of movement behind her made her turn. She found herself face to face with Donovan. He was emerging from the shower room, a towel fastened round his waist, shirtless. The bruises were still visible on his torso.

"Hi, Samira. First you find me in the bedroom, now it's in the shower. We'll have to stop meeting like this. People will talk."

Samira quickly raised a hand to her mouth. "I'm sorry. I didn't realise you were –"

"It's fine. It's fine. Are those the boat keys?"

Samira tried not to make it obvious that she was eyeing his body. "Yes. I forgot to return them. I'm sorry. I meant to do it earlier."

Anne called across from the office. "Donovan, are you going anywhere near Northampton today?"

"Yes, Grayson's. We've got to talk cameras. Also seeing a friend. Why?"

"What time are you going?"

"Aiming to arrive around eleven."

"Perfect. Samira needs a lift."

Donovan turned to Samira. "Would you like me to take you?"

Samira grinned. "Bedroom, shower, alone in your car. Why break the trend?"

****

At his uncle's house in Luton Javid was on the phone. He had checked the small ad pages in the local paper to find the names of car hire firms. One of them had a Mondeo available for that day and could let him have it for a week. He arranged to collect it first thing.

It was not the cheapest car in their range, but the only one not currently out on hire. The manager of the firm assured Javid that the Ford Mondeo was comfortable and reasonably economical. For Javid the most important detail was that he could collect it straight away.

****

As soon as Samira got in the car, Donovan could feel the vibes. There was something animated about her. He wondered if she was maybe nervous about travelling alone and unchaperoned with a young man who was not a relative. But in truth he was past caring. If Samira wanted a lift into town she could have it. He just did not want to have to take on board all the extra baggage she carried with her wherever she went.

"Where do you want me to drop you?" he asked as they reached the edge of town.

"Do you know the bus station in the centre?"

"Hard to miss. It's a huge monstrosity."

"Would it be convenient for you, Donovan? I don't know where the camera shop is."

"It's fine. And I'm not going to the shop first. I'm meeting a friend in Grace Street."

"What's in Grace Street?"

"The mosque," Donovan said casually as he negotiated a roundabout.

Samira stared at him, incredulous. "You're going to the mosque?"

"Yep. I'm going to meet the imam."

Samira's mouth was half open as the car came to a halt at traffic lights.

"Your friend is an imam? I didn't know that."

Donovan put the car in gear as the lights changed to green and the traffic began rolling.

"No, I'm meeting his son, Azim. You know, the guy who came to Glebe Farm the other day. He's going to introduce me to his father at the mosque. Ah, that's the bus station on the right. I can't park anywhere here, so I'll just pull over and let you out."

"Why?" Samira asked.

"Why what?"

"Why are you meeting the imam?"

Donovan shrugged. He was anxious about blocking the road as traffic was approaching from behind. "It's a long story."

197

Samira stared at him, shaking her head. "What is it with you? I just don't get it. I can't make you out." She fumbled with the door handle and struggled to release the seat belt as she pushed the door open.

"Man of mystery, me," said Donovan lightly. "Anne always says so. What about returning? When shall I pick you up? Shall I meet you here?"

"Don't worry. I'll make my own arrangements."

Donovan's heart sank as he watched her hurrying across the road. She didn't look back. Sighing, he put the car in gear, found a gap in the flow of traffic and pulled away from the kerb. Rounding the corner from the bus station, he pulled into a side street and took out his mobile. He rang Anne's number. She sounded cheerful.

"Good timing, Donovan. Just finished a meeting. You've delivered Samira safely?"

"Yeah well, that's just it. I've delivered her all right, but I have a sneaking suspicion I've spooked her. I'm worried she might have gone walkabout again."

"I don't believe it! What did you do?"

"She asked me where I was going and I told her the mosque. I think she took fright."

"Oh hell."

"I know. Look, I'd better be going or I'll be late. I'll ring you when I'm through."

****

Javid agreed with the man in the hire firm's office. The Mondeo was comfortable and smooth to drive. He parked about forty metres down the street from the Khans' house and settled in to wait for as long as it took. Twenty minutes or so later he saw Rashida leave the house. She glanced quickly up and down the road and set off at a brisk pace. He waited until she reached the end of the street before starting the engine and driving after her. At the T-junction he spotted her in the distance. Two cars passed and he turned right to slip in behind them.

198

Javid had done his research. He knew not only the position of the bus station but the number of the service for Northampton and its schedule. Rashida arrived in good time to catch the next bus. Javid found a parking space in a nearby street from where he could observe the station. The National Express left punctually, and Javid was sure that no-one on board knew they were being followed. To be absolutely certain, he held back and, when the coach emerged onto the motorway, he fell back even further.

It was only when they approached the junction leading to the town that he overtook the coach and made his way towards the bus station. He found a multi-storey opposite the terminus building. His plan was to park there and follow Rashida. Then she would lead him to Samira.

It was in that last phase of the master plan that things went wrong. He had not anticipated that the car park might be full at that time on a Tuesday morning. Market day. Aghast, he found a small queue of cars lined up for the entrance. Cursing under his breath, Javid looked down the road to see Rashida's coach pull into the bus station. He thumped the steering wheel with his fist.

What now? The new plan formed itself rapidly in his mind. What else could he do but wait inside the bus station for as long as necessary? He guessed – or rather hoped – that Samira would eventually accompany Rashida back there. Then he would confront the woman destined to be his wife. Romantic encounters were not Javid's style, and Northampton bus station was certainly not the place for one, but it was his best option, his only option.

And he was determined that this plan would not fail.

****

Not a hundred metres from where Javid was queuing for the multi-storey, Donovan was consulting the town plan. He saw that Grace Street was not far from the centre but to reach it involved criss-crossing the maze of Victorian terraces through the area known as Little Warsaw. It brought back painful

199

memories as he traced a route with a fingertip, memorised the way and set off.

Approaching his destination, Donovan turned from a main thoroughfare into a side road and found his way blocked. A row of red and white bollards stretched across the entrance to Grace Street. Beyond them, police cars were parked on either side of the road. As he drew to a halt and reached for the town plan on the passenger seat, Donovan became aware of a shape looming up. He raised his eyes to find himself confronted by a policeman in uniform. The officer indicated that he should lower his window. Donovan wound the handle and the glass descended smoothly.

"Sorry, sir, you can't come this way." He pointed towards a deviation sign. "You'll have to take an alternative route."

"But Grace Street is where I need to be," Donovan said calmly.

"Are you a resident?"

"No."

"So where might you be going?"

"To the mosque."

The policeman stared at Donovan, making no effort to conceal his disbelief. With a light complexion, blonde hair and clear blue eyes, Donovan didn't look like someone who had a connection with a mosque.

The constable spoke slowly. "You want the mosque?"

"Yes."

"And what business might you have there?"

Donovan suspected that the question was out of order, but he had learnt that it was better not to argue with the police.

"I'm meeting the imam."

"You are?"

"Well, not directly. I'm here to see his son who wants to introduce me to his father."

"What name do you have for this ... *son*?"

"Azim. I don't know his surname."

"One moment."

200

The officer turned and walked slowly away, his head inclined, speaking quietly into the walkie-talkie attached to his jacket. Donovan wondered what was going on. He looked down the street, half expecting to see smoke rising in the distance from a burnt-out building, but everything seemed quiet. The officer returned and, without a word, moved two bollards aside. He signalled to Donovan to go through.

As he rolled forward, another policeman raised a camera and photographed the car. Donovan stopped and leaned his head out of the window.

"What's that for?" he asked.

"Routine, sir. We're keeping a record of every vehicle admitted."

Donovan frowned as he wound up the window. He drove slowly, peering out for any building that might be the Islamic Centre. His attention was caught by movement on the pavement up ahead. It was the distinctive figure of Azim, indicating a space where Donovan could pull over. He parked behind a police van, aware of constables on the pavement wearing hi-viz yellow jackets, one of them speaking on her walkie-talkie.

It was the usual greeting. As soon as Donovan climbed out of the car, Azim embraced him warmly. The only difference Donovan noticed on this occasion was that Azim was not smiling.

"What's up?" said Donovan.

Azim shook his head. "It's not good. There's been trouble."

"The mosque vandalised?"

"And the rest. We have a small Muslim section in the borough cemetery in Far Cotton. The headstones have been sprayed with red paint, all of them."

"So why is Grace Street blocked off?"

Azim pointed across the road. The façade of the Islamic Centre was daubed with obscenities, also in red paint.

"That's why I'm here, Donovan. I've had to give a statement. My father's gone to the cemetery with some of our board of directors. It's a right mess, the whole lot. We'll have to get a

201

contractor in to clean everything up. Sorry to bring you here for nothing. My father was looking forward to meeting you."

"Look, just tell him there's no need to thank me. He's got enough on his plate. Please tell him I'm really sorry about what's happened."

"I will, but I know he'll want to meet you and as soon as he can." Azim looked across the street at the defiled mosque. "So much for security. The new CCTV cameras have been trashed. It's hard to know what to do about all this aggression and hatred. Despite what some people think, Islam is fundamentally a religion of peace."

They crossed the road together to stand outside the mosque. Donovan grimaced at the red spray-paint obscenities. "The people who did that had other ideas."

Azim put a hand on Donovan's shoulder and spoke in a soft voice.

"Things have been especially difficult for many of us since the Gulf War. It's as if people think all Muslims support Saddam Hussein. Many of our community have made their lives in Britain precisely to get away from tyranny and violence."

Donovan nodded towards the defiled building. "Obviously not everyone sees it like that."

"That's what I'm saying, Donovan. Yet on the whole we feel that Britain is tolerant of our religion."

Donovan looked Azim in the eye. "I'd like to think that, too, that Britain is tolerant, but I think it's because Brits are basically indifferent to religions. This has become a secular country. I think most people don't care what religion you are, as long as you don't shove it down their throats."

"On the whole," Azim said with a wan smile, "I think tolerant indifference is preferable to violence."

Donovan looked up at the remains of the cameras. Someone had climbed up, sprayed them with paint and torched them.

"Sometimes you have to fight fire with fire," he said. "It's the only way."

Azim stared at him. "I thought the Christian community believed in turning the other cheek."

"Who's saying anything about the Christian community?"

"I just meant it's a Christian country. The queen is the head of the church as well as the state, isn't she?"

"You can't make assumptions just like that, Azim. I gave up on religion years ago. For me it's all superstition and hocus pocus. Sorry if you find that offensive."

"But you're a good man, Donovan. You came to my rescue, and to help those women in *niqabs*. Wasn't that an act of Christian charity, coming to our aid even though we were Muslims?"

"Nothing Christian about it. It was personal. Azim, I'm fine about you being Muslim. It's cool. I respect you and your religion. You've got a right to believe what you think. It's just not for me. I don't want to be told what to think. I don't want to be indoctrinated."

Azim said, "Even if enlightenment comes from great prophets?"

Donovan said, "Knowing me a little better, are you sure your father would really like to meet me?"

"He'll respect you for your goodness, Donovan. He will value that and appreciate you for what you did."

Donovan held out his hand. "Good luck for the future, Azim."

Azim ignored the hand and embraced Donovan as before. His expression was still grim.

****

Rashida spotted Samira as soon as she climbed down from the bus. She ran towards her sister, arms opening to embrace her. To her surprise, Samira virtually shrugged her off, taking her by the arm and hustling her away.

"What's the matter?" Rashida said breathlessly, as her sister rushed her out of the bus station and down a side street. "What is it?"

Samira didn't break stride. "I don't want to be seen."

Rashida stopped sharply and gripped Samira by the arms. "I don't understand. You think some nasty person is lurking in Northampton bus station on the off-chance that you might drop by so they can whisk you off to Pakistan?"

"You're right, Rashida. You don't understand. Let's get to the coffee shop, then we can talk. You have no idea what's going on."

With that, Samira set off at a rapid rate, leaving Rashida trailing in her wake.

****

Donovan drove to the far end of Grace Street and found another row of bollards blocking his way, but this time a policewoman watched the Beetle and stepped out to move two of the bollards from his path. In the next street he stopped the car and pulled out his phone.

You've reached the voicemail of …

Damn! Anne must be in another meeting. He waited until the recorded voice stopped.

"Anne, not sure when you'll get this. My meeting with the imam is off. Vandalism at the mosque and the Muslim cemetery. On my way to the camera shop now. Ring you later. If you hear from Samira, leave me a message if I can't speak."

****

Samira and Rashida bundled into the coffee shop and found a short queue at the counter.

"You get a table, Rashida. I'll get the coffees. Cappuccino?"

"Fine. There's a table just come free by the widow. I'll grab it."

Samira looked aghast. "No! Not there. Find one further back."

"But –"

"Please, Rashida, just do it. Okay?"

Shaking her head, Rashida managed to find a table in the furthest corner of the café. When they were seated she looked quizzically at her sister.

204

"Are you going to explain what's going on? You look ... I don't know ... *haunted*."

"That's exactly how I feel. You'd be the same in my position."

"What position is that?"

"They're wanting to marry me off – you know that – and by rejecting that, I'm no doubt regarded as bringing dishonour to the family. Now Javid's actually coming here has made everything a whole lot worse. You said that yourself."

"And what are you saying, Samira?"

"I fear for my life. Is that clear enough for you?"

"You mean you're worried about ..." She mouthed, *honour killing?*

"Of course I am."

Rashida sat back in her seat and stared at her sister. "Samira, this is modern-day Britain. We don't live in a tribal area up in some remote valley near the Khyber Pass. Mum and dad wouldn't ..." She shook her head. "I think you're being paranoid. You know an *arranged* marriage isn't a *forced* marriage."

"Yes, well," Samira said. "We all know that old saying about being paranoid doesn't mean they're not out to get you."

"Who?" said Rashida. "Who are *they*? You're not making sense."

Samira composed herself. She loved her sister and did not want to spend these precious minutes with her arguing.

"Maybe not," she said wearily. "I'm in a very confused place right now. I'm really scared, but I am trying to make sense of things. It's just hard to see a way forward, to see how things are going to end."

Rashida said, "I'm sure things will turn out for the best, at least I hope so. And maybe ..."

"What?"

"Do you think it might help if you at least *met* Javid? You never know, you might like him."

"Enough to want to give up my life, my career in England and go to live in Karachi or Lahore or some other place where I'll be treated as a chattel?"

"It might not be as bad as that, Samira. You haven't even seen him yet. You don't know what Javid's like."

"I saw him when I was eight years old and he must have been about fifteen."

"He's certainly changed a lot since then," Rashida said, smiling.

"So you've seen him. Was it the man who came in the taxi?"

Rashida nodded. "Yes. And he's been to the house since then and talked to mum."

"You haven't told him –"

"I haven't told anyone anything. I made tea and sat quietly without saying a word like a good little girl."

"What's he like?" Samira asked.

"Well, he's very good-looking, I'd say quite handsome. And he's a successful businessman. He has his own firm making parts for the aircraft industry. You'd be marrying someone who's on the way to becoming a millionaire!"

Samira looked pensive. "I can't believe someone who's running a big company would travel all this way just on account of me. It doesn't make sense."

Rashida said, "There is more to it. I heard him tell mum he has business meetings at Luton airport and with aerospace companies in Hertfordshire."

"So this trip is a tax-deductible expense!" Samira laughed. "Huh!"

"No, no. He really has come to see you. The meetings here are just a sort of coincidence. It's you he really wants."

Samira shook her head. "Rashida, I'm not impressed. I couldn't possibly accept someone just like that."

"All right. I get the message. Let's change the subject."

"Good idea." Samira blew across the top of her coffee. "So how are things at home? How is everybody?"

"Well, it's not very relaxed. You can guess the main topic of conversation."

"Me?"

"What else? Though that's not strictly true. Mum and dad are both worried about Tariq."

"You said he's getting over zealous about religion?"

"More than that. To tell you the truth, Samira, I'm worried about him too. In fact I'm finding him a little bit weird these days."

"He's hardly going to run off and join the Mujahideen."

"Wouldn't surprise me."

Samira shook her head. "It's a phase. He's a teenager."

"I'm a teenager too, Samira, and you were one not many years ago."

"It's not the same for girls."

"You haven't seen him lately. He's just so *intense*."

Samira studied her sister for a long moment. "Then maybe it's just as well I'm not at home."

They sipped their coffee in silence.

Eventually Rashida said, "So how are things with you, anyway, apart from being scared out of your wits the whole time?"

"It's not the whole time." Samira permitted herself a half-smile. "I do miss you all badly, but I'm staying in a nice place and I have some lovely new friends. It's not the same as a family and they do have a very different outlook on life, but at least I feel safe with them."

"That's something, I suppose."

"They're very patient with me, though I feel guilty about one of them. He's a bit strange and I'm sometimes unsure about him, but in some ways he's been the most helpful of them all."

Samira watched Rashida sip her coffee. In her mind she saw *XO2* moored under the willow trees on the far bank of the canal, inaccessible, secure. She pictured the cupboard and fridge on the boat laden with provisions, all freely given. She saw the still water of the canal in the moonlight and remembered that feeling of sublime peace and serenity. But then with a sinking sensation in her stomach she saw Donovan's bewildered expression as she jumped out of the car and said she would make her own way back to Glebe Farm. More than bewildered, he looked hurt as his offer of a lift home was rejected, thrown in his face. He deserved better than that, she thought.

"Have you finished your coffee, Rashida?"

"Yes."

"I ought to get going. I'll walk with you back to the bus station."

****

In the bus station Javid walked up and down the row of buses and coaches lined up at an angle, facing the pavement. He could taste the diesel fumes as he picked his way past queues of passengers waiting to board. Every few minutes another bus would rev its engine and reverse out before making for the exit onto the one-way system. After half an hour he could bear the noise and stench no longer. He hurried through an exit which led into a covered shopping precinct. Perhaps Samira and Rashida would come this way. Or perhaps he would miss them if they entered from some other direction. Reluctantly, after patrolling from one end of the shopping centre to the other, he retraced his steps.

****

On the way back to the bus station arm-in-arm with Rashida, Samira had a sudden thought. She stopped abruptly, causing Rashida to stumble.

"What is it?" Rashida asked. "You're not going all spooky again, are you?"

Samira reached into her bag for her mobile. "No, but I am in a jam. I more or less ran out on Donovan. Now I've got to grovel for a lift back."

"Donovan? You've not mentioned him before."

"He's a sort of friend of people at the place where I'm staying."

"*Sort of* – what does that mean? And where are you staying?"

Samira made a gesture, brushing her sister's questions aside as she focused on the mobile. Lifting it to her ear, she said to Rashida, "Do you know what time your next bus leaves?"

Rashida checked her watch. "Quite soon. We've got time to –"

Another gesture from Samira. She spoke into the phone. "Hello, Donovan, it's …" She sagged. "Voicemail! What a nuisance. Perhaps he's already on his way home."

"Where's home?" Rashida asked.

Samira grimaced, then had an idea. She quickly began pecking out another number on the keypad. "Anne, is that you?"

Rashida stood in silence, wondering who these people were – Donovan and Anne, and the others who had entered Samira's life – and listening as a conversation took shape. Evidently not voicemail this time. Samira was speaking to a live person.

"I've tried ringing Donovan but it went straight to voicemail. I really need to reach him. Can you try his number and see if he can pick me up from the bus station. … Oh thanks, Anne. I'll be there until he comes, unless I hear from you. Thanks a lot. Bye."

"That's not logical," Rashida said. "You could just as easily ring him yourself, surely."

Samira made a face. "Yes, but I think Donovan is probably fed up with me, and I wouldn't blame him. He and Anne are an item, so I think it might be better if she asks him rather than me."

Rashida looked unconvinced. "I suppose that makes sense."

"Come on," said Samira. "Let's get going. I'm sorry it's all such a rush today. Perhaps when Javid has gone home to Pakistan I'll be able to get back to a normal life and get on with my new job."

They hurried along and had covered barely thirty metres when Samira's mobile rang. Samira listened, thanked Anne profusely and hung up.

"That's a relief. Donovan can meet me in ten minutes."

"How can he meet you? There's nowhere to park at the bus station."

209

"He'll find a way. You don't know Donovan."

"You're right, Samira. I don't know him. In fact, the more I think about it, I don't know anything. I don't even know how I can reach you. It's as if you don't trust me."

"No, Rashida. It's not like that. It's just that my situation is so …" Samira reached into her bag again and pulled out a business card and a pen. She hastily scribbled a number on the back. "Look. This is a new mobile. No-one else has it. You can use it to contact me, but only when you can do it in private. Okay?"

Rashida took the card and read the number. "Well, it's a start, I suppose. Thanks."

More relaxed now, Samira smiled at her sister as they approached their destination. "Don't worry," she said. "All will be clear one day … I hope."

"If you say so."

They made their way through the shopping centre and into the bus station. The departures boards were showing that a bus for Luton was imminent, and they hurried to the furthest bay in time to see a National Express coach pulling in.

****

Javid looked at his watch and promised himself he would give it just five minutes more. Then another five minutes came and went, and another and another, and so on. He walked to the end of the station, looking up at the electronic departures boards for services to Luton. None was visible. Then, just as he reached the far end of the walkway, the name Luton appeared on the list of destinations. As luck – or misfortune – would have it, that bus would be leaving from the opposite end to where he was standing. Not for the first time that day he cursed.

In the distance he could see a National Express easing into the furthest bay. And then, unbelievably, there they were at the end of the crowded concourse. At least he was sure he recognised Rashida. The two of them were hastening towards the last bay where they joined the short queue boarding the

210

bus. As he drew nearer he got a good view of the young woman standing beside Rashida. They embraced before she climbed aboard. In that moment, he could do nothing but marvel at the woman who had been promised to him in marriage by both their families. He was completely smitten.

Javid stopped in his tracks, holding back while Rashida boarded the bus. He wanted to meet Samira alone, to talk to her quietly without Rashida in the way. He saw Samira wave an elegant hand and blow a kiss towards the bus. For a few moments Samira stood watching it pull away, giving one final wave.

Now Javid's time had come. He would have preferred a more salubrious venue for their first meeting as adults, but he knew he had to seize the opportunity while it presented itself. Not wanting to accost her breathless with exertion, he collected himself calmly and began walking without haste, knowing that Samira would have to come towards him either to leave the bus station or catch a bus.

For a few moments he lost sight of her in the throng. Then, three things happened in quick succession. Javid heard a faint sound in the distance: a car's horn. Straining forward he saw a dark bulbous shape on the approach road into the bus station; it flashed its headlights twice. Javid saw Samira again, but now she had turned and was hurrying away. He was certain that she had not seen him and was bewildered by her sudden change of direction. Was she reacting to the car's horn? He speeded up in time to see Samira reaching the car. It was distinctive and reminded him of those old Volkswagen cars from times past. He saw the passenger's door swing open, and Samira jumped in, slamming the door behind her as it sped away from the kerb.

Javid knew that the VW would have to follow the one-way system past the bus station. He turned to run as fast as he could to the far end to try to see the car's direction of travel. As luck would have it, the VW had had to stop at traffic lights. It was in the right hand lane. The signboard beside the lights

211

indicated that that route was heading for the ring road. From there it would probably lead out of town.

Desperately, he raced across the road, prompting a staccato chorus of car horns, and into the multi-storey, found the Mondeo and took off, the tyres squealing on the exit ramp.

****

Donovan made a sharp turn to the left from the bus station approach road and swung out into the traffic lane. Beside him, Samira leaned back against the head-rest and breathed out heavily. Donovan shot her a quick glance as he changed into third gear.

"Seat belt," he said.

"Oh, yes. Thank you for coming, Donovan. I apologise for my behaviour earlier on. You must think me —"

"Don't worry about it. I know you're jumpy. I'll explain about the mosque when we're on the open road. Back to Glebe Farm?"

"Please. You got a message from Anne?"

He stopped behind two cars held up at a red light.

"She said to meet you here pronto. I'm glad I spotted you in the bus station. Otherwise I'd be driving round the one-way system till you showed up."

Just then movement caught his eye in the rear-view mirror. Some madman in a light grey suit was racing across the road in the direction of the multi-storey. Donovan shook his head. The madman was really taking his life in his hands, dodging in and out of the traffic. A cacophony of horns trumpeted him on his way. Samira noticed Donovan's expression.

"What is it? Is everything all right?" She strained to look over her shoulder.

"Just some nut-case doing a *kamikaze* run across the road behind us. Lunatic."

"I don't see anybody," said Samira.

"He's gone now. I think he made it ... just."

The lights changed to green and the cars began rolling forward.

"Are you in a hurry to get home?" Donovan asked.

212

"Not particularly. Why?"

"I have to tank."

"To what?"

"Sorry, that's German slipping in. I have to stop for fuel, petrol. I need to fill up."

Minutes later Donovan pulled in at a filling station on the main road out of town. Each pump was occupied and they took their place behind a van. Its driver was already hanging up the nozzle. They only waited for a minute or two before the driver came out of the shop, tossed his wallet into the van and drove off. The Beetle moved forward to take his place.

As Donovan climbed out, Samira asked if there was anything she could do.

"No, you're fine. I won't be long."

He closed the driver's door and reached for the pump.

Just sit there and look beautiful, he muttered under his breath. *I'm sure you'll manage that.*

****

Javid's mind was in turmoil. First, because he couldn't get the vision of Samira out of his head. Second, because he had allowed her to slip through his fingers.

When he last saw her in Pakistan, she had been a small child, he had been a teenager. Back then his world was made up of cricket – he was a devoted fan of Imran Khan – his school work, especially his favourite subjects, physics and maths, and football – he was a dedicated follower of Manchester United. An eight-year-old girl had been of little interest to him. But the woman she had become was magnificent in his eyes. He had not exchanged a single word with her, so how was he to find her and persuade her to return with him to make a new life in his country? He gritted his teeth, determined to do just that.

Javid was musing along these lines, trying to concentrate on driving as he nosed out of the exit ramp, wondering how on earth he was going to make it into the outside lane where the black Volkswagen had positioned itself. Then the first of two remarkable things happened. As the lights turned to red the traffic slowed and left a gap for him to cross into the further lane. If he had attempted that manoeuvre in Karachi he would have been blasted by a fanfare of horns.

Once the traffic was on the move he opted to go with the flow of cars heading away from the centre. He had no clear plan but simply took the path of least resistance and found himself following signs to the motorway and the ring road. Why not? He could think of no better idea.

And then the second remarkable thing happened. He was slowing on the approach to yet another set of traffic lights when he saw it. Beyond the junction was a service station, and standing at one of the pumps was the unmistakable shape of that old black VW. Even as he noticed it, the car began pulling out of the forecourt. Perfect. He would be able to follow it discreetly with three cars between them, and the driver would never know he was there.

****

Donovan was happy now with a full tank of petrol and was pleased that the lights at the junction fifty metres behind had created an opening for him. He lined up with the exit and pulled forward. Beside him, Samira was fastening her seat belt. She had gone into the filling station's shop while Donovan was busy at the pumps. As soon as the car turned onto the carriageway Samira spoke.

"Er, Donovan?"

"What is it?"

"Did I see shops in that side street near the traffic lights back there?"

Donovan eased back on the accelerator. "I think so. Why? D'you need something?"

"I do."

"What d'you need?"

Samira hesitated. "Personal things."

"Is it urgent?" Donovan asked. "If you want, I can do a U-turn here. It's wide and there's no traffic. But you have to decide straight away."

214

"Please. If you wouldn't mind."

In one fluid action Donovan braked, changed down a gear and pulled a tight U-turn. He accelerated towards the lights and took the left-hand lane as they changed to red. He brought the Beetle to a halt and a movement caught his eye in the rear-view mirror. Almost at once the filter arrow shone green and he made the turn, his attention now fully focused on finding a parking slot.

"Is this okay?" he asked when he stopped at the kerb.

"Perfect. I won't be a minute."

"D'you need any help or shall I wait in the car?"

"I'll be fine."

Samira was true to her word. In no time she emerged from a shop clutching a carrier bag, but as she did so a sudden squall of rain came down. Donovan spotted her and quickly leapt out of the car to open the door for her to climb in.

"Thank you, Donovan. You're very considerate."

He gave a mock salute and inclined his head. "Happy to oblige, ma'am."

As Donovan gunned the engine, Samira smiled and fastened the seat belt.

She said, "I can see why Anne is so fond of you."

She looked across at Donovan but he was not smiling. She was dismayed to see him not just looking serious but scowling.

"Oh, I'm sorry, Donovan. That was very forward of me. I shouldn't have spoken like that. Please forgive me."

Donovan's reply surprised her. "Do you know anyone who has a Ford Mondeo?"

"Do I ... Sorry, I don't follow."

His next reply surprised her even more. "No, but somebody does."

Samira saw that he was glancing repeatedly in the mirror. She turned in her seat to look over her shoulder, but saw nothing out of the ordinary. There were cars in the street travelling in both directions. She knew the name, Ford Mondeo, but to her, one car looked much like another.

"Are you always so enigmatic, Donovan? Is that why Anne calls you a *man of mystery?*"

Her question was met by another cryptic utterance.

"We'll go through Far Cotton."

"What does that mean?" Samira asked.

"It's the part of town we're coming to."

Samira saw terraces of small Victorian houses as Donovan wound his way through a modest residential area. Eventually they ran uphill, following signs to the ring road. Slowing for a roundabout, Donovan changed down and gestured to their left. A marked police car was parked outside the entrance to the cemetery.

"The cemetery has a Muslim section somewhere in there," he said.

Samira felt her stomach turn. "How do you know that, Donovan?"

"I heard it was vandalised yesterday."

"You heard that at the mosque?"

Donovan stared at the rear-view mirror as he braked for the roundabout. More frowning.

"Yes, from Azim. He's the imam's son. I told you. The imam wanted to thank me for helping Azim when he was in a fight with some thugs."

"Did you meet him?"

"No. Let me concentrate here." Donovan swung the car round the roundabout and accelerated firmly to turn right onto the ring road. He held the car longer than usual in each gear, and Samira could hear the engine running faster than before. She knew they were exceeding the speed limit.

"Why are you going so quickly?" she asked.

"Don't worry about it, but we seem to have a friend." He spoke calmly, though it was obvious from his stance at the wheel that he was driving with total concentration. "Coming back to your question, no, I didn't meet the imam. He was inspecting the damage in the cemetery that we just passed."

Samira looked back over her shoulder. "By a *friend*, you mean someone's following us? Are you sure of that? Is it the Mondeo you asked me about?"

Another roundabout. Donovan braked hard, studying the signboard. He slipped into the left-hand lane, changed down and swung the wheel over. Samira felt the pressure as the Beetle skated round the bend. More firm acceleration, more growling from the exhaust.

"Is a Mondeo quicker than your car, Donovan? Is that why you're driving so fast?"

Donovan ignored her questions. He was busy overtaking a lorry and trying to read the next signboard.

"I need to pay attention here, Samira."

He pulled ahead of the lorry just as the Slow Down sign appeared for another roundabout. Behind them, the lorry signalled and pulled into the outside lane. Donovan followed suit and, with the lorry about twenty metres behind him, turned hard into the roundabout and followed the sign to Services. Samira stared at him, bewildered.

Donovan slowed at the entrance to the motorway service area and cruised slowly to the end of the car park. He slotted the Beetle into a space between a van and a Range Rover. To any casual observer they were completely hidden. He turned off the engine.

"Donovan, we're in a car park."

"Yeah, I spotted that."

"I mean seriously. I thought you were trying to go quickly."

Once again his reply was enigmatic, but she was accustomed to that now.

"Chinese proverb: if you want to hide a tree, plant it in a forest. Or something like that."

****

Javid was now completely frustrated and confused. In town, the VW had doubled back on itself as if the driver knew they were being followed. But then the car had parked just round the corner after turning at the traffic lights, and in his haste

217

Javid had almost missed it as he gave chase. He turned into a street further along the road just as it started to rain. As he turned to retrace his route he caught sight of the driver climbing out of the VW to open the door for Samira. It was definitely a man. Disgraceful!

Moments later the VW pulled out from the kerb and went on its way. This necessitated another turn in the road by Javid – during which manoeuvre other drivers patiently waited – and he took off back in pursuit. His one consolation was that Fords were not uncommon cars in Britain, and the behaviour of the VW driver led him to believe that he didn't suspect he was being followed.

Javid drove as fast as he dared through streets lined with houses until he saw signs indicating the ring road ahead. Left or right; east or west? It was a guessing game, and he had no clue to guide him. One of the options was a blue sign for the M1 motorway to the west. For want of any better idea, Javid took the westbound turn. He kept to the outside lane and swung the Mondeo to the right.

As soon as he straightened up, Javid strained to see up ahead. His heart sank. The distinctive dark shape of the VW was nowhere to be –. Wait! Was that it in the distance? He caught sight of something that could have been the Beetle negotiating another roundabout some way away. He pressed the accelerator and saw the speedometer needle climb quickly towards the top of the dial. At the same time he noticed a speed limit sign: 40 mph. To hell with it! His future life was at stake.

One more roundabout, another motorway sign, this time to the left. He took it. Then in quick order came more options: a trunk road to Oxford; the motorway itself, signposted North to Birmingham, South to London; a service area. Rather than hare off down a motorway, he opted for the Oxford direction, A43. His expression grim, Javid skated round the roundabout. He knew that somewhere in this region was the woman on whom he hoped to base the rest of his life. He pressed the accelerator pedal to the floor.

****

Donovan was a strange one, Samira thought. Small wonder that Anne called him a man of mystery. Sitting in the Beetle in the car park of the motorway services, she looked at him beside her. He sat back resting against the head restraint with his eyes closed. The shower had now passed, but the windows were covered with raindrops. Donovan had sat there for some minutes without speaking, without moving. She felt churned up inside after their dash out of town, but Donovan could hardly have been more composed. In one sense Samira felt reassured by his inner calm, yet part of her was desperate to be away.

To her surprise, he suddenly raised a hand to his mouth and yawned. He looked at his watch.

"Six minutes," he said. "Okay. Let's get going"

"Are you sure the coast is clear, Donovan?"

"Who knows? But we can't stay here all day."

"You seem pretty relaxed about things."

Donovan turned to look at her. "If our pursuer's gone on the motorway he's miles from here in either direction and can't change his mind very easily. If he's headed down the A43 we're a long way behind him."

"And what if he's here in the car park?"

Donovan smiled grimly. "He would've found us by now."

Samira took a deep breath, turning her head from side to side, scanning the area for any sign of their pursuer. Donovan meanwhile was pulling on a pair of black leather driving gloves, rows of perforations running down the backs of each hand. Every move he made was purposeful, measured.

"You're very precise, aren't you, Donovan?"

"Precise?"

"And your style of driving is the same. I bet you passed your driving test first time … with flying colours."

"Do you drive, Samira?"

"I can, but I haven't had much experience."

"Did you pass first time?"

Samira smiled and nodded. Donovan continued.

"After how many lessons?"

219

"I had a course of ten."

"That's pretty good."

A modest smile. "Yes. My instructor said I was a natural."

Donovan started the engine, flicked on the wipers to clear the windscreen and reversed carefully out of the slot. They rolled slowly past the rows of parked cars towards the exit. There were no blue Mondeos in sight. Donovan drove up the slip road to the roundabout and took the exit for the A43, direction Oxford. The engine gave a throaty rumble as he accelerated firmly, concentrating simultaneously on the road ahead, on the rear-view mirror and on the traffic around them. While Donovan was occupied with driving, Samira said nothing but cast occasional glances in his direction. She realised she was becoming at ease in his company. Her upbringing had brought her little experience of men outside her immediate family, and it surprised her to recognise that, for all Donovan's strangeness, she was growing to trust him.

****

All the way home on the coach Rashida's mind was a jumble of anxieties, thoughts that haunted her, reflections on things she could have said, *should* have said. Stepping down in the bus station, she set off on the walk home. A shower had come and gone leaving the pavements wet but, despite the possibility of more rain to come, she walked much more slowly than on her outward journey, going over again and again her conversation with Samira. She loved her sister but now her feelings were dominated by fears for her well-being. How would it all end? Instinctively she felt a dread in the pit of her stomach that things were not going to turn out happily.

Arriving home, she was reaching forward to put the key in the lock when the door flew open and Tariq burst out. He only just managed to stop himself crashing into his sister.

"There you are!" he exclaimed. It sounded like an accusation. "Where have you been?"

"I've just … well, I had things to do … I … More to the point, where are you going in such a hurry?"

"Haven't you heard? There's been trouble in Northampton, serious trouble."

"Is that where you're going? What are you going to do there?"

"No, I'm going to see some friends. We have to decide what to do. We can't just sit back and take all this shit. It's blatant persecution, that's what it is."

Tariq pushed past her and hustled up the street, leaving her on the doorstep wondering what trouble might have taken place in the town she had only just left. Anxiety flooded over her. What if Samira had been caught up in it? She rushed into the house anxious to log onto local radio. In the hall she stopped dead. Through the kitchen door she could see her mother sitting at the table, holding her head in her hands.

She walked quickly into the kitchen and knelt beside her mother.

"What is it? What's happened?"

A sad face turned slowly towards her. "Your brother is so headstrong. I worry that he's going looking for trouble."

Rashida nodded. "I saw him at the door. He said he's off to see some friends. I expect they'll just talk."

Her mother sighed. "I try to persuade myself that it's his age, being a teenager, a boy."

"That's what –" Rashida stopped herself just in time. "That's what I think, too."

"I think," her mother began. "I think our family is falling apart."

****

Javid could feel his shoulders were tense and realised he was gripping the steering wheel as if he wanted to crush it. He forced himself to relax, or at least try to calm down. One deep breath, two, three. A shake of the head from side to side. Of the black rounded shape of the old VW there was no trace. He glanced down at the speedometer as he passed a sign depicting a traffic camera. Going much too fast, he took his foot off the accelerator and let the car ease back to a respectable rate for

221

half a mile. It was no use. He knew he was on a fool's errand, but he had done all he could.

He passed the traffic camera at exactly seventy miles per hour and felt quite smug, though he could not understand why in Britain such cameras were painted the most conspicuous bright yellow. Did the authorities *want* the motorists to be forewarned? Concluding that it had to be something to do with the strange British notion of fair play, Javid turned his attention to a signboard. Evidently he was approaching a place called Towcester. He had no idea how the name was pronounced. The main road seemed to by-pass the town, skirting it at a large roundabout controlled by that other British institution, yet more traffic lights.

The lights turned to green while Javid was changing gear, and as he pressed down on the accelerator, he made up his mind to turn back at the next opportunity. Another roundabout loomed up a short distance ahead, and he moved into the right-hand lane ready to turn through one-eighty degrees. He would travel back to the outskirts of Northampton and pick up the M1 southbound to return to Luton. The car had cruise control. Javid set it to seventy and chugged steadily along, pondering his next moves.

And then it happened.

On the other side of the dual carriageway, beyond the central barrier, Javid saw the black Volkswagen Beetle travelling south. He wondered if he had misjudged it. Old it must have been, but it seemed low-slung and somehow purposeful, speeding along, gripping the tarmac as if on rails, its bodywork shiny like new. In a matter of seconds it cruised past, and there was no way of turning in pursuit. Javid recalled that there were no more roundabouts for several miles. But he now had one consolation. He had narrowed down the area in which he was hunting, and hunting he certainly was. Samira had been promised to him. She had gone to ground, but he would find her. He *would* find her. *Yes, he would.*

****

After the family meal that evening Rashida withdrew to her bedroom on the grounds that she needed to revise for her exams. She cleared the table and filled the dishwasher while Tariq went upstairs to read car magazines in his bedroom. It was decorated with posters of Imran Khan, sports cars and Manchester United football club. Their parents were still at the table talking together in low voices when she climbed the stairs.

In her room, Rashida left the door open a crack and listened. Muted voices mingled with the babble from the television rose from downstairs. Closing the door, she pulled the mobile phone from her school bag and quickly pressed buttons, mentally crossing her fingers that Samira would have her own phone to hand.

"Hello?" The voice was unmistakably Samira and unmistakably nervous.

"It's me, Samira. Can you talk?"

"Can you?"

"I'm in my room. I might have to break off suddenly."

"How is it at home?"

"Not wonderful. We've just finished eating. As usual mum made a great dinner, but we ate without anyone speaking. It was a really strained atmosphere. Tariq looked sullen the whole time. He's always like that these days. Tonight he's even worse, if that's possible."

"Why d'you think that is?" Samira asked.

"I don't know. He went out when I got home and only came back just before we sat down to eat. I don't know where he went but I think he's up to something."

Samira sighed. "I wish I could come to see you all."

"You always could get round Tariq, Samira. He idolised you. But even you might not get through to him the way he is now."

"What do you mean by that?"

"Like I told you, he's so intense. It's like he's got religion really bad."

"You think he wouldn't approve of my actions."

223

"Of course he wouldn't, especially if he knew you were gallivanting around in a car with some man none of us has ever heard of."

"All perfectly innocent," Samira said.

Rashida's turn to sigh. "You don't get it, do you? We none of us match up to his standards these days, and least of all you, Samira."

"I don't know what standards are —"

"Sorry. Gotta go."

The line went dead. Samira found herself listening to air. She pressed the red button to disconnect. *Thanks for the call, Rashida*, she thought. *You've really cheered me up.* Samira went and stood by the kitchen door looking out into the small patio garden. It was dusk outside, and she saw only her own reflection in the glass, a solitary ethereal figure. She was haunted by the thought that things had just become even worse than she had ever imagined.

Chapter 21

Surprise

Early on Wednesday morning Donovan was lying in Anne's bed, persuading himself that it was time he got up, when his mobile began warbling. He grabbed it from the bedside table and pressed the green button.

"Donovan."

"Good morning. This is Azim. I hope I'm not calling too early."

Donovan hoped his voice didn't sound too sleepy. "You're fine."

"My father wishes to apologise for yesterday. He wants to invite you again to meet him. Would you be able to come today?"

"Is it so urgent?" Donovan asked.

"You know he wants to thank you personally for coming to my aid."

"I told you, there's really no need, Azim. It was no big deal."

"Ah, but it was. You don't understand, Donovan. For us it's a very big deal. Please say you'll come. He wouldn't like to think he'd offended you by missing you yesterday."

"Well, since you put it like that ... Okay, I'll be pleased to meet him. Same place?"

"Perhaps not. The mosque is still under police guard. There's an unused school building just off the Wellingborough Road. Do you know it?"

"Yeah, I think so."

"We're hiring the hall for meetings on a temporary basis. What time would suit you?"

They agreed on ten o'clock. Donovan was making a note on the pad he kept by the bed when Anne came up through the trap-door opening and announced that the shower was free.

****

225

It was a morning of unexpected calls. After breakfast Marnie was working solidly on a design project when the office phone rang. Anne took the call.

"Walker and Co, good morning."

"Anne, it's Angela. Is Marnie about?"

"I'll see if she's in. Please hold."

Anne put the call on hold. "Marnie, it's our friendly local vicar. I think she wants to save your soul."

"Good luck with that. Put her through."

There was a click on the line. Angela Hemingway said, "What's all that about *I'll see if she's in*? Your desks are only twenty feet apart and you're facing each other."

"We like to convey an impression of corporate grandeur. What can I do for you, Angela?"

"Have you heard the news?"

"Keep going."

"There was trouble in Northampton yesterday afternoon. Some vandals set fire to a church hall. On local radio they said it might have been an attack by Muslim elements, a reprisal after the desecration of the mosque and the graveyard."

Marnie was incredulous. "They think the earlier vandalism was carried out by born-again Christian hooligans?"

Angela sighed. "Apparently eye witnesses saw young Asian men running from the scene."

There was a pause. "Why are you telling me this, Angela? You have me down as a suspect?

"Marnie, I'm not joking. I was thinking about Samira. I wanted to warn her. There could be disturbances in town."

"Why would anyone —"

"On the radio they were interviewing young men, wanting their reactions to the arson attack. They were talking about ... oh dear, it sounds awful."

"What did they say?"

"There was likely to be an outbreak of ... I can hardly bring myself to say it ... Paki-bashing." Silence. "Marnie, are you there?"

"And this would presumably be in town, would it? You're not thinking trouble might spread out here?"

"No, Marnie. I just wanted Samira to be aware, in case she was coming out of the village."

"I'd better warn Donovan."

"*Donovan*? He's not likely to be affected, surely."

"He was saying at breakfast that he's going to Northampton this morning to meet the imam."

"Whatever for?"

"Long story. I'll fill you in some time. Thanks, Angela. I'd better tell him before he sets off."

"Marnie, just one thing before you go. I've got involved in this because I'm the designated ecumenical liaison person."

"What does that mean? Another committee or something? It didn't do much good last time there was trouble."

"No, it's more informal contact with other religious and social groups."

"You're hardly based in the town, Angela."

"We're covering the area roughly from Northampton to Milton Keynes, so we're more or less central down here."

"Hold on a sec." Marnie put the phone down and called across to Anne. "Can you pop over to the house and tell Donovan to watch out for trouble when he goes into town. This time it's a church hall – arson attack. More worries for the imam."

"That's not something you say every day." Anne was already on her feet and hurrying towards the door.

Marnie raised the phone again to her ear. "Angela, did you say *we* just then? Should I be reading anything into that? Put it another way: why am I feeling suspicious?"

"Oh Marnie. It's just that you're always so helpful in difficult situations."

"Meaning what exactly?"

"I'm supposed to liaise with – among others – the police, for example."

"And?"

"The local CID liaison officer wants a meeting to agree on a sort of collaborative approach, seeing as how faith groups are involved. It'd be great if you could be there with me ... moral support, you know."

"When? My diary is very full at the moment."

Hesitation. "She wants to come – sorry for the short notice – tomorrow morning, actually."

"And who is this liaison officer? Did you say *she?*"

"Yes. It's detective constable Cathy Lamb. You've known her a while now, Marnie. You've always got on very well. Could you spare an hour perhaps?"

Marnie had the diary up on the screen. There were no meetings on Thursday morning. She sighed.

"I heard that. You're free, aren't you? Can I tell Cathy we'll see her? She said she has something of interest to show us."

"I can hardly wait."

****

Donovan was not desperately keen to meet the imam, but he admitted to himself that as he drew nearer to the venue, the more curious he became. On the other hand, he didn't feel that thanks were really necessary. He had thought it was stupid of Azim to charge in against a gang of yobs without any kind of weapon or support. It was asking for trouble, and that was exactly what he got.

He slowed and signalled to turn right off the Wellingborough Road into the side street where the old Victorian school was located. He knew it well from the time when it was used as a base for community activity a couple of years earlier. It also occurred to him that back then it had been the scene of violent rioting. Same old, same old, he thought.

He parked the Beetle, set off across the playground and straight away saw Azim waiting for him in the entrance. After the usual hug, Azim led him inside. In the lobby Donovan removed his shoes, aware that the building was being used as a Muslim place of worship. Azim thanked him and pushed open the inner door to the hall. The imam looked younger than

228

Donovan expected, though there were a few traces of grey in his beard and he stooped slightly as he rose to receive his visitor. No-one else was present and, although three folding chairs were set out in a corner of the hall, the imam asked Azim to leave them to speak in private. He gestured to a chair and waited for Donovan to be seated before taking his own place.

"First, I must apologise for yesterday. I know you understand the circumstances."

"No need, sir."

The imam smiled. "And no need for formality. My name is Abdullah and I am in your debt for what you did, rescuing my son."

"And I'm Donovan, but you know that already. There's no need to thank me. I was just in the right place at the right time to help. As I've said to Azim, it was no big deal."

"Donovan, for people of our faith what you did was certainly a big deal. I don't want to embarrass you, but you put yourself in harm's way to help Azim and also the young women who were being molested."

"Well, I'm glad to have been able to help them."

"What you did was outstanding. It is written in the holy Koran that if any one saved a life, it would be as if they saved the life of all people. It's a sentiment common to all people of the book."

Donovan was uncertain how to respond. The imam went on.

"You have explained to Azim that you are not a believer."

"That's correct."

"I do not wish to impose our beliefs on you, but I would like you to know that Islam is a faith based on peace. Your intervention, though violent in its way, was merciful in essence and so would be regarded by us as a blessing. I thank you from the bottom of my heart."

The imam extended a hand, and Donovan shook it.

"Thank you, Abdullah. I'm very touched." Donovan sat back in the chair, his expression thoughtful.

229

The imam said, "There is something on your mind, something you would like to ask, perhaps?"

"It's … I don't want to cause offence, imam … Abdullah."

"Donovan, there are many misunderstandings about Islam. If there is anything that I can clarify, please do ask me. I promise you I will not be offended."

"It's about … honour killing. Does Islam approve of it?"

"No." The imam's tone was emphatic. "It is strongly prohibited."

"But it happens."

"It does, and there are many old and new reasons for it, some of them going back to ancient times and some to more recent laws, which I'm sure would surprise you."

"I always thought it was a feature of Muslim life."

"It is strictly forbidden to take a life without lawful reasons. No-one may take the law into their own hands. Those who commit murder are condemned to eternal Hell and damnation."

"But if someone is seen as bringing shame on the family?"

"No." The imam shook his head. "That is no reason in Islam to justify killing another. Sometimes *honour* is used to conceal a murder committed for other reasons. No saying of the Prophet Mohammad – peace be upon him – sanctions such crimes."

"You mention more recent laws that justify it?"

"I think you will be astonished, Donovan. Some countries in the Middle East and South Asia have adopted laws that in different ways have served to condone honour killing."

"But not arising from the practices of Islam?" Donovan said.

The imam looked him in the eye. "Do you know the term in French, *crime passionnel*?"

Donovan nodded. "A crime of passion."

"Did you know that under French law a husband was allowed to murder his unfaithful wife and her lover? As it was regarded as a crime of passion, the husband would not be prosecuted."

"I've vaguely heard of the concept."

"It was enshrined in the Napoleonic Code of 1810."

"I was thinking more in terms of modern-day crimes, rather than history."

"The law was repealed in France as recently as 1975," the imam said quietly.

"Really?" Donovan was astonished, but quickly gathered his thoughts. "I'm not sure how that relates to honour killing nowadays."

"That and other French laws were copied by many Arab countries, and in some of them it still applies. France has for a long time had considerable influence in the Arab world. This has influenced thinking throughout Islam. It has created attitudes that persist to this day. By analogy, that is how such dreadful concepts as honour killing have pervaded thought in many communities."

"You're saying the blame lies with the Napoleonic code and French laws?"

"I'm saying that they have created attitudes that survive even now."

"There are no factions, sects, religious leaders that have contributed to such thinking?"

"No true Islamic leader or scholar has ever sanctioned this kind of murder to preserve the so-called *honour* of a family."

****

On the way back to Glebe Farm Donovan had to use all his concentration to drive with the precision that Samira had described the previous day. His mind was awash with thoughts and ideas. What the imam had told him opened his eyes to a different way of looking at Samira's predicament. She was trapped in a system of values that was widely held by her community even though there was no justification for it in their religion. Was it all underpinned by the *Code Napoléon* from 1810? If those Muslim countries had taken that law into their constitutions, they had had plenty of time to expunge it.

Having spoken with the scholarly imam, he was willing to believe that Samira was not the victim of religious dogma or extremism. Even so, there was one thought that he could not

231

erase from his mind. Whether the concept was justified or not, one thing was certain: when you were dead, you were dead.

Chapter 22

CCTV

Thursday morning was again overcast and blustery with the threat of rain. It seemed appropriate for a visit by detective constable Cathy Lamb. To be fair, the woman herself was pleasant enough. For Lamb's part, she had to admit she had a soft spot for Marnie. It probably dated back to the time she had sat at her bedside in Intensive Care when Marnie's life hung in the balance. When Marnie's readings started to improve, and the consultant said she was out of danger, Lamb had to wipe away a tear. That was something she would forever keep secret.

On that grey blowy morning Marnie was concentrating hard on completing a design before her visitors arrived. Consequently she overlooked the need to check the biscuit tin. It was Anne of course who noticed it was empty when she began gathering together the crockery for coffee.

She grabbed her bag, yelled "Biscuits!" like an esoteric war-cry and headed for the door.

Marnie glanced up, understood and refocused.

Yanking the door shut behind her, Anne turned up her collar against the gusting breeze and pointed her nose towards the field track. At that moment Samira came out of her cottage. Without breaking stride Anne called out: "Coming for coffee?"

Samira stalled and watched Anne striding out. She began, "That would be —"

"Ten minutes," Anne called out over her shoulder and was gone.

Samira went back into cottage number three, happy at the prospect of coffee with her friends. She had no inkling that they would be joined by detective constable Cathy Lamb.

****

By the time Anne made it back to the office barn Angela Hemingway and Samira were already installed on visitors' chairs. They were chatting happily while Marnie was busy with the cafetière in the kitchen area at the rear of the office.

"I hope you got some dark chocolate digestives," Marnie called out.

Anne was taking off her jacket. She pulled a face and held up the carrier bag. "Rural deprivation, I call it. Molly had sold out of chockie digestives. I got Hobnobs and custard creams and ..." Her expression brightened. "... a Battenberg cake."

"Good thinking, Battenberg man!"

Samira stood up and took the bag from Anne. "Let me help," she said. "Where do you keep plates?"

Marnie pointed to a cupboard under the workbench. "Down there. We'll need five."

"Five?" Samira looked round. "Oh, of course. Ralph."

"Not this morning. He's got a deadline to meet. This is for Angela's benefit, so it's just us."

"And Cathy," Angela added.

"Can't forget Cathy," Marnie said.

Samira put tea-plates on a tray together with larger ones for biscuits and cake. "Cathy is another friend?" she asked.

"Not exactly."

Before Marnie could elaborate, the door opened and Cathy Lamb stepped in. A laptop case hung from her shoulder.

"Hi everyone. Cor, there's an unseasonal chill in that wind. Ooh, do I smell coffee?" Anne took her jacket. "I've always thought you make the best coffee in these parts, Marnie."

"Absolutely," said Angela.

"That probably explains why you so often come down trying to arrest me, Cathy." Marnie said light-heartedly.

"Arrest you?" Samira looked puzzled.

Lamb turned towards Samira, noticing her for the first time.

Marnie said, "Let me introduce you to Samira, Samira Khan, my new tenant in cottage number three."

"Hello. I'm Cathy." She held out her hand and they shook. "Cathy Lamb."

"Detective constable Cathy Lamb," Marnie added, setting down the tray on Anne's desk. "Please help yourselves."

Anne brought a knife from the kitchen and began slicing the cake. Marnie poured coffee.

"Where can I set up the computer, Marnie?" Lamb asked. "On your desk?"

"Sure. Why do we need it?"

"I want to show you some CCTV footage from Northampton."

"I thought you wanted to talk about this inter-faith initiative," said Angela.

"I've brought a list of names of people involved. It includes the usual suspects – metaphorically speaking – namely vicars, the odd rabbi, a couple of imams. The idea is that you keep in touch with each other and tell your respective flocks to keep an eye out for any trouble."

Marnie looked thoughtful. "So how are CID involved in a community thing?"

Lamb looked up from the computer. "Vandalism and arson are serious crimes, Marnie. They often provoke violent reactions."

"Are you expecting reprisals for the vandalism and arson attack in town?" Marnie said.

"It's already happening. That's why I want to show you this footage. We're releasing it to the news media, asking for anyone who recognises people on the screen to come forward."

While Lamb fired up the laptop, the others dragged chairs across the room to sit in a semi-circle facing Marnie's desk. They proved to be highly skilled at balancing plates on their laps, nibbling biscuits and Battenberg held in one hand while simultaneously clutching mugs of coffee in the other.

Anne wheeled her desk chair over and placed it near the computer for Cathy Lamb. The latter finished fiddling with the machine and turned to face the others.

"Okay, so here we have a mixture of filming taken from cameras near the town centre. Some of them are a bit blurred, but people should be able to recognise faces and clothing. The footage was taken in broad daylight in the afternoon."

She tapped on the keyboard and a series of images flickered into view, some in colour, some in shades of grey, some in focus, some fuzzy. All of them showed young men, hurrying across the screen. In the background of some sequences a blazing building could be seen. Identifying anybody was made difficult by the fact that they were all wearing hoodies, though in some cases the hoodies slipped off as the young men ran from the scene. While they watched, Lamb gave an intermittent commentary, explaining where the cameras were located.

Marnie was sure she was not the only one of them to notice that all the young men on the screen – some of them seen more than once from different camera angles – were of Asian or Middle Eastern appearance.

Lamb said, "This next lot of film is pretty clear."

The view changed to a high-quality colour scene. As men ran towards the camera they came sharply into focus before flashing past. One of them was struggling to keep his hoodie in place, and it obligingly slid backwards a second or two before he vanished below their field of vision. Moments later the sequence ended and the screen went blank. Lamb leaned over and switched off the computer.

As she did so, her audience felt a chilly draught and all heads turned towards the door. It was half open, swinging gently in the breeze. Anne hurried across to close it. As she did so, Marnie noticed that Samira was no longer in the room.

****

Donovan had opted to miss coffee that morning. He had no desire to cross paths again with DC Lamb. She had in the past tried to get him arrested on suspicion of murder. A prominent far-right politician had been gunned down in the street at an election rally, and Donovan was her prime suspect. Nothing was ever proved, and he always denied it.

While the detective was giving her film show in the office, Donovan was up in Anne's attic room reading a text book for his university course. He was finding it difficult to concentrate on the development of post-war Italian cinema and was curious to know what exactly Cathy Lamb was showing her audience down below. Her commentary was giving tantalising snippets

236

of information: *This is looking towards the hall from the north; these young men seem to have a dark complexion, and they all have beards; we'll get a better view when we see some whose hoodies have slipped.*

After the show had been running for several minutes Donovan thought he heard a gasp. Soundlessly he crept across the room and peered down through the trap-door opening. Cathy Lamb was standing, leaning towards the laptop, her attention focused on its keyboard. The others were still facing towards it, all except for Samira. Wide-eyed and with a hand held up to her mouth, she stood silently and turned to leave. No-one seemed to pay her any attention as she left the office, pulling the door silently behind her. It was only when it swung open that everyone turned to face it. Anne was quickly on her feet, rushing to close it. Turning back, she caught a glimpse of Donovan's face a split second before he withdrew.

From his vantage point at the top of the wall-ladder, he was fleetingly able to see Samira hustling across the courtyard and retreating into her cottage. *Why the escape act?* he asked himself.

****

Lamb folded the laptop shut and slid it into its carrying case. Marnie and Angela were shifting the chairs back to their normal places while Anne was loading the tray with crockery.

"What happened to your friend, your tenant, Marnie?" Lamb asked. "Something scare her off?"

Marnie shrugged. "Probably remembered something she had to do and didn't want to disturb the show, so she just left discreetly. I'll pop over and see her shortly."

"No, don't bother. I'll go."

Marnie tried to look relaxed. "Okay. Thanks for coming. I'm not sure there was much we could do to help with your enquiries."

"Early days, Marnie. Thanks for coffee." She looked across at Anne. "And for cake and biscuits."

Anne smiled back. "Only reason you came. You can't fool us."

"I learnt that long ago, Anne." Lamb turned to Angela and said, "Keep in touch on the inter-faith liaison."

Lamb stepped out into the breezy courtyard and checked the brass numbers on the doors of the cottages. Number three was just opposite. She advanced and pressed the bell. The door eventually opened a crack and one eye looked out.

"Samira, isn't it? Can I come in?"

"What do you want?"

"A word."

The door opened wider and Samira stood aside to show Lamb into the small sitting room just off the hall. She gestured to an armchair but the detective remained standing.

"I didn't get a chance to ask if you recognised anyone before you dashed off," Lamb said in an even tone.

"I, er ... needed to go to the bathroom. I didn't want to interrupt your ..."

"There's a bathroom at the back of the office. I once used it myself."

"There were some things I needed over here," Samira said, looking down.

Cathy looked at her speculatively. "Did you recognise anyone on the screen, Samira?"

"Like you said, most of the images were blurry, and the men were wearing hoodies."

"But not all of it and not all of them."

Samira shook her head. "I didn't."

Lamb reached into a pocket. "Here's my card. Contact me any time if you have any information or anything you want to get off your chest. Okay? My mobile number's on there."

"Thank you, but I hardly think it's likely."

"Believe me, Samira, you never know what's around the corner."

****

The blue Ford Mondeo pulled out of the slip road into the first lane of the motorway. At the wheel, Javid was in a bad mood. He had been in a bad mood since arriving in Britain. That

238

morning he was scowling at the dreary country in which he was obliged to do business and with which so much of his personal life was bound up. He heartily disliked the weather which, even in the supposedly 'merry' month of May, fluctuated as if out of control. One day it would be sunny and almost warm, the next it would be grey and squally or grey and windy or just grey. The relentless cheerfulness of his British business contacts also irked him, opining that if it was rainy one day, it could be bright the next.

Javid knew he had to snap out of this gloom. He had meetings arranged in the cluster of aerospace companies in Hertfordshire. Contracts were at stake; there were deals to be clinched. A positive countenance was needed. But all the while he found his thoughts straying to Samira. It angered him that her family seemed unable to honour the arrangement that had been agreed. It was disgraceful that she should flout the wishes of her parents, as if the family counted for nothing. His feelings for Samira – even after just one sight of her as a grown woman – combined tenderness and annoyance plus, he admitted to himself, a fair degree of lust.

Javid knew he had to tread carefully and not antagonise Samira's family for fear that they might react violently towards their daughter. Although in present circumstances they seemed powerless even to find her. And yet there was one clear link that he could pursue: the sister. She knew how to contact Samira and probably even knew where she was staying. One way or another she had to be persuaded to reveal what she knew. After all, the honour of the family was at stake. Someone in that household had to see sense.

Javid's train of thought was interrupted. The signboard indicating the junction where he had to leave the motorway flashed past, glimpsed fleetingly in a gap between heavy lorries lumbering southwards. Was it the one-mile or the half-mile board? He couldn't risk being stuck in the middle lane and missing his turn-off. He braked and aimed to slot into a space between two juggernauts. For a second he hesitated. Was the gap sufficient to allow him to squeeze in? The car behind him hooted, a long angry blast at his dithering, rushing up to fill his rear-view mirror. He went for the gap. More hooting, this time the deep bellow of a truck horn and the furious flashing of headlamps.

Another signboard loomed up: half a mile to the junction. Javid fumed as he sat in the slow lane with an enormous juggernaut almost attached to his rear bumper.

****

Detective constable Cathy Lamb had only just reached her desk in the CID office when DS Marriner came over.

"I've got a job for you, my girl."

She tried not to wince, roll her eyes or show any sign of irritation at this mode of address. She had known worse, but not usually from him.

"And what's that, sarge?"

"We've had a huge response to the pictures and video that went out this morning."

"What, already?"

"You bet. There's a pile of messages to go through. I think you're going to spend some time on the phone today, checking them out. Lucky you."

"Lucky me," Lamb groaned. "What proportion are likely to be crank calls?"

"Nearly all of them," Marriner said cheerfully. "I'll bring them over."

240

Chapter 23

Pursuit

I t could only be Azim. No-one else phoned that early. Donovan was dozing in the shallows between sleep and waking and reached out from under the duvet to locate the mobile on the bedside table. He could hear Anne breathing rhythmically, and he moved swiftly and smoothly so as not to disturb her. His groping fingers settled on the phone, and he pressed what he hoped was the green button.

"Donovan."

"Good morning. It's Azim. I hope –"

"No, you're fine. How are things?"

"Very well. I wanted to say that my father was really pleased to meet you. He liked you."

"Even though I'm an infidel?"

Azim laughed. "We don't use that word very much. It's not like that film, *Lawrence of Arabia*. We don't have to spit every time we talk to you."

"That's a relief. So what can I do for you?"

"I was hoping we might get together again some time, maybe have coffee or something? Are you coming into town?"

"I am, but it's this morning, so rather short notice."

"This morning would be okay. I have to be at the mosque for prayers later on, but otherwise I can make it. What time are you coming?"

They settled on ten-thirty at a coffee shop in the town centre. Donovan disconnected and quietly replaced the mobile. He had conducted his conversation *sotto voce* and was encouraged that Anne's breathing pattern was unaltered, a steady rhythm of long slow inhalations and exhalations. Slumber. He settled his head gently on the pillow, closed his eyes and breathed in deeply, ready for at least half an hour of snooze before it was time to get up. Donovan was drifting off when a soft voice spoke from the next pillow.

"It could only have been Azim."

241

At that moment, over in the farmhouse, Marnie was turning on the shower. She and Ralph had arrived home at around midnight after a formal dinner at his Oxford college, and had fallen into bed feeling pleasantly drowsy. Despite the late night, Marnie had awoken at her usual time and slipped silently out of bed leaving Ralph still sleeping. There would be much to do that day, designs to complete, clients to see, suppliers to phone. She was thinking about her schedule, revolving under the hot jets, when the shower door opened and Ralph stepped in.

"I didn't like to think of you in here all by yourself. I thought you might like some company."

"Thank you, kind sir. How thoughtful."

"I was thinking we might have a talk."

"I suspected you had an ulterior motive. Were you thinking of anything in particular?"

"Our wedding, actually."

"Really?" Marnie's tone was jagged with suspicion. "Would it be the bit about *With my body I thee worship*, by any chance?"

Her suspicion was not entirely unfounded as Ralph had set about lathering her all over.

"That got me thinking about Samira."

"This is starting to sound kinky," said Marnie. "You're not confessing you've become some kind of perverted deviant, are you?"

Ralph's expression became serious, though significantly his hands did not stop moving.

"It seems to me that this arranged marriage lark must have struck her as really shocking."

Marnie was also doing her fair share of lathering Ralph's body. "What brought this on?" she said.

Ralph looked down. "I'd have thought it was rather obvious," he observed, deadpan.

Marnie gave him an old-fashioned look. "I meant these thoughts about Samira and arranged marriage."

242

"Oh that ... Well, she's obviously an intelligent young woman who wants to succeed in her career, yet once she's been married off, and probably taken to live in Pakistan, she'll always be in the shadow of her husband."

"It sounds quite mediaeval," Marnie said, squeezing more shower gel onto her hand.

"But don't forget," Ralph began. "It isn't all that long ago that the marriage vows in this country included: *love, honour and obey*." He stressed the last word.

"I'm glad you're obviously not thinking of slipping that into our wedding when we manage to get it organised."

"I wouldn't dream of it," Ralph said firmly.

"Pleased to hear it."

"Absolutely. I'm much keener on the *with-my-body-I-thee-worship* bit. Which reminds me. Could I have that shower gel when you've finished with it?"

****

Donovan left Graysons' at ten-twenty and arrived punctually at the coffee shop to find Azim standing by the door with two other young Asian men. Only Azim was wearing the traditional *shalwar kameez*. His friends were both in blue jeans, though all three were wearing parkas with hooded tops, like Donovan himself. The day was overcast and threatening rain. May was proving to be a gloomy month.

Azim introduced Bashir and Muhammad, friends and fellow-students. On entering the café, Azim insisted that Donovan was his guest and asked him to find a table. The coffee shop was crowded, but they were in luck. A group of women were vacating a table, and Bashir quickly took possession of it as they walked out. Azim soon joined the others, carrying a tray.

"You did well to find this table," he said, handing round mugs. "Never seen the place look so full."

Bashir sniggered. "With our looks we'd only have to shout *Allahu Akhbar* and we'd have the choice of any table we wanted."

243

Donovan and Muhammad laughed out loud, but Azim scowled disapprovingly. A moment later his frown turned into a smile.

"Bashir, that was wicked." He wagged his finger but was still smiling.

"I thought it was pretty good," Donovan admitted. "I'll remember it next time I'm in a crowded bar."

Muhammad said, "You might need to get a suntan first and dye your hair."

Very soon the conversation turned to the clean-up works at the mosque and cemetery. Azim asked Donovan about how he and others tackled the vandalism the previous year against the Polish community, but Donovan didn't want to go into detail.

"I don't think there's much similarity," he said. "The Poles were attacked by New Force, you know, the far-right organisation, fascists. I get the impression the trouble we have now is just common-or-garden prejudice carried out by hooligans."

"*We?*" Azim said, with a twinkle in his eye. "You identify with us now, with Islam, even though you have no religious faith?"

"I'm against any violent bigotry or discrimination, and I'm sure this bout of hatred has nothing to do with any other religion."

"They're not Christians, you mean," Muhammad said.

Donovan shook his head. "It's not the crusades all over again. It's just stupid ignorance."

"Yet you fight it on our behalf," Azim said quietly.

Donovan shrugged. "When push comes to shove ..."

When the time came to leave the café they exited to find a squally shower had set in while they were in the warm and dry. They huddled together under the awning, zipping their parkas up to their necks.

"Anyone need a lift?" Donovan said. "I'm parked up the road."

His car was nearest, and they all accepted. They pulled up their hoods against the rain and set off at a steady jog.

Rounding a corner in the pedestrian zone they found themselves confronted by two uniformed police constables.

"Whoa, whoa, what's your hurry?" The officers spread their arms wide, barring their way.

The group skidded to a halt, bumping into each other. Afterwards Donovan thought it was unfortunate that first in line was Azim, conspicuous in his *shalwar kameez*, even under a hoodie. Also unfortunate was the attitude he adopted.

"So where are you lads running to or maybe running *from?*" one of the officers asked.

"We're doing nothing wrong or unlawful," Azim declared. "I don't think you have any right to stop us like this."

"Well, perhaps we ought to discuss that at the station."

Donovan was on the point of pulling down his hood to reveal his non-Asian appearance, when he noticed the other constable looking beyond the group. Donovan turned to see two more officers approaching from behind. The rain now began falling more heavily as the police shepherded their presumed 'suspects' in the direction of the station.

****

It was coffee break time in the office barn. Marnie was alone at her desk when the phone rang.

"Walker and Co, good morning."

"Marnie, hi. It's Cathy Lamb. Got a minute?"

"Sure, but I'm busy meeting a deadline, so I'd be glad if it wasn't much more than that."

"I'll come straight to the point. One of the young men on the CCTV has been identified. We think his name is Tariq Khan. He lives in Luton."

"Uh-huh?"

"Any ideas, Marnie?"

"I don't think I know anyone who lives in Luton."

"Let me repeat. His name is *Khan*. Ring any bells?"

"From what little I know of Luton, Cathy, I'd imagine that name might not be uncommon."

245

"It's not uncommon in Knightly St John these days, either," said Lamb.

"Look, Cathy, I don't want to be difficult but this really isn't anything to do with me and –"

"Do you know if your tenant, Samira *Khan* ..." she stressed the surname, "has a brother or other relative of that name living there?"

"I don't interrogate my tenants about their background."

"Marnie, you saw her reaction when we were viewing the CCTV footage. Didn't it strike you as odd?"

"And didn't you go over to speak to her afterwards, Cathy? You must have a better idea than I do about why she left like that."

"She said she needed to use the loo." Lamb sounded unconvinced.

"That's also not uncommon."

"There's something you're not telling me, Marnie."

"I'm sorry. There's nothing I can add to what you know already."

"Okay, if you say so. I'll let you get back to work."

After disconnecting, Marnie sat for a minute deep in thought. Anne returned to the office carrying an empty tray. She had been taking coffee to the men working in the farmhouse garden.

"Stuck for ideas?" Anne said. "Not like you."

"I'll tell you later." Marnie got up. "I need to have a word with Samira."

"I'll have coffee ready when you get back."

****

Azim spoke rapidly in a whisper. "What should we do, Donovan?"

They were grouped in front of the desk in the police station being booked in by the duty sergeant. Donovan and Azim were standing behind Bashir and Muhammad. The latter was spelling his name slowly and clearly.

"Just tell the truth," Donovan said quietly. "It's always easiest and, in any case, we have nothing to hide. We've done nothing."

"Should I tell them my father's an imam?"

"Sure. It can't do any harm. Just don't be confrontational, okay?"

Azim nodded. After giving names and addresses – Donovan gave his as the narrowboat *Exodos* and explained that it was spelt *XO2* – they were separated and escorted to different rooms for interview. Donovan waited for almost half an hour before the door opened and a man wearing a suit came in. Donovan stood and offered a hand. There was a moment's hesitation before the officer took it.

"I'm detective constable Trentham. What do I call you? You seem to have an unusual assortment of names."

"In Britain I'm always just called Donovan."

"Not Donovan Smith? I notice you specified no hyphen."

"I'm half German, hence Nikolaus. The other half is a mixture of English and Irish. Donovan works well enough in this country."

"Okay, Donovan. Your friend Azim –"

"Before you go on, can I just ask on what basis you're holding us? Clearly we've not been arrested or cautioned or anything like that."

"We just want to ask you a few questions. You must be aware that there are tensions in the town following recent vandalism and arson. My colleagues encountered four young men, apparently Asian, in hoodies running through the streets and naturally became ..."

"Suspicious?" Donovan suggested.

"Let's say *curious*. Why running like that?"

"It was raining," Donovan said in a reasonable tone. "And we were just jogging along."

Trentham nodded, "And no further incidents have been reported today."

"So we're free to go?"

"We have no cause to detain you. Just one thing. Your friend Azim says he first met you recently in a fight."

"He'd gone to the aid of some young Muslim women who were being molested."

"As did you, I gather."

"I couldn't just stand by and let it happen."

"Okay. Can you describe the women?"

Donovan grinned. "This is a joke?"

Trentham was not smiling. "Why would I be joking about such a thing?"

"They were wearing *niqabs*," Donovan said slowly. "You know those tunics? They were covered in black from head to foot with just slits for eyes. So there's my description."

"So how did you know they were *young* women?"

"Their legs looked young."

"You saw their legs even though they were in these *niqab* things?"

"Their assailants lifted their dresses up high. That's why Azim got involved. Me too."

"So you saw their legs. Can you tell me anything else about them?"

Donovan sighed. "They wore clean white knickers."

Trentham leaned forward. "Did you know them?"

"What do you mean?"

"Had you met them before … been on intimate terms with one of them perhaps?"

"Mr Trentham, they were *Muslim* women. We were in a Northampton street in broad daylight. Not exactly the conditions for any kind of relations, let alone *intimate* ones. I do realise you are just winding me up, you know."

Trentham stared at Donovan for a long moment. Then his face relaxed into a smile. "Sure. You're free to go."

Donovan stood and offered his hand again. This time the officer took it without hesitation.

****

Samira was in the kitchen filling the kettle when she heard the doorbell ring. She hurried along the hallway into the sitting room and peeped through the front window. Marnie was on the doorstep looking at her watch. In seconds Samira released the two Chubb bolts, unhooked the security chain, turned the Yale lock and opened the door.

"Marnie, hi. Come in. Is everything all right?"

Marnie made no reply until they were settled in the sitting room.

"Cathy Lamb, the detective, has just been on the phone. She's the one who came to show us the CCTV footage."

"Yes, I know who she is."

"It appears that one young man has been identified, though I'm not sure if they're absolutely *certain* who he is. His name is apparently Tariq Khan. He comes from Luton. Ring any bells?"

Samira stared at Marnie, wide-eyed. "You say they're not certain of his identity, Marnie. Why do you think that?"

"I'm not sure how these things work, but I got the impression Cathy was fishing."

"She was *what*?"

"Testing me to see how I'd react. If she was really convinced who that person was, I reckon she'd have come here straightaway to talk to you."

"Why me?"

"Oh, come on, Samira. Please don't play games. You have a brother, Tariq? He lives in Luton?"

At first there was no reaction, then a slight nod and a reply little more than a murmur. "He's fifteen, Marnie, just a boy. I can't believe he'd commit a crime, certainly not a violent crime. He's not a vandal. We've always been close."

"You recognised him on the CCTV?"

"Is this just between you and me, Marnie ... I mean private and confidential?"

Marnie looked thoughtful. "I'm not sure I can give that sort of guarantee. It's not like I'm bound by the rules of client confidentiality. I think I know what your answer is, so don't say any more."

249

"Why have you come to tell me this, Marnie?"

"I suppose I wanted to warn you that Cathy Lamb is highly suspicious of your brother and you."

"*Me?*"

"I think it's a crime to withhold evidence from the police."

"What if I said I didn't recognise that young man as my brother? The police couldn't *prove* otherwise, could they?"

Marnie shrugged. "It's up to you, Samira. But I'm telling you, just be careful."

After Marnie had left, Samira went through the usual routine of bolting and locking the door. She hated living like that, though she knew that in any other circumstances she would enjoy having such good friends around her, such a pleasant cottage as her home, such a delightful environment. She sat at the kitchen table with a mug of tea and pondered her situation. It was obvious and inevitable what her next action should be. She went upstairs to her bedroom, found the mobile phone and pressed familiar buttons. Rashida answered on the third ring. She sounded breathless as if she had had to hurry upstairs to the privacy of her room to take the call.

Samira brought her sister up to date on everything that had happened, including Marnie's warning.

"Was it Tariq on CCTV?" Rashida asked.

"Yes, but the image wasn't very clear. I could deny recognising him, and they couldn't say I was wrong if I stuck to my guns."

"I think your friend Marnie was right to warn you to be careful."

"I know that. Rashida, I think I should come home, just for a quick visit. I want to talk to Tariq, tell him to keep away from people who are a bad influence."

"No, Samira. Not a good idea. You don't know how he's changed these past few weeks. I'm pretty sure he's been ..." She lowered her voice. "... radicalised."

"What does that mean?"

"I told you. It's like he's been indoctrinated. He thinks we all have to behave in a certain way, like him and his friends, to be true Muslims. You must be careful, Samira, after what you've done. There could be consequences for you."

"You're not saying –"

"I'm not sure what I'm saying. But that little boy who always followed you around like a lamb, he's not the same any more. He's growing up in a way that scares me. I think you should stay away, Samira. Don't come home ... for your own good."

****

Anne was concentrating hard on the phone. She could hardly believe what Donovan was telling her.

"I didn't say I'd been *arrested*, Anne. I was just – *we* were just – asked to go to the police station to answer a few questions. You could see their point."

Anne groaned. "I'm glad you can because I can't. Why should they pick on you? It doesn't seem at all reasonable."

"Look, the two cops saw a group of Muslim men running through the street with hoods up. Remember, there'd been what seemed to be a revenge attack on a church hall just the previous day."

"Muslim?" Anne repeated. "Did you convert recently? Have I missed something?"

"I was behind Azim who was in his fancy gear. They didn't get a proper look at me till we got to the station and took our hoods off. It was raining at the time."

Anne sighed. "So what now?"

"I've dropped the others off at the multi-storey. Azim had parked there. Now I'm heading back. See you in half an hour."

Marnie returned from Samira's cottage as Anne was ending the call. While she was making Marnie's coffee she explained what had happened to Donovan and his new friends. Marnie took the news calmly.

"You know Donovan, Anne. He can certainly fend for himself."

"I suppose so, but I did –"

251

Anne was interrupted by the phone ringing. She went to her desk and picked it up.

"Walker and Co, good –"

"Anne, it's me."

"Hi, Donovan. Everything all right?"

"Sure. Er, listen. I've got to make a detour. I may be delayed a bit. I'll be back as soon as I can."

"What detour? Where?"

"Can't stop. The lights are changing. See you when I see you."

The line went dead. Anne put the phone down and relayed the conversation to Marnie.

"What d'you make of that?" she asked.

Marnie shrugged. "I wouldn't worry about it." She smiled. "That's Donovan for you, our man of mystery."

✱✱✱✱✱✱✱

Donovan pressed the red button, dropped the mobile onto the passenger seat and engaged first gear. His eyes strayed to the rear-view mirror. There it was again, four cars back in the queue at the traffic lights. How popular was metallic blue for the Ford Mondeo? Was this a coincidence or was it the same car that had been following him and Samira on Tuesday? If that was the case, although Donovan might entertain some doubts on his side, the driver of the Mondeo could have little uncertainty about the black 1970s VW Beetle. It must be the most conspicuous car on the road.

Donovan considered his options. Ahead lay the main road south out of town. In a mile he would reach the roundabout on the southern ring road where he would normally turn right and travel westbound to meet the A43 dual carriageway, direction Towcester / Oxford. The Mondeo driver might expect that from past experience and certainly had the power to keep the Beetle in his sights. Donovan could be leading him straight to Samira's door.

Donovan changed down to third for the run up the hill past Delapre Abbey but, instead of hugging the right-hand lane, he

252

stayed in the middle and followed the road round to continue southbound.

Donovan stayed in the nearside lane after the roundabout and pushed the Beetle up to seventy. That was the speed limit, but there was no shortage of cars and vans lining up to overtake him. The blue Mondeo was not one of them. It maintained a gap of around a hundred metres all the way down to the next junction, another large roundabout, this time connecting with the M1 motorway. Donovan slipped into the left-hand lane signposted M1 South / London. As he expected, the Mondeo moved into the same lane just as the lights turned to green.

Donovan accelerated up to seventy again and kept to the left-hand lane. His plan had worked so far, but he knew that fate had not dealt him the best hand. He was in an under-powered machine more than twenty years old, and the route he had chosen for his getaway offered no scope for changing direction, at least none that he could attempt without being seen. And if he did try to be creative – such as taking an exit road and then driving straight back down onto the motorway – he would reveal that he knew he was being followed. That might lead to all sorts of complications.

There was nothing for it but to sit back, maintain a steady rate of knots and see what happened.

After fifteen minutes he saw the one-mile sign for the turn-off to Milton Keynes. Worth a try? On balance, Donovan thought not. The self-proclaimed New City was a grid-work of dual carriageways and roundabouts offering little chance of losing his tail. He pressed on. The Mondeo followed.

Another junction, same result. Then another. No change. Hare and hound continued their procession. Donovan was starting to think he'd be travelling all the way to London and was working out a route through the great city that would enable him to lose the Mondeo without making it too obvious.

He had formed a mental image, turning onto the North Circular Road and heading into the maze of curving streets through Hampstead Garden Suburb when a new signboard loomed up: the first junction for Luton. The name brought his mind back to Samira. Somewhere in that town her family was worrying about her. From the day she had come to Knightly St John she had transformed their lives, turned them on their head. Now here he was forming plans to escape some phantom stalker that he didn't know and who certainly didn't know him.

And then quite suddenly everything changed.

Slow lorries rolling down the slip road to join the motorway pushed Donovan into the middle lane. He flashed a quick glance in the mirror to check there was a gap in the flow and caught sight of the blue Mondeo peeling off to take the exit road. His first thought was: bluff! The Mondeo driver was testing him. He would leave the motorway, go up and over the roundabout and drive back down to press on in the same direction as before. He would creep gradually close enough to observe the Beetle, hoping that his prey would have relaxed and dropped his guard.

But no.

Donovan stayed out in the middle lane, cruising past a procession of lorries. From there he could observe the highway for a fair distance behind. He studied the mirror as closely as conditions permitted. There was no metallic blue Mondeo, of that he felt certain. He was still working out a plan when the next junction came and went, the turn-off for Luton airport.

The Beetle was designed to cruise all day in fourth gear at its top speed of around seventy-six miles per hour. When Donovan came up behind a gaggle of cars travelling a shade slower, he pulled into the outside lane and pushed the accelerator to the floor. The car responded willingly despite its not inconsiderable age and burbled along merrily, gobbling up the other vehicles. A quick glance in the mirror revealed two things. The first was a BMW racing up behind him at tremendous speed. The second was a clear view of much of the traffic behind. There was no blue Mondeo.

Turning his gaze rapidly ahead, Donovan saw a road sign, another junction a mile off. He signalled to move over, just when the BMW driver angrily flashed his headlights. Donovan pulled into a gap and kept up the momentum to reach the nearside lane as the half-mile sign shot past. Now the choice was either to turn through one-eighty degrees on the roundabout and head north back up the motorway or travel across country and find an overland route to Knightly St John.

He chose the old Roman road, Watling Street, the A5, which would lead him back to Milton Keynes. It would be slow but steady. Donovan was past caring. The hare had already outrun – and outfoxed – the hound.

****

Javid was fuming. It seemed to be his default setting ever since he came to this wretched country. Everything and everyone conspired against him. If it was not for the vision of the beautiful young woman who had been promised to him in marriage, he would quickly conclude his business and fly back to Pakistan.

He had wasted his time following a car that he had convinced himself was the one in which he had seen Samira riding a few days ago. Instead it was going in a completely different direction, obviously heading for London. Another waste of his valuable time. Perhaps those old Beetle cars were more common in Britain than he realised.

Seeing a sign to Luton on the motorway, Javid gave up the fruitless pursuit. His patience at an end, he would go to the Khans' house and have it out with them. He would demand that they find Samira and make her honour their obligation. The other daughter must surely know her sister's whereabouts; he had seen them together in Northampton. It was time for a showdown.

****

Anne was thinking about lunch. It had been a strange morning. First, there was Donovan's call from Azim leading to their meeting in Northampton. Then Cathy Lamb trying to get information out of Marnie, followed by Donovan's sudden change of plan to make a mysterious 'detour' on his way back from police custody. How they were supposed to run a business when all this was going on, she had no idea. At the front of the office Marnie was working on a design project, deep in her usual concentration. Anne was loath to interrupt her but noon had already come and gone, and an urgent decision was required about a matter of importance.

"Marnie?"

No reaction.

"Earth to Marnie, Earth to Marnie, are you receiving me? Come in, please. Over."

Still nothing. Anne was about to pick up the phone to call her when it started ringing. Absent-mindedly Marnie's hand began reaching slowly towards the receiver. Anne beat her to it.

"Walker and Co, good –"

"It's me, Anne."

"Donovan, where are you? What's going on?"

"Tell you later. Is Samira at home?"

"I suppose so. We haven't seen her. Why d'you ask?"

"Things are developing. It's important she stays put."

"What things? Look, Donovan, you can't just keep us in the dark like this. You're obviously worried about something. Spill the beans."

"Yeah, okay. I was followed by what I think was the same car that followed Samira and me the other day."

"How did that happen? I mean, how did he know where to find you?"

"He must have been cruising around on the off-chance. Just bad luck. I've got rid of him and I'm on my way back."

"Got rid of him?" Anne's voice was edged with suspicion.

"Not like that. He just sort of gave up and went his own way."

"So where are you now?"

"MK in a lay-by. I'll be back in twenty minutes."

"We'll expect you for lunch."

Anne disconnected and looked up to find Marnie standing by her desk.

"Did you get any of that?" Anne asked.

"Spell it out for me."

Anne outlined the conversation. Marnie sat on the edge of the desk, lost in her thoughts. Eventually she spoke.

"If he's so close, why did he bother phoning?"

Anne suggested, "First opportunity to pull over and use the mobile?"

Marnie looked unconvinced. "How did he sound?"

"Same as always: calm, unfazed. You know Donovan."

Marnie stood abruptly and headed for the door. "Even so, not like him to fret. I'm going to check Samira's in the cottage."

"Shall I start to organise lunch?" Anne asked.

Marnie stopped by the door. She nodded. "Make it for four."

"You're inviting Samira?" Anne said.

Marnie pulled the door open. "Best way to keep an eye on her."

"You're worried too?"

"No, it's nothing," Marnie said. "Just … paranoia. My default setting these days."

****

Drizzle was falling again by the time Donovan made it back to Glebe Farm. He gave a brief account of his morning while they laid the table. Marnie was convinced he was playing things down so as not to alarm Samira. She was also convinced that his stratagem was not successful.

They were all glad to be having lunch by the Aga, though two of them seemed less than enthralled. Samira was on edge, as usual, and seemed constantly on the brink of speaking. She said nothing but focused distractedly on cheese and biscuits. Donovan was half-heartedly working on a bowl of soup while consulting his filofax. He was also frowning.

"What's up, Donovan? Problem?" Marnie asked.

He groaned. "I knew there was something I had to do."

"Work for college?" Anne suggested.

"Nothing so simple. *Exodos* is booked in at the boatyard next week: safety certificate inspection and hull blacking."

257

Samira looked up. "For what? Blacking?"

"The hull has to be reblacked."

"Can't you do it here?"

Marnie said, "You have to book well in advance. You see, the boat has to go into a dry dock or be craned out of the water so that the hull is exposed and dry."

"So what's the problem?"

Donovan shook his head. "It's not so much a problem. It's just that *Exodos* has to be down in London at the boatyard by the end of next week. She has to be inspected and passed by the engineer. Without that I could lose my boat licence."

"Can you get there in time?"

"If I leave soon. The thing is, I wanted the boat to be here in case you needed it again, Samira. I should've thought."

"Don't worry," Marnie said. "You've got to get those things done. They're important. We're here for Samira."

Anne asked, "When are you thinking of setting off?"

"We sail on the morning tide." Donovan's expression was deadpan.

"*Tide?*" Samira said.

Anne rolled her eyes. "It's okay, Samira. He's just gone into U-boat mode again."

Chapter 24

Bashir

The normal Saturday morning routine of Walker and Co, design consultants, was interrupted by preparations for Donovan's departure. Straight after breakfast Marnie and Anne made *Sally Ann* ready to take Donovan on the first leg of his journey. Ralph decided to tag along for the tootle north up the canal to rendez-vous with *XO2*.

Sally Ann slipped her mooring with Marnie at the tiller at around eight-thirty. With the engine rumbling beneath their feet, the crew of four stood together on the stern deck under lowering clouds. As the boat passed beneath the nearby accommodation bridge, they took stock of their surroundings. In the fields on either side of the canal sheep and cows were nibbling wet grass. The air smelled of damp vegetation, and there were puddles on the towpath. At least the air was mild.

After cruising for half an hour Anne called out. "I can see *Exodos*! Look there, under the willows."

Marnie parked *Sally Ann* alongside *XO2*, and Donovan heaved his bags across from one boat to the other. From there the crews split up. Marnie and Ralph decided to turn and head back to base where work awaited them. Anne opted to travel down with Donovan as far as Cosgrove lock. From there she could walk back to Glebe Farm in little more than twenty minutes.

Donovan reversed out from the willow-cave while Anne heaved firmly against the bank with the barge pole to push the stern free across the canal. With the prow nudging the water's edge, Donovan pressed down the accelerator and threw the tiller hard over. Pivoting from the bows, the boat swung in an arc until the stern was pointing northwards. In the distance Anne could see *Sally Ann* vanishing from sight, rounding a bend on her homeward run. With fluid movements Donovan slipped the gear lever into neutral then reverse. Drifting back to within a yard of the bank, he engaged forward gear and accelerated, leaning on the tiller to bring the boat round in

259

mid-channel, pointing to the south. The whole manoeuvre had taken barely a minute. They were underway.

With no locks ahead for the next forty-five minutes or so, Anne went down into the cabin. She emerged soon afterwards with mugs of Donovan's German coffee and a packet of half-chocolate Leibniz biscuits.

"It really is just like being on a U-boat here," she observed, passing a mug to Donovan.

"I don't think the U-boat service went in for *Jakobs Kaffee* and *Bahlsen Choco Leibniz* biscuits," Donovan said in a neutral tone. He added, "And it probably wouldn't work to try to submerge in these waters."

Anne stuck out her tongue. "I wouldn't put it past you to try."

"Nonsense," Donovan's expression was serious. "I'd never get the periscope to function."

Anne's tongue returned and blew an enthusiastic raspberry.

When they reached Glebe Farm they saw *Sally Ann* safely installed in her dock. Donovan asked if Anne wanted to change her mind and disembark, but she chose to stay aboard as far as Cosgrove lock. Twenty minutes later the lock-beams came into view. With a routine born of much practice they swung into action; Anne drove *XO2* into the lock while Donovan dealt with the gates and paddles. They were through and down to the lower level in fifteen minutes. With promises to keep in touch by mobile every night, they kissed and parted company. Anne waved Donovan off and climbed the steps to the side of the lock chamber to begin the walk home.

The weather stayed dry, though there were still random puddles along the towpath. Anne needed to watch where she trod, which distracted her from noticing the men until they were no more than twenty-five yards away. Looking up from the ground, she hesitated in mid-step and almost over-balanced.

"Careful!" one of the men called out. "Don't want to end up in the drink."

His companion laughed. They continued walking towards her at a steady pace. Both men were wearing woodland pattern camouflage gear with field glasses slung round their necks. Anne froze. There was nowhere to hide.

****

It occurred to Marnie afterwards that Samira must have been looking out for her. She had barely had time to turn on her desk lamp and switch on the computer when she heard a knock on the door and Samira stepped in. She was opening her mouth to speak when she noticed Ralph filling the kettle in the kitchen area at the back of the office.

"Oh sorry. I didn't see you – I mean I didn't know you were here … didn't mean to intrude."

"That's okay," Marnie said. "Come in."

"Would you like coffee or perhaps tea?" Ralph asked.

Samira hesitated on the threshold. "Er, I …"

"Did you want to speak to Marnie in private? I can easily trot off to *Thyrsis*."

"No, it's just –"

"Why don't you just come in, Samira. I'm sitting in a draught here."

"Sorry, Marnie."

Samira came in and closed the door behind her. Marnie waved her to a chair, and Ralph repeated his offer.

"Tea would be lovely, thanks."

"So what can I do for you?" Marnie asked.

Samira looked down at her lap and replied in a quiet voice. "I'm very worried about Tariq, my brother. I don't know what to do about him."

Marnie said, "Is there something we can do to help or do you just want to talk about it?"

No reply. Samira was struggling for words.

"Can you tell us what the problem is?" Marnie prompted. "Is it to do with the CCTV images?"

Samira looked up, her expression desolate. "My sister, Rashida, thinks he may have been … radicalised."

261

Ralph walked over with a tray. "How old is your brother?"

"Fifteen. He's the youngest in the family."

"And what do you have in mind?"

Samira sighed. "I was thinking ... perhaps I could just go and talk to him."

Ralph passed round the mugs of coffee. He said, "Do you think going to see Tariq would be wise?"

"Tariq and I have always been close, Ralph, ever since he was little."

"But if, as you say, he's become extreme in his attitudes, might that not apply also to your behaviour?"

Samira raised a hand to her mouth. "You're saying you think he might do me harm or even ...?"

Marnie interrupted. "I don't think Ralph is suggesting anything sinister, but don't you think your brother might be – how can I put it? – *disturbed* by your actions of late? From what you're telling us, he's hardly going to approve, is he?"

Ralph said, "I'm not sure we're being much help, are we? You say you want to talk to him. What does your sister think of the idea?"

"Rashida? She's dead against it."

Unfortunate choice of words, Marnie thought.

****

Anne turned sharply to make a run for it. If she could outpace the men as far as the lock she might be able to attract Donovan's attention and –

Splat!

Her feet slithered on the muddy ground, and she fell forward to land flat on her face. Another few inches and she'd be drinking a puddle. Struggling to get to her feet, Anne heard hurried footsteps behind her. A moment later strong hands fastened round her arms and she was hauled upright. She found herself looking into the faces of two middle-aged men whose expressions revealed nothing but concern. They released their grip.

"Are you okay, love?" one of them said.

"Apart from feeling really stupid ..." Anne began.

"Sorry if we alarmed you," the other one joined in.

He reached into a back pocket. Anne watched him warily, but he pulled out a large cotton handkerchief, pristine and white, and held it out to her.

"It's all right," he said. "It is clean. I haven't used it."

Anne took it meekly and stared at it for several seconds.

The first man said, "You might want to ..." He indicated her jacket.

Anne gazed down at her clothes. The man had a point. She looked like a contestant in a mud-wrestling competition.

"I couldn't possibly." She passed the handkerchief back to its owner. "It'd make a mess of your hanky. It's only mud on my clothes. I'll brush it off when it dries and put them in the washer. Thanks, anyway."

"We really didn't mean to startle you."

"I'm sure you didn't. It was just a shock seeing you again like that."

"*Again*? You've seen us before?"

Anne wondered if she had said too much. "Sorry, a slip of the tongue."

"Where did you see us?" the first man asked.

Anne pointed over her shoulder. "There's a spinney about a mile that way on the opposite side of the canal near an accommodation bridge. Weren't you there a short while back?"

They nodded. The first man said, "We were. Do you know who owns it?"

"You wanted to know who owns it?"

The man's eagerness shone through. "Perhaps I should explain. We're part of the CBS."

"The record company?"

They both looked bewildered. The first man said, "The County Birdwatching Scheme. You've probably heard of it."

"I don't quite see what it has to do with ... Ah ... you mean you were looking for birds?"

"Not really. We're looking for places to set up CCTV cameras for observations. It's part of a year-long project to record bird life all over the county."

"And that's why you were in the spinney?"

"It would be ideal, only there were no signs up to say whose it was. We've started making enquiries about various sites, but it's not easy."

It was Anne's turn to reach into her back pocket. She drew out a business card and offered it to the man who was still holding the handkerchief.

"That's the number you should ring. Ask for Marnie Walker. You need to speak to her. Now, if you'll excuse me, I'd better go home and get out of these muddy clothes."

With that, Anne turned and headed back along the towpath. Watching her go, the men in camouflage gear had the strange impression that they heard laughter.

****

Samira finished her tea and put the mug down on the desk. There was silence in the office. Marnie and Ralph were staring at her, wondering what they could say to lighten her mood. Samira sat with her gaze averted. It was an awkward moment.

"I'm sorry," Samira said. "I shouldn't burden you with my problems. You've been so good to me."

Marnie said, "It's not the problems that concern us – well, they do obviously cause us concern – but our inability to do anything to help."

As Marnie was speaking a sudden movement distracted her at the edge of her field of vision. Someone had walked briskly past the office window. A moment later the door opened and Anne came in. She looked as if she had crawled back through a field of mud. For all that, her expression was cheerful, even elated. She was grinning, seemingly unaware of the mud attached to her chin.

"Hi everyone," she chirped. "I'm back, and I bring good news."

"You've discovered the world's biggest chocolate cake?" Marnie suggested.

Anne looked down at her clothes. "What? Oh well, yes, sort of. I did have a mild *contretemps* on the way home."

"So what's the good news?" Ralph asked.

"I ran into the men in camouflage gear who were in the spinney that day. You remember – the ones that Donovan spotted?"

"*Ran* into?" Marnie said. "At speed, judging by your appearance."

Anne rubbed her chin. "That was running *from*, so to say."

"Why?" Samira spoke for the first time. "What were they doing?"

"It's all completely innocent. Donovan was right. They were twitchers."

Samira looked horrified. "They were *what?*"

"Birdwatchers," Ralph explained. "You spoke to them, Anne?"

Anne gave a potted version of her conversation on the towpath, ending with, "I hope you don't mind, Marnie. I gave them a business card and said they had to get permission from you."

Marnie nodded. "That's okay. Can't do any harm."

"I'd better go and change," Anne said. "All right if I hang my muddy things in front of the Aga to dry?"

"Sure."

They stared for a moment at Anne's mud-smeared clothing, all except for Samira who appeared to have lost interest in the subject. Marnie hoped that Anne's news about the watchers in the spinney might reassure Samira. But no. When Anne turned towards the wall-ladder to climb up to her attic room, Samira excused herself and headed back to the cottage, preoccupied as ever.

****

The blue Ford Mondeo rolled slowly along the quiet suburban street In Luton. Javid was still seething with pent-up anger

265

after the frustrations of that morning and he was absolutely ready to off-load it all on the Khan family. He would demand that they take every action necessary to bring their outrageous daughter to heel. She was promised as his bride and that was an end to it. If they failed at this point to meet their obligations, they would not only bring dishonour to both their families, but would bring total disgrace down on them all.

He was musing in this way when he caught sight of a car in front of the Khans' house. The car had blue and yellow squares on the side, red and yellow chevrons at the rear and other markings on the roof. When he saw the word POLICE in large letters he braked heavily and almost stalled the engine. Quickly gathering his wits, he changed down into first and accelerated as unobtrusively as he could towards the end of the street. There he turned the car round and parked in a spot where he could watch from a discreet distance.

Minutes passed slowly. More than half an hour elapsed before the front door opened and two uniformed police officers appeared, one man, one woman. They climbed into the car and pulled away from the kerb. Javid slid down in the seat as they came by. When he heard the engine sound die away, he wriggled himself upright and turned the ignition key. He had barely reached third gear when he arrived at the short path to the Khans' front door.

In response to his ringing of the doorbell, Rashida appeared. She looked flustered. Javid spoke without preamble.

"I've come to see your parents."

He made as if to step forward, and was surprised when Rashida did not move aside.

She shook her head. "No."

"*No?*" This was outrageous. Had this entire family lost its collective mind? "What do you mean – *no?*"

"Not a good time, sorry. My parents have just had the police here. They're both very distraught."

"Why?"

"It was a really upsetting experience."

Javid was losing his patience. "I meant why were the police here? What's going on?"

Rashida hesitated. "I don't know if I can –"

"Look, Rashida. We are almost family. You can *certainly* tell me what has happened."

Rashida looked over her shoulder and replied in a quiet voice. "It was on account of my brother."

"Go on."

"Did you know there was an arson attack in Northampton the other day ... a church hall or something?"

"What does that have to do with your brother?"

"He ... he ... well, it seems he looked like someone spotted on a security camera, running away from the scene."

"The police suspect him?" Javid was mortified. "Have they charged him?"

"No, no. The picture wasn't clear enough to be certain. He denied that it was him."

"Why did the police think it might be your brother in the first place?"

"I can't say any more."

Rashida made to shut the door, but Javid was too quick for her. Rashida sighed, looked over her shoulder again and muttered, "We're all worried that he's becoming extreme in his views."

"What views?"

"About religious matters."

"I see. Where is he now?"

"Father sent him to his room."

"What is his name, your brother?"

"Tariq."

Rashida waited for the next question but it didn't come. Instead, Javid looked thoughtful. Eventually he said, "Tell your parents I was here and I will return."

"When?"

"Soon."

Javid turned abruptly, went back to the car and drove away. Rashida closed the door quietly and climbed the stairs to her room. So it was that she didn't see the blue Mondeo come to a halt at the end of the street. Javid adjusted the rear-view mirror so that he could see down the road all the way to the Khans' house. He sat and waited, biding his time.

****

Anne climbed down the wall-ladder with a duffel bag slung over one shoulder. She had changed into pale blue jeans and a white sweatshirt. Ralph had gone back to *Thyrsis* to work on his new book, leaving Marnie engrossed in a scheme design for a country pub. She looked round as Anne's feet touched the floor.

"You've put your mucky clothes in that nice duffel?"

"Yes, but they're in a plastic bin liner. It'll be all right."

"Good thinking, Batman."

The phone began ringing. Marnie picked it up.

"Walker and Co, good —"

"It's me, Marnie. Just heard something on the news: more trouble in Northampton."

Seeing Marnie's expression cloud over, Anne came and stood beside her.

"What kind of trouble, Ralph?" Marnie asked.

"I only caught the tail end of the bulletin, but I gather someone has been attacked and ended up in hospital. It was a young Muslim man, as far as I could tell."

"Any other details?"

"None that I heard."

"So you don't know how badly injured he was."

"No. Probably worth catching the lunchtime news on local radio."

Marnie glanced up at the office clock and sighed. "This is just what we need."

When they ended the call Anne said, "Should I tell Donovan?"

Marnie shrugged. "Not much he can do about it. He's well on his way south by now."

Anne said, "I was just thinking it might be someone he knows. He has such a lot to do with that community these days."

Marnie sat back in her chair. "True, but Northampton's hardly a small village, is it? Chances are, the person attacked will be a complete stranger."

But she was wrong.

****

Javid was aching with impatience. Everything he did that day seemed to backfire. Now he was sitting in a hired car, staring into a mirror in a street of no character or prestige, and he had no certainty of any likely result that would improve matters. Yet what else could he do? The more he thought about it, the less sure he was that Samira was now even the right woman for him. He had seen her in the company of another man, someone obviously not suitable for her in any way. What was she thinking of?

Javid's thoughts were wandering. His mind was wandering. His eyes were –

What was that?

He sat up in the seat. In the distance, back down the street, there was movement. Someone was coming out of the Khans' front door. Could he be sure of that? Javid strained his eyes. Yes, a young man, a teenager, was leaving their house. Javid watched as the boy turned and began walking in his direction. Was there more than one brother? No. Rashida had simply said 'my brother', and he took it to mean she had only one. At last something was going right that day.

As Javid watched in the mirror the boy – what was his name? Yes, Tariq – left the pavement behind the Mondeo and began crossing the road. He was halfway across when Javid lowered his side window and called out.

"Hello! Are you Tariq?"

The boy stopped and looked at Javid without speaking.

"You are Tariq, Tariq Khan?"

"Who are you?" Tariq said, his tone wary.

"My name is Javid Shah. I am to marry your sister."

"My sister?"

"Samira."

"What are you doing out here?" Tariq asked.

"I was hoping to have a word with you. Do you have a minute?"

"I'm on my way to see some friends."

"I won't keep you long," Javid said.

A car had turned into the street from the far end and was coming towards them. It was a moment of decision for Tariq. He had to decide which way to turn. After some hesitation he walked back and came round the front of the Mondeo. Javid stretched across and opened the passenger door. Tariq climbed in. Javid offered a hand and they shook.

"I'm very pleased to meet you, Tariq."

"What do you want to talk to me about?" Tariq asked.

"Samira, of course." He smiled. "Do you feel like a cup of tea?"

****

It was no good. Marnie couldn't bring herself to wait until the lunchtime news on local radio. From the other side of the office Anne could sense Marnie's impatience.

"Do you think it's likely to wear out?" Anne asked.

Marnie stared across at her, uncomprehending. "Mm? Do I think what's likely to wear out?"

"The clock." Anne indicated the wall clock with a nod of her head.

Marnie frowned. "Don't know why it should. It's a good make and we've only had it ..." Light dawned. She sighed. "You're such a joker."

"Well, the number of times you've looked up at it, it's a wonder the surface hasn't worn away or the hands dropped off."

"It's just that —"

"I know, Marnie. You don't have to tell me. I keep thinking about it too."

270

"The Muslim guy who was attacked?" Marnie said.

"Yeah. How can we find out who it was?"

Marnie shook her head. "I'm not phoning Cathy Lamb."

Anne looked thoughtful. "No, of course not. Who else might know?"

"We could try Angela. She always knows what's going on from her contacts."

"Good idea."

Marnie reached for the phone, but Angela beat her to it. It had hardly begun to ring when Marnie picked it up.

"Walker and Co, good morning."

"It's Angela, Marnie. Have you heard the news?"

"Try me."

"A young man has been attacked in Northampton. I was wondering if he might be a friend of Donovan."

"Did you get a name?"

"I think he's called something like Bashir ... not sure if that's the right pronunciation, but that's what it sounded like."

Marnie relayed this across to Anne. She nodded and mouthed 'yes'.

"Anne recognises that name, Angela. Did you gather what condition he's in?"

"Fairly knocked about, I think. Is Donovan still with you?"

"On his way back to London by boat. We'll let him know, though there's not much he can do about it."

But Marnie was wrong again.

****

Tariq suggested a café on the other side of Luton. It was located in a street full of Asian-owned businesses. It took Javid a while to find a parking space, and they had to walk some way past shops selling saris, materials in exotic designs and colours and food from India, Pakistan and Bangladesh. The café was not quite up to the standard to which Javid was accustomed, but they had no trouble finding a table for two, and the tea was good. Javid offered spiced cake, but Tariq declined. He knew of Javid, in the sense that he had heard his name mentioned at home, usually in hushed tones, but they had never met before. It was the first time he had heard that Samira was to marry this man, and he was intrigued.

"So what do you want from me, Mr Shah?" he asked.

"I want you to help me find Samira. And it's Javid."

"How do you think I can do that? She's run away. I have no idea where she is. Neither do my family, as far as I know."

"Were you aware that we are to be married?"

"No."

"It was arranged a long time ago. How old are you?"

"Fifteen."

Javid nodded thoughtfully. "It was around the time you were born."

Tariq too was thoughtful. "Samira is nine years older than me. She must have been very young when this promise was made."

"She was eight, and I was about your age. That is how such things are arranged between families. You must know this."

"Yes."

"And you know that this is an ancient tradition in our community."

"Yes."

"Do you agree that it's right?"

Tariq paused for thought. "It's how our society has worked for a long time."

"So you do agree?"

"I agree that a daughter should do what the family wants, especially if it's been agreed with another family."

Javid nodded again. "Good. You must see that if a daughter doesn't comply with the wishes of the families involved then she could bring dishonour by her actions."

"That's how it would look," Tariq said.

"*Great* dishonour!" Javid said.

To emphasise the point he slammed his fist down on the table. The gesture was possibly stronger than intended. It caused other customers to turn and stare at him and made

Tariq wince in surprise. To cover his feelings Tariq took a sip from his cup. Over the top of it he gazed speculatively at Javid.

"I don't know how I can help you, Javid."

"Tariq, do you have your own mobile phone?"

"Yes."

Javid took a business card from a pocket and slid it across the table. Tariq picked it up. The writing on one side was in Urdu, on the other it was in English.

"There is my mobile number," Javid said. "Think about what I've said and ring me. Make it soon. I need your help."

Tariq looked puzzled. "There's no way I know of finding out where Samira is living."

"Oh, but there is a way," Javid insisted.

"How?"

"You can find out from your sister."

"My sister?"

"Rashida knows. She can lead you – and me – to Samira."

****

Donovan had set himself the ambitious target of reaching Leighton Buzzard on the first night of his journey south. It was well after sunset before he found a mooring and tied up, too weary by then to think of preparing a meal. He stepped down into the cabin, poured himself a measure of *Asbach Uralt* German brandy, flopped down on the banquette and reached for his mobile. He pressed the buttons for a number he knew by heart.

"Hi," Anne said. "Had a good journey?"

"Yeah, but I'm bushed. Know any good places to eat in Leighton Buzzard?"

"You've got that far?" Anne sounded incredulous. "I don't believe it."

"Yep. So now I need to grab a meal."

"There's a chippy on the Linslade side of the canal, that's the west bank."

"Any good?"

"My brother's favourite."

"Problem solved."

"Er, Donovan, listen. One of your chums – a guy called something like Bashir? – he's been attacked."

Donovan sat up straight. "Bashir? How bad?"

"Concussion, damaged ribs, lacerations. The news said violence was breaking out all over Northampton."

"Damn! I'd better get back. Can you come and fetch me?"

"Are you sure? There's not much you can do."

"I can't ignore what's going on."

A pause.

"Okay. I'll come for you in the morning. Nine o'clock okay?"

"Fine."

"Now get some rest and go find that chippy."

Chapter 25

Luger

Donovan stood on the bridge over the canal at Leighton Buzzard under a heavy sky that Sunday morning. From there he had the best view of the road in both directions. Watching out for Anne's red Mini, he was surprised when a Freelander flashed its headlights and came past. Marnie was at the wheel and she was travelling alone. The car pulled into the kerb a short distance beyond the bridge, with hazard warning lights flashing. Donovan jogged along and climbed in beside Marnie. He fastened his seat belt, clutching the rucksack on his lap.

Marnie smiled at him. "Did you manage to get a good night's sleep?"

"Certainly did. Out like a light."

There was hardly any traffic on the road. Marnie pulled an unhurried U-turn and headed back the way she had come.

"I was surprised to see you," Donovan said. "Is Anne all right?"

"She's fine. I came because I want to have a talk with you."

"Okay."

Marnie negotiated a roundabout and turned towards the by-pass. She waited until they were settled on the main road before she spoke again.

"I can understand why you want to get back to see your injured friend."

"Have you any more news about him?"

"Not so far. It's a worrying time."

Donovan said, "That's for sure. I'm worried about Bashir; you're worried about Samira."

Marnie sighed. "I thought we were *all* worried about Samira."

"Preoccupied," Donovan suggested.

Marnie glanced quickly sideways. "I'm worried about you too, Donovan. I have to say I think you should be very wary of getting drawn into this conflict involving your Muslim chums. I know you get on really well but the situation's dangerous and could get worse."

"I realise that, Marnie. Do you remember when I first came up here?"

"Of course. You wanted to take direct action against the neo-Nazis."

"And for a time you all thought I was one myself."

Marnie said, "Well, you did look the part." She laughed. "Come to think of it, you still do."

Donovan looked down at his black bomber jacket, black jeans and lightweight black boots. His rucksack was the same colour. They all contrasted starkly with his light complexion and short blonde hair.

"I came up that time because I thought it was important to fight extremism and prejudice. Remember, my own German family was persecuted by the Nazis."

"Would you feel the same animosity towards Muslim extremists?"

"If they were violent, sure. But Azim and his friends aren't at all like that. They just want to live normal lives in peace."

Marnie nodded. "I can see that, but Donovan, please be careful." She smiled at him. "Can you manage to do that?"

He smiled back. "I'll try."

They were making good progress in light traffic as they approached the Milton Keynes ring road. Donovan watched the miles tick by, wondering what awaited him back at Glebe Farm. He knew he would try to take care, but being careful wasn't always an option, wasn't always enough. As he sat holding his rucksack he was absent-mindedly running the side of his thumb up and down a bulge in its side.

****

Unlike many boys of his age Tariq was not a late riser even at weekends. No Sunday lie-in for him, especially since his new-found zeal for spiritual matters. When he came down to the kitchen that morning his parents had already eaten, and only Rashida was still at the table. This suited him well; he had a lot on his mind, and he suspected that only Rashida could answer his questions. She looked up as he entered.

"Hi," she said. "You'll probably have to boil the kettle for a fresh pot of tea."

"No problem. How's the revision going?"

Rashida shrugged. "Oh, you know ..."

"You're lucky. You'll have finished all your exams before mine even get started."

Tariq filled the kettle and lit the gas. While he was waiting for it to boil, he poured cornflakes into a bowl and went to the fridge for milk. He looked back at his sister. As usual she had her nose in a book.

"Rashida?"

"Mm?" She did not look up.

"I want to ask you something." His tone was serious.

Rashida raised her eyes. "What?"

He lowered his voice. "Do you know where Samira's living?"

"Why are you asking me that?"

"Do you?"

She shook her head. "No."

"I met Javid Shah yesterday. He thinks you do know where she is."

"How did you meet him?"

"It doesn't matter. I just did. He says you know more than you're letting on."

"Well he's wrong."

"He said –"

The kettle began whistling. For a few minutes Tariq occupied himself with making tea. He poured milk into his cereal bowl and took a seat opposite Rashida. She had returned to her reading, but now looked up again.

"I don't care what Javid Shah said. I don't know where Samira's staying. End of."

"Javid said he'd seen you both together in Northampton."

Rashida gasped. "When?"

"So you don't deny it."

Rashida picked up her cup and sipped her tea. Her mind was a jumble. She struggled to look Tariq in the eye.

"I saw her recently. We had coffee together, that's all. She wouldn't say where she was staying, only that it was with friends."

"If they were friends we'd know them."

"These are new friends. We don't know them."

"They're not from Pakistan."

"Nor are we."

Tariq scowled. "You know what I mean."

"What makes you say that?"

"Javid saw one of them. She was travelling with him, a man … unaccompanied."

Rashida frowned. "It's how things are here. It doesn't mean anything wrong."

"It's not our way, Rashida. It's not the proper way for a woman to behave."

Rashida glared at her brother. "You think the proper way to behave is to be given away when you're a child, to be married off to someone you don't even know?"

"Having your marriage arranged by your family is part of our tradition. It's been that way for generations. Wasn't their marriage agreed according to custom? Doesn't Javid have rights too? Don't you think a girl should follow the wishes of her family?"

"Let me ask you something, Tariq. Have you ever thought about what such an arrangement might mean to a girl?"

"I'm not a girl, so how should I know about such things?"

"Then let me tell you that for a girl to be given – yes, *given* like a piece of property – to a man, who could be a total stranger, that's … well, it's just like a form of abuse."

Tariq was exasperated. "But a man has a duty to take care of his wife and provide for her. That is our system, and it works. We know it does."

"From a man's perspective it works very well, Tariq. But does anyone ever ask the girl if she approves? And what if she doesn't?"

278

"You've become very westernised, Rashida."

"I'm a girl, too, unless you haven't noticed. And I don't need someone else to tell me how to think or behave."

Tariq protested. "It can't be so bad for girls. They don't all run away and hide, like Samira."

"You don't get it, do you, Tariq? If a girl – we should call her a *woman* – doesn't want to accept such a marriage, it must be *awful* for her. Just think about it. It must be like a form of *rape*."

Tariq had never heard his sister speak like this before. He was shocked by such ideas and by the very language she was using. Confused and muddled, he looked away. Rashida stood and put her breakfast things in the dishwasher. Without another word she picked up her book and left the room. Tariq watched her go and returned to brooding over his breakfast.

****

Marnie and Donovan arrived back at Glebe Farm and converged with Ralph on the farm house doorstep. Entering the hall they became aware of a delicious smell emanating from the kitchen. Anne was busy at the Aga.

"Pancakes anybody?"

Marnie groaned with pleasure while Donovan walked over and kissed Anne on the cheek. While the pancake orgy was in progress Anne brought Donovan up to date on Bashir.

He had been walking home alone in the evening after seeing Azim when a gang of hoodies cornered him in a side street. They bundled him into a doorway. Luckily for him the people heard a thud against their front door, and the man of the house rushed out. He was big, brawny and bristling with indignation. As soon as the hoodies saw him they ran off. Seeing Bashir lying bleeding on the ground, the man rang 999. The police arrived within minutes, but Bashir couldn't identify his attackers.

After breakfast Anne and Donovan stayed behind to clear up. When they were alone Anne said, "Marnie was keen to fetch you herself this morning."

"Yeah. She wanted to warn me off. She said things were getting dangerous around my *Muslim chums* and I should keep out of it."

"Good advice. Will you?"

Donovan said, "Let's clear the table. Then I have to make a phone call."

****

Azim offered to collect Bashir from hospital that morning and drive him home. His parents were glad to accept the offer. They had a shop to run with no other staff, and it was open every day from early in the morning till late in the evening.

When Azim presented himself at the nurses' station of Bashir's ward he was surprised to find a police constable waiting there. They were about the same age. The officer looked Azim up and down before speaking.

"Are you family?" he asked.

"A friend of the family. I've come to take Bashir home."

The policeman shook his head. "You know you're asking for trouble going around like that."

"What do you mean?"

"You're not exactly gonna blend in wearing that gear, are you? Or is this meant to be some sort of statement?"

Azim glared at him, indignant. "This is how I choose to dress. It's part of who I am."

"And it's asking for trouble, like the women who go round in those yashmak things."

"Bashir was wearing western clothes when he was assaulted. Or do you think he should get his skin dyed lighter … to blend in?"

"I'm only saying, it's for your own good."

"And I'm only saying, I will not let hooligans dictate what I wear or how I live my life."

The constable shrugged and walked away. "Your funeral."

Azim felt the mobile vibrating in his pocket and stepped out into the lobby to take the call. It was Donovan. Azim outlined the situation and assured Donovan there was nothing he could do to help. They arranged to meet in town for coffee.

Azim returned to the nurses' station to see Bashir walking unsteadily out of the ward. He looked battered and bruised and held himself awkwardly, but attempted a smile. They made slow progress towards the exit and spoke little on the journey. Arriving home, Bashir's mother fussed over him and ushered him up to his bedroom.

Azim drove away with a heavy heart and found a parking space near the town centre. As he locked the car and set off for his meeting with Donovan, he failed to notice the young man watching him from across the road, a young man who pulled up the hood of his parka as he followed in his footsteps.

****

Azim first noticed the hoodie when he checked both ways to cross the road. A few moments later he spotted him again, a reflection in a shop window. Azim admitted to himself that he was afraid and, more than that, he didn't know how to cope with the situation. He murmured a silent prayer as he walked along. This helped to calm his nerves, and he began looking for some way of eluding his pursuer. Preoccupied in this way, he failed to notice the second hoodie homing in on him.

Rounding a corner he saw a gap between buildings not far ahead. He speeded up, glanced over his shoulder – all clear – and slipped silently into the alleyway. Too late he discovered it was no more than a yard for storing wheelie bins. He turned to retrace his steps. At that moment his pursuer appeared at the entrance. He began walking slowly forwards, his features in shadow. Azim was desperate. There was nowhere to run, nowhere to hide, no means of escape. Then a voice came from inside the hood.

"Thought you'd got away did you? Too bad."

The voice was low, deep, filled with menace. As the man advanced, he drew a knife from under his jacket, a long knife with a wide blade. It gleamed in the shadowy yard. If the man's aim was to terrify Azim, he succeeded. Azim backed away, only to find himself up against a wall. For a brief moment he wondered if he could heave one of the wheelie bins at the aggressor and make a run for it, but he knew that was unrealistic. The man in the hoodie spoke again.

"I'm gonna fucking stick you like a lump of halal meat, you piece of shit."

As he spoke he noticed Azim's focus shift from his face to somewhere over his shoulder towards the entrance to the alley, an obvious desperate bluff. Hoodie wasn't fooled. Then he heard a voice behind him.

"I don't think so."

It was a quiet voice, its tone moderate, almost conversational. The hoodie hesitated. He inclined his head to the side, but the hood robbed him of lateral vision.

"Put the knife down." The voice was eerily calm, pronouncing each word slowly and distinctly.

For a few seconds the hoodie remained motionless. Then he twisted fully round to face the intruder. The first shock was to see a man dressed entirely in black standing in a braced position with his feet apart, holding a Luger pistol. The second shock came when the stranger racked the pistol with a purposeful movement. It gave a loud click.

Donovan lowered the pistol, pointing it at hoodie's legs. In the same quiet tone he said, "I'm counting to three and you'd better believe I'm not joking. If I hit a femoral artery you could bleed to death ... quite slowly."

The hoodie recognised the Luger from countless films and war games he had seen. In the hands of this stranger it made him shudder. But it made no sense. This was no Paki confronting him.

"Why are *you* –"

"One ..."

"What?"

"Like I told you. I'm counting to three."

"All right, all right." After a moment's hesitation he dropped the knife on the ground.

"Now take five steps to your left," Donovan said.

The hoodie complied. Donovan stepped slowly forward.

"That's good so far. Now face the wall and get down on your knees."

"What are you gonna do?"

"You heard me." No reaction. "Two …"

The hoodie almost collapsed to his knees. Donovan reached down and picked up the knife. The pistol never wavered in his hand.

He said, "You want to know what I'm gonna do? I'm going to give the knife to my friend here. He can decide. He's probably already got a fair idea."

Azim said, "The holy Koran forbids –"

"Not what I've heard," the hoodie muttered.

Donovan said, "Then you'd better hope you've heard wrong because I'm handing him the knife now."

Azim shook his head. He looked at Donovan who nodded and took out his mobile phone. He walked round to stand in front of the hoodie and looked down at him.

"Take that stupid hood off." No reaction. Donovan held out his free hand. "Give me the knife, Azim."

Azim passed the knife handle first. Donovan replaced the Luger in his pocket, took the knife and weighed it in his hand.

"Now are you going to take the hood off or do I take it off for you? Your choice." As the hood came down, Donovan said, "Look at me." He held up the mobile in his other hand and pressed a button. He took a second photograph and checked them both on the tiny screen. "Good. Now lie flat and stay there till I say you can move."

This time there was no hesitation. When the young man was prone, Donovan reached down and raised the hood, dropping it so that it covered his head. Then he nodded towards the street and followed Azim out with silent footsteps. They left hoodie lying sprawled on the ground and hurried quietly on their way.

****

"Why do you think Donovan came back like that?" Ralph asked. He had returned to the office barn from his study on *Thyrsis*.

They had agreed to take advantage of the dry weather and get out in the fresh air.

"You know Donovan," said Marnie. She closed down the computer and tidied the papers on her desk. "Once he gets an idea in his head he just goes for it. Right now he's fixated on opposing the thugs who are threatening the Muslims."

"He's really taken their situation to heart," Anne said from across the office. "I suppose it's like the way his German family stuck up for Jewish people in the Hitler time."

"It didn't do them much good," Ralph observed.

"Who?" Marnie said.

"His family ... or the Jewish people, come to think of it. But that isn't an argument for doing nothing, of course."

Anne said, "Donovan's not capable of doing nothing. He says you have to fight fire with fire. That's what worries me."

Suddenly they heard car tyres crunching on the gravel beside the farmhouse. Moments later a shape came past the shop-front window of the barn. The shape was wearing a clerical light grey dress and dog collar over a long thin body. Angela Hemingway knocked and entered.

"Hope I'm not interrupting anything," the vicar said.

"Come in, Angela. Are you on strike? I thought Sunday was your day of work."

Angela grimaced. "Actually I've finished my services for today. There's a curate from Northampton coming to take evensong as part of her development."

"We're going out for a picnic," Marnie said. "Care to join us?"

"Kind of you, but I'm visiting old and sick people this afternoon. I heard that young Muslim chap has been discharged from hospital, and I wondered if you'd heard anything else."

"We didn't even know that," Ralph said.

Marnie said, "Donovan's gone to see him. If we get any more news I'll be in touch."

After Angela left, Ralph gazed out of the window while Marnie fetched the office keys from the board in the kitchen. She watched him standing there.

"What is it, Ralph?"

"Mm? Oh, I was just thinking."

"Something you'd like to share?"

"Wars and religion, basically. So many wars have been about religion or leaders who claimed they had God on their side."

Marnie said, "I'm no believer, but not *all* wars are down to religion, surely."

Ralph shook his head, "No, but can you name one conflict where atheists have gone to war against agnostics on the grounds that they didn't *not* believe enough?"

Marnie and Anne looked at each other and laughed.

Marnie said, "I don't think there's an answer to that, Ralph. Are you ready for a picnic?"

Ralph grinned. "I think that's a good enough answer. Let's go."

Anne was pressing buttons on her mobile as they went out.

****

Donovan and Azim were sitting in silence in the Beetle after leaving hoodie spread-eagled on the ground. Donovan guessed that Azim was deeply troubled by what had happened. They had given up on the idea of coffee.

"Tell me about it," Donovan said.

"About?"

"What happened to Bashir."

Azim reflected. "This gang cornered him in a side street, just like I was back there. One of them asked his name. He said he was called Bashir. He said they thought that was funny. They said it was a good name for someone who was going to get a good bashing." Azim looked urgently at Donovan. "Why do people act like that?"

"The worst side of human nature," Donovan replied. "Maybe it derives from fear of the unfamiliar."

Azim said quietly, "You really think you have to meet violence with more violence, Donovan?" Donovan said nothing. Azim went on, "Would you really have shot him?"

285

"Azim, I intervened to stop you getting knifed. What would you have had me do? D'you think I should just have asked him nicely to let you go?"

Azim shook his head. "I'm confused. Grateful to you of course, Donovan, for rescuing me again. But I must say I was shocked to see you holding that gun."

Donovan reached into a pocket and pulled out the Luger. He flicked a switch on the side, and the magazine ejected itself from the handle. He passed it to Azim.

"You know what that is?" he asked.

Azim said, "No."

"It's the magazine where you put the bullets. Look closely at it. How many bullets do you see?"

"I can't see any. Are they inside?"

"It's empty. There are no bullets. And before you ask, I have a licence for it. It was found in my grandfather's house in Germany after the war."

Azim knitted his brows. "So you were bluffing."

"Yes."

"Wasn't that taking an awful risk? What if he'd called your bluff?"

Donovan raised the pistol and pointed it at Azim's face. Azim flinched.

Donovan said, "I made you jump, even though you have the empty magazine in your hand and you're my friend. How d'you think he felt?"

"And when you gave me the knife," Azim said, "was that a bluff as well? Did you know I wouldn't use it?"

Donovan smiled and winked. "What do you think?"

Just then his mobile began warbling.

****

Anne phoned Donovan while Marnie and Ralph loaded the hamper into the Freelander. It rang several times before he answered. He was out of the car being hugged by Azim before he went on his way.

"Did you see Bashir?" Anne asked.

286

"No. He was at home with his family, so I chatted with Azim instead."

"Is Bashir okay, then?"

"Rather the worse for wear, but generally all right, I think."

"And you had a nice chat with Azim?"

Donovan laughed. "Most congenial."

"Then why are you laughing?"

"I'll tell you some time. Were you just calling for an update on Bashir?"

"No, you're invited to a picnic." Silence on the line. "Donovan?"

"I'm here."

"What's up?"

"I really should be getting back to the boat. Not sure I've got time for a picnic."

"We're not tootling on *Sally*, just driving up to Knightly Woods."

"Samira coming?"

"Not this time. It's just us. If you want to stay long enough to eat, I'll take you back to Leighton Buzzard in the Mini afterwards. You can leave the Beetle here."

A hesitation. "Deal."

"Good," Anne said. "A nice restful Sunday before you set off again."

They disconnected. Donovan thought of the hoodie threatening to butcher Azim in the yard. He thought of the Luger in his rucksack and hoodie's terrified expression. In his mind's eye he saw the hoodie lying face-down in the dirt. He wondered how long he stayed there before he realised he was alone. Reaching into a pocket for his car keys, Donovan's fingers brushed against the brass cases of a dozen bullets. Anne's words were rolling round his brain when he climbed back into the Beetle and started the engine.

A nice restful Sunday. Sure. With a wry smile he engaged first gear.

Chapter 26

Marnie's Plan

Mondays had never been a problem for Marnie. She loved her work; she loved her surroundings. On that last Monday in May she had the office to herself for the first part of the morning. Anne had gone into college, leaving instructions on refreshments for the men restoring the farmhouse garden.

When the phone rang shortly before ten-thirty, Marnie expected it might be Anne reminding her of coffee time. It was Anne, but her voice had a serious edge.

"What's up, Anne?"

"Donovan just phoned. He's had a call from Azim. Bashir collapsed last night. They rushed him to hospital. Oh Marnie ... He died early this morning. There was nothing anyone could do to save him."

"Oh my God! What was it?"

"They think it was a brain haemorrhage. They were getting him ready for an emergency operation when he ..." Anne's voice failed her.

"What's Donovan going to do?" Marnie asked.

"I think he knows there's nothing he can do."

"Where is he right now?"

"He was on the Tring Summit, somewhere near Bulbourne. He sounded very downcast."

"Not surprising. Anne, I don't think there's anything we can do, either."

"At least ..." Anne paused. "I know it sounds crass, but at least with Donovan away, there's no danger of him doing anything hot-headed. You know what he's like."

"Direct action?" Marnie said. "Fire with fire?"

"Exactly."

Marnie added, "I only hope Donovan's friends will leave everything to the police and not take matters into their own hands."

"I don't know them, Marnie, but from what Donovan says, I don't think they will."

After ending the call, Marnie had a mental image of Donovan sitting in the cabin of his boat, head in hands, lamenting the death of one of his *Muslim chums*.

****

In the middle of the morning Javid's mobile rang while he was parking the car at the factory of Melville Aero Systems in Stevenage. He was hoping to line them up as suppliers of avionics to his own firm in Lahore. Tariq wanted to report back on his conversation with Rashida.

Javid cut him short; he had business matters on his mind. They would have to speak later and agreed to meet outside the school gates in Luton at four o'clock.

Javid had a spring in his step as he crossed the car park and entered the office building. He was convinced that at last things were starting to go his way.

****

Because of Anne's phone call Marnie was behind schedule. When she returned to the office barn from taking refreshments out to the workmen, she found Ralph in the kitchen area preparing coffee. She broke the news about the death of Bashir.

Ralph shook his head. "That's awful. Donovan's going to be *so* cut up."

Marnie said, "He likes those lads. They've hit it off right from the start."

"Small wonder. Donovan probably saved Azim from serious injury … or worse."

Marnie took the mug of coffee from Ralph. "Anne said a funny thing. She was glad Donovan was out of the way. She'd otherwise worry he might do something impetuous."

Ralph considered this. "Well, he believes in fighting back, but he's no fool. I don't think he'd do anything extreme."

"What about Azim and the others?"

289

"I've never met them, so I've no way of judging how they might react."

"Anne thinks they're not disposed to be violent. At least, that's what Donovan's told her."

"Let's hope she's right. A death like this can spark off all manner of troubles. Things could turn very nasty indeed."

Marnie sipped her coffee and shuddered.

****

Tariq had had a grey cloud hanging over his head all afternoon at school. More than one of his teachers had to tell him to buck up and concentrate in class. One of his few friends asked him what was bugging him, but got no reply, just a shrug of the shoulders. Then as soon as the bell sounded at the end of lessons, Tariq confronted the cause of his misery. Parked just a short distance from the school entrance he saw the blue Mondeo.

Javid started questioning him as soon as he climbed into the car. "So what have you been able to find out, Tariq? I want good news."

"I haven't got any news," Tariq said in a low voice. "I tried to tell you on the phone. I just wanted to say I'd spoken with Rashida."

"I knew that already. And?"

"She insists she doesn't know where Samira's staying."

"You believe her?"

There was a long silence before Tariq replied. "I don't know, but I don't think my sister's a liar, although ..."

"What?"

"It was just a feeling."

"Tell me."

"She could be covering up for Samira."

"Of course she's covering up!" Javid was almost shouting. It startled Tariq. "That's the whole point, Tariq. Covering up, lying ... what's the difference? There is none."

Javid stared at Tariq who fell silent, gazing down at his hands. This was not the conversation he had expected. When the boy said nothing, Javid went on. "I came here thinking – *believing* – that you had something to tell me. But I'm no further forward. So why did you bring me here?"

Tariq spoke softly. "I said I'd speak to Rashida and I did. I wanted you to know I'd done what I promised."

"No." Javid was emphatic. "There's more. You know that the honour of your family is at stake, and there are consequences."

"What do you want me to do, Javid? What do you expect of me? I can't force Rashida to tell me anything. I'm not even sure she knows anything."

"You do realise, Tariq, that to go against the wishes of your parents and refuse an offer of marriage is a very *serious* matter. It's worse if a woman goes off with another man, especially if that man is totally unsuitable. You do know this, don't you?"

"Rashida says Samira is not involved with another man, *any* man."

Javid was looking straight ahead through the windscreen, his voice dark and menacing. "I don't believe that. I've seen them together with my own eyes, and I can tell you he's not one of us."

Tariq didn't know what to say. He looked across at Javid and was alarmed to see him gripping the steering wheel so tightly that his knuckles were turning white.

****

At the same time the phone rang in the office at Glebe Farm. Marnie glanced at the caller ID and pressed the hands-free button.

"Hi, Donovan. How are things?"

"Okay." A pause. "Well, not okay at all actually. I'm really angry about Bashir, the more I think about what happened to him. I've got to come back up. There's nothing for it."

"Donovan, listen. You've got to go to London. There's nothing you can do here."

In the background they could hear the boat's engine running.

291

"Nothing I have to do in London can't wait, Marnie."

Marnie protested. "Think about it. Your boat has to be licensed."

Anne chimed in. "Marnie's right, Donovan. You've got to sort out *Exodos*."

"I agree," Ralph said. "At least think it over."

Donovan began, "It's just ..." His voice faded leaving only the subdued rumble of the engine on the line. He continued. "I can be in Berkhamsted tomorrow. The trip will give me time to think what's best to do."

"Berkhamsted?" Marnie immediately got the implication.

"Yeah. I can catch a train to MK from there. I'll be in touch. Lock coming up. Gotta go."

****

Rashida regretted that she had called out 'come in' when she heard a knock at her bedroom door. Tariq looked in.

"I want to talk to you," he said simply.

"Can't it wait? I'm trying to learn quotes for my exam."

"It won't take long. I just need a quick answer. Where is Samira staying? That's all I want to know."

Rashida sat back in her chair and stared at her brother. He was standing just inside the room looking a picture of misery. She eyed him with suspicion.

"How many times do I have to tell you?" She spoke slowly. "I do not know."

He flared up without warning. "She should be here, not running off like that! It's not the right thing to do, Rashida."

"Why is it so important to you?" she asked.

"There's a reason why things are done the way they are. We're a family. She should behave like a member of the family."

Rashida thought he was trying to sound convinced. Instead, he came across as confused. Before she could respond he stormed out, slamming the door behind him.

"I don't know where Samira is," she said softly to herself. "I wish I did."

****

Donovan had never felt so frustrated. He was seething with anger and indignation, desperately trying to calm down. On that remote stretch of canal, he was aching with irritation and despondency. Ahead, he caught the first glimpse of the balance beams of the next lock. Irrationally he felt a strong urge to charge the gates and blast through.

Get a grip, he told himself. He reached down to reduce speed and as he did so, he saw the Luger pistol on the chart shelf. Lying beside it was a cluster of bullets in shiny brass cases.

****

Rashida realised she had read the same stanza more than once and could remember none of its meaning. So much for revision! The words just floated past her eyes without registering. Tariq's interruption had ruined her concentration.

What am I to do? she thought ...

To spit out all the butt ends of my days and ways

Oh, so there was something that had stuck after all, but the rest of the sinister quote was meaningless to her. *Sorry Mr Eliot, sorry Mr Prufrock*, she thought. With her mind growing dizzy and cloudy she felt there was no-one she could turn to for help or support. Or was there?

Rashida rummaged in her bag and found the business card that Samira had given her on the way to the bus station that day. She hastily grabbed her mobile and pressed buttons. It responded straight away.

The number you are calling is not available, please try later.

Rashida sagged in despair and the card fell to the floor. It had fallen face-down, but as she picked it up, she saw that it was not one of her sister's cards from the office. This one belonged to a firm of design consultants, Walker and Co, with a PO Box address, an e-mail address and a landline number. Rashida wondered why Samira had the card of an interior designer. She had no home of her own ... or did she? Could she have some other connection with the firm?

Rashida turned the card over and over in her fingers, trying to work it out. She figured there was nothing to lose by trying the number. It was after all a working day and within normal office hours. Once again she began pressing buttons. The reply was almost immediate.

"Walker and Co, good afternoon." A young female voice.

"Oh, hello. Can I speak to Mr Walker, please."

A hesitation on the line. "Mr Walker? Can you tell me what it's about, please?"

"I believe he might know … a friend of mine."

"And your friend's name is …?"

"Look, I'd rather not explain myself. Could I just have a word with him, please?"

"One moment. Please hold the line."

Rashida heard a click followed by a few moments of silence, then another click and another female voice.

"Marnie Walker. Can I help you?"

"Marnie?"

"Yes. My colleague said you have a friend who knows us. Have we been recommended to you … or is there perhaps some other connection?"

"I … You see …"

The *Walker person* spoke again. "Is this a business matter?"

After hesitating for a moment, Rashida said quietly, "Er, not really. It's more … a personal matter."

Marnie waited for further explanation. None came. She tried a shot in the dark.

"Does the name Samira mean anything to you?"

There was an intake of breath. "Yes."

Marnie said, "The connection is?"

Rashida spoke softly. "She's my sister."

"Do you mind me asking how you got this number?"

"Samira gave me a card. It was your card. On the back she wrote her new mobile number."

"I see. And your reason for getting in touch is …?""

Rashida felt desperate, completely unsure of what was going on around her. Yes, she did have a reason for being in touch, but she was having difficulty in putting it into words. The voice on the line was kindly, unthreatening. Of course Samira would hardly trust a malevolent person. And so it all came pouring out.

"Samira ran away because she couldn't face an arranged marriage with someone she hadn't seen since she was a child. Now this man is in Britain and he's stalking her, or at least he would be if he could find out where she was living. Instead he's been trying to coerce me into helping him. I can't; I won't. And he's putting pressure on our younger brother to try to get him to find out her address. Tariq – that's our brother – is fifteen and getting more and more extreme. We think he's being radicalised, though in fact he's probably just as confused as the rest of the family. It's all so awful. It's tearing us apart."

"Hey, hey, slow down," Marnie said. "You need to take a breath." She heard a gasp that turned into a sob. Marnie said quietly, "You know I'm Marnie. What's your name?"

There was a sound of ragged breathing. Marnie waited patiently.

Eventually, "I'm Rashida, Rashida Khan."

"You all have such pretty names."

Marnie's voice had a genuine ring of kindness. It touched Rashida deeply. She found herself crying down the phone. "I don't know what to do, Marnie. We're all so mixed up. I know I can't ask you to tell me where Samira's staying –"

"No, I can't do that, not without her permission, but perhaps I can help in some other way."

"Really? Like what?"

Marnie hesitated. "Could I perhaps speak to your brother?"

"What would you hope to achieve by that, always assuming he'd even agree to see you?"

"I was wondering if I could just talk to him about the situation, try to get him to be more supportive."

"I don't know."

"What sort of things interest him?" Marnie asked.

"Religion." Rashida's reply was immediate.

"Nothing else?"

"You want to find some common ground so that you can get through to him."

"Exactly."

Rashida pondered this question for a long moment. Eventually she said, "Well, he doesn't have any interest in design or things like that, unless you count cars."

"What sort of cars?"

"In his room he's got posters and pictures of sports cars, you know, Lamborghinis, Ferraris, Jaguars, that kind of thing."

"Old ones?" Marnie said.

"Some, but I don't know the makes."

"Okay, Rashida, listen. See if you can get Tariq to agree to see me. Give me a date and time. Presumably he's at school this week?"

"No, we're all off this week for exam revision."

"So can you do that?"

Rashida sighed. "I'll try."

****

Ralph came into the office to find Anne sitting beside Marnie's desk, the two of them locked in conversation. He drew up an extra chair.

Marnie said, "Sorry, Ralph. I hate to interrupt your work, but –"

"No problem. What's so important that you come between me and the latest *magnum opus*?"

"I've just spoken with Samira's sister. She's worried that Samira's being pursued by this man they've lined her up to marry. Now he's pressing their younger brother to try and find out where she's staying."

"Tell me about the brother."

"He's fifteen, his name is Tariq and they think he's becoming radicalised."

"So you're involved how, Marnie?"

Marnie sat back in her chair. "I, er ... I've asked Rashida – that's the sister – if she can get Tariq to agree to see me."

Ralph sat forward. "With the aim of ...?"

296

"I thought that if I could talk to him, I might be able to get him to back off."

Ralph steepled his fingers and murmured slowly, "A radicalised fifteen year-old faced with the dishonour of his family."

Marnie said, "You think the idea's crazy."

"It's certainly bold."

Anne joined in.

"If Donovan was involved, I think he'd go."

"No doubt about it," Ralph said.

"And I'd go with him," Anne added.

"No doubt about that, either," said Ralph. "It would be typically bold. Yes, *bold*, I think that's definitely the word."

Marnie looked at them both without speaking.

****

Donovan cleared up after supper that evening and sat out on the stern deck. He rang Anne's mobile and she brought him up to speed on the latest in the Samira saga.

"I think Ralph thought Marnie's plan was a hare-brained idea," Anne said, "but he didn't say it out loud."

"He probably thought it was the kind of thing I'd do," Donovan said.

"Typically hare-brained," Anne agreed.

"Thanks."

"Well, it is … I mean the kind of thing you'd do. I said as much to Ralph. He described it as *bold*. That's fair enough, isn't it?"

Silence on the line. Anne checked the tiny screen on her mobile; the seconds were ticking away.

"Donovan, are you still –"

"When's this meeting due to take place?"

"I think Marnie's hoping to go tomorrow."

"Where exactly?"

"Samira's family live in Luton. I thought you knew that. What's on your mind?"

"I don't think she should go alone."

297

"That's what I told her, but she said I'd have to stay and mind the shop."

"I wasn't thinking of you."

"Donovan, you said you'd get back to London to take care of the boat."

"I wasn't thinking of me, either. I have a better idea."

"Who? Ralph can't go. He's got meetings in Oxford all day."

"Not Ralph either. Leave it with me. I'll phone you later."

And he was gone. Anne sat looking at the mobile, wondering what he had in mind. Whatever it was, she suspected it would be bold.

****

The number rang several times before there was a reply.

"Azim, it's Donovan. Hope I'm not phoning too late."

"Donovan, no it's fine. We were just watching the news on TV. What can I do for you?"

Donovan explained Marnie's plan to try to reason with Tariq about Samira.

Azim said, "They think this boy's been radicalised, worried he might use violence against his sister?"

"Or worse."

"Seriously?"

"I think so."

"I find that very worrying."

"You're not the only one," said Donovan.

"And you're ringing me because ...?"

"I wanted to get your take on the idea of Marnie meeting Tariq. Do you think an approach by a woman would be acceptable?"

"Obviously I don't know this young man, but I've met Marnie and I can't imagine she'd be confrontational."

"Azim, I want to ask you something. What do you think of arranged marriages?"

"I can see that it's something difficult for people of other cultures to understand. I must admit in some ways I'm ambivalent myself. I was born and brought up here and I've always lived here, but for our community it's an old tradition, so to me it doesn't seem strange. The family is very important to us. But I think you're touching on a rather different subject, aren't you?"

"You think I'm wanting to ask about honour killing."

"Are you?"

"Only by implication. I wouldn't want Marnie to walk into a situation where she might face danger through asking the wrong question."

"Is this Tariq known to be violent?"

"Not to my knowledge."

"You know that such killing is forbidden in the holy Koran."

"I do know that. Your father told me."

"And you know, perhaps, that arranged marriage exists in other societies as well. The Jews for example have the tradition of the matchmaker. In some communities Catholics and Protestants only marry within their own faith, they don't inter-marry."

"Yeah. I realise it's complicated. So what about my original question?"

"You and Marnie want to try to reason with Samira's brother."

"No, not me. I'm on my way back to London."

"You mean Marnie's thinking of going alone?"

"That's her plan. You sound doubtful, Azim."

"When is she thinking of doing this, do you know?"

"Tomorrow, I think."

A pause from Azim, then, "I'm just wondering ... Look, Donovan, the more I think about it, the more convinced I am that she should not go unaccompanied."

"My thought exactly. So ..."

"Ah, I see what you're getting at. Do you have Marnie's mobile number?"

****

Ralph came out of the bathroom rubbing his hair with a towel. He found Marnie sitting on the bed staring down at her mobile. Both were in white towelling bath robes.

"Thinking of phoning someone?" Ralph asked.

Marnie shook her head slowly, only partly paying attention. Ralph crossed the room and sat beside her.

"What is it, Marnie?"

Marnie turned to look at him. "It's odd. While you were in the shower I got a call. Do you remember that chap who came here once, the son of an imam?"

"Azim, yes. He came looking for Donovan. They'd been in a fight with some thugs attacking Muslim women."

"That's him. Well, he phoned to say he wants to go with me tomorrow to meet Samira's brother."

Ralph looked thoughtful. "I detect the hand of Donovan in this."

"Correct. Donovan told him about my plan to see Tariq and gave him my number."

"What do you think of his suggestion, Marnie?"

"Not sure. I said I'd think about it, but he more or less insisted – very politely – and in the end I sort of agreed."

"Sort of?"

"As in, reluctantly. And I can't help thinking Donovan might gate-crash the party."

"Surely he doesn't know where Samira's family live in Luton."

"Wanna bet? If anyone can find out, Donovan can."

"And that would worry you?" Ralph asked.

Marnie thought for a moment. "Donovan has a knack of attracting trouble, of taking things head-on. That would worry me."

Chapter 27

Impressions

On Tuesday morning Marnie waved Ralph off to a two-day seminar in Oxford. She then spent an hour tidying her desk and issuing instructions to Anne. Outwardly she seemed calm. Internally she was a jumble of confusion, doubt and misgivings. When Samira crossed the courtyard and appeared in the office, Marnie felt close to panic.

In contrast, Anne was a model of cool. "Hi, Samira. You got my message?"

"Thanks, yes. I'd be delighted to join you for lunch."

Marnie tried to suppress her bewilderment. She surreptitiously mouthed *lunch?* to Anne across the room.

"It will just be the two of us," Anne explained to Samira. "Marnie and Ralph will both be out at meetings."

At that moment, Dolly jumped up onto Anne's desk, made a warbling sound and curled up under the lamp. Anne reached over and stroked her thick-pile fur.

"Don't worry, Samira," she said. "I'll make sure Dolly doesn't jump on your lap."

Samira laughed. "That's kind of you. I'll let you get on."

After she left, Marnie stared at Anne. "What was that about?"

"Think about it," Anne said. "Would you want Samira showing up unexpectedly at her parents' home in the middle of your chat with Tariq?"

"*Sneaky*," said Marnie. "Was this Donovan's idea?"

"Nope. I can do sneaky all by myself."

****

Tariq couldn't concentrate for any length of time. He was supposed to be revising for end-of-year exams, but it was hopeless. Sitting in his room at home, he knew that across the landing Rashida would be ploughing through her work with dogged concentration, just as Samira had always done. Girls were different. They saw things differently and did things differently. Now there was a question: why did girls always seem to work harder at school, get the best marks, yet accept to be told everything they could and could not do? Life could be so complicated.

Checking files of schoolwork on his laptop, he inadvertently pressed the wrong key and deleted a whole document. *Oh no!* He forced himself not to do anything to make matters worse. He would restore the default settings. Ironic, really, he thought. His own default setting these days was confusion. If not confusion, it was total bewilderment.

He looked up at the posters on his wall. His favourite was the yellow Lamborghini or perhaps the bright red Ferrari. A tough choice. And there were plenty more, classic cars from all ages: Aston Martin, Jaguar, Porsche, Alfa Romeo, exotic names. They were also the reason why he didn't invite friends to visit him in his room. Such machines, such images were probably decadent and materialistic. Were they a sign that he had become too westernised? He had resolved to take them down, even to destroy them. But not today, he thought. Today was all about exam revision.

He could remove them some other time.

****

A faint mist hung over the surface of the water. Donovan looked out at it through a porthole in the sitting area on board *XO2*. He was brooding with a mug of coffee in his hands as the sun came out. Normally he would be well underway by that time, but on Tuesday morning he had dawdled. Now, he gazed out from his overnight mooring in Berkhamsted. Across the road that ran parallel with the canal for a short distance, he could see the railway station. He could be back in Milton Keynes in half an hour on the train.

It was against his nature to sit back and let others tackle problems while he fretted on the sidelines. Not that Marnie was incapable of taking charge of a situation and doing the right thing. He had more than once heard her described as *dashing*, and she was certainly that. She looked every inch the woman of action, though he also admired her reasoned approach, her capacity for empathy, her steadiness. He finished his last mouthful of coffee and put the mug down on the table, close to reaching a decision.

He knew Marnie had always trusted him, given him her support when he was planning some bold action. Now he had to decide if he would trust her judgment and leave her to handle that local difficulty by the name of Samira Khan. He washed the empty mug and left it to drain beside the sink.

Shaking his head, Donovan walked through the boat, stepped up onto the stern deck, switched to starter battery and turned the ignition key. He hopped down onto the bank to untie the mooring ropes, satisfied with the rhythmic idling of the engine and the pale grey puffs of smoke clouding around the exhaust pipe.

On the simple instrument panel the red light was glowing. He switched back to leisure battery and revved the engine for a few seconds till the light went out. The volt meter was indicating a solid charge. All readings were normal as Donovan pushed *XO2* clear of the bank. He smiled to himself, hearing Anne's voice in his head in her customary U-boat mode: *full ahead both*. Presumably both cylinders. He chuckled, remembering her next customary command: *steer course two-two-zero*. He answered inwardly: *Jawohl, Herr Kapitän-Leutnant.*

The smile faded. Up ahead he saw the black-and-white balance beams of the first lock of the day. There would be plenty more to come. His decision was taken: no turning back.

Would he come to regret it?

****

From inside the office Marnie heard the sound of a car manoeuvring close by. She turned and looked out of the window to see a Ford Fiesta reversing, its tyres crunching on the gravel drive beside the farmhouse. Quickly she shut down the computer, stood up, grabbed her shoulder-bag and waved a cheery goodbye across the office. Anne wished her luck and held up crossed fingers. Marnie tried not to grimace.

Closing the office door, Marnie met Azim hurrying towards her. He smiled and wiggled his car keys.

"Would you like me to drive?" he said.

"No," Marnie said firmly. "You've driven down here. Now it's my turn. If you'd like to wait here, I'll bring the car round. Won't be a mo."

"Quite a nice day for a drive," said Azim.

"Just as well."

Marnie's enigmatic reply gave Azim food for thought as he stood waiting for her to re-appear. Somewhere beyond the office barn he heard an engine come to life, its note bubbly and throaty. Moments later it drew nearer. As the car turned the corner and came to a halt, Azim's mouth opened and his eyes widened. Marnie gestured to him to get in.

****

Javid had second thoughts as he climbed into the blue Mondeo. His first intention had been simply to drive across town and call in on Tariq. He would press Samira's brother to help resolve matters once and for all. But then it occurred to him that Tariq might be at school, and that his journey might be wasted. He pressed buttons on the mobile and was mildly annoyed when Rashida answered.

"It's Javid," he said tersely without preamble.

"Oh yes," said Rashida. "Well, my parents aren't here this morning. My father's at work and my mother's visiting a friend."

"And Tariq?"

"He's here but we're both revising for exams."

Rashida hoped that Javid would take the hint and realise that a visit would not be convenient or welcome. She was to be disappointed.

"Will you tell him that I'm coming to see him."

"Now?"

Surely he would recognise the discouraging tone in her voice. Evidently not.

"Now," he said firmly.

Rashida opened her mouth to reply but it was too late. The line had gone dead.

****

Azim was impressed with Marnie in more ways than one. As soon as he had climbed into the car she had presented him with a printed itinerary, giving precise street-by-street directions to the home of Samira's parents in Luton. When they reached the town he quickly learnt that the most efficient way to give directions was by a series of hand-signals, rather than raising his voice above the sound of the engine. It came as no surprise to him when they reached their destination without difficulty. Azim pointed ahead.

"There, Marnie. You can park behind that blue Mondeo."

Marnie nodded and pulled over. She blipped the accelerator twice and switched off the engine. As she did so she recalled that Donovan had at some point said something about a blue Ford Mondeo.

****

Donovan was making good progress. Soon after leaving Berkhamsted he had found himself travelling in convoy with a boat operated by a husband-and-wife crew. The husband was happy to handle the locks, leaving Donovan free to steer without having to jump ashore at regular intervals. At one lock near Hemel Hempstead the boats had to wait while the chamber filled before they could advance. Donovan used the delay to phone Anne for a news update.

"Nothing to report so far," Anne said. "Dolly and I are running the office and it's all quiet. How about you?"

"I'm travelling breasted up with some other guy's wife." Silence. "Hello? Anne?"

"I'm giving you the Death Stare."

"Sorry, I missed it. I must've been looking the other way. Oh, gotta go. The husband's waving us on. Will you give me a ring if you have any news?"

"Sure, if I'm still speaking to you."

"Great. If you're not, just make hand signals."

Anne was making appropriate hand signals at the phone when she disconnected.

****

Tariq really didn't want this conversation. The whole business with Javid and Samira was messing with his mind. No-one seemed to understand that these exams were important, the last step before his GCSEs next year. Javid acted as if nothing mattered except his marriage to Samira, and that plan seemed to be going nowhere. Worst of all, Rashida played the role of the dutiful daughter of the house and left the room to make tea for their visitor, abandoning him, Tariq, face to face with the man who had become his tormentor.

And then quite suddenly there came a change for the better. The doorbell rang. Tariq had never leapt so quickly to his feet. With a breathless *I'll get it!* he rushed from the room, narrowly overtaking Rashida as she emerged from the kitchen. He opened the front door to face a barrage of surprises.

The first was a woman, white but attractive, wearing a suede jacket and blue jeans. The second was the view over her shoulder.

"Wow!" he said. "Is that your car?"

The woman looked him in the eye. "You know what it is?"

Tariq's eyes narrowed. "MG TC, 1947?" He smiled at her, pleased with his display of knowledge.

"No."

Tariq's smile vanished. "It isn't?"

The woman shook her head. "Good guess, though. It is an MG, but it's a TA, 1936." She held out her hand and smiled. "And I'm Marnie Walker. I'm not telling you what vintage I am."

As they shook, Tariq became aware of his third surprise. Standing beside Marnie Walker was a young man dressed in traditional *shalwar kameez*, complete with *kufi* skullcap. Marnie released Tariq's hand and indicated her companion.

"Let me introduce Azim. His father's an imam in Northampton."

Azim inclined his head towards Tariq and raised a hand to his chest. "*Salaam alaikum,*" he said.

After a moment's hesitation Tariq repeated the gesture. "*Wa'alaykumu as-salaam.*" He tried to appear confident but his expression remained confused.

"What are you doing, Tariq?" The voice came from behind him. Rashida was holding a tea caddy.

Marnie introduced herself and added, "I'm guessing you're Rashida. We spoke on the phone."

Rashida looked from Marnie to Azim and back to Marnie. "You came," she said.

"That was the idea. And I've brought a friend. This is Azim."

Azim and Rashida exchanged greetings.

Tariq said, "His father's an imam in Northampton."

"Really?" Rashida said. "Well, please come in. We already have a visitor."

"Oh?" Marnie glanced quickly back at the blue Mondeo.

Ushering their latest guests inside, Rashida explained. "Yes. I'll introduce you." She looked pointedly at Marnie. "It's Javid. He's hoping to marry my sister."

Marnie nodded. When they trouped into the living room Javid stood up. Introductions were made, and everyone except Rashida sat down. She retired to her tea-making function in the kitchen.

Tariq announced, "This lady has a *really* cool car, a pre-war MG."

"How nice," Javid said. He glanced at Azim and spoke to Marnie. "You are a friend of the family?"

"A friend of Samira. I came to assure everyone that Samira is well. She's having some time out to take stock of her life before starting her new job."

Javid looked puzzled. "New job?"

"Yes. She's earned a promotion but it involves a move to a different branch, and the post isn't available for a short while."

"I see." Javid looked at Azim. "You also know Samira?"

"Not really. I came to reassure her brother and sister that Samira was safe and well, that's all."

"Presumably, Azim, you know where she's staying?"

Marnie jumped in. "We do, but we've promised to respect her privacy while she decides what direction to take."

Javid nodded. "Of course. Did you know we have an understanding between our two families?"

"I'm not really *au fait* about that side of things," Marnie said.

"Nor I," said Azim. "I realise that such arrangements are not uncommon. I can also understand that sometimes people need a breathing space when faced with great changes in their lives."

Javid turned back to Marnie. "Is it your impression that Samira just needs a little time to herself?"

"Probably. I rather agree with Azim."

Javid said, "I wouldn't want to rush Samira. It's understandable that she needs to think things over calmly. I would only ever want what was best for her. I'm convinced I could offer her a good marriage, with financial security and a high standard of living at home. I would like her to know that." He smiled modestly. "I am a man of some means with a prosperous future."

"That's encouraging," Marnie said. "I'll pass it on."

At that moment the door opened and Rashida came into the room carrying a tray.

"Tea," she said. "It's nice to see you all getting on so well."

There were smiles all round.

****

Back at Glebe Farm Marnie drove the MG into its slot in the garage barn, and they climbed out. Azim declined the offer of lunch; he had things to do that afternoon.

308

"Thanks for coming, Azim. It was good of you. I really appreciate it."

"It was worth it, just for the ride in your car! Though I'm not sure I helped much in Luton."

They began walking back towards the farmhouse.

"Oh, I think you did. In fact just having you there made a big difference. What did you make of Javid?"

"He seemed reasonable enough. I think he wants to provide Samira with a good life, though whether she wants to go and live in Pakistan is another matter. I've heard of girls who go back to the old country to get married and find it hard to adjust to its ways and customs."

They parted with a handshake, and Marnie watched Azim's car climb the field track and disappear from view. Back in the office, Anne was desperate to know how they had got on.

"First," Marnie said firmly, "messages, orders, commissions?"

Anne handed over a lengthy list plus a clutch of yellow post-it notes. Marnie stared at them.

"Sorry I asked. Is there anything urgent in that lot?"

Anne shook her head. "Basically routine stuff, nothing that can't wait till you've told me about your meeting. How was Samira's brother?"

Marnie drew a breath. "Well, it wasn't just her brother. When we arrived we found Javid was there. Yes, the man who wants to marry her."

Anne gaped. "No way! So what happened?"

"Actually, it was all quite civilised. I think it helped having Azim there in his *shalwar kameez*, son of the imam and all that kind of thing."

"And this Javid, what's he like?"

"He's a bit older than Samira, somewhere around thirty at a guess."

"So, ancient then," Anne said.

"So, a little younger than me," Marnie added pointedly.

"Oops. Sorry. Go on."

309

"He's rather good looking in a rather aquiline, chiselled way."

"He wasn't annoyed you'd come, didn't think you were interfering in his affairs?"

"He didn't give that impression. He seemed to think it was okay for Samira to have some time to think things over. And, thinking of Samira —"

"Marnie ..." Anne stood up and perched on the corner of her desk. "Has it occurred to you that we may have been getting the wrong impression about this man?"

"You mean seeing the whole situation through paranoid sunglasses?"

Anne nodded. "Well, through Samira's eyes, at any rate."

Marnie reflected. "I suppose that was inevitable from the start."

"So what now?" Anne asked. "Where do we go from here?"

"I think that's pretty clear," Marnie said.

Anne grinned. "Now you're sounding like Donovan."

"Be that as it may, the next step is to talk to Samira."

Anne looked surprised. "Really?"

"Yes. I promised Javid I'd tell her what he's thinking."

"Best of luck," Anne said. "And I mean it."

****

Samira was upstairs putting a set of sheets in the airing cupboard when the doorbell rang. She skipped into the front bedroom, stood to the side of the window and peeped down, careful to keep out of sight. She relaxed. Marnie was standing back from the doorstep. Samira hurried to the top of the stairs and made a rapid descent.

Once inside, Marnie wasted no time. "Samira, I've got something to tell you. I've spoken with Tariq ... and Javid."

Samira looked stunned. "You've spoken with ...?"

"Yes."

"Marnie, I hope you won't mind me saying this."

"You don't think I should've gone to see them."

"Well, it is all a bit surprising. Can I ask why you did it?"

310

"I thought I might be able to reason with your brother. That's why I went. I had no idea Javid would be there."

"How did Javid react?"

"He listened to what I had to say about you needing some time and space to think about your future."

"How did he respond to your ..."

"Interference? Meddling?" Marnie suggested.

"I was going to say involvement, or maybe intervention."

"He seemed to understand, took it quite calmly. Did you expect a different reaction?"

"I don't know what I expected, Marnie. I really don't."

****

Tariq spent much of that evening in his room wrestling with quadratic equations. He was on the brink of Enlightenment when the mobile began trilling. His near-euphoria with algebra was dimmed as soon as he heard the voice on the line.

"Tariq, it's Javid."

"Er, nice to hear from you. I'm glad the meeting went well this morning."

"Went well?"

Tariq was surprised at Javid's tone. "Yes. It seemed quite sort of ... amicable." Not a sound came from the mobile. Dead air. "Javid?"

"Frankly, Tariq, I was *horrified* to see how things are developing in Britain."

"But I thought –"

"Unbelievable that someone should be tolerated – and a *woman* – to come and interfere in our private affairs. She was not only unrelated but not even from our community. It shows how low standards have sunk in this godless country."

Tariq was perplexed. He understood perfectly what Javid meant and was in many ways in sympathy with his views. And yet ...

"Are you listening?"

"Yes, Javid, of course I am. I just don't know what –"

"Nothing has changed. Do you understand me?"

"I'm not sure I do. In fact I don't think I'm sure about anything."

"That's why we have standards, customs, traditions. There are such things as rules we have to live by. I thought you knew that."

"Well yes, of course."

"Then you'll understand what has to happen next."

"I will?"

"I said nothing has changed. You must still do all you can to find out where Samira is staying. That Marnie woman definitely knows. I wouldn't be surprised if she was hiding Samira somewhere. You must discover where Marnie lives or works and let me know. You can leave the rest to me."

"What if I can't find out?" Tariq asked, close to panic.

But the line was silent again. Dead air.

****

Anne was sitting up in bed writing a birthday card for her mother. The mobile lay on the duvet beside her, and she picked it up at the first ring.

"Do I hear music playing, Donovan?" she asked.

"Mozart's Clarinet Concerto, Jack Brymer and the Academy of St Martin in the Fields."

"You sound a bit tired."

"It's all this fresh air."

"Where are you now?"

"In bed."

"Ha … ha," Anne said slowly. "Try again."

"Cassiobury Park in Watford. It's not too far to the station. I could be back by midnight. No, forget that. I could be back first thing in the morning."

"No need for that."

"So what news from the front?"

"Marnie went to Luton to try to get Samira's brother, Tariq, to see reason."

"Really? That was … bold. How did it go?"

"Marnie got quite a surprise. Javid was there, you know, the man who thinks he's going to marry Samira."

"Blimey! Obviously not part of Marnie's plan."

"Absolutely not. He was just there when she arrived."

"That was awkward."

"Actually, Marnie said Javid seemed quite reasonable and receptive. He accepted that things are different here and was even open to allowing time for Samira to sort out her ideas."

Donovan said, "That's not the impression we got from Samira."

"That's what we thought, Marnie and I."

"Surely Samira was totally spooked by the whole idea of Javid."

"I know. Anyway, you can relax and forget all about coming up here. Javid has backed off and Samira's more relaxed about things ... well, by her standards. We'll still be keeping an eye on her, I expect."

"Mm."

"Sounds like you're relaxed enough already, Donovan. Get some rest. That's an order."

"*Jawohl, Herr Kapitän-Leutnant. Gute Nacht.*"

Donovan suspected he heard a raspberry as they disconnected. He yawned. The fresh air and activity of the day were taking their toll. The soft music and subdued lighting in the 'U-boat' were making him drowsy. With eyelids drooping, he switched off the cassette player and turned out the light.

Just one thought flitted through his mind as he drifted off. Was everything really going as smoothly as it seemed?

Chapter 28

Contrasts

Azim was fighting back tears. He stood in the small gathering in the Muslim corner of the cemetery watching Bashir's coffin being lowered into the ground. Earlier, during the reciting of the *Salat al-Janazah*, the funeral prayer, he had avoided eye contact with the other participants, especially members of Bashir's family. They were practically overcome with grief and sorrow. He had been grateful indeed that only men attended the burial. The outpouring from Bashir's mother, aunts and sister would have been unbearable to witness. And when the time came for him to pour three handfuls of soil into the grave, it was as much as Azim could do to mutter the traditional prayers without his voice failing him.

It appalled him to think that only a few days earlier Bashir had been a happy, lively companion with a cheeky sense of humour. Now he was gone, and Islamic custom required him to be buried with the minimum delay, even in Britain. Azim shuddered at the thought of why in hot countries burial took place normally on the day immediately after death. Even so, he found the suddenness of departure brutal, however sensible it might be.

As a lifelong friend, he had been asked by Bashir's father to hold the burial wreath. He knew it was an honour, but regretted that it meant he would have to stand close by the grave until it had been filled in and patted into shape. Then it would be his duty to lay the wreath on the mound. Sometime in the next few days a small headstone would be placed at one end of the grave, and that would complete the earthly farewell to his friend. Soon, Bashir would be nothing but memories and the inscription on the marker.

Standing alone at the graveside, Azim wondered for how long Bashir's headstone would remain untainted by vandalism.

****

Donovan was cruising steadily that morning. It seemed as if the waterways were conspiring to lure him southwards. One after another he found the locks through Cassiobury Park and around Watford set in his favour as he approached them. Few other craft were on the move that day, and the air smelled fresh and clean.

Little did Donovan know that at that very moment, barely twenty-five miles away in Stevenage, a blue Ford Mondeo was just pulling into a reserved space in the car park of an aeronautics factory. Javid, the cause of so many of their problems, was about to embark on another round of business meetings. He was trying hard to focus on the matter in hand and not let his thoughts wander to the woman of his dreams.

****

Marnie had been having misgivings all morning about her visit to Luton the previous day. Had it really been a good idea, or had she gone too far? It was one of those moves that some would call *bold*. A less charitable opinion would be that she had intervened – *interfered* – in the private family matters of the Khans and the Shahs. Worst of all, she may well have made things even worse for Samira, the one person she had tried to help.

The thought preyed on her mind until, shortly before coffee break time, she got up from her desk and announced to Anne that she was going across to have a word with Samira.

"I wondered how long you'd hold out," Anne observed.

"Was it so obvious?" Marnie asked.

"It was the glazed look that gave you away ... that, and the occasional sigh."

"Hold the fort. I'll probably not be long."

"Search party if you're not back by dawn tomorrow."

With a final valedictory sigh Marnie left the office and crossed the courtyard.

To her surprise, she found Samira surprisingly calm. The front door of cottage number three opened without the customary clanking of locks, bolts and chains. And something

315

about Samira told Marnie that she was at peace with herself, or at least compared with her hitherto habitual anguish.

"Not disturbing you, am I?"

Samira actually grinned. "That's usually my line, Marnie. Come in. I was just sitting on the sofa with my feet up, watching the BBC News channel. Would you like some tea?"

When they were settled comfortably at the kitchen table armed with tea and biscuits, Marnie received a further surprise.

Samira took a sip of tea and said, "Marnie, I've reached a decision."

Marnie braced herself. "Go on."

"You gave me the idea when you said you thought Javid had softened his attitude, that he might be sort of ... understanding of my position."

"Did I say that?" Marnie said.

"Something like it. Anyway, I took it as an encouraging sign."

"Where's this leading, Samira?"

Samira took a breath. "I thought I might go and see him."

"Javid?"

"Yes. I want to explain how I feel. I want to put things right between us."

Marnie frowned. "Why do you think that's a good idea?"

"Didn't you say you thought he was being reasonable, Marnie?"

"I may have got that impression, but it might be different if he sees you."

"Why should he be any different to me compared with how he behaved when he met you?"

"Well, for a start, he didn't think there was an understanding that I was going to marry him."

"You think that would make a difference?" Samira said.

Marnie sighed. "Not to mention the fact that he obviously has strong feelings for you that he doesn't have for me."

"Obviously."

"And, on a practical note, Samira, how do you imagine setting up a meeting with Javid without giving him the wrong idea? Had you thought of that?"

"Wrong idea?"

Marnie said, "How about this: *hello, Javid, it's me, Samira. I think we ought to meet for a chat.*"

Samira looked puzzled. "Actually, Marnie, that's more or less what I thought of saying. What's wrong with it?"

"What's his reaction going to be?"

Samira shrugged. "He'll probably want to know what I have to say, won't he?"

Marnie sat back and breathed out audibly. "Samira, he's come thousands of miles to see you. He's expecting to whisk you off on a magic carpet to be his bride. Doesn't that give you a clue?"

"I thought he might be willing to understand my point of view."

"Think again, Samira."

"But you said –"

"Look, I had an impression based on a single conversation on the one and only occasion when I met this man. I could hardly claim to know how his mind works. And you certainly don't know him. You've made that quite clear."

"Absolutely right, Marnie. I had nothing to do with anything."

"So it's just your families that are close?"

"Yes, in some ways. But Javid and I are from different worlds. He grew up in Pakistan and, apart from outward appearances, I'm an English girl from Luton."

Marnie made no reply, but sat sipping her tea. The two of them lapsed into silence for a full minute before Marnie spoke.

"You must do what you think is right, Samira, but I do have misgivings if you're acting on what I told you after my brief contact with Javid."

"I wouldn't want to do anything rash, Marnie. I'll sleep on it before I reach any decision."

"That sounds like a good idea."

317

Chapter 29

A normal Day

Thursday was to be a quiet day, with a full schedule of designing for Marnie, the joys of analysing statistics for Ralph and a programme of reading and course work for Anne. Dolly would keep the office under surveillance from her usual vantage points.

Marnie reported Samira's latest brainwave to Ralph the previous night when he returned from Oxford. His misgivings about Samira's meeting with Javid were as strong as hers.

The first part of the morning followed the routine pattern until Anne made an announcement.

"You do realise we need to go shopping."

Marnie looked up from her drawing board. "We?"

"Okay, *someone* needs to go shopping."

"For?"

"Hadn't you noticed we're running low on basics?"

"Such as?" Marnie still sounded unconvinced.

Anne pondered. "Quinoa, quails' eggs, salted caramel ice cream."

Marnie kept a straight face. "Okay, but no panic buying. We don't want to start a riot in Waitrose."

"Seriously, Marnie, we do need quite a few things. Can you even remember the last time we did a food shop?"

Marnie's turn to ponder. "Fair enough. All I seem to worry about these days is Samira. Would it be foolish to ask you to draw up a list?"

Anne waved a sheet of paper and raised an eyebrow.

"Why am I not surprised?" said Marnie. "Would you mind going on your own while I finish off this scheme?"

"Sure. And before you ask, I agree with you."

"About what?"

"That we should find out if Samira needs anything or wants to come."

Marnie leaned back in her seat, stretched and rubbed the back of her neck, turning her head from side to side. Yawning, she said, "Okay. I'll go over and check. She's bound to need some stuff."

Anne was on her feet in a trice. "I'll pop up for my outdoor shoes." She was heading for the wall-ladder as Marnie made for the door.

When Anne descended from her attic room, booted and kitted up for the great expedition, she found Marnie standing in the office looking puzzled.

"What's up?"

"It's odd," Marnie said. "Samira's not in the cottage."

"Did you go in?"

Marnie held up her key-ring. "Yeah. I keep the key together with mine now."

"Well, she won't have gone far," said Anne.

Marnie picked up the phone from her desk and dialled Ralph's number on *Thyrsis*. Had he seen Samira this morning? He hadn't. Did he have any bright ideas as to where she might be? He didn't. He offered to patrol the environs – his wording – and try to track her down.

While Marnie was on the phone, Anne went to the kitchen area to retrieve her car key from the board. She returned as Marnie was replacing the phone on its cradle.

"Ralph's going to have a look for her," Marnie said.

"We're not really worried about her, are we? I mean, we don't think she'll have done a runner again ... do we?"

"I don't know. I have an uneasy feeling."

"Where's Ralph looking?" Anne asked.

"I'll check." Marnie grabbed the phone. She pressed the buttons for Ralph's mobile. It rang several times.

Anne heard it on speakerphone. "He probably forgot to take it with him," she said.

Marnie agreed. "He's the most intelligent person I know but sometimes –"

"Hello?" There was a click and Ralph's voice sounded loud in the office.

"Ralph, it's Marnie. I was unjustly maligning you."

"Sorry. I forgot which button to press."

319

Marnie suppressed a laugh. "Or perhaps I wasn't."

"What d'you mean?"

"Nothing. Listen, Ralph. We're going to look for Samira, too. Where are you searching?"

"Don't bother. I've solved the mystery."

"You've found her?"

"No, but I know what's happened. Anne's car's missing. I think Samira must've taken it."

"Damn!" said Marnie. "Where the hell can she have gone?"

"Try her mobile," Ralph suggested.

Marnie scrolled down and found the number. She pressed the green button. Straight to voicemail.

"Probably switched it off because she's driving," Ralph said.

"But where to?" said Anne.

Marnie turned on her heel. "Let's check the cottage again."

In the cottage they found an address book with an open notepad and a pen beside it. On the page facing them was a to-do list including reminders to make phone-calls: Rashida, the bank, head office. It also contained a list of food to be bought and, touchingly, 'flowers for Marnie'.

"Do you think she's just gone shopping?" Anne asked, incredulous.

"Doubt it," said Marnie. "Look. She's not taken her shopping list."

"I can't imagine she'd have just taken your car like that," Ralph said.

Marnie said, "Why not? She's got form. Remember how she took Donovan's keys and stowed away on *Exodos*."

"What's bothering me is how did she get the key?" Anne asked. "How did she know where to find it?" She gasped and raised a hand to her mouth.

"What is it?" said Ralph.

"Stupid me!" Anne said. "I told her where I kept the spare key in the garage barn, under the oil can. I never thought she'd —"

Marnie shrugged. "Okay, so where is she and what's she doing?"

320

Marnie picked up the notepad and studied it again.

"This isn't much use," she muttered and held it up for Ralph. "Am I missing anything here?"

Before Ralph could take it, Anne pointed at the reverse page.

"What's that?" she said.

Marnie turned the pad over. On the other side was a series of what appeared to be doodles. In amongst the jottings was a list, two words repeated several times over. Close inspection revealed that the words were a name: Javid Shah.

"That's him," said Marnie.

Ralph was looking thoughtful. "Marnie ..."

She nodded. "Yes, that's what I was thinking."

Anne said, "I think I've turned over two pages at once. Have I missed something?"

Marnie picked up the address book and began turning pages. "Samira was talking about going to see Javid. I asked her to think it over before doing anything rash. She knew I thought it wasn't a good idea."

Ralph completed the sentence for her. "But she'd made up her mind."

Marnie waved Samira's address book. "Shah ... Here it is. There's only one entry for that name, and it's in Luton."

"You think that's where she's gone?" Anne said.

Marnie said, "Where else?"

****

They had agreed that Marnie should make the trip solo to the Shahs' house in Luton on the grounds that nothing was likely to be gained by the arrival of a deputation.

On her way round to the garage barn, Marnie suddenly stopped and asked herself why she wanted to get involved at this stage. In a moment of self-doubt she questioned her motives. What did she expect to find in Luton? Probably Samira confronting Javid. How might that turn out? Had Marnie accurately interpreted Javid's state of mind on the basis of one short encounter?

321

Nothing was clear-cut, but she had come a long way with Samira in her struggle to cope with the problems forced upon her against her will. Marnie now felt strangely compelled to see things through. It might be the only way to bring everything to some kind of conclusion. In her head Marnie heard a long-remembered quote from school days about taking arms against a sea of troubles and, by opposing, ending them. She shook herself free from this reverie and concentrated on practical matters.

Marnie climbed into the Freelander and fed the address and postcode for the Shahs into the satnav's memory. While it calculated route and timing, she fastened her seat belt and made ready to set off.

The journey passed without incident, with the traffic flowing steadily on the motorway. Marnie was amused and impressed to find herself arriving at journey's end at exactly the time forecast by the satnav. She was less pleased to see no sign of Anne's Mini near the house where she knew Javid was staying. But something stirred in her memory, a feeling of *déjà vu* as she pulled up behind a blue Ford Mondeo parked at the kerb. She knew she had seen it before, parked outside the home of Samira's parents on the other side of town, the day she met Javid.

Marnie took a deep breath, summoned up all her courage, resolved to take arms against a sea of troubles and climbed out of the car. With as much confidence as she could muster, she strode towards the front door and pressed the bell. It sounded inside the house. Marnie stepped back a pace to await results. But there was no response. She rang again, and again there was no response. Tempted to look through the letterbox, she spotted a path leading past the attached garage, presumably round to the back door. On impulse, she followed it.

At the end of the path, her way was barred by a wooden gate. Marnie reached over and slid back a bolt. She pushed the gate open and walked into the garden. It had a simple layout, a lawn with narrow borders containing shrubs. What to do? Beside her was a semi-glazed door leading into the kitchen, which looked clean and neat, testimony to a house-proud family. But for Marnie something wasn't quite right. A strange silence hung over the neighbourhood, and it filled her with foreboding. Afterwards, she couldn't explain what made her try the door handle. The action was smooth, and the door was unlocked. It swung inwards without a squeak.

"Hello?" Marnie realised that her voice was little more than a whisper. She cleared her throat and tried again, this time louder. "Hello?"

No result. Marnie wondered what she would say if the owners of the house suddenly returned and found a complete stranger standing in their kitchen.

"This is not a good idea," Marnie muttered under her breath, wishing she had never come.

She turned and made to leave, but as she did so, her foot knocked against something on the ground. Automatically, she stooped to pick it up, suddenly aware of external sounds, a wailing in the air, growing louder by the second. Sirens. She bent down and picked up the object, her head turned now towards the back door, her attention completely distracted by commotion outside in the street. A squeal of tyres, several squeals of tyres, followed by the rushing of feet. Moments later men burst into view from the garden, men in uniform.

"Put it down! Drop it! Now!"

Marnie froze, uncomprehending. *What the hell was going on?* Everything had become surreal.

"Put down the weapon!" The command was delivered in a firm clear voice.

Weapon? What weapon? Marnie looked down at her hand and saw that she was holding an ordinary kitchen knife. She wanted to explain that it wasn't a weapon, but the words failed her. With a shrug she set it down on the worktop. Only then did she realise that it had an unpleasant sticky feeling. She was staring down at her hands when two of the men rushed in and seized her by the arms. The whole scene was bizarre. The palm of her hand and her fingers were bright red. It *was* a weapon. The handle was bloody, the blade was bloody, and

323

where it had been in contact with the floor, that too was stained red. Blood. It was more than a weapon. Marnie knew at that moment that it was a *murder weapon*.

She looked into the eyes of the man on her right. His expression was a mixture of shock and loathing.

Chapter 30

Witness

Marnie woke on Friday morning and wondered if she had slept through a nightmare. She turned her head slowly on the pillow to look at Ralph. He was lying on his back with his eyes open, staring up at the ceiling.

"It wasn't a dream, was it?" she said quietly.

"No. It really happened."

Marnie breathed out audibly and reached across under the duvet to take Ralph's hand. He squeezed hers gently.

"You know, Ralph, I have very little recollection of what happened yesterday from the time Roger brought me home."

"Not surprised. You were in a daze."

"Did Roger bring me back from Milton Keynes?"

"That's right."

"Why not Luton?"

"I gather the Thames Valley police force is bigger than Bedfordshire's, and they were over-stretched, so you were taken to MK police HQ."

"You know, Ralph, I'm still hazy about what happened at the police station. One minute they were grilling me about everything that's happened since Samira came here; the next minute, it's all change and I'm out of the door. Can you make any sense of it?"

"When you came back I put you to bed. You were completely drained of energy and fell asleep at once. I'd made Roger a cup of coffee and when I joined him in the kitchen he told me all about the interview."

"Interrogation."

"Okay, interrogation. He'd been thinking while I was getting you into bed and he thought there could be only one reason why they'd let you go like that."

"I'm innocent."

"That's as good a reason as any."

Marnie eased herself up into a sitting position and looked at the clock. Six-fifteen. "So what led them to that conclusion?"

"Roger said – and I think he's right – that the forensic evidence must have backed you up. It had to be that, given that there were no witnesses, presumably."

"So that's it? I'm off the hook?"

Ralph pulled himself up, swivelled the pillow upright and sat back against it. "They'll no doubt need your testimony and a statement, since you were on the spot."

Marnie shuddered, thinking back to the bloodstains on the floor. She looked at her hands. They were clean. "Did I wash last night?"

Ralph shook his head. "I, er ... cleaned you up with a wet-wipe."

She turned her right hand over and inspected both sides closely. "You did a good job." She leaned over and kissed him.

"How d'you feel, Marnie?"

"Like I've slept too long."

Ralph smiled. "About ten hours, more or less."

"Blimey! Did it make the news last night?"

"Not that I saw. I had to catch up, so I worked late."

"Now there's a weird thing," Marnie said.

"What?"

"No-one actually ever told us who was murdered. Do you know?"

"No, but I expect we'll soon find out."

Marnie let out a long sigh. "So all we do know is that the police accept it wasn't me. If the forensics were in my favour, they presumably can't argue with that."

"Seems a reasonable assumption," said Ralph.

Marnie smiled for the first time that day. "Spoken like a true academic."

****

DCs Driscoll and Rabjohn were sitting in despondent silence at their desks, facing each other in the outer office. They were the only two officers in the room. Everybody else was out on house-to-house enquiries, and they would be joining them shortly. But for now they were mulling over the conversation they had just had with the senior investigating officer.

Rabjohn leaned forward and spoke softly. "I don't see why we couldn't have kept her in for forty-eight hours. We might've got a confession if we'd played it right."

Driscoll made a face. "Forensics are forensics."

"Sure, but we had her prints on the knife," Rabjohn objected.

"I know that. We saw her holding it. That's not in question. The fact is, her prints were only found *on top* of the blood, not under it. It bears out her saying that she only handled the knife when she picked it up from the floor."

"But there's bound to be –"

Rabjohn stopped abruptly as the door of the SIO's office opened and DCI Craig came out.

"Just had a call," he said. "A witness. She says she saw a woman lurking outside the Shahs' house for about twenty minutes before going round the back."

Driscoll said, "Walker said she'd just arrived before we did."

"That's the first chink in her armour," said Rabjohn. "Do we have a description, sir?"

"Dark hair is all I've got so far. Go and fill in the rest of the details."

The detectives were heading for the exit before the DCI's door had closed. Rabjohn had picked up the photo they had of Marnie Walker. He waved it at Driscoll.

"And I bet she was thinking she was in the clear."

****

Marnie was finding it hard to concentrate. By mid-morning she gave up and announced that she was going for a walk by the canal. Anne offered to hold the fort. She would use the time to go over Marnie's latest designs. Marnie stood up and began walking in Anne's direction.

"Aren't you going the wrong way?" Anne said. She pointed towards the door. "The great outdoors is over there."

"Slight change of plan," Marnie said. "I'm going to look in on *Sally Ann*. Haven't been on her for a while. I don't want her to feel neglected."

Anne smiled. "Fourteen tonnes of steel and you're worried about her feelings."

"She's a boat. Boats have character, so they must have feelings. It's a well-known fact."

"Absolutely," said Anne. "Silly me. I'd get the keys for you, but I'm incapacitated."

Marnie looked concerned. "How come?"

Anne sat back in the chair and pointed at her lap. Marnie looked down to see Dolly curled up, apparently sleeping.

"Does she often do that?" Marnie asked.

"It's her latest habit. As soon as I get back from delivering coffee to the workmen, up she jumps. I think she started after that time she gave Samira a scare."

"Samira," Marnie repeated, shaking her head. She looked at Anne as if about to speak, but said nothing. She took the boat's keys from the board and went out.

****

Ralph as usual had no trouble immersing himself in work. He was concentrating intensely, preparing for a conference on the developments leading to overheating in certain economies in the Far East. When the mobile on the desk began trilling, some seconds elapsed before he noticed it and picked it up. Confronted by the keypad, he pressed what he hoped was the right button and raised it to his ear.

"Hello? Lombard."

"It's me, Ralph, Anne. You do remember me, don't you?"

"The name seems vaguely familiar," he said slowly. "Speak words."

A pause on the line. "Have you seen Marnie at all?"

"Not lately."

"You couldn't see if she's on *Sally*, could you? Roger Broadbent's on the office line, and Marnie seems to have left her mobile behind."

"You think she's on the boat?"

"That's where she went about half an hour ago."

"Tell Roger she'll ring him back. I'll pop across now."

As soon as Ralph hopped ashore he saw Marnie refitting the engine cover on *Sally Ann*. He called out to her.

"You're wanted on the phone. It's Roger."

Marnie leapt down onto the bank and began walking briskly towards Ralph with her hand out in front of her. He shook his head.

"No, not here. You're to phone him back pronto. He rang the office."

"Oh gawd," said Marnie. "What is it now?"

"I'll walk back with you." Ralph held out a hand, and they turned towards the spinney. "Actually, while I think of it, there's a file I left in the car."

They skirted the spinney and took the side path that led to the garage barns.

"Are you feeling any better?" Ralph asked.

Marnie sighed. "It's hopeless. I can't focus on my work. I keep thinking of Samira. Anne mentioned her just before I came out, and my stomach turned over, knowing she could be dead. You haven't heard anything on the news, have you?"

"No. I've been up to my neck in figures this morning."

They reached the first of the two barns where the cars were kept and stopped abruptly. Ralph felt Marnie's grip tighten on his hand. They both stared forward, eyes wide.

"Oh my God ..." Marnie said.

****

DCs Driscoll and Rabjohn pulled up with a squeal of brakes close to the incident tape that cordoned off the crime scene house. Rabjohn grabbed the nearest PC in uniform.

"Where's DS Prentiss?"

"Gone to the autopsy. Left ten minutes ago."

"The witness?"

The PC pointed at a nearby house. "Number forty-seven. Name is Mrs Grose."

Mrs Grose was a short woman with mousy hair going grey, pulled back in a bun. She looked about fifty and not one who took great care of her appearance. The detectives flashed their warrant cards, introduced themselves and asked if they could come in. They were shown into a sitting room and offered a sofa. Mrs Grose sat opposite in an armchair.

"Can you tell us what you saw, Mrs Grose?"

"I've already told the other bloke, the toffee-nosed one."

The detectives managed to control their features, but inwardly conceded that she had a point.

"I think you mean our sergeant," said Driscoll in her most reasonable tone. "DS Prentiss has been called away. You're an important witness, so if you'd just go over things one more time ..."

Mrs Grose made a sound somewhere between a sigh and a snort. She explained that she had noticed a woman standing on the opposite side of the road to the *murder house*. She was there for quite a while and seemed to be watching it. Some time later Mrs Grose was upstairs making the bed in the front bedroom when she saw the woman go round the side of the house.

"Can you describe her, please, Mrs Grose?" said Driscoll.

"Like I told your sergeant, she was quite tall, slim, dark."

"Long hair?"

Mrs Grose tapped her shoulders. "Down to about here."

Driscoll looked at Rabjohn who produced the photo of Marnie taken when she was arrested. He held it out to the witness.

"Is this the woman you saw?" he asked. "Take your time. There's no rush."

Mrs Grose stared at the photo before looking up at the detectives. She scowled.

"Is this a joke?"

Rabjohn was stunned. "Sorry?"

Both detectives looked dumbfounded.

"I said she was *dark*. I meant dark like them over there ... a Paki."

Marnie didn't know what to do first. As soon as she saw Anne's Mini back in its place in the garage barn, she wanted to rush round to the cottage.

"Samira must be back!" she exclaimed, hugging Ralph in relief.

Then she remembered that she was supposed to be returning to the office to phone Roger. She was a bundle of emotions.

"What to do first, Ralph?" Marnie looked close to tears. "I don't know if I'm coming or going."

"Suppose you go to the cottage and satisfy yourself that Samira's all right. I'll phone Roger and find out what's going on. Is that a plan?"

"Oh yes." Marnie's voice was weary but edged with relief. "It's definitely a plan."

They walked quickly on and separated when they reached the courtyard. Marnie rang the bell at the cottage and looked through the letterbox. She called out.

"Don't hurry, Samira. It's me, Marnie. No rush."

Marnie could feel her heart pounding. She was suddenly overjoyed, exhausted and overwhelmed all at once. She rested her forehead against the door, breathing deeply with eyes closed. Gradually she became aware of sounds inside the cottage, and took a step back. At that moment two things happened at once. Behind her, Marnie heard a sound as the office door opened. In front of her, the cottage door clicked open and a uniformed policewoman appeared. She wasn't looking at Marnie but rather beyond her across the courtyard.

Marnie turned and saw Ralph standing in the office doorway. One look told her that all was not well.

****

Anne was aghast. She couldn't understand how she'd missed everything. She had popped to the rear of the office to use the loo. By the time she had washed her hands and put the mugs out for the workmen's afternoon tea, it was apparently all over.

The police had come to the cottage and taken Samira away with them, leaving two uniforms behind searching the house. Anne only knew of the visit by the police when Ralph returned and phoned Roger Broadbent.

"How did they know where to find Samira?" Marnie asked.

Ralph said, "Roger told them. He said he had no choice. It would do no good to anyone to lie to them when they asked if he knew where she was staying."

"I suppose not. So what happens now? Can Roger act for Samira? Are they charging her with murder?"

"Roger said the police had taken her in for questioning. They apparently have a witness."

"Presumably we now know who the victim was. Or do we? Did Roger say?"

"He says it was Javid."

"Bloody hell!" Marnie's voice was little more than a whisper.

****

Roger phoned again at close of play. He sounded tired and, Marnie thought, a little dispirited. Yes, he said, he would be acting for Samira, at least initially. Yes, the victim was definitely Mr Javid Shah of Lahore, Pakistan. He had been stabbed through the heart with a long kitchen knife. The senior investigating officer had told him that the case against Samira was pretty solid. She had been seen watching the house; some of Mr Shah's DNA had been found on her clothes; there were tiny traces of his blood on her shoes. The fingerprint evidence was inconclusive; too many smudges. So far, Samira had not offered any explanation for these facts, nor did she dispute them. Roger would be meeting a barrister in the morning and would then return to see Samira. She had been held overnight in custody in Luton.

Marnie, Ralph and Anne were shattered. They were sitting in a Zombie-like state of trance when one of the men came in from working on the farmhouse garden project. He was carrying the tray with mugs on it.

"Oh, sorry," he said, when he saw their expressions. "Er, I brought the tray back." He looked at Anne. "Only you usually come to get it when we finish and, er ... anyway."

"Thanks. If you'd like to put it on the desk, I'll deal with it."

"Okay." Self-consciously he set the tray down and withdrew. "I'm sorry," he said as he went out. "Whatever it is ..."

After he left, Marnie said, "I never dreamt things would turn out like this. It's all so horrible. I just couldn't imagine Samira ..."

"Perhaps she'll say it was self-defence," Ralph said. "I'm sure it must've been."

Marnie said nothing. Anne got up and collected the tray.

****

Anne's mind was still in turmoil that night, as she sat up in bed reading – or trying to read – waiting for Donovan's regular phone call. She could scarcely imagine how she would put into words everything that had happened. How can you explain something that you don't understand yourself? she wondered. As it turned out, there was no need of explanation.

"I heard it on the news," were his first words after Anne picked up the mobile.

"What did you make of it?" she asked.

"It's all pretty ghastly. What do *you* make of it? You're closer to events than I am."

"It's what you'd expect. We're stunned, can't believe it."

"But it's true? You think Samira did kill the guy who'd been pursuing her?"

"Roger Broadbent says the police reckon they've got sufficient evidence."

"Mm ..."

"You don't sound convinced, Donovan."

After a few moments' hesitation he said, "Look, I'm a million miles away, sitting in a boat in a peaceful stretch of the canal. Everything's quiet here, and I can picture Samira the way I knew her. On the radio it said he was killed with a single blow to the heart. It's just ..."

"Perhaps it all simply got too much for her," Anne said. "Who knows what anyone will do if they're provoked far enough?"

"Yeah. Who knows indeed?"

"So you can believe it?" Anne said.

Donovan's reply was typically enigmatic. "Fight or flight. Sometimes you don't get much choice."

Chapter 31

Statements

By Saturday morning Marnie's sleep pattern had returned to normal. Always an early riser, she slipped out from under the duvet without disturbing Ralph. Minutes later she was washed and dressed and preparing breakfast in the kitchen. With Ralph still snoozing upstairs, she wandered across to the office barn while coffee was filtering. There she checked the answerphone, the fax and e-mails that had come in since the previous evening.

As usual the office was neat and tidy; Anne's 'good going-over' on Friday night. Marnie was reflecting pleasantly how much Anne contributed to the firm when the phone began ringing. It brought her back to reality. It also gave her a surprise. She rarely received business calls on a Saturday morning.

"Walker and co, good morning."

"Oh, I'm sorry to disturb you at the weekend, but this is the only number I have."

The voice was vaguely familiar.

"Who's calling, please?"

"It's Rashida, Rashida Khan … Samira's sister?"

At the mention of Samira's name, Marnie had the impression that the caller might at any moment burst into tears.

"Of course, Rashida. What can I do for you?" There was no reply for a long moment. "Rashida? I'm sorry that you're upset. It's an awful situation, but I want you to know that my solicitor will do everything possible –"

"It's not me, Marnie. I'm concerned about Tariq, our brother. He's absolutely distraught, doesn't seem able to make sense of what's happened. Ever since he was little he's always worshipped Samira, his beautiful big sister. And now this …"

Marnie felt scarcely better herself and when she replied she realised how lame it sounded. "It's understandable in the circumstances."

"Honestly, Marnie, it feels like our family's falling apart."

Marnie wanted to ask Rashida why she had phoned, but was hard pressed to find words that would not sound harsh. In the end Rashida saved her the trouble.

"The reason I'm calling you is that we don't want Samira to feel isolated or abandoned."

"Of course you don't. Is there something I can do to help?"

"We were wondering if you knew whether we could go and see her? There must be rules about visiting, but we have no idea what to do, or even who to ask."

Marnie closed her eyes and concentrated. Searching her brain, there was nothing in her experience that gave a clue to procedures.

"Frankly, I'm in the dark too, Rashida. But I'll tell you what I'll do. I'll phone my solicitor and find out how it works."

"And you'll get back to me soon?"

Marnie glanced up at the wall clock. "Sure. But you do realise it's very early. Probably best if I wait until at least a respectable time after breakfast."

Rashida gasped. "Oh yes, sorry. Yes. I've been awake all night. I hadn't twigged how early it was. It's really nice of you to –"

"Don't worry about it. Leave it with me and I'll be in touch as soon as I can. In the meantime, I suggest you get something to eat. Try to relax. Same goes for Tariq. Okay?"

****

It was a morning for early calls. Donovan was on the point of reaching for the accelerator on *XO2* when he felt the mobile vibrating in his back pocket. He pressed down just far enough on the lever to make headway and pulled out the phone. It was Azim.

"You're an early bird," Donovan said in a cheerful tone. "You okay?"

"Not really."

"What's up?" Donovan said.

336

"First of all, I'm sorry to phone at this time. I know you're an early riser ... thought you wouldn't mind."

"No problem. I've been underway for half an hour. Tell me what's on your mind."

"You know Samira has been arrested for the murder of Javid Shah?"

"Yes."

"Can you believe it?"

"I want to say no, but she's been pushed pretty hard. Who knows what anyone would do if forced into a corner?"

"So you think it's possible?"

"Possible, yes. But her nature is more flight than fight."

"So the opposite of you, Donovan."

"I suppose. Azim, why are you phoning?"

"I just wanted to get your view of things. I respect your opinions, and I know you don't rush to judgment."

"Especially when I don't know all the facts or circumstances."

"Is there anything we can do?" Azim sounded desperate.

"*We?* You mean the Muslim community?"

"I'm serious, Donovan. I meant you and me."

"I wasn't laughing. Listen, all we can do is let the police and the lawyers get on with their work. It's in their hands now."

There was silence on the line. Donovan wondered if the signal had dropped.

"Azim?"

"I ..."

"What is it? Come on, tell me."

"I don't know how to say ... Donovan, I think I've started to have feelings for Samira."

Donovan thought, *As if things weren't complicated enough already.* He said, "Have you spoken about this to Samira ... or anyone else?"

"No. I can't. It wouldn't be the right thing to do."

"I can see how it might make matters worse. You'd be stepping outside the ... whatever."

"Exactly."

"But these *feelings* are making you want to do something for Samira. Is that it?"

"Yes."

"You're feeling frustrated."

"In the sense that —"

"Yes, I know what you meant. That's what I meant, too. Well, the fact is, you just have to be patient. There's nothing you can actually do at this moment. Sorry for stating the obvious, but that's how it is."

"You're wise as always, Donovan. Thank you. I'll try to contain myself in patience."

"Azim, I've never been in your situation, but I do understand how you feel. If I find out anything that I think you should know, I'll contact you straight away."

"And if there's anything you think I could do, you'll tell me."

"You've got it."

They ended the call, and Donovan pressed down on the accelerator. As *XO2* reached cruising speed, he rewound the conversation in his head. He added one unspoken sentence:

But don't hold your breath.

****

"Roger, you are a miracle worker!" Marnie stared at the phone in wonder. "How did you do that?"

Marnie had phoned Roger Broadbent at home and asked if he could possibly get permission for Rashida and Tariq to visit Samira in custody. Twenty minutes later he rang her back with the news that a short visit would be permitted.

"The police want statements from the sister and brother anyway," Roger explained. "So if they present themselves at the station for that purpose, they'll be allowed in to see her, but only briefly. And an officer will be present the whole time, so they can't compare notes."

"I'll make that clear to them," Marnie said. "And I'll bring them along myself. What about Samira's parents? Will they have to give statements, too?"

"I doubt there's anything they can contribute really, but the police will send someone to interview them at home. Just take care of the siblings."

****

Marnie arranged to meet Rashida and Tariq at home at around two o'clock and drive them to the main police station in Luton where Samira was being held. She knew they could make their own way there but wanted to give them moral support.

It was Rashida who came to the door when Marnie arrived. Tariq followed and shook hands with Marnie, but without making eye contact. They climbed into the Freelander and set off. As soon as they started out Marnie could see that Rashida was fighting off tears. Briefly she reached across and squeezed her hand. There were no words that could comfort her. On the back seat Tariq sat in silence.

As they took the turning at the end of the street Marnie said, "You do understand that you can only see Samira for a short time, don't you?"

"Are they keeping her in a cell?" Rashida asked. "Is that where we'll see her?"

From the rear, Marnie heard an intake of breath from Tariq. It was close to a sob.

"I expect you'll meet in an interview room," Marnie said.

"What will they have done to her?" Rashida's voice trembled as she spoke.

"Nothing unpleasant," Marnie assured her. "They'll have asked her a lot of questions, but they're not monsters. I've been questioned myself more than once. They're persistent but not aggressive."

"You've been questioned about Javid?"

Marnie hesitated before replying. She was checking the mirror, pulling out to pass parked cars. "Yes. I was initially regarded as a suspect."

"*You* were?" Tariq was leaning forward, straining against the seat belts. "Why were *you* a suspect?"

"I'm not really supposed to talk about it," Marnie said, "but I was at the house hoping to find Samira at the time when the police turned up."

"So you got arrested?" Rashida said. "Actually *arrested?*"

"Wrong place, wrong time."

"But they decided you weren't guilty and let you go?"

"The evidence was on my side."

"But they've got evidence against Samira?" It was Tariq again.

"I suppose they must think they have."

"Evidence can't lie, can it?" said Rashida, close to tears again.

Marnie said, "Try not to dwell on it. I know it's difficult but —"

"I don't believe she could do something like that," Rashida blurted out. "I just don't believe it." The strength of her outburst caused Marnie to jerk the wheel. The car swayed. "Sorry. Didn't mean to distract you. I'll be quiet."

Nothing more was said on the journey, and they reached the police station in a tense silence.

****

At Glebe Farm Anne was in her attic room trying to read a biography of the German architect Walter Gropius, founder of the *Bauhaus*. That spring it had been a feature of their existence that their normal pattern of life would be disrupted by Samira. That day was no exception. Desperate to clear her head, Anne rang Ralph in his study on *Thyrsis*.

"Same here," he said. "I'm blowed if I can concentrate on these damn figures."

"Sorry to interrupt your concentration, Ralph."

"What concentration? I'm on the brink of giving up."

Anne sighed. "I just wanted to ask, do you really believe Samira killed him? I mean *really* believe?"

"Frankly I can't imagine anything less likely. But ..."

"I know. The police have to go on the facts and the evidence. I take it you haven't heard anything from Marnie since she went off to Luton?"

"Nothing so far. Have you been in touch with Donovan lately?"

"Only last night when he rang as usual. But he's no wiser than the rest of us, is he? Fancy a cup of coffee, Ralph?"

"Good idea. See you in a few minutes."

"I'll put t'kettle on." Anne said it in what she hoped passed for a north country accent. The aim was to lighten the atmosphere. She didn't quite succeed in either ambition.

****

Marnie parked close to the enquiries entrance at the police station. For a few moments nobody moved. Now that they'd arrived, no-one was keen to enter the building.

"Come on, then." Marnie tried to sound encouraging. "Remember, we have to put on a brave face for Samira's sake." As she spoke she felt her voice starting to break. She swallowed.

The three of them stood quietly together beside the Freelander, gathering their strength to face what lay ahead. Marnie wanted to suggest a group hug, but was unsure whether that would be appropriate or acceptable. She still didn't even get eye contact from Tariq.

"Come on," she said again and thought *to hell with it!* She put an arm round both their shoulders and guided Rashida and Tariq towards the door. Neither resisted her contact. Marnie hoped both were comforted.

Once inside the station, Marnie turned to suggest that her companions let her approach the duty officer while they hung back. But to her surprise Tariq ignored her completely and strode towards the desk. The sergeant on duty looked up at him expectantly. When he spoke, both Marnie and Rashida were stunned by his words.

In a clear voice Tariq said, "I wish to confess to the murder of Javid Shah."

341

Anne was pouring coffee into mugs when the office phone began ringing.

"I'll get it, Ralph. You have your coffee." She walked from the kitchen area to her desk and picked up the receiver. "Walker and Co, good morning."

"Hi, Anne. It's Beth. How's things? Marnie around?"

"Not at the moment. How was your holiday?"

"Just got in this minute. Crete was *wonderful*. We had fabulous weather, great food, lovely wine. Thought I'd see how things were out in the sticks, show off my tan."

"On the phone?" Anne's tone was dubious, but she had known for some time that Marnie's sister had a curious logic all her own.

"In a manner of speaking."

Anne let it pass. "Marnie should be back later this afternoon. Can I get her to call you?"

"Thanks, Anne. So what's the latest in Knightly St John? All quiet? Last thing I heard was that your tenant was trying to keep out of the way of her family and that guy who wanted to marry her. Any news there?"

"Er ... well, since you last heard, Marnie's been arrested for attempted murder but released through lack of evidence. Meanwhile Javid – *that guy*, the victim – has now died, so it's a case of *actual* murder and Samira has been arrested for it. Marnie is at this moment taking Samira's sister and brother to visit her and give statements to the police. So, all in all, it's just another quiet day in rural Northamptonshire."

Silence.

"Beth, hello? Are you there?"

More silence. Anne turned to Ralph. "I think I've lost the connection."

"No, I'm here," Beth intervened. "But barely conscious. How do you do it?"

"Do what?" Anne asked.

"All this, this ... murder and mayhem."

"We don't do it on purpose, Beth. It's not like a hobby."

"What was that name, the victim?"

"Javid, Javid Shah."

"And Samira actually –"

"I think you'd better get the whole story from Marnie, when you speak to her. She'll have the latest news."

Beth sighed. "I can hardly wait."

When they ended the call Anne scribbled a post-it note for Marnie – *Ring Beth* – and took it over to her desk. On her way back across the office Ralph made a gesture to her, pointing towards the window. She heard the sound of car tyres on gravel. Moments later Angela Hemingway hurried past. With a brief tap on the door, she came in.

"So sorry not to have come sooner," she said breathlessly. "I've been out of touch these past few days. Is it true about Samira? She's really been arrested for ...?"

"Murder," Ralph said. "Yes. She really has."

Angela looked around the room as if seeking Marnie.

"Marnie's at the police station now," Anne said. "She's taking the sister and brother to visit her."

Angela flopped onto a chair. "Oh, my dear Lord! This is *terrible.*"

Anne nodded. "Yeah, it's a bum – I mean, an awful situation."

Angela was shaking her head. "I can't believe it. She seemed such a gentle person."

"Would you like coffee, Angela?"

"Oh, no thanks. Can't stay. I'll look in later. I'm supposed to be visiting sick parishioners. Better get going."

She floated out, tall and thin in clerical grey. They heard her car start up and roll away over the gravel.

"It's really odd," Anne said.

"This whole business with Samira, you mean?" said Ralph.

Anne stared at him. "No. That's the first time I've ever known Angela refuse coffee."

****

Marnie and Rashida sat in the reception area without speaking. Both were dazed, catatonic, in a trance. Since Tariq had been led away by a custody officer, they had sat in a companionable stupor with no idea of the passage of time. They re-surfaced simultaneously when a woman detective walked towards them, her expression serious. She introduced herself as DC Scudamore. Rashida and Marnie rose to their feet.

"What's happening?" said Rashida.

"We've interviewed your brother and we'll be needing some of his clothes – the ones he was wearing on Thursday. We'll be sending –"

"Wait a minute," Rashida interrupted. "You mean you *believe* Tariq, that he really did ... you know?"

Scudamore stared at Rashida as her voice faded.

Standing beside her, Marnie asked quietly, "Do you have any results from your tests at this stage?"

Scudamore looked at her. "Fingerprints aren't helpful. DNA will take a while."

"But you're going with Tariq's confession?" Marnie said.

Scudamore nodded. "Yes, for now."

"What will happen next?" said Rashida.

"One of my colleagues is taking a statement from your sister."

"Are you letting her go?"

"Yes. She'll be changing back into her normal clothes when she's finished. Then we'll be releasing her."

"And you want a statement from me?" Rashida looked desperate and drawn.

"If you feel up to it." Scudamore turned again to Marnie. "Didn't realise you were still involved, Mrs Walker."

"I've become the local taxi service," Marnie said in a matter-of-fact tone.

"Will you be taking Samira Khan home?" Scudamore asked.

Rashida glanced at Marnie.

"It will depend where she wants to go," Marnie answered. She turned to face Rashida. "Whatever's decided, I'll get you home."

"No need," Scudamore said, looking at Rashida. "Mr Khan is coming to collect you. I think he expects to be taking both you and your sister home with him."

Neither Rashida nor Marnie made any reaction. At that moment neither knew what to say.

****

It was later in the afternoon that Anne heard a car – perhaps more than one car – coming down from the field track and turning towards the garage barns. Instinctively, she got up and went to the kitchen area to put the kettle on. Her next move was to pick up the phone and ring through to Ralph. He announced that he would come at once. Anne was dealing with the kettle when the office door opened, and she turned to see Marnie and Roger Broadbent. Both looked drained. As she passed her desk Marnie glanced at the pile of messages waiting for her, shook her head wearily and walked by.

"Ralph's on his way," Anne said. "No Samira?"

Before they could reply, Ralph burst into the office behind them.

"What's the situation?" he said without preamble. It was not a day for preambles. "Where's Samira?"

Marnie said, "She's gone over to the cottage, wants to lie down for a spell. She's whacked, poor girl. It's been quite an ordeal for her. In fact, it still is."

"Not just for her," Roger added. He sat down on the nearest chair.

"You all look as if you could use some coffee," Anne said.

Ralph snorted. "Sod coffee! Isn't there a bottle of brandy back there somewhere?"

"I know where it is," Anne said turning away.

"It's only basic brandy, *eau-de-vie*," Marnie observed. "It's not real cognac."

With a sigh Roger said, "I'd settle for meths, if it was on offer."

In the background a tinkling of glasses could be heard, and moments later Anne re-emerged with a tray containing the bottle of supermarket brandy and a motley assortment of glasses.

"No fancy cognac *balloons*," she said. "Just water tumblers."

"I'll drink mine out of a bucket if necessary," said Roger. In his mind he heard his wife Marjorie muttering darkly. He added, "Second thoughts, I'll be driving. Better make mine a small one." More dark muttering sounded in his head. "Very small."

When they were all settled with a mug of coffee and a measure of brandy, Marnie asked Roger to set out what had happened. As he collected his thoughts, she switched on the answering machine and turned off the ringing tone.

"While I think of it," Roger said, "Tariq confessed to being present when the arson incident happened."

"So it definitely was him on the CCTV footage that Cathy Lamb showed us," Marnie said.

Roger nodded. "He said he was running from the scene because he hated the violence that he saw."

"Will anything come of that?" Ralph asked.

"No," Roger said emphatically. "The police won't be taking any action on that score."

"And the murder?"

"The details will all come out soon enough," Roger said. "The main thing is that Tariq has confessed to murdering Javid Shah, and all the evidence seems to point to him."

Roger took a sip from his mug then his glass, allowing time for the situation to sink in. "I sat in with him when he was interviewed. He said he originally went to Javid's house to support him. The teaching he'd received lately had convinced him that Samira should do what her family wished and marry the man chosen for her. He seemed pretty certain that the old traditions should be upheld, but it was clear to me that he was prone to some confusion."

"Did something happen to make him change his views?" Ralph asked.

"Oh yes, it certainly did. He'd gone to the house deliberately knowing that Samira would be there and, as I said, he was

346

going to argue in favour of the arranged marriage. What surprised him – *startled* him, he said – was Javid's attitude. Samira had hardly begun explaining her point of view when Javid flew into a rage. He apparently banged his fist down on the table and demanded, yes *demanded*, what he saw as his rights.

"Tariq was shocked and tried to reason with Javid, who initially calmed down a little. Then Tariq tried to reason with Samira. He asked her at least to think things over. Marrying Javid, he said, might not be a bad thing. But Samira refused. It was clear; her mind was made up. That was too much for Javid who lunged at Samira and tried to seize her by the wrist. She pulled away and ran into the kitchen. Javid chased her, shouting and screaming.

"Tariq thought Javid had lost all self-control and was seriously concerned for the safety of his sister. When Javid grabbed her by the arms, Tariq took hold of a kitchen knife and threatened Javid. In the struggle that followed, Javid was stabbed in the chest. Tariq said Javid was grappling with him to take the knife away when it happened. Javid staggered back to the living room where he collapsed. Tariq was in a daze and Samira took the knife out of his hand. He rushed out of the house and rode home on his bicycle. Samira herself was deeply shocked. She dropped the knife on the floor, ran out and drove off."

"That's how her prints came to be on the knife handle," Marnie said.

Roger nodded. "Yes, on top of the blood. There's loads of forensic evidence in the house, on the bike … oh and in your car, Anne. I'm afraid there'll be traces of blood on your steering wheel. You haven't noticed anything?"

Anne shook her head. "I haven't been in the car at all since it came back."

"Well, don't touch it for now. The police will be sending people to examine it."

"So that's it," said Marnie. "Samira's sad story has come to an end. And what will happen to Tariq? Will he be put on trial?"

Roger said, "Yes, in a juvenile court."

"And presumably he'll be found guilty, given all that evidence?" said Ralph.

Roger raised a hand. "Let's not get ahead of ourselves. I've already spoken with a barrister, and we both think we could make a pretty good case on the grounds that Tariq was acting in defence of his sister who was being violently assaulted and threatened with a deadly weapon. In the scuffle, Javid took a blow to the chest."

"What are Tariq's chances?" Anne asked.

"Really too soon to say, but at least he is in with a chance."

"I'll drink to that," said Marnie.

"So will I." Roger raised his glass and downed the brandy – what was left of the *very small* brandy – in one gulp.

****

Anne felt drained that night and could hardly keep her eyes open to read her book, much as she admired Walter Gropius and thought his life story fascinating. She was relieved when Donovan rang earlier than usual.

"You feeling tired too?" she asked.

"Not particularly. Why?"

"You usually ring after ten. I thought you might be wanting an early night."

"No. Azim phoned me a short while ago, and I've got a pizza warming in the oven. Thought this might be a good time to ring you. Is that okay?"

"Sure. What's this thing you've got going with Azim?"

"No cause for concern. He's not my type."

"Glad to hear it. So why did he phone you?"

"He'd heard on the News. Samira was released by the police but someone else was being questioned, a youth. They wouldn't give a name as the person in question was a minor. I thought I'd check with the local oracle."

"It's Tariq, Samira's brother."

"Blimey! That came out of the blue. How did they catch him?"

"He confessed when Marnie took him and Rashida to see Samira."

Donovan said, "Samira had said nothing in her defence?"

"No."

"So she was protecting him."

"Seems like it."

"And he confessed without being put under any pressure?"

"Yeah. Apparently he came straight out with it, said he did it to protect his sister."

After a pause Donovan said, "Ironic, isn't it?"

"How d'you mean?"

"Well, they were both protecting each other. Don't you see? In a roundabout way this turned out to be an honour killing of a sort, Tariq defending the honour of his sister. Not what we expected or feared."

"I hadn't thought of it like that," Anne said.

"If Tariq hadn't confessed, Samira could've been in real trouble," Donovan said, adding, "though I expect the evidence would probably have come out in the end."

"Will you tell Azim about all this?"

"Probably not. Best not to say too much. He'll have to wait till it comes out in court."

"He wants to be your friend, doesn't he?"

"Seems like it. We get on pretty well. Got off to a good start, I suppose. Like brothers in arms."

"Even though you're an infidel," Anne said.

Donovan laughed. "Even so."

"D'you think he wants to convert you to Islam?"

More laughter. "Fat chance! But listen, Anne. Whatever you do, don't tell Angela!" He almost added, "For Chrissake", but thought better of it.

Chapter 32

Aftermath

Marnie was up early as usual on Sunday. She loved the quiet of the countryside on those mornings, a time to refresh the mind and spirit, ready for whatever the week to follow had in store. On that morning she felt relaxed, relieved that the long episode of Samira's anguish was finally, it seemed, at an end.

She turned her head to look at Ralph, barely visible under the duvet. *Sleepyhead*, she thought. For all the pressures that were his constant companion, he seemed able to cut himself off and sleep the sleep of the just; or was it the sleep of the contented? It hadn't always been like that. When she first knew him he was at his lowest ebb, with a career that had been blighted by controversy and conflict. He had thought of ending it all, even tried to take his own life but now, his international reputation greater than ever, he seemed to sail on, serene and strong. And in that moment of insight, Marnie realised that she played no small part in his rehabilitation.

And for Samira? Had Marnie and her friends helped her cope with her personal dilemma? Or had things turned out almost as badly as they possibly could? At least Samira was safe and, for now, free of marital pressure. But Tariq was in custody, facing a trial for murder. Marnie wondered if Roger and his barrister colleague could make out a case in his defence. Some time would elapse before they knew how successful that strategy might be. In the meantime, what would Samira do?

Marnie had an answer to that question before the day was out.

****

They were in the kitchen finishing breakfast when the doorbell rang. It was mid-morning and they were taking things easy. Ralph was skimming through the Sunday papers; Marnie was reading an article in a magazine and Anne was pouring herself another mug of coffee.

"I'll get it," she said and hurried out into the hall.

"Any bets on who it might be?" Marnie said quietly.

Ralph glanced across at her. "No takers."

A good decision. Moments later Anne returned followed by Samira. She was wearing a pink sweatshirt and skinny pale blue jeans. Even with only the lightest make-up, she looked sensational, though also drained and weary.

"Coffee or perhaps tea?" Marnie said, getting up and kissing Samira on the cheek.

"Not just now, thanks."

Marnie gestured to a chair, but Samira shook her head. "I've come to ask a favour. You'll probably think I've got a nerve, but ..."

"Go on," Marnie urged.

The faintest of smiles. "You always say how restorative the waterways can be. I was wondering if you had any plans to go for a tootle today."

"We hadn't got so far as making plans," Marnie said, "but a tootle wouldn't be out of the question."

"Far from it," Ralph added.

Marnie said, "How about a picnic lunch on the boat?"

****

When Samira emerged from the spinney at noon she was impressed by the activity around *Sally Ann*'s docking area. Ralph was on the bank near the bows loosening mooring ropes, while Marnie was on the stern deck starting the engine. One of the sections of decking was open, and Samira surprised herself by knowing that, with the engine running, Marnie would be switching from starter to leisure battery. Through the window in the centre of the boat Samira could see Anne busy in the galley. Everything was ordered, purposeful and now familiar, and just the sight of them made Samira feel relaxed among friends. Looking up, Marnie saw her and waved, smiling. Samira quickened her pace.

"What can I do?" she called out.

Marnie pointed down to the bank by the stern. "Mooring rope."

Samira was pleased to have a role as part of the crew, not just a visitor.

They headed north that day and chose a place to tie up for lunch close to the spot where Donovan had concealed *XO2* for Samira as a refuge. They sat out on the stern deck, enjoying the mild weather. It was the usual cheery gathering, with simple country fare – quiches, salads, cheeses, fruit and well-chosen wine for the others – and, while they ate, Samira found her thoughts wandering between her brother, languishing somewhere in a cell, and memories of the events that had enveloped her since coming that first day to Knightly St John and Glebe Farm.

"So, Samira, have you come to any decisions, plans for the future?" Marnie asked.

Samira took in a breath of fresh clean air. "I think I'm ready to resume my life, Marnie. I don't think things will ever be quite the same again, especially with Tariq's situation to sort out. But that's all beyond my influence. I just have to trust your solicitor and his barrister friend."

"I'm sure Tariq's in good hands," Marnie said. "He'll get the best help possible."

"I'm sure of that. I feel strangely optimistic about it all. Can't think why. But Tariq was trying to protect me, which should count in his favour. And I'll testify to that. There is one thing I have to ask you, Marnie."

"Don't worry about it."

"I haven't told you what it is yet."

"It's the lease for the cottage that's on your mind."

"That's right."

"I guessed. Don't even think about it. You've paid till the end of the month, and I'll have no trouble letting it again once you don't need it."

Samira sighed. "You've always been so kind to me. I only hope your next tenant won't cause so much trouble for you."

"You can say that again." Grinning, Marnie raised a hand to her mouth. "Oops, did I really say that out loud?"

They laughed, friends together, enjoying a spring picnic lunch on a quiet English waterway on the good ship *Sally Ann*.

After lunch Samira took the tiller for the homeward leg of the tootle. It would be her last cruise as skipper, and she performed well. The other members of the crew complimented her on her prowess as a boatwoman. For Samira it was another milestone in her progression that spring. When she had first met Marnie she had been a fugitive, taking flight from a situation she found unbearable. Now, thanks in large measure to Marnie and Ralph and Anne – and yes, Donovan too – she felt an inner strength that she had never believed possible. But of course Marnie didn't know the whole story. Perhaps she never would. Or perhaps she should.

"Well done, Samira." Samira was roused from her reverie by Marnie who was pointing forwards. "Shall I take over from here, or do you want to guide *Sally Ann* into her slot?"

"No thanks, I know my limitations. Let me rest on my laurels, Marnie."

Samira stood aside and looked on with admiration as Marnie controlled the boat with tiller and accelerator to make a perfect re-entry. As she pressed down to increase revs in reverse, the nose button gently nudged the end of the dock and *Sally Ann* came smoothly to a halt. To Marnie's surprise, at that moment Samira reached forward and kissed her on the cheek.

"Thank you, Marnie," she murmured softly, "thank you all, and thank you, *Sally Ann.*"

Marnie smiled at her. "Our pleasure."

Samira declined the offer to join the others for tea in the farmhouse, opting instead to walk with Marnie through the spinney while Ralph and Anne finished attending to the boat. No words were spoken as they made their way along the footpath, but Marnie accompanied Samira to her front door where she put the key in the lock.

Marnie said, "You must be glad you made your point and stood up for your principles, Samira. Things haven't turned out perfectly, and at times it's been a hard struggle, but you've come through it all and now you're ready for a new start."

Samira stared at Marnie. "Yes. It will be good to start the new job. I'm ready for it now." She paused for a few moments and added, "I hope I've come through, but I know I still have a long way to go. My life isn't resolved yet."

Marnie nodded. "You mean Tariq."

"Not just that, Marnie." She lowered her voice. "There's more to it ... much more."

"In what way?"

Samira swallowed and turned her head to look away. When she turned back she said quietly, "You see, all along there's been something else."

"Something else?" Marnie repeated. "More than the pressure of the arranged marriage?"

"In a way. You see I've always known that could never work out, and it's not only, or even really, a matter of principle."

"I don't follow."

Samira frowned. "Marnie, I think I've always ... preferred women to men."

"You mean ...?"

"Yes. I think I'm probably ... gay."

Samira turned the key and went into the cottage, closing the door behind her without another word. Marnie found herself staring at her reflection in glossy deep blue paintwork.

About the author

When not writing novels, he is a linguist and lexicographer. As director of The European Language Initiative he compiled and edited twelve dictionaries in fifteen languages, including English, since the first one was published by Cassell in 1993.

They include the official dictionaries of the National Assembly for Wales (English and Welsh), the Scottish Parliament (English and Gaelic) and a joint project for the Irish Parliament and the Northern Ireland Assembly (English and Irish).

For the record, the others are specialist dictionaries in Basque, Catalan, Danish, Dutch, French, German, Greek, Irish, Italian, Portuguese, Russian, Scottish Gaelic, Spanish and Welsh.

Since 2015 he has devoted his time entirely to writing fiction.

He lives with his wife, cookery writer Cassandra McNeir, and their delinquent cat, Marmalade, in a three hundred year-old cottage in a Northamptonshire village. Delightful as it is, it bears no resemblance to Knightly St John.

Books by Leo McNeir

The Marnie Walker Mysteries

Book 1 - Getaway with Murder
Book 2 - Death in Little Venice
Book 3 - Kiss and Tell
Book 4 - Sally Ann's Summer
Book 5 - Devil in the Detail
Book 6 - No Secrets
Book 7 - Smoke and Mirrors
Book 8 - Gifthorse
Book 9 - Stick in the Mud
Book 10 - Smoke without Fire
Book 11 - Witching Hour
Book 12 - To Have and to Hold
Book 13 - Beyond the Grave

Author's website **www.leomcneir.com**

Printed in Great Britain
by Amazon

70900198R00208